Harper Errant 3

The

Mermaid Stair

Maggie Secara

Since once I sat upon a promontory,
And heard a mermaid on a dolphin's back
Uttering such dulcet and harmonious breath
That the rude sea grew civil at her song.
And certain stars shot madly from their spheres,
To hear the sea-maid's music.

--William Shakespeare
A Midsummer Night's Dream

Popinjay Press   Los Angeles

for
Steven Gillan
Scholar, Craftsman, Chief

Books by Maggie Secara

THE HARPER ERRANT SERIES

The Dragon Ring
King's Raven
The Mermaid Stair

THE RAVEN AT RANDOM SERIES

Black Dog, Grey Lady

ROMANTIC ADVENTURE

Molly September

HISTORY

A Compendium of Common Knowledge 1558-1603:
Elizabethan Commonplaces for Writers, Actors, & Re-enactors

The Mermaid Stair…fuses elements of fairy tale, urban fantasy, historical fantasy, and time-travel to tell a unique story …Secara's poetic prose and tantalizing imagery paint picturesque vistas that remind me of the gorgeous view of Rivendell
Fantascize.com (Dec 2014)

Maggie Secara's impeccable research brings rich detail to both history and legend, and her characters are a delight to read.
Sharon Cathcart

The most intense of the Ben Harper series...beautifully written and grabs the imagination.

Plenty of twists and turns to the plot, as well as satisfying characters. Even the bad guy...is rendered understandable in Secara's capable hands; she keeps getting better and better.

I stepped into The Mermaid Stair today, ensorcelled by prose that put me right in the book with our heroes and now my weekend is over…with housework undone, errands not run, overdue letters unwritten, and the cat miffed at being ignored.

Chapter & Verse

Part Three ❧ Londinium

Part Four ❧ London

The Ata'rathi Scroll

Acknowledgements

This book would not have been possible without Dr Ari Berk's delightful *A Secret History of Mermaids*. The professor's profound knowledge of the sea-folk and occasional uplifting phone calls kept me hearing the Atami song clear and true on many a weary night.

Also beta readers Sandy, Kathleen, Jess, Robert, Judith, Annye and Debra. And my darlings in the Under the Tiara support group on Facebook for help and inspiration with so many things, and for singing along.

My patient editor, Sue Barnard, surely deserves a special mention for putting up with delays, stubbornness, and my idiosyncratic spelling habits, as does compulsive research badger and oldest friend of all, Nan Earnheart,

My appreciation for the support of my darling husband, JimDear, can't even be measured.

Addendum

Respectful thanks to Laurence and Stephanie Patterson at Crook Cat Publishing who encouraged me to complete the series and waited patiently through wind, rain, and appendicitis to get it.

M.S.
April, 2017

Dramatis personae

ENGLAND, JUST THE OTHER DAY

BEN HARPER, an ex-pat American with a new career

DR MELLIS POWELL, his musical wife

RAVEN FITZROY. his whimsical friend

PADDY CASEY, skipper of the *Darling Girl*

JOHN, Ben's driver

KRISTIN POWELL, a convenient landlady, also a cousin

GLAS AP GWYDION, an inconvenient friend

FAERIE REEL, the members of Ben's folk & roots band, headed by Dinah Shorland

SINADUBH, a girl who dances

LONDON, 1595

SIMON CAREW, a tormented scholar

SIR FRANCIS BROWNE, an affable gentleman in service to Lord Aubrey

SIR RAFAEL FITZROY, a dangerous fellow also in Lord Aubrey's service

NAN HETHERINGTON, innkeeper

WILL SHAKESPEARE*, a poet

BEN JONSON*, a player

RAFE SILVER, a clown

RICHARD MARTIN*, RICHARD CAREW*, JOHN DONNE*, and other scholars, lawyers, and antiquaries, habitués of the Mermaid Tavern

MR ROBERT COTTON*, gentleman scholar and antiquary

MARTIN, a boy in his service

WICKIT, a waterman

JOHN DECKER, a sergeant of the Queen's guard

WILLIAM CECIL,* Lord Burghley, the Lord Treasurer

SIR ROBERT CECIL, his son. Also Principal Secretary of State, the Queen's spy master *

LORD AUBREY, a gentleman of the Court

RANKIN FOY, a scrivener and part-time jackman

DRUSILLA and CALPURNIA, easy but not cheap

A number of players, poets, lawyers, and soldiers

OF FAERIE

ORIANA, a mysterious nymph

AMADIS, a mysterious gentleman

OBERON or AUBREY, king of Faerie

RAVEN, one of his principal gentlemen

DIGGER, a wee small man

TAMESIS, the River Thames, lord of the waterways of England

LUTHER, a helpful otter

LLYEA, a helpful mermaid

TEIFI, CYFLA, and ISSA, each the nymph and goddess of the rivers Walbrook, Fleet, and Dart, respectively

MEROPË, a mermaid of the sea

AMPHITRITE, Neptune's consort, chief of the Atami Lore Mothers

ATA'RATHI, the Star of the Sea

LONDINIUM, 175 CE

ANTONIUS ATIUS CORAX, a noble Roman with a wondrous toga

FESTUS, his freedman

FLAVIA PAULINA, the Procurator's tipsy wife

SEPTIMIUS PLACIDUS, a traveller from Dumnonia

HILARION GALLIO, a prosperous *negotiatore*

VALERIA LUCILA, sometimes called Veloriga, his brittle wife

MARINA, their marriageable daughter

TITUS, their pimply son

SLAVES in Hilarion's house

~Barates, the *promus* or steward

~Eporedorix, a short-tempered Gaulish cook with
  long moustaches

~Milia, a kitchen maid enamored of French cooking

~Perfidius, a bad-tempered undercook

~Hardalio, a gossipy footman

~Dafy, the pot boy

FLORA, possibly an old woman selling apples

CRATIUS, a seller of luck

SENUA, a seller of new and used clothing

Part One
London

London, thou art the flower of cities all!
— William Dunbar

I hate London when it isn't raining.
—Groucho Marx

1
Thursday: Thames Valley

The Thames is liquid history.
—*John Burns (1858-1943)*

Gaudy as a gypsy caravan, beaded curtains rattling at her windows, the narrowboat *Darling Girl* danced a bit as her skipper cut the engine and let her coast into the launch lock on momentum alone. With only the lightest squeal of rubber bumpers, she slipped in snug between two others just like her. Paddy Casey signaled that he was in; exchanged greetings with his counterpart across the way.

The lock at Teddington would be packed like a tin of sardines before they could move on into the lower reaches of the Thames. Behind them sat a tour boat; then some kind of pleasure cruiser with a scowling captain chomping on an unlit cigar; and at the very last, like the cork tamped into the bung hole, an outsized houseboat with only inches to spare between its bumpers and the concrete curbs. In short order, the lock started to fill.

Paddy tied down the helm and called to Ben Harper sunning himself among the coiled ropes and herb pots on the beetle-green crown of the roof.

"Oi! Hollywood! Are y'all right?"

Rising up like a banner, a tanned, well-muscled arm and hand appeared clutching a beer bottle, reversed. A pleasant voice called, "It's broken."

A moment later the empty bottle came rolling to the edge of the roof and dropped off into Paddy's hand. The brosey Irish face broke open in a grin. He still didn't know how the American managed to do that, though his grandmother could probably have told him. "Faeries," she might have said. Paddy just knew it was a good trick.

"And you want me to fix it, yeah?"

No answer.

He might have heard a sound that might have been a grunt. Or not.

"Just me, then," Paddy said, and ducked down into the dim closeness of the galley.

"Hang on!"

Ben Harper's sandy head popped up blinking, fringe falling across his eyes, wire-rimmed glasses askew. He straightened one and brushed back the other, and vaulting to his feet, he sauntered back to Darling Girl's helm and followed.

For weeks, he had hauled his harp into every folk club and wedding ceilidh in the Thames Valley, or so his aching fingertips told him. He'd made a whole lot of music, traditional and brand new. He'd made friends too, and gotten some rare child-free time with his wife, whenever Mellis could spare a few days from her summer teaching schedule.

He loved it, no question, but it wasn't for fun. Instead of being overworked producing and presenting a popular TV programme for the organizationally challenged, he was chatting up his new recording studio down in Devon, pushing the band's first CD, and still over-worked, and never at home. Only the hours were different. Plus he no longer had an assistant and the mighty BBC behind him, at least not for much longer.

Sure, it was fun, but he was starting to feel almost as fraught as he had before a kick in the arse a coupe of years ago from his friend Aubrey, who was incidentally Oberon king of Faerie, had turned his life around. So when Casey, a gypsy guitarist from Clapham Road, had offered a slow ride into the City, Ben had jumped at the chance.

One does not just walk away from television at the top of a show's popularity. It's not that easy. Ben had to be at the studio on Friday morning for a day of voice-over and ADR looping for his last episode of Now or Never. And film the hand-off to his replacement. And sign a contract for a guest appearance. So yeah, he'd be there, no question. But right now he wanted to put his feet up in touristy bliss and watch long patchwork stretches of England roll by at a leisurely three knots. The river did not encourage haste. Neither did the speed regulations.

A happy passenger, he settled into a deck chair on the compact deck at the bow in the warmth of a fading afternoon. He could ignore everything else while he sipped on a beer and watched the light go all golden and soft around him as the boats spread out and separated as they spilled through the lock. From Teddington to the sea, the river was a breathing thing, rising and falling with the tides. A place of transitions, a gateway, a point of departure and arrival. Ben felt a new tune coming on, taking shape in front of him, bouncing in and out of the laughter and gossip.

The lock opened. Paddy goosed the engine, and they danced out—a sedate, leisurely pavane—into the tidal and ever-widening Thames. Ben let his head drop, conjuring his harp in front of him with half closed eyes. Lightly, lightly his fingers moved through the air as though the strings buzzed beneath them, trying a passage, altering, trying again, following the strain. Long minutes passed, the river and the music.

A cloud of dragonflies hovering near the shore skimmed the bronze surface of the river. They paced the Darling Girl for a few minutes in the dappled light of overhanging leaves, diving in and out of the sunlight. And while they did, they called out in a high piping language of their own, which meant they weren't dragonflies at all. One of them zoomed up to Ben, a tiny opalescent, humanoid form with the wind of its wings a soft crackle like tinkling ice. It stared at him out of a pinched, almost human face. Inquisitive eyes met his, making them cross.

"Hullo," Ben murmured, and inclined his head in a kind of bow from where he sat.

The creature started a bit, surprised perhaps that he could see them, then dashed back into the long shadows and disappeared.

The plop of a fish, or maybe a falling leaf, broke his concentration as if a bell had sounded. Curious, he got up and leaned over the starboard rail, squinting into the bouncing light. He pushed his glasses up his nose with one finger. A long, dark shape in the water was matching speeds with Darling Girl—an otter maybe, or a dolphin of some kind. The changing light tricked and baffled the eye. Then trailing willow leaves shattered the image entirely.

Ben's mouth drew into a curious frown, aware of the tingle of magic. Kneeling on a wet locker he hooked an arm through a looped cable, and leaned as far over the side as he dared. Blinking, he peered into the leaf-littered water, dark in the sliding shadows, clear as ice.

With a low cry, he rocked back.

"What's that, eh?" Paddy asked around the pipe in his teeth.

"Ah," said Ben carefully. "Uhm, nothing. Slippery, is all."

"Aye, I did say so. Mind the gap."

He smiled at the misplaced warning and leaned forward again, and felt something in the universe shift, just slightly. The riverine world closed in: the rich green smells of the mossy bank, the chuckle and lap of the water, the rise and fall of insect hum all brightened around him. And there it was, floating slightly under the surface: a young woman's body lying in repose mere inches from the hull, the pontoon to his outrigger.

He swore, then blinked and cleaned his glasses on his t-shirt. He looked back at Paddy, calmly at his post far away. From where he stood, his friend shaped a bare outline in a kind of mist, as if a mantle of fog had been drawn around him. Or perhaps just around Ben, cutting him off from the mundane world. Passing terraces of expensive flats, docks, restaurants disappeared as well, and all the other watercraft but one—the big blue houseboat. With the ease of stepping through a beaded curtain into another room, Ben had crossed over, just a little, into Faerie.

Resigned, he leaned out and looked again, really looked. She was still there, only clearer, brightly hued and very fair. Only it was no woman that skimmed along a few inches or maybe a few feet beneath the surface. Pale hair that might be blonde and might be shades of teal and gold swirled over small, quite naked breasts, haloed her head, breathed back and forth across her childlike face like seaweed on the strand, caught in the draw stream of the canal boat. It curled and twined down to the tips of her green, webbed fingers.

As his eye travelled along her length, he could see where the soft rounding of her belly changed gradually from pink-edged celadon to iridescent jade into what Ben thought at first must be a mermaid's tail. When he looked properly, though, he saw the tail divided into two slender legs, deliquescent with jewel-like scales. Not a woman, no, but no mermaid he'd ever heard of, either.

Pale hands floated calmly beside her, as if she only slept. Like Ophelia in the river, she lay surrounded by eglantine and violets, and trailing nameless vines. Her black eyes were open, sad and staring.

Words came to his lips almost without realizing.

> *There, on the pendent boughs her coronet weeds*
> *Clambering to hang, an envious sliver broke;*
> *When down her weedy trophies and herself*
> *Fell in the weeping brook. Her clothes spread wide;*
> *And, mermaid-like, awhile they bore her up:*
> *Which time she chanted snatches of old tunes...*

Ben whispered, half-quoting, half-overwhelmed.
"She is drowned. How can she be drowned?"
A rush of long silver fish swarmed between them. The world shifted again. Paddy goosed the engine, and flung Darling Girl into the midstream sunlight. The Borderland fell away. The mortal world snapped into place with its busy sounds and sharp edges. Ben swung back inboard and sat down hard on the rust-colored locker, shaking his head. Among his

several talents he could, as Aubrey said, hear the bells of Efland; the doors of Faerie were open to him. He'd been in some strange places and seen a lot of strange stuff, but this was new. Quite new, and troubling.

For a moment, he sat back and stared into the middle distance, trying to figure it out.

"What am I supposed to do?" he muttered. Then he looked up and shouted into the afternoon, "What am I supposed to do?"

Only echoes returned from the opposite bank. Paddy, grinning, answered,

"Drink more beer!"

Ben ignored him. Just ahead, the fancy blue houseboat was tying up on the northern bank. Gates of Dawn, she was called. A white-bearded grandfatherly type on the deck turned when Ben shouted, laughing like Father Christmas. Whatever he thought Ben had hollered, he waved and shouted something back. It sounded a bit like, "Trust the water!" whatever that meant.

Ben smiled and waved in return, making all the usual gestures to indicate he couldn't hear or didn't understand. After a few fruitless exchanges, they both shrugged and went back to their own business, and Darling Girl motored on. Ben turned around and sank into the music of the river lapping at the hull, the hum of insects, the shrill cry of a hawk in the distance, and closed his eyes. A few minutes later, he opened them again.

Celebrity, musician, entrepreneur, Ben Harper was also the king of Faerie's sworn man. If Aubrey needed him, he would call or send his Raven. Right now Ben needed to find some paper and catch that new tune before it got away from him. Just in case.

2
Friday: London, Crystal Palace Park

It had been a long day at BBC White City, if not quite as long as Ben expected, ending in a late lunch made largely of champagne and sentiment. When he burst at last into the daylight, he was shocked to find it was only about three o'clock in the afternoon. The train home wasn't for hours yet. Time on his hands, he felt like a walk in the park.

His driver let him off at the southern end of Crystal Palace Park by the artificial lakes where the dinosaurs still roamed.

"When shall I pick you up, sir? Don't want you to miss your train."

Ben smiled and took his hand for one last farewell. The man had been his studio driver since Now or Never's second series.

"I'll find my own way, John. You go on home. And thanks for everything. Enjoy your retirement."

"Thank you very much, sir. I know I will, if the missus don't mind." John touched his cap in his old fashioned way. "All the best."

With that gesture and the solid rumble of the engine, Ben Harper's old career more or less drove off along Thicket Road.

A pastoral footpath wound its way around the mossy verge of the lower lake, so he shouldered his backpack and followed it around to where the dinosaurs, their 1850s designs long out-dated, still lounged on their island and in the shallows. Dark green and shimmering brown touched with blue, the water bounced the sun's westering reflection into his eyes as he walked.

Other sounds quickly muffled by water and a light wind rattling in the overhanging trees, the city fell away. Even with the modern Sport Center looming beyond the trees further up the slope, all sense of the suburban neighborhood that surrounded him faded and disappeared till there was nothing but the hum of insects, songbirds, and the excited trill of children in the play-park. While he stood there, even that vanished. Not too concerned, he looked, really looked, to left and right. He scanned the untidy islands noticing only that as the shadows lengthened, the monstrous statues were less amusing, almost menacing. For a moment, almost...

Overtaken by the tick and growl of advancing skateboards, he stepped aside. Three shouting boys passed him, full of noise and life. He was only thirty-five, but it did make him feel a little old just thinking how close his own son was to that age.

A chime of laughter rang from somewhere nearby but, as usual, out of sight. Little folk, faeries, reminding him how young he was, all in all.

Old, so old, Ben Harper! they sang out.

He strolled a bit further, appreciated the scenery in brief and blissful solitude with yesterday's vision more on his mind than plans for tomorrow.

"I wonder if the King's Raven is busy today," he wondered casually, as if it didn't matter much.

Ho ho ho!

Who knows?

I'll go!

The plop of a fish, a falling leaf, or something, drew him off the path, giving attention to the water at his feet. It was fenced to keep the kiddies from tumbling in, of course, trying to get at the giant statues. Easy enough for a determined grown-up to deal with, but weeds and wildflowers, a stand of golden anise, were also in the way. Man-made or not, the frowsy lake edge was natural enough to give way under Ben's feet. He put one knee to the muddy ground and pushed aside an armful of reeds.

Just below the surface, cloaked in her long hair, a pair of

Maggie Secara

moonstone eyes stared up at him out of a dull, lifeless face framed in golden scales.

Not again.

Ben caught his breath, sat back on his heels. When he dared to look again, there was nothing but deep pink water lilies rocking on their broad flat pads.

"Going for a swim, then?"

This time the voice behind him was unquestionably one he knew, though with a Cockney twang he wasn't used to. He turned, patting down his jeans to dust away the damp leaf litter and mouldy detritus. On a park bench he hadn't known was there, and perhaps it hadn't been, sat the languid, perpetually youthful person he knew as Raven.

When it suited him, Raven gave a rather good impression of Gainsborough's Blue Boy, vain and arrogant, no more than sixteen. Today he was more of a young solicitor gone rogue, dressed in blue pin-stripped suit and thin leather tie, with designer sunglasses perched on the jet-black curls. Shoulder-length, as usual, he had tied them back with a silver jewel: a raven on a silver branch set with table-cut sapphires that he had made himself, by his own hands, four hundred years ago.

"I was just thinking about you," Ben said, slapping the muck from his hands.

"So they tell me." Oberon's principal gentleman leaned back expansively, arms wide, legs crossed. "And why is that?"

"Mermaid."

"Mermaids live in the sea, Ben," said Raven solemnly. "This is a lake. Technically, it would have a naiad, if it were a real lake. But as it isn't…"

"Not living."

"Oh?"

"Mmm. Drowned, I think."

"Interesting. I don't believe mermaids can drown, you know."

"Yes, well, that was my understanding," Ben agreed in his best presenter's voice, and sat down. "But I am starting to wonder."

They sat in silence for a moment looking at the scenery,

then Raven sprang up, his narrow tie flying as he strode to the water's edge to see for himself. Disappointed, he turned to Ben.

"I thought you were done with London?"

"Final cleanup at White City. And what are you doing hanging about a public park in the middle of a working day? Eyeing little girls with bad intent?"

The familiar sideways glance from hooded eyes.

"I have things to do, as you do. I keep busy."

Ben raised a prompting eyebrow, though without much hope. The fae can be very stingy with explanations. But perhaps the moon was in the seventh house or something, because the boy went on talking, the Cockney diction thickening till he sounded like a young Michael Caine.

"If you must know, I've been giving guitar lessons to a bloke who don't know how good he is and needs some encouragement. By the time I'm done, he'll be playing the Palace. The actual Palace."

"So you're his muse?"

"In a manner of speaking. And his manager."

"Why not? Titania sings for Gilbert and Sullivan, his Grace builds recording studios."

"Every immortal boy needs a hobby." The accent dropped back into his own unique cadence.

"And this guy doesn't mind being represented by a teenager?"

Raven shot his cuffs, dropped the dark glasses onto his nose and sauntered away following the rustic path, with a slight air of Reservoir Dogs. Ben shook his head and caught him up.

"So this mermaid thing?" Raven said after a bit.

"Naiads?"

"Nymphs of a watery kind. Is this the only vision you've had?"

How did he always know?

"Well…"

"How about Chinese?"

Ben thought about that for a moment, then said, "English, by preference."

The boy grinned.

"Dinner, you idiot. I feel like Mandarin."

"I know the perfect place."

3
1590 Bankside

Swaying slightly, Simon Carew planted himself on the muddy platform at Winchester stairs, pretending he had not become a whoring drunkard. But what other sort of man stood in broken boots in the last light of an April day, with drizzling rain trickling down his collar and his guts ripped out with aqua vitae, swearing at his fate. He dragged the borrowed cloak tighter around his bony shoulders, cursing the river, the boatmen, and the mud flats uncrossable between them. In the mid-stream, beyond the mud, dozens of lighters, wherries, and barges cut swiftly through the Thames, as unattainable as the slopes of Heaven.

He hated the river. He had always hated it, not only Thames but all the others: rivers, streams, babbling brooks—those, perhaps, most of all with their mocking voices. Hated, feared and, to his daily shame, was drawn to them as some men are drawn to violence or pretty boys, even when it gave him no pleasure. Scripture said that running water washed away the stain of sin. Why, hadn't Jesus Christ himself been baptized in a river? That alone should have made flowing waters sacred and so worthy of his admiration.

Go to, a pagan notion. No more sacred than the fairy harlots that tended them.

Unemployed scholar, cypherist, translator, bawd, he paced a while then stared out again towards London sprawling fat, complacent and inaccessible on the other side. A hundred church spires stabbed the sky, a thousand chimneys streamed with smoke moved by the same breeze that dashed the stinging rain into his eyes. He was only five-and-thirty, too young to have fallen so far. The voices whispering in his head agreed. With any luck, it would kill him.

God, he hated the river.

And if there was anything he hated more than the endless crossing and recrossing by boat, it was crossing by London Bridge. Almost a city in itself, a jumble of houses and shops occupied most of its length. From the great gate house at the Southwark end, where traitors' heads and quartered parts spiked the air, a wide passageway bored through the shops of milliners and drapers, a few fine houses, even a church alternating with open space as crowded as any street in London and twice as noisy. The very sound of the waters rushing beneath the Bridge's nineteen stout oak piers made his stomach churn. Not even the clamor of squawking housewives, bawling costermongers, dogs scuffling over a bitch or a bone could drive out the sound of it. The river whispered, rumbled, rushed at him with all its ghosts, and no escape. If he could have grown wings and flown across like the kites and gulls that soared shrieking over all, well, he would have shat on housewife, monger, and dog just as the birds did, and been the happier for it.

But the hour was growing late and the fog rising and, while the god-forgot river stood at such low tide, not a single swearing waterman could come in to the landing for him, nor could he get to them. The city gates would be closing soon. Options were few.

He'd had enough of vulgar Southwark for the day, belike for all time. He swore he would not be back. He swore it every time he stumbled, weeping and cursing, out of the Three Tuns, or the Bell, or the Pope of Rome. He knew it was a lie. When a man has no soul to lose, what matter where he spends himself?

So here he stood, stranded in the rain on the muddy verge of the river he despised, despising himself and ignoring the voices in his head. He could, as some good men might, retreat to St Saviour's, the cathedral that stood hard by, and occupy the time in virtuous prayer. He could pace about in the damp and wait for the tide, wishing he still had a scrip from the Palace as he used to, good for the use of any boat on the river, though it still wouldn't make the tide come in. He could go back to the Bell... God, no. He could curse Lord Treasurer Burghley for the latest Court economies that had cost him his place and his privileges. Or he could betake himself to the Bridge, and walk over.

***

Simon Carew, bent under his cloak like a hunchback, set his ill-shod foot to the oaken planks of London Bridge longing for peace and finding only noise. London was always noisy, Southwark no better; one got used to it. But the Bridge! The sound of the river rose up at him, echoing in the hollow spaces beneath, ripe with curses. Head down, he shouldered his way into the chattering crowd, avoiding eye contact: a salmon swimming upstream, if ever a salmon dreamed such poisonous thoughts as he. Seven hundred and fifty paces to go.

Christ's wounds, he hated the river!

He knew that all about him the world joked, complained, condoled, and gossiped yard by yard, but he heard only the uproar, the tread of boots, the clip-clop of horses' hooves, and he opened himself to it, reveling in the racket that drowned, however briefly, the whispers that always followed him. The voices that disappeared when his mind was teasing meaning from a cypher, or puzzling over an inscription in some antique scroll. The voices that, sniggering, never failed to find him when he had given in to base desire.

Let them whisper, Simon thought, and dived into the dark, echoing chamber of the first arcade. Ahead of him, a gang of idle apprentices hooted to make the echo, and someone else shouted a name though anonymity was only imperfectly secured. Light leaked from office windows and delivery doors cut into the walls.

"Randall loveth Mary Perkins!" cried a boy, and his friend pummeled his shoulders, laughing.

Some unbearable time later, though it can't have been more

than a minute or two, Simon emerged blinking from the Chapel House onto an open deck that had once been the bascules of the drawbridge that was no longer used. Like everyone else he clutched his hat to his short-cropped skull and leaned against the cross-breeze to keep from being tumbled over the railings.

The next passage worked through a dozen or more half-timbered buildings three and four stories high, cantilevered out over the edge of the bridge to make up for the space lost in the tunnel. These were mostly the offices of great merchants, the tallow chandlers, silk mercers, men who dealt in flax and train oil and furs. He had found work there after coming down from Cambridge, but the endless awareness of the river had been more than he could bear.

Someone swearing inventively thrust past him, with a dog at his heels. A whore gasped, plying her trade with urgent efficiency in a shadowed doorway. Hugging bony elbows to himself, Carew winced and hurried on to keep his gorge from rising, and the rest of his body from responding in any other way.

Sooner than he expected, he was in the open air again in what was, or should have been at the Bridge's mid-point, the wide space they called The Square. But it couldn't be. It smelled of sunlight and cinnamon, and the wholesome scents of bruised thyme and bay. He was still aware of the crowd pressing past, broad shoulders, sharp elbows and hard baskets; horses with creaking panniers, a rattling hand cart. How was it then that, phantomlike, they moved around him as if he were a tree or a statue? As if they, or he, had slipped behind a curtain of gauze? He stopped still, hardly daring to breathe. It smelled, he thought miserably, like Dartmoor. Like his home.

He looked around, frowning. To the west, as it should be, lay the open deck and a dim view of the city as far as the Bridewell, where the sluggish Fleet emptied into the Thames. To the east, downstream, the tall masts of great ships clogging the Pool of London filled the sky. Here at the Bridge's edge, a painted wooden hoarding screened the bank of privies that jutted out over the water for the ease of travellers. All that was quite as it should be.

But to Simon's astonishment, some enterprising soul had planted a market garden in the open space. Rows of turnips and cabbages, climbing beans and peas blossomed in wooden frames. In the midst had been set an apple tree in a vast wine barrel: a tree planted so long ago that it had grown old, the trunk twisted and gnarled, and stretched out limbs thick with leaves and blossoms, though it was nowhere near apple time. A few hesitant steps took Simon under its boughs, though he blinked and rubbed his eyes, knowing it could not be true. Many a time he'd drunk himself raving, to be sure, but not today. He'd run out of money and friends before delirium could take hold.

Witchcraft, then, or worse.

Almost directly above his head, a branch shook setting a shower of blossoms adrift on the breeze. From high up within the masking leaves there came a sigh, a young woman's muffled squeal, the throaty laughter of a lover with his face buried in her cleavage. Entranced, Carew ventured warily towards the sound, then stopped at the sight of two pairs of naked feet pressing pink toes against a branch.

Some pissant 'prentice and his poxy wench must have clambered up the ancient tree to laugh and fleer at honest folk, he thought. And worse, to fumble under their clothes, to whisper and moan when their lust peaked.

Carew shuddered, his guts wrenching with shame and disgust even while his blood stirred. He meant to back away, to run, but he couldn't move. Shame became outrage and boiled into fury.

"Ho, there!" he shouted. "You there, in the tree! Come down at once, thou knave. Come down and bring the whore with you."

The girl's voice squeaked a sound like "Oops!" but the boy just cackled.

"Bugger! We've done it again."

"Not now, my love, we… Ah, ah, Amadis! Stop!"

Bile scourged Simon's throat.

"Come down, I say."

A small, brown-spotted apple sailed out of the leaves and

almost before he saw it smashed him square on the bridge of his nose. Simon cried out and clapped a hand over the spot, the red-rimmed eyes watering. He called out,

"Help ho, the Bridge Warden! Help!"

Did no one hear?

A face warped with mischief, surrounded by a halo of dark gold curls, thrust through the leaves.

"What's that you say, you staggering, puke-dribbling ale worm! God's Eyes, man, call you that a beard? Say, is it a beard, sweeting, or a gravy stain?"

The girl's face, heart-shaped and wide-eyed, framed in a fall of gilded hair, peered out next to the boy's. She blinked owlishly.

Recognition raked across Simon Carew's heart as sharp as a carding comb. His brain whirled. How could he not have known what she was? The profane music in her voice should have branded her at once. Oh, there was more here than sluttishness and riot. The scent in the air was not cinnamon, but sulphur.

"Faith, we've upset him. I think we should go, love," she said, and started to descend.

"Stay!" The boy grabbed her arm. "Oriana, my heart, let him come to us."

"Amadis, stop it!" She sounded more annoyed than frightened, or threatened.

"Say, is that a ruff about your neck, grandsire, or is it a dish clout? Faith, it's so yellow, I took it for a cheese!"

The dark, the stinks, the damp, the noise, the reality of the Bridge, of London, of the world slammed back into Simon Carew like an avalanche, rocking him where he stood. But where a weaker man, or a sober man, might have fallen back in fear, he reached for righteous anger. Buffeted by passers-by, he unbent from the miserable customary posture and drew up to his full height.

"I know you, foul creature," intoned Carew, a long finger pointing to the west.

The last veil shredded away. To bewildered travellers, he seemed to have appeared out of the thin air: an annoyed, middle-aged scholar blinking in the fog and muttering to himself.

One man slowed his pace to stare, cursing when the next caught up with him too suddenly. They stopped, perforce, and others too. A trio of apprentices in dull blue caps peered out of a glover's shop, and two clerks from the counting house appeared with quills behind their ears.

"Stay me not!" said one in annoyance. "Go on!"

"Do you know me indeed?" said the boy called Amadis, dropping down through the branches to land on his feet, now fitly covered in slashed leather shoes of the finest make. They matched the wine-colored jerkin winking with deep green gems. Which set off the doublet of black velvet, the jet-black trunk hose, and the lace-edged ruff tight under his chin and at his wrists, one of which was cocked over the swept hilt of a superb Spanish rapier.

Simon swallowed his astonishment. Not witchcraft. This was far more magic than he had expected, and of an utterly different kind. Who were these people?

The boy, the gentleman rather, struck a pose and said, "I pray you, what am I, little man?"

"Not you, my lord," he stammered. "I mean the harlot there who has bewitched you. Come down, witch!"

"Witch?" The word sped through the crowd, echoing through the passages. "Where? There's a witch on the bridge! A witch in the apple tree."

Traffic finally ground to a halt, except for the last grumbling drayer who didn't care if the Devil himself were in the apple tree, it were none o' his business. The road ahead cleared rapidly, and if none followed, why then, the sooner home. A neighbor snatched a wobbly toddler out of the way of the relentless hooves.

"A what?" said the girl, as she slid to the ground herself, her naked skin glowing pink and white. With her came a fall of apple blossoms that caught the breeze and swirled around her, fluttering, folding, dazzling the eye until she minced forward as gallantly, as impossibly appareled as her lover. The rosy lips set in a thin line.

"What did he call me?"

"A witch, my love. A sorceress. An enchantress, and that perhaps I will not deny him." He captured her little hand and kissed it.

A deep inhale, a quick exhale bounced her delightful bosom, making passers-by smile who couldn't even see her.

"A witch, am I? A witch? Why, thou poxy boggard! I will not... I mean, I am not... Oh, fie!"

She was not supposed to giggle, but how could she help it? Had it not been for the deeply pointed, smoothly corseted waist, the carnation silk taffeta tucked and pinned to the vast wheel farthingale, the reticella and point lace collar winking with diamond sparks at her throat; had it not been for all of these restraints, her perfect shoulders would have risen to her ears in a little girl shrug. She settled for the stamp of one dainty red-heeled shoe.

"I have forgot what thou toldst me to say, my love. I thought he said 'bitch'!"

"Madam," sneered Simon Carew, though his bowels turned to ice. "I say thou art a witch, a creature from Hell, a demon. You turn men's heads with your pretty voice and your wanton shape. You lure them to sin then abandon them to melancholy and self-slaughter."

He knew full well she was nothing of the kind. In fact, he knew exactly what she was—how could he not when his mother had been of the same faithless race: a water nymph, a pagan sprite as soulless as himself. She should be destroyed, hanged, burned as he had been burnt, though the flames had spat him out. Red fire rose up in his eyes, the crackling and the roar of flames licking the straw in the walls, the coal in the bin, melting his skin all down his left side. She should be scarred as he had been scarred; scream as his father had screamed when four strong men dragged him from the blazing forge.

He would denounce her with the words folk understood. Cry up her many crimes in ways they dared not ignore. Even threaten by implication to recognize her accomplices within the swelling crowd.

Goodwife Tapster and Mistress Merchant glared back at

him and went on their way. A country woman gathered her children and disappeared behind a friendly door.

Only one thing was odd, he thought in a moment's shocking clarity. The man and the girl, whoever they were, had been walking towards him the whole time, as if from very far away, not merely from the tree that couldn't be there but from within Faerie itself. The man's clear grey eyes bored into Simon's, pinning him to the spot. The man, if he was a man, looked to be speaking or chanting, perhaps singing, Simon couldn't tell. He could see the lips move but heard nothing.

The noble Amadis appeared to pause, gathering the audience to him with his gallant patience, and now his voice carried beautifully as the fog—the true fog—crept across their feet. He could have reached out and laid hands on the bastard.

"Fellow, go to bed. You're drunk, and—" He leaned forward to take a long sniff, then grimaced, waving an aristocratic hand before his nose. "A' God's name! You stink of the brothel and the shit house. Certes, someone has been wanton enough, though his revels have ended."

The glance he tossed out, sharing the joke, won the crowd to him, even the whores. Adorable, noble, and sweet-witted, too, and when the handsome face went stern and sharp as the landlord's on quarter day, they respected that.

"But if you speak of my wife again in any wise, I shall have you in the Clink Prison. Or mayhap these fine fellows will toss you into the river for me."

"This monster is a witch, my lord. If she is your wife, I pity you. If you defend her, you are either her victim or her hell-bound accomplice."

Sweat gathered under the band of his hat, in his armpits, in the hollow of his chest though the fog grew thick and chill. Was it the fog, or had his vision clouded? Why would no one do anything?

"My masters, can you not see it? Will ye not help me! I have evidence against her! Will no one bind them over? By our Saviour's bleeding wounds, where is the Bridge Warden?"

The crowd shuffled, muttering. They saw only a grandly dressed pair of courtiers being harangued by some canting

Puritan with spittle flying from his lips. There were witches in the North, some said, surely not here in London. As all knew, foul countenance bespoke a foul heart. And look at her! A sweet-faced young wife no older than their own daughters, and prettier too. The husband, bless him, was clearly a man of parts, and more patient than that great coxcomb, the Earl of Essex, and his friends.

And what about this Carew, this skulking knave, with the terrible weals all down his side and the top of his arm. His left side. The Devil's side. Burns, he said. Aye, and so they would be. Claimed for Hell already, then. Well, there you have it.

With blossoming horror, Carew understood what he should have realized from the start: that no one else had seen the nymph and her minion come out of the tree. By whatever spell or charm this so-called Amadis had sung under the cover of the river's voice, not a man among them of any degree had reason to believe him, Simon. Not even the men he knew.

Amadis. What sort of name was that? Oh, of course. The Spanish book called him Amadis of Gaul. And as any Englishman could tell you, Spaniards are wicked, dishonest, false, and Frenchmen worse.

"I think I know a witch when I see one," one man grumbled, glaring at Simon.

"Aye," said another, sneering. "And I know a drunkard for a puking, ditch-born measle!"

The lady Oriana looked sweetly at her lover. He lifted her hand to his lips, and murmured,

"Now."

Almost under his chin already, she reached for Carew's forearms, buried her fingers in each greasy sleeve at the elbow. Her head went back and her voice split the air with a heart-stopping scream as she threw herself at his chest. Every downcast pair of eyes swung up to see the pinch-faced ranter clutching the fairest lady in all the world to his chest as if he would carry her off.

"Unhand my lady, foul recreant! Ah-ha!" cried Amadis, his rapier hissing from its sheath, and began laying about the fellow with the flat of the blade. The expression that curled across his handsome face might almost have been giddy laughter.

Carew's showed only misery, hatred, and terror as the 'prentices and their masters, even the ballad seller, all rushed forward.

"No!" he shrieked. The girl's body, smoothly naked, pressed up hard against him; her fabulous gown, the lace and jewels, were nothing but illusion. "No, it is all false! They are not what they seem. They are not what they seem!"

He cried out again as the barest flick of steel laid his cheek open scant inches from one eye. Limpet-like, Oriana still clung to him, screaming in the fog, until her lord's arm came round her slender waist. She froze, relaxed. Round blue eyes glanced up into Simon's, and she said, "I will greet your mother for you at the Mermaid Stair. She must be so proud."

She let go her hands.

In the instant he was free of her, they dragged him away. Carew went down under a hail of cuffs and kicks, still yelling for aid and swearing terrible oaths.

He hated the river. He hated every river, and every lying, faithless, whoring naiad, nix and goddess ever spawned in a well. As consciousness fled, the voices, his voices, promised him revenge.

Unseen by any mortal man or woman, glittering Amadis swept his beloved away to the apple tree. At the base, carved into the wine barrel, the mermaid badge waited only for his tracing caress to take them into Faerie, and the tree with them.

"Well, *cariad*," he observed, "that's another place we can never go back to."

In the morning, the blood had been sluiced away and a barber surgeon found for the mad scholar. And though the story was the talk of the Bridge, none could say exactly what the noble couple had said, or done, or what they had been like, though all agreed they had been very fair and well spoken. Names? No, no names that any had heard.

The ballad seller assured her blind old mother that their clothes had shimmered with the most delicate shades of sky blue and sea green. And surely they were as much in love as any folk in a story.

"Hmph," the old woman snorted. "There's no good can come of that."

4
Fleet Bridge, the next day

When a man understands that he has no soul, unlike his fellow men, it changes things. How should he live? What governs his relations with the world? On whom should he call when humiliated, derided, driven to the ground by blows? When he staggers up the creaking stairs to his two sad rooms, with no more damage than a cracked crown and a mosaic of bruises startling in their color and variety, whom should he thank?

It was a mercy, surely, but whose? The silk mercer's widow who made sure Simon ended up on the right side of the river, and found the cart and driver willing to take him there? The barber surgeon, who had patched him up and dosed him with willow bark, then sent to the apothecary for a tincture of opium to stave off the pain? Certainly. Their rewards would be in Heaven, though he still owed the widow six shillings. But to God, Simon Carew was himself invisible. He had long suspected this, and now, leaking tears in his sorry bed, he knew it was true. If he died in the night, not even Hell would care.

It was not that he had lost his faith. No, for thirty years and more he had been all too sure of God's dominion. But Christ's mercy was for Mankind, not for the soulless legions of Faerie. And what was he, Simon Carew, but a sorry simulacrum of a man: half fae, half human, wholly lost. A man could not have half a soul.

As for the nymph on the Bridge: just as Carew had seen her true nature at once, so too had she seen his. She had known him for what he was, a cripple pretending to be whole, and she had laughed. Any mortal would have been horrified.

The whispering voices told him it was so. He had heard them in his cradle and every day of his youth. A pretty brown thing she was, his mother, or so he had heard, fair as a speckled trout. A step as light as leaf on tree, both in the village dancing and even the while she carried him under her heart. He knew what that meant now, though he hadn't as a child. A faerie woman. A damned, deceitful, soulless faerie incapable of love. And true enough, three months after the child came, she had gone away as smiling and as careless as she had come.

You could see, they said as well, her mark on the child, who slept through his christening as no human child does—then woke up and bit the priest with tiny, shell-like teeth, but he never cried. The old women said that meant there was no soul, neither, to drive the devil out of. And they grumbled, as old women will, and never missed the chance to remind him of it.

If only he could somehow destroy the faerie half of him, cut it away and leave the human side whole and clean. Aye, the blacksmith, his father, had tried to save him that way once; he remembered, and it filled his dreams.

As a child of eight, Simon had waked in the dawn to find himself naked and bound, bent like a bow over his father's workbench. He had looked up in terror to see the huge man looming over him, sinewy arms raised over head, hands knotted around the black knife, praying, black-eyed and terrible, as Abraham had prayed over Isaac.

With an iron dagger, Giles Carew would have cut away the evil for good and all. But interfering neighbors had broken down the door and wrestled the blacksmith to the hard earth floor.

It had taken four of them, and none came away unhurt, but they had managed eventually to bind him and take him away. After that Simon had gone to live with the vicar and his wife, who taught him Latin and a little Greek. That, together with a tenuous link to a Carew of greater consequence, and another to the Guildhall, had allowed him to go up to Cambridge to study properly.

They should not have stopped the smith, Simon thought, as he had so many times before. It would have worked, he knew that now. Iron is anathema to the faery kind, and the dagger Giles had forged from sky-fallen ore and his anger and his betrayal—that knife would have cut out the wickedness. If only they had not stopped him. If only, poor bedeviled man, the smith had not run away and hanged himself from the old bridge that spanned the River Dart.

"Fool," he snarled, though at himself or his father was unclear.

He was doing it again, sending himself down that terrible path. That way lay only madness and death. It would not do.

It would not do.

What he needed was a course of action, something to do, not more of this melancholic despair. He needed the knife, and it was here, somewhere among the chaos of his belongings. Somewhere… And then he understood what the whispering voices were telling him. He finally heard them, plain as a pikestaff. The knife, of course.

Throwing himself out of bed to look for it, he got as far as the floor, where tangled in the sheet he lay near an hour eaten up with frustration and self-loathing. Perhaps it was the opium working in his blood, or perhaps his spinning brain had at last discerned a path.

What if he could purge that vile nature from him another way, atone for it somehow? Oh, not by rattling beads, or sitting through endless sermons, or pattering prayers his awkward God would not hear. No, no, they were right, his voices. With God all things are possible, even…

Even a creature such as he might earn a soul and become wholly human. If he could do but one great service in God's name, surely that would shrive his heart till it was truly human, worthy of grace. He would kill the mermaids and all their immoral kin: naiads, sirens, nymphs, whatever their heathen names.

One more thing niggled and gnawed at his mind.

Oriana had said, I will greet your mother on the Mermaid Stair. But what was that, besides a conundrum? What use had a mermaid for a stair? A secret, then. A cipher. He was very good with ciphers, none better. Perhaps it was the road to their obscene kingdom. Well, he would study to find it out, whatever it was, and whatever it took. And then he would destroy it, burn it, cutting the wickedness from the body of the world.

A worthy goal, but he could do nothing without money. He would need money for books, and travel, and decent apparel; his meager savings were all but spent. And that meant he must give over his despair and find a decent position again, restore his fortunes.

He clambered back to his bed with painful slowness, listening to the ropes creak under the sagging mattress, and settled his mind. He needed to mend his life, which would be hard, and his fortunes, which might not be so hard at all.

In the morning he would make himself get out of bed, take his breakfast of bread and small beer. Then dressed cleanly and soberly, with care, he would betake himself to where the Court lay at Greenwich to beg an interview with Sir Robert Cecil, the Queen's new spymaster since the death of his old master. Cecil could not, as Walsingham had done, employ him daily in an office—the hunchback's father, old Lord Burghley, hated paying salaries—but Walsingham had given assurances along with that last quarter's salary. Providing Simon could keep himself sober and out of the stews, something could be done for him, a place might be found. It had not seemed possible a few weeks ago, but now...

For the first time in years, Simon Carew slept peacefully, even poisoned with alcohol and bruised to the bone; even while he dreamt of murder.

5
Friday: Lambeth North

"The name is against it, I know," Ben said, looking up at the neon sign glowing crimson and blue in the afternoon.

Mr Wong's Authentic Every Flavour Chinese "We Deliver."

Raven shrugged.

"It's Lambeth."

"But the food is excellent. One of Mellis's cousins has a B&B around the corner. We used to come here all the time before we bought the flat in Kensington."

"The one you just sold?"

"You see my point."

In the rattle and clatter of a busy restaurant, they could talk about anything without being overheard or remarked on. He pushed open the door. Somehow they managed to be seated at once.

"So, where's your boss?" Ben asked, after half a dozen dishes and a lot of questions to which Raven had no answers. "He'll have something to say about this, whatever it is."

Raven looked thoughtful while poking among the noodles for a last honey walnut shrimp. Finding it, his chopsticks struck like a heron's beak. He glanced up and grinned.

"Yorkshire, 1920, I think," he said. "Wreaking havoc among the populace with an enormous camera, a couple of teen-aged girls, and Arthur Conan Doyle."

Ben stared, then snorted with delight as the penny dropped.

"Cottingley!" he said when he had stopped laughing. "Cottingley, seriously? So they really did see faeries!"

"I'm afraid so. Pity is, it's very hard to take pictures of the little folk, especially with those old slow cameras. And really quite impossible to catch my lord's image at all."

"I suppose Aubrey provided the picture books? You know, for the cut-outs."

"And possibly the camera," said Raven with a particularly elvish twinkle. "It remains to be seen, doesn't it?"

"Poor old Conan Doyle."

"So before we bother him, and speaking of Sherlock Holmes, why don't we see what we've got, and what we can figure out on our own?"

"You mean before he makes it an assignment?"

"Knew you were clever."

The American shook his head a little doubtfully, and signaled the waiter for another bottle of Tsing Tao.

"So what do we have? Some kind of vision in the dinosaur lake, and a major one around Teddington."

"Where the river meets the tide!" Ben declared, quoting the town's trademark phrase around a pork rib.

"Which fact," Raven added, "might be significant, though I can't say why. Something is trying to get your attention, that much is clear."

"Well, they've got it." Ben picked up the bill, automatically checking the math.

In the instant, the room fell into one of those awful moments of silence usually filled by someone embarrassing themselves. This time, the room held its breath, the whine of Chinese folk music asserted itself for that suspended second, and the chatter closed over them again.

The fae stopped suddenly and cleared his throat.

"Time to go," he said abruptly, and shoved back his chair.

Ben followed his nod in the direction of a waiter who was giving them more attention than they were paying for. Huddled with two others near the kitchen door, the man was muttering rapidly in Chinese. In a moment, all three were talking, and staring too.

The tell-tale aura of Faerie is hard to see even to those who have that gift, unless the light is right. Ben swung round in his seat, checking the windows, and oh yes. From where he sat the cloud-filtered light was perfect. He could make out the faint aura without much effort. Evidently, the waiter could, too. From the nervous looks and gestures, Ben guessed not only could the man hear the bells of Elfland, as they say, they were jangling in his ears, and he didn't like it. The staccato of Chinese was getting louder. Some of the customers were starting to pay attention.

"Mental note," Ben murmured, pulling out cash instead of a credit card. "Avoid red lanterns and gold foil when dining with the lords of Faerie."

"Oh, and tip generously but not extravagantly, or they'll know you're Chu Pa-Chiai and you'll never be able to eat here again."

"Chu Pa-Chiai?"

"The celestial pig fairy!"

The boy dodged the incoming punch with subtle skill, and smirking, left the tip himself.

They strolled through Lambeth's dinnertime bustle through the mingled smells of diesel and curry, the rattle of green leaves and a dozen accents. What had been a noisome swamp in the first Elizabeth's time had long ago been drained, built over, and improved. Now the hollow sounds of television, the beeps and clicks of video games, fell from open windows as if the bones of the old marsh were not still lurking a few meters below their feet. Only the grey-edged clouds piling into fabulous towers over the city remained the same.

"So what next?"

"Are you going home tonight, or can you stay in town awhile?"

"Let's see what Cousin Kris says."

Cutting through a neighborhood park, Ben shuffled through fallen leaves, tasted the air, holding his thoughts. A few fat raindrops stained the concrete path beside him. The scents altered, the lively air of rain edged with something like cinnamon, something like thyme, wrapped in a tendril of a girl's perfume. Oblivious, a pair of young lovers entwined on a bench between a pair of apple trees, their faces masked by the cascade of the girl's long blonde hair. They caught Ben's eye only because Raven stopped suddenly to glare at them tightlipped, as if he didn't like what he saw.

"What?" said Ben as they crossed Austel Street. "You've seen kissing before. I've seen you kissing before, come to that."

"Mmm," the boy grunted and moved along, his swift stride efficiently leaving the lovers behind while his expression cleared. "Where are we going?"

Austell Mews, facing the park, sounded more upscale than it was. Still each narrow, red-brick house in the row retained a faded elegance, and a pair of tall plaster pillars framing a door between bay windows.

"Come on, it's just along here."

Finally Raven deigned to remark,

"Consider, human child, that there may be more to a thing that what you see. Our sense of what is right, like our emotions and appetites, is not as clear-cut or as simple as yours."

"Mine?"

"Mortals, aye. With us, these things are…" He sighed bleakly. "Complex."

Ben snorted. "Harm no one? Do unto others? How complex can it be?"

"I'm sure you're right," said Raven.

Avoiding the iron palings on either side, he followed the harper up the sober bricks to Kristin Powell's front door as the first rumble of thunder rolled over their heads.

ii

Of the houses in Austel Mews, Number 7 was not alone in having a sign reading Bed and Breakfast in the front window with "No room" in front of it. But Mellis's red-haired Cousin Kris was waiting for him with a big smile and a tiny room at the top of the stairs at the back, garden view, just for the one night. Breakfast between half-six and half-eight and no later, mind.

"Well, maybe for you, love," she said, and kissed Ben's cheek, beaming. She never noticed Raven at all. Once or twice she blinked a puzzled look straight through him. He winked at her with boyish charm, and she looked away, shaking her head.

Kristin gave Ben the room key, and one to the front door in case he came in late, and repeated the house rules: no smoking, no loud music, please use your mobile phone for external calls, and check out by 10:00 a.m.

"No problem," he assured her, accepted all her smiles and love to the family, and headed up the steep, narrow stairs. Many landings later, he turned the key in the lock and went in. And stopped dead.

He had walked through a neat white door in London and into a darkly comfortable, clubby sort of chamber in what he supposed must be a wing of the king's Great House in Faerie: all leather-bound books and forest-green walls, which might have been actual forest by the fragrance. Billiard table, club chairs, a guitar in a corner, a silver flute on a stand, a gleaming well-used fiddle on a shelf under a big flat-screen TV. Behind folding doors, a kitchenette.

The door on the opposite wall presumably led to the bathroom. Imagination quailed at what luxuries faerie magic might have arranged there. Ben couldn't even pretend not to be impressed.

"Damn," he breathed. "It's…"

"Isn't it, though?" Raven grinned, eyes alight with mischief as he pulled a couple bottles of very good beer out of a gleaming chiller that Cousin Kris didn't know she had. His black hair shook out to his shoulders as he stood up and held out a beer.

"Close the door, please, Ben. Were you born in a barn?"

One of the best parts of Faerie, Ben thought as he accepted the bottle, was the abundance of beer. In his youth, he'd spent all of his summers at the Renaissance Pleasure faire in northern California, and a good few springtime weekends at the one in L.A. After that, four immersion seasons at Farthingale Hall in Kent had refined his understanding of how to be an Elizabethan gentleman, and, incidentally, how to drink like one. So he was accustomed to thinking of beer as one of the four major food groups.

The fae, being immortal, as Raven had pointed out before, eat only for pleasure. As he said, for food there is honey, for dreams there is wine. And for sustained problem-solving, there is beer.

"This may be a three-bottle problem."

Ben tipped the bottle back and drank gratefully, then headed for the shower.

"Look, the real question is…" Ben began when he emerged pink and damp half an hour later.

Raven stepping out of a shadow handed Ben an armful of clean clothes, then flung himself onto the fat leather sofa and switched on the TV to some nature show.

"Phone call," he said.

"Yes, mother. What phone call?"

"God, I love David Attenborough!"

The programme featured birds—flocks and flights and herds of birds—which always tickled him silly. Attention fixed, Raven said only,

"Phone your wife."

"Why, what time… Oh."

Ben Harper sat down with his mobile at a massive desk in a sort of alcove or bay facing a wide, diamond-paned casement window. Beyond it, the view was definitely not London, or probably England in any age he was familiar with. Soft rain fell over a flower-studded garden, wherever it was.

Ignoring it, he dialed home.

"Did you miss your train?" Mellis asked in the breathless way she had when she'd been playing a particularly energetic piano concerto. Ben could hear the strings still resonating.

"Yes. I mean, no, that is, not exactly."

"Oh, good start."

"I know," he said contritely, and he meant it. "I'm sorry. They threw me a party and—" Raven threw him a frown. "And well, Raff stopped by, and we got some dinner. So, yeah, I did."

"I see." He heard the cover come down over the keyboard

with a firm but controlled crack. "Where is Oberon sending you this time?"

"What?" He threw a panicky glance at the sofa, but Raven was busy smirking at the flamingos. "Uhm, what do you mean?"

Mellis didn't know—couldn't, shouldn't, wasn't supposed to know—that their stylish friend Aubrey was anything but what he seemed to be: an industry friend who knew some interesting people. After her own part in the magic, Aubrey had all but promised the memory would fade, and the fae can't lie.

He couldn't lie, but he could be wrong. A Devon woman to the bone, Mellis Powell didn't believe in faeries any more than any other ordinary highly educated modern woman, not consciously. But when she wasn't actually bewitched herself, as she had been last Christmas, she could see what was right in front of her. What if...

"Are you there?" she asked a little anxiously. "Sorry, pet, it's the connection. I asked if Aubrey was sending you to hear another band?" But he could tell her voice had changed.

"Uh, no. I missed the train. It's all right, Kristin took me in. Home in the morning. Are you all right?"

She didn't sound all right.

But they exchanged news, and how Sparrow was getting excited about the new school term starting on Monday, and so on; the usual domestic chat without further reference to anything uncanny.

"Kisses, I love you." Mellis rang off.

Perhaps he'd misread her after all.

Or not.

Still, when he snapped the phone closed and tucked it away in a jacket pocket, Ben found himself strangely relaxed, almost light-hearted. With all the mundane busyness of his life organized, stamped, filed or finished, he had only one task left.

"So," he said at last, collapsing into the club chair at Raven's elbow. The beer on the end table, he noticed, was still cold; the light in the room, though it had no obvious source, was set to a level his strained eyes appreciated. The TV was still on, but went off as the boy turned toward Ben.

"So," he agreed. "Let me show you something."

What Raven handed across the coffee table was a fragment, no larger than his hand, of a manuscript so shattered with age it should have fallen to dust even under the fae's weightless touch. Across it, three lines of a script Ben had seen before, wedge-shaped forms like little arrowheads, and others that looked a bit like Greek. With the fragment ripped or slashed from its source at an angle, none of the lines could be complete, but there was magic in it. Ben could feel it as a warmth, a kind of tingle that reached for his hands as he took hold of it. Magic that came from the words, but even more from a drawing at the bottom: a blank-faced figure with interlaced strands that might be hair and legs, or tails.

"I've seen that before," Ben murmured.

"Oh?"

"Yeah, one of the bands I'm working with at Diamond Hall, they're called Pictish Mermaids. That's their logo, more or less"

Raven coughed, laughing. "Great name for a band."

"Where did this come from?"

"The little stream at the edge of your property," the raven-boy said thoughtfully. "Sparrow and I were fishing. Didn't catch anything of course. And this was wedged under a rock. And yes, it's a kind of mermaid. The one everybody knows about is carved on a Pictish stone in Scotland, but it's older than that. From what I understand, far older."

"Anything else?" Ben asked, which made Oberon's henchman laugh.

"Yes, now that you ask. A girl's face, very pale with eyes like pearls. And music, singing, coming from the water. Very sad. In one of the old modes. The sea folk, all the Atami really—the water fae—they use something called Icthylean mode. Here."

He paused, then went to the shelves and took down the violin and set it under his chin. After a few uncharacteristically halting measures, he stopped, shaking his head.

"Something like that. It can be beautiful but weird. Sparrow said it must sound better under water."

"Clever boy." Ben thought about this a moment, and asked, "Does Sparrow know what you are?"

If he could have blushed, Raven might have considered it.

"I wondered when you were going to ask. Oh look, chocolate!" He reached for a pink glass candy dish that hadn't been there before. Unless it had. His eyes rolled up in abject bliss as he bit into a dark brown bon-bon. "Gods of earth, toffee. You really have to try this!"

"So that's a yes?"

"Uhm, yes, of course he does."

"How long?"

"Honestly, I think since the first time we met."

"At the studio?"

"No, Ben." For a moment he almost looked guilty. "On the moor. Before I met you, actually. He must have been about six. And before you get angry, yes, I was watching him. On my lord's orders. Usually from a tree—I didn't want to alarm anyone, least of all him. He's an extraordinary boy, your Sparrow."

"I appear to have an extraordinary family." Ben paused, fiddling with the label on the beer bottle, peeling a strip of paper along one wet edge. "Mellis just said something…"

"You're not really surprised? My lord did take her into Faerie, and she helped you restore the dragon ring."

"You don't get it. Aubrey said she'd forget. It would fade and she'd forget." He hated to think of her carrying around the burden of memory, the fear and violence from that spring, unable to talk to him, protecting him. "She didn't have the gift before then."

"Or she did as a child and, as most mortals do, she rejected it. You did the same, as I recall, for a long time. Look, it will be all right. We'll go talk to her tomorrow. Right now…" He got up and from some twist of reality produced two more beers. "We have a vision of a dead or dying mermaid in the Thames just where the tidal river begins and ends. And another in the city in a place we've been together. Another at your home on Dartmoor. All magical places. And this scrap of paper, papyrus, whatever."

"You know my methods, Watson," Ben said, sitting back with a grim smile. "What can you tell us about this slip of papyrus with the unusual markings?"

Raven laughed and as usual laid his own interpretation on the character.

"Let me see, Holmes."

Ben watched his friend keep his physical self occupied while his mind worked. He took the scrap to the little table that now stood in the casement window in place of the desk, and gestured Ben to come along where the light was better. For Ben's sake, of course, not his own. For his own sake, Raven opened the window latch over a garden fragrant with herbs under a clearing sky. The green smells rose up on the twilight air, and the fae breathed deeply once or twice, taking it in.

Then he sat and spread the ancient fragment on the table between them, smoothing out the creases.

"The symbol is sometimes called morforwyn, sometimes morven, in the old Celtic tongues, though it has much older names. Much older. It's a marker, and…"

"What?"

Raven pursed his lips.

"Set that aside for a moment. Some of this is in Greek, I think, but very old. This line is in what they call Linear B. I can read it, but I don't know what it means."

"I beg your pardon?"

"No, I can read it, of course, but it doesn't seem…" He cleared his throat and pointed to the first line. "This bit is about a staircase in a place of waters. This here is the name of a goddess, if I recall. But the rest, the letters are Greek, but I think the language is Akkadian!"

"Arcadian? You mean Cajun?"

"Hardly." The boy glared, and went on. "No, the tongue of the men of Akkad. It's very old, Ben. I mean, seriously ancient. Older than I am."

"Older than the king?"

An eyebrow lifted.

"So what does it say?"

"It's only a fragment, no way to be sure. But this last line—I think it's an invocation." He grinned. "Shall we see what happens?"

Gently, he turned the fragment over, hiding the text, and lifted away his hands. Ben saw the pale pointed face with the long sapphire eyes take on an expression he associated with deep magic, more perilous than the daily glamours and sleight of hand one quickly got used to.

"You'll think I'm being melodramatic. Humor me, please."

Ben nodded, glad he'd been allowed to stay.

Raven took a breath and spoke a phrase he knew for safety, begging whatever powers he might inadvertently address to be gracious. Then he chanted,

"Rabbatu atiratu yammi."

Nothing happened. A long minute passed. Traffic sounds rose from the open window, somewhere a dog barked, and in the floor below them water rattled in the pipes as someone started running a bath.

"Well!" said Ben at last.

Raven slowly bent forward until his brow touched the cool burnished oak of the table, and closed his eyes. Better than banging it.

"Well, indeed," he said, straightening with a slightly embarrassed chuckle. "That was…disappointing."

It was a good thing, Ben thought, that he'd gotten over the idea Raven couldn't be taken by surprise. In fact, he half wondered if the boy had entirely recovered from their mission last Christmas.

"Are you okay?"

"I'm fine." The boy waved away the question, his wide gaze still on the papyrus. "Look! Something's happening!"

In a ragged curve along the bottom edge, a string of tiny markings was fading into view, rising so swiftly out of the papyrus that Ben thought at first it must be mould, and started to cry out, until he saw shapes appear. More Greek letters grew from thin, muddy scratches into a black so clear it might have been written that morning. Then a huge grin split the fae lord's face and set free his laughter.

"What is it?" Ben demanded. "What's so funny?"

"It's an address!" Raven couldn't seem to stop chuckling, walked away to catch his breath. "I don't know who made this, or how, but it's an address. In London! Get yer coat!"

6
1591 Blackfriars

For months now, Simon Carew had had good work and money in his pocket. As promised, Sir Robert Cecil had provided an introduction and a modest purse to help him to a new suit of clothes and the services of a barber. He had even intimated that there might still be some need of his skills in the Queen's service. If he proved temperate in his living. So now he went each day to Robert Cotton's fine house in Westminster where he spent his days happily translating, cataloging, and writing in the antiquary's growing library.

It couldn't have been more to his liking. The work itself suited his gifts, and he and his master rubbed along well together. They were two like-minded scholars with esoteric interests, and Cotton didn't mind if Simon pursued his own researches as well.

Oh, the younger man—Cotton was only five-and-twenty—he smiled a little. Mermaids, forsooth! Oh yes, Pliny the Elder had written an account in the first century, though he never claimed certain knowledge of his own eyes. But there was lore enough, whether anyone living had seen one or not, and who could really say? Perhaps in his journeys here and there Simon could collect such tales as he found, perhaps even compile a book.

From time to time Simon travelled up and down the country and in time even abroad to buy rare books or delve into ancient curiosities; a statue found in a well, or fairy gold ploughed up in an old field. His gift for the intricacies of Latin and Greek, even the subtleties of Hebrew, gave him an advantage in valuing whatever was on offer. His French and modest Italian served to make the bargaining sweeter. And indeed, now and then, these trips doubled with some assignment of Cecil's: delivering a purse of money, collecting letters, observing a royal ward or her guardian.

And all the while, he read and studied, pursued obscure clues through scroll and codex, ever eager for more. Sober, chaste, silent, he prepared for his holy task.

He might have taken better lodgings in a safer part of the city—a less noisome part of the city, at least—where he could bring home the books and documents he worked on without exposing the often fragile pages to mildew and damp. He would have enjoyed staying up late with a puzzle of translation from time to time. But it was not important. He was good at the work and it delighted his mind, but nothing was as important as his mission, which restored the tiniest fraction of his heart every day that he was called to do it. For his true calling, never forgotten, rode over all other inclinations.

He lodged, as he had done since coming up to London, at the top of a sagging timber-framed tenement that must have been old when the Earl of March took the city for the Plantagenets. That it had not yet collapsed and slid down Ludgate Hill below was something of a wonder, if not a miracle. There were no miracles.

He lived there in a solitary asceticism almost hermit-like, as if at any moment he might throw on a hair-shirt and take up residence on a pillar like one of those old desert saints. It was no wonder everyone thought him a puritan. Two narrow windows in what the landlord was pleased to call the parlour looked down over the noisome channel that was the River Fleet, deceitful even in its name. The window near the door gave him clearance to empty the jordan, the chamber pot in its padded box, almost directly into the ditch without the bother of carrying one stinking mess to the other. If sometimes he missed, few noticed. The neighbors all did the same, and some of them were tanners.

A proper river once, so old books said, Fleet was now little more than a charnel ground for filth, dead cats, and the occasional unwanted mother-in-law. If it had once had a goddess, she was surely gone now, or asleep, or dead. For sure, no watery nymphs lurked on its banks to taunt him. He would have laughed to piss on their heads. He would have liked to put his questions to them: Who was my mother? Who is Oriana? What is the Mermaid Stair?

Surely he could do better, but this terrible place, this Gehenna, was the reminder of his purpose. He would bear its proximity while he worked his way into God's favour. Fleet would be his hair-shirt until he had earned his reward.

7
Friday: Edgware Road, London W1

When a man is tired of London, he is tired of life,
for there is in London all that life can afford.
— Samuel Johnson

Pressing aside the veils of Faerie rather than waste time on bridges or trains, Ben and Raven walked out of an alleyway fragrant with cardamom and rotting cabbage into the Edgware Road and the district sometimes called Little Cairo. The glare and the music wailing out of a dozen doors beat at them for attention.

Shops crowded together, a transplanted bazaar in a neon explosion of light and noise: sweet shop, greengrocer, Café Helen; shisha cafés, chip shops, and an all-night dentist—all open and throbbing with life. Raven grinned, exhilarated by the night and the nightlife, inhaling deeply and letting it go with a long sigh of pleasure.

"Lovely Barnet," he said, as if remembering something. "This was part of a Roman road once, you know. Watling Street, though I don't suppose the Romans called it that."

"Via Watling? Watlingus?" Ben said cheerily, coughing slightly on the mingled scents of shwarma lamb burgers and fruity tobacco.

"Probably not."

Two men arguing earnestly in Farsi nearly ploughed

through him in a headlong march gods-knew-where. Pausing only briefly at the corner, they crossed the street with hardly a glance. Brakes squealed in the rain-slick street. A cabbie swore at them in Arabic, shaking a fist more out of custom than any intent; they didn't seem to notice. In moments they had all melted into the night.

"I'm not sure I'm cut out to be Sherlock Holmes," said Ben, raising his voice over the din. He loved this city, but in self-defense he stepped back into the unlighted alcove of the only closed-up shop in the street.

"Sure you are. You have a mystery, a clue, and an amiable sidekick. What else could you possibly need?"

"A keen, incisive intellect? A Persian slipper? A seven-percent solution?" He was kidding. "A clue?"

"Elementary," said the fae lord, nose quivering. "Do I detect coffee? Oh! And baklava!"

Ben frowned, smelling only rain and diesel as a classic red double-decker omnibus pulled up to the curb. Coffee was not the point. With an ancient papyrus in his hand and a haunting tune in his head, he had followed an undeniable pull to northwest London. Fine. Now they were here—what?

He started to ask, and was immediately cannoned into by a scantily dressed young woman of graceful aspect who had just launched herself from the omnibus, though it might easily have been the Tube station across the way, or from the moon, for that matter. Being half-dressed in London was no surprise, but the look of panic on her heart-shaped face was startling.

"Whoa!" Ben said, catching the winsome bundle in his arms. Waist-length ropes of golden hair fell like seaweed across his hands. "What's the matter, love?"

She shrieked, black eyes wild.

"Stay me not! He will kill me!"

"What? Who?"

He looked up at once, seeking a villain, but there was no sign of pursuit, not even a sulking bully pretending not to care. Nothing, except the belch of exhaust trailing behind the Number 16 bus, and the haggard figure that stared from the rear platform as it pulled into traffic. But every bus has those.

Still the girl struggled, frantic as an eel.

"Please let me go!"

So of course, he did.

"Sure. It's okay, you're safe." He backed away from her and lowered his voice and his hands, radiating peace. *See, not a threat. Safe.*

She didn't care. Raven was reaching for her arm meaning only to ease her mind when something sizzled between them, and she screamed—a thin, inhuman wail that threw both men back and opened Raven's fingers before they could close.

"No!"

"Oak and ash!" Raven breathed, shaking the sting out of his hand.

Before Ben could move, she had reached for the shop door and, without actually opening it, she vanished. He stopped, stared, turned to look out into the busy street where chattering pedestrians with mobiles at their ears dodged the cars cruising for a place to park. He looked down towards Marble Arch and its flashing neon, then up towards Tyburn, drowned in residential dark. But she hadn't doubled back, or she'd have run into him again. And if she could flit into a locked shop, what on earth was she afraid of?

"Now that's odd," Ben muttered.

The kid was still shaking his hand and frowning, unnerved. He never did deal well with pain, even when he knew it wouldn't last.

"Maybe she was too afraid to think. Nymphs tend to have the attention span of a goldfish. But I've never heard of... What's odd?"

"Well, look. Egyptian-British Friendship League on one side, doors wide open. Hookah cafe on the other, smoking on patio only, busy as ever."

"Pet shop in the middle. There is in London all that life can afford, as Dr Johnson said."

"The pet shop is our address, and it's shut when every other place on the street is jumping."

Ben jiggled the latch, still wet with the girl's touch. When he put his hands up to the tinted glass to peer inside, glowing lights showed two rows of fish tanks and darting, jewel-like fish, but no sign of a girl.

"Did you happen to notice, she was soaking wet?"

"Wet?"

"All right, severely damp, and not from running."

"Ah," said Raven. "That would be because she was a naiad, I believe."

"Of course. Wait… What?"

"Naiads, the river nymphs. They can, apparently, hit a harmonic that rings my chimes. At least that one can."

"A naiad on a bus," Ben grumbled, frustration growing. "Aren't we a long way from the Thames?"

"London has more rivers than Thames, my lad," the raven-boy said thoughtfully. "Most of them long lost underground, used as storm drains or sewers like the Fleet, or repurposed like the Regent's Canal, or just buried. Now what's this?"

He crouched down in front of a low recess cut into the tiles below the shop window. Framed in an oval niche, a smooth flat stone was almost buried in blown plastic cups and Starbucks wrappers. Once polished like marble, now partially broken, the granite was so old even the broken edges had been blackened and smoothed with time.

On alert, Ben watched a police panda car roll by without giving them a second look. Even the roar of the city had muted since the girl's appearance, and not returned. Raven must have done something, he realized, to divert the flow of people—and attention—to the other side of the street. Whatever, he was grateful.

"Come look at this," Raven said, tracing a finger along the Roman capitals carved in the stucco frame: MORVEN. "Our Pictish mermaid again. This is older than the building, Ben. Probably older than the street."

Even softened by faerie magic, the flaring lights picked out a coiled shape carved in the stone that sprang up clear and identifiable under his touch.

"Another mystery."

"Or that clue you're looking for."

Curious, Ben pushed up his glasses and hunkered down

beside him. With harper's fingers he traced the path of the interlaced lines, sensing the music that had gone into their making, the music that maintained it. A kind of buzz tingled his fingertips, as sweet and insistent as the taut vibration of a plucked harp string, or the familiar tug at his chest that set him on the trail of some lost treasure.

Their eyes met. Raven nodded and touched Ben's arm, and they were inside the pet shop tasting the fragrance of sawdust and animal warmth, feeling the floorboards give slightly under their feet. On one wall, a clutch of sleeping puppies whimpered in their dreams, sensing an otherworldly intrusion, but did not wake. One ginger kitten did, in a cage on the opposite wall, but only stared, owl-eyed, saying nothing. From the tanks and their unearthly glow, aerators burbled, heaters hummed while the fish, their bright colors flashing, ignored them completely, serene among the swaying fronds, the treasure chests and hovering deep sea divers. But no nymph, nor any sign of one, except the small damp footprints of a running girl that vanished half way up the main aisle.

"Can we follow her?" Ben asked

"Well, we can't stop here."

Ben stooped in the eerie light to touch the last damp footprint before it vanished into the sawdust, and knew at once how to go. With a nod to his friend, he took the first step.

How odd. In a day already at its limit for oddness, he felt the changes begin, and almost stumbled. So often he had felt the veils of the worlds pass over him like a silken curtain caressing his cheek; or the varied textures of a painted wooden gate, a wicker hurdle, even woven light that filled his hands as he pushed them aside with the tinkling shimmer of wind chimes. Brief glimmers of other times and places opened and closed as he went. This was none of those. A glance told him even Raven was surprised, and that was oddest of all.

Faerie is always a place of marvels, but this was new. Before there was anything to see, a place came to his mind like a taste in his mouth or a thrill in his chest, like leaping through a waterfall and finding the sea: salt air danced on his tongue, and curious melodies marked their passing.

In the next heartbeat, they stood blinking on a grassy island in the arms of a sun-drenched river hedged with fern and light-fingered trees, smelling warmly of green grass and cinnamon under a high blue sky. And from everywhere came the sound of water rushing, pounding, sighing into placid pools, tinkling over stone.

"Caer Fannel?" Raven wondered softly. "In the Brecon Beacons there's a place quite like this. See where the river hisses and sings through the fern over shelves of stone. And a wooden footbridge like that one there, only not so fair."

But Ben was looking elsewhere, back the way they'd come, where another ladder of water and stone tumbled through some other course.

"Costa Rica, maybe. Place called Tabacón. My mother loves it. But it can't be both, can it? I mean, how can it?"

With deliberate slowness he turned on the spot, trying to take it all in, until he had come round to where he began. Barely visible through the screen of leaves and golden light, the river split into threads and spindles and trickled down the rocky face of a low cliff, while another higher up, or possibly another stream altogether, burst over a impossibly lofty ledge, falling through mist and rainbows to some unknown bottom masked in evergreens.

"The Bridalveil." Ben murmured. "In Yosemite."

When he looked away he found Raven, in a gaudy Hawaiian shirt and white linen trousers, rolled to the knee, lounging on an old-fashioned wooden deck chair. He was sipping a yellow drink with an umbrella in it, and grinning like an idiot.

"Really?" said Ben

"Why not," the boy said, then pointed away to his left. "Wherever she is, she's here, so she must be all right."

"What do you mean?"

Raven swore colorfully and touched two long fingers to his friend's forehead.

"Clean your glasses, human child, and look again!"

Ben batted the hand away, then polished his glasses with his t-shirt and slipped them back on. And he looked, really looked.

"Oh my God," he whispered.

Raven cackled. "The double-take was worth the whole price of admission, sir."

Shouting and playing, cavorting in pairs and trios and parties of nine, at last Ben saw them. At every level of every fall or pool, anywhere water splashed, flocks or schools or hazards of pretty nymphs and mermaids played, diving and sliding like otters, and most of them, like otters, clad only in their innocence.

Seeing them, the air came suddenly alive with the tinkling laughter of girls pearl pink as the dawn, green as the river where it meets the shore, blue and iridescent as the sea. Among them some sturdy lads with startled eyes kept them company: speckled like a trout, or sleek as seals; cobalt, grey and malachite, and every combination of jade and gold. The laurels on the bank and the long limbs of willows draped the Atami where they frolicked. The girl from the Edgware Road saw them and frowned, then someone tagged her shoulder and pulled her laughing into a game.

When the others noticed the king of Faerie's gentlemen, they squealed and waved, calling for them to come and play. At least, Ben thought that's what they were saying. The roar of the water and the blood singing in his ears made it hard to be sure.

Raven sucked down the last of his drink with a crash of ice, and banished the glass.

"See?"

Ben Harper, who was never at a loss for words, who had once chatted comfortably with the Prince of Wales, for godssake, rubbed his eyes and fought not to stammer.

"How could I not have seen them? How could any man straight or gay not have registered a double handful, if you know what I mean, of more or less naked women right in front of him?"

"Been married too long?"

"What the hell is this place?"

Raven laughed, shaking his head.

"Sir, I have no idea."

8
On the Stair

"This, gentlemen," said Aubrey, "is the Mermaid Stair."

You half-expected a swell of violins or a brass fanfare when confronted suddenly by the king of Faerie. But lacking that, you could settle for birdsong and playful laughter descanting over rushing water.

Tall, dark and rock-star gorgeous, three thousand years crowned king of Faerie, Aubrey successfully dragged their attention away from the frolicking nymphs.

"Ah!" said Raven. "Of course."

Ben blinked and nodded, still taking in the ferny ledges and shelves and steps of stone that tipped and pooled the waters.

"Yes, your Grace. I can see that. But… what is it, sir?"

The king had his enigmatic face on, something between amused and annoyed, as if his two favorite pupils had been caught in a prank.

He still affected the clothes, cap, and photographic gadgets of 1920, where he had himself been complicit in a charming fraud, "photographing" fairies for *The Strand* magazine. An efficient-looking fellow in pleated bags and collarless shirt with the sleeves rolled up over trim, muscular arms. Black hair nipped short, for him, but charmingly bohemian for the Nineteen-Twenties, parted around the slightly pointed tips of his ears. Neat round glasses perched on his nose, while above them, the glimmer of a golden coronet laced across his brow, shining in the clear light of Faerie's perpetual summer morning. His pose, however, bespoke nothing but majesty.

"It is a playground for the Atami, as I think you can tell. Their refuge from the mortal world. When springs dry up, or a river is paved over or polluted beyond help, this is where their nymphs come to bide the time until they find a new home, or the world changes. Otherwise they would fade and die. The question is," he went on with a slight smile. "What are you two doing here?"

"Well, he's a mermaid," Raven said lightly. "And I—"

"Merman," Ben corrected. "I left my tail in my other coat."

"Just so."

Obviously tolerance was called for.

"Chair," said the king of Faerie, shaking his head.

A canvas director's chair unfolded on the grass behind him as he sat, now classically draped in white like Zeus in judgment. The boys could stand a little longer. He clicked his tongue glancing from one to the other, leaned the noble jaw on one fist.

"Try again."

Ben took point. Quietly, efficiently, counterpointed by birdsong, he counted off the visions in the Thames and the dinosaur lake, Sparrow, the papyrus, and the pet shop girl.

"I can't leave you two alone, can I?"

"Sir!" Ben objected.

"My lord!"

"It's not as if we go looking for trouble."

"And yet it seems to find you."

Their shrugs were nearly identical, though one of them of supernal grace in spite of the Hawaiian shirt.

"Very well, what's this about a papyrus?"

Ben handed over the fragment. "I guess this didn't come from you, then."

Raven moaned, and not for the first time, then folded into a cross-legged position on the ground.

"I miss Dartmoor."

Oberon regarded his gaudy Raven briefly, then went back to examining the scrap. Another seamless shift, and they stood in the borderland of Faerie where it overlapped Hisley Wood.

Well, Ben stood; Oberon retained his chair, and a few yards away, the boy was walking heel-toe along the wall of a hump-backed medieval bridge where it curved over the stream. The number of nymphs had reduced to one, and she was hiding.

For his part, rocking a little with the change of footing, Ben felt a sense of relief he was pretty sure was unwarranted. At least he knew where he was, for the time being.

"When I want you, I am quite straightforward, as you well know," the king took up where he had left off. "Someone else sent this, and not by accident. Certainly this bit along the edge was meant to lead you to the Mermaid Stair, but why? The delivery was roundabout, the method unreliable—you don't read Greek, as I recall?"

"Not a word," Ben confirmed with a nod.

"And yet it managed to find you—and my Raven. For the rest, it is very old, indeed. The text even more so, though this is not the first transcription. That was made so long ago, it was pressed into clay and rolled into a cylinder."

"Ha!" Raven crowed. "Akkadian. I knew it!"

"Yes, you're very clever. There was a scroll made once, transcribed into this old Greek script without translation, as this is. The last I heard of it, it was at Alexandria, but I would have thought it burned with the library."

He paused to look closer, then drew a long breath across it and closed his eyes.

When he opened them, the world had shifted again, and the three men ranged around the table in the chrome and art deco glass of Aubrey's recording studio.

Ben put a hand out to catch himself on the back of an egg-shaped Eames era chair, just as Raven, accustomed to this sort of thing, unfolded out of it and headed for the computer desk.

"This is part of that scroll, I believe. A remnant snatched from the fire," said the king. "Ben, are you all right?"

"I'm getting dizzy."

"Sit. Have a drink."

A tall glass of iced lemonade waited for him on the beveled glass table. Ben sat, sipped, grateful for the shot of Jameson's that was Aubrey's special touch, and asked:

"What did you mean, sir? Just as well it burned?"

Oberon looked up, but not at Ben.

"Raven," he said. "I'm sure you haven't told Mr Harper everything you know about this."

"My lord, I thought it best. It was not a name I wanted to conjure without knowing more."

"Very wise." To Ben's interested expression he explained, "The goddess named in these lines is Ata'rathi. She was the first of the sea goddesses to arise in this quarter of the world. Her people are the Atami of every sort: mermaids, selkies, nereids, and all the nymphs of lake, river and well, like the naiad you encountered. They call her the Deep Mother, Sea Wife, the Star that Fell to Sea, though she has many other names, including some you have heard. In a way, she is the sea itself, though it isn't hers alone. Very remote, she seldom speaks directly, and never to mortal men—not in five thousand years."

As good as forever.

"With good reason, I guess," said Ben, combing his fingers through his sandy hair. "So this is from her? What does she want with a musician? Or is that a silly question?"

The forthright brown eyes met the glittering blue ones. Even in linen slacks and silk shirt, businesslike among stylish furnishings and surrounded by the best sound equipment known to man or fae, there was no mistaking the majesty that clung to him.

"I can't say, but you have made a name for yourself in the twilight realms, Ben Harper," he said.

Ben chuckled.

"Hired gun? Troubleshooter?"

"Bad ass," Raven hooted from the computer desk, while laying waste to hideous alien hordes.

"King's man."

Pleased, Ben tilted his head in acknowledgement. It was a name he could live with.

"I believe," the king said thoughtfully, "she is asking for your help, though you can never be sure with these eldest gods."

Ben Harper, king's man, considered a snappy retort, and rejected it.

"All right," he agreed.

He got to his feet and felt a change slip over him as it did every time he accepted the king's warrant, as he thought of it. Spirits lightened, easy with his duty, whatever it was, he stood like a king's musketeer with a sword at his hip.

"How can I be of service?"

Aubrey produced a cigarette from somewhere, tapped and lighted it with a vintage Zippo, moving deliberately through the motions. A long draw, a satisfied exhalation, blue smoke swirled away without troubling his mortal companion, who had given up the habit years ago.

"It appears," he said at last, "that the Atami of England are disappearing. Not retiring or falling asleep, as many have done. It's as if—"

"As if they were dying, sir?" Ben filled the pause as the truth came home.

"Yes. And not dying well. There are dark threads in the water's song such as I've never heard before, crooked and untuned threads in the pattern, even at the Stair where all waters run clear."

That would be why he had brought the conversation indoors, away from the chattering rivers.

"And this document. What is it, exactly?"

Aubrey turned to the other man.

"Have you worked it out yet?"

"Not exactly, headmaster," Raven said dryly.

"Ah, so promising in his youth, such a disappointment to his parents," said Aubrey, who might or might not be Raven's parent. Ben still wasn't clear on that.

He held up the fragment between two long fingers.

"Although you may not be interested, careless boy, I believe this may be the last remaining piece of the Ata'rathi Scroll."

The boy spun away from his game with a laugh.

"But that's a myth!"

"So are you, yet here you sit drinking my single malt and trying my patience."

Maggie Secara

"Is someone going to tell me what it is, this scroll?"

"I would rather not, just now," the king said cagily. He reached forward slightly to tap the cigarette against a heavy carnival glass ashtray.

"Okay." Ben exhaled sharply. "I guess we need to talk to the goddess, then?"

"You can't go to her directly."

Both of the younger men rolled their eyes and chorused, "Of course not!"

"Of course not." Aubrey smiled over the gin & tonic that had appeared in his hand. "But you can talk to Tamesis. In fact, I think you must. He'll tell you the rest."

"Tamesis is the old Roman name for the Thames," Ben said with a slight chuckle, and got raised eyebrows in response. "Fine. I have to talk to the river. Any particular stretch?"

"A placid one, I hope. The trouble appears to be centered along his valley and its tributaries. It's his patch, though he is lord of all the waterways of England. These are his people, his sisters and his children. It would be best to hear it from him, along with whatever else you need to know."

Ben the scholar frowned. Dealing with Faerie and its monarchs and its folk light and dark had not quite prepared him for encounters with ancient gods, especially gods he had never heard of.

"But you're the king of Faerie, sir. Doesn't that include all the mermaids and…?" Aubrey's amused gaze suggested otherwise. "I don't entirely understand what Faerie is, do I?"

Coolly purposeful, the faerie king tapped out his cigarette, set the last of the smoke free.

"This is where the human metaphor breaks down, I'm afraid, of kings and kingdoms. If we persist with it, you might think of Tamesis as a kind of client king, though I wouldn't say as much to him. Our realms overlap. He is a force of nature real and present. He has his own dominion and cares. Unlike Odin, whom you have met, his time will never be over until the sun goes cold. Such spirits have their own weapons and notoriously short tempers. You'll need to be as mindful of his dignity as you are of mine."

If there was a twinkle in Aubrey's eye as he said this, Ben missed it.

"Of course, sir."

"Good, that's settled then. Can you leave at once? I have a feeling he is waiting for you. What is it?"

Ben, stifling a yawn, looked uncomfortable, but it was Raven who put down his drink and answered.

"My lord, there is one other thing."

"And what is that?"

Ben shrugged.

"Just a few things I should do at home first."

The kid turned a significant gaze on his friend.

"Ben, you have to tell him."

Aubrey rolled his eyes.

"Gentlemen!"

"It's Mellis, sir," the harper said as the echoes died away.

"She's all right, isn't she? She's a steady girl."

"Of course, sir, but you remember, after the dragon ring, you promised... Well, not promised, but you said she'd forget it. That it would be like a dream."

"Ah," said Aubrey. "So she remembers."

"Oh, yes. She didn't mean to say anything. A slip of the tongue. She backtracked immediately. But yes, I believe she does, and she isn't happy. I have to go home anyway to get my things. I mean, I've been away for weeks promoting the band and the new album." He chuckled ruefully. "It's almost as crazy as when I met you."

"And now I'm sending you off again."

Ben nodded. "You see my point. I can't just walk away."

The air in the room had altered, charged with the smell of ozone. When a sudden damp chill swept through, Ben had the distinct impression that someone else had arrived, a watery presence whose patience was not unending.

"Someone thinks you must," said Raven, shutting down the computer.

"Half a day!" Ben snapped, staring around for the source. "Tonight and half a day, that's all!"

"Done," said Aubrey, echoing a voice only he had heard. "Go

quickly, then, Ben Harper. Go home."

As they stood, Ben found that new tune in his head again, unlooked for. He had forgotten to mention it, and now it seemed pointless. Perhaps it would be useful along the way.

"Oh! And you might want to take the little harp, or maybe the cittern. It packs well."

"My lord, I will." Ben bowed as though he had stood up in doublet and hose.

A moment later he was stepping into the vast music room downstairs or wherever it was, elsewhere in the king's great house.

"Look for the mermaid badge" said the kindly voice in his head. "It will guide you to the Stair at need. Otherwise, follow your gift."

Ben smiled uneasily as he chose what he needed from the carved and jewelled cases and pigeonholes in the wall.

"I will, sir."

He was already singing the path away from Faerie when the king's voice added, "Take the diary!"

"Yes, your Grace!"

"And take Raven!"

"Gramercy, my lord, so shall I!" he laughed.

And he was home.

9
1592 Holborn

Carew had always known how to find them, his mother's people. Where water moved freely, even deep underground, even in London, he could track them by the ache in his belly that no caudle nor no surgeon could soothe, only drown in aqua vitae or spend between a woman's thighs. Well, he had given those up, so he would learn to live with the nausea, for the sake of his great undertaking. The closer he was, the stronger the gnawing in his gut, the more clearly he could hear their voices.

In city or country, fountain or fetid marsh, if water moved through it, he could see them, hear them. They danced everywhere but not to proper music, such as one heard amongst honest folk, neither in the taverns nor the homes of the great. To his ear it was no more than warbling in some strange key, like the Morescos whose wailing echoed in the narrow alleys of East Cheap. It was alien, inhuman, the unsanctified songs of Hell. Which he, being who he was, could hear even when others could not.

As he crisscrossed the city on his master's errands he listened to his innards growl, mapping the lost rivers by the roiling of his bowels.

*

The first killing was rushed and hideous, though it began so well.

On a Saturday, Simon spent the day on his knees, either in prayer or puking, and called it purification. When the moon rose near midnight, he dressed in his oldest doublet and trunk hose, and fortified himself with wine—he had sworn off spirits, but a man must drink something. The iron knife he hung on a thong around his neck under his shirt. Mindful of footpads, he kept his usual dagger at his waist and a shuttered lantern in his hand, though the full moon itself would surely keep all but the most determined ruffians in their dens.

He took the path along the gurgling Fleet, though the stench as he crossed behind the tannery nearly knocked him down. When the stream vanished into a conduit below Holborn, he turned aside unmolested to the swampy fields on either side of Drury Lane, until he saw a flickering light, and tracked it to its source.

Fragile, vain, alone, draped in some filmy garment woven of moonbeams, she knelt over a shallow pool, posing and smiling, trilling a little song to herself. A pair of tiny wings fluttered between her shoulder blades. Suddenly, she leapt up dancing, her little toes dimpling the water's surface.

He crept up less silently than he supposed, every nerve on fire, heart pounding so fast he felt like a student again, fumbling with his first whore. Even his hands were sweating. Heat rushed into his face like a blush of shame, and hardened his cock.

He expected a scream when he grabbed her round the waist and threw her to the soggy ground. Instead, horribly, she laughed as if welcoming a new lover, and stretched out her arms to him.

"How now, Cousin! Dance with me!"

Fury surged through him white-hot from brain to groin as it had that day on the Bridge. An incoherent cry gurgled with the spittle from his lips. Furious, his arm went up; the iron knife clenched in his fist drove down into her white throat.

The beautiful eyes startled wide. The lips moved but made no sound. Again and again he struck out in his anger, slashing and cursing until he collapsed, sick with revulsion. He hadn't known such creatures would have blood like mortal women, and so much of it oozing molten silver in the moonlight, cooler than the air. All of it, even the blood on his hands, lifted away from his skin like a silvery mist as she died. He had asked her nothing.

Horrified, he staggered back to the midnight streets where even the Shoreditch whores would have none of him. By the time he crawled shivering into his own stifling rooms, he was drenched in sweat.

He would have to burn the clothes. He would need another plan.

10
Saturday: Iveston, Diamond Cottage

If you've ever had a lesson from Mellis Powell, you crossed through the warm country kitchen at Diamond Cottage and went down two steps into a small but tidy room with white walls and a wide picture window, filled with music stands, a few chairs, a piano, a harpsichord, and an electric keyboard.

You might have found her working on schedules and email at the tidy Queen Anne desk with a lamp and a small bookcase. The walls shone with framed certificates and awards, BAFTA and Academy nomination letters, and photos of Dr Powell shaking hands with conductors, academics, and a few notable actors; some had been her students, if only briefly, in this very room. Also a Lord Mayor of London.

But when you knew her really well, or if you happened to be a favoured student, you might have taken those two steps and almost immediately turned right to follow the spiralling stair behind an arched wooden door down into her sanctum, her real work space: the baby grand and the functional desk, along with the big computer, music sampler, multiple monitors and assorted devices that daily taxed the power limits of the Grade II listed cottage.

Between the tree-shaded windows, cases of books and notebooks crowded the warm ivory walls from the Navajo rugs on the flagstone floor to the tuned acoustic panels in the ceiling. On every horizontal surface, stacks of music scores poised ready to slide, whether bound, hand-scrawled, or printed out, bright with colored Post-its. Somewhere in the clutter on the lid of the baby grand was the golden mask of a BAFTA award for a film score she swore she'd created in a dream. Which she may have done.

Mellis's famously organized husband, whose opinion of her office was usually expressed in archaeological terms, had been haunting her thoughts all morning, to the point of interrupting her work at inconvenient moments. She was only adding notes to a lecture she'd given a dozen times, but she kept staring out the window wondering where he was.

It would not be the first time Ben had rolled in at lunchtime looking as if he'd slept in his clothes—because he had. For the twelve years of their marriage, the twenty cumulative years of their friendship, both their careers had involved madly unpredictable timetables, so the hour, by itself, did not signify. Working at her own desk under an open window, the soft autumn air filled with music for which she'd won a major award, the time hardly mattered. The problem was not time, as such. The problem was magic.

And like magic, he appeared. He stood on the whitewashed spiral steps with an old cittern at his side. A very old cittern she'd never seen before.

"There you are!" Ben said, somewhat warily, she thought.

"So I am, and there you are!" she replied with a smile. Covering the unexpected attack of nerves, she got up and threw her arms around his neck. "How neatly it all works out."

Mellis sat at the big wooden table and watched her handsome American moving efficiently about the kitchen, getting down the tall cafetière, measuring out coffee, reaching for two mugs, all while humming a peculiar tune. She'd always loved the way he moved with a kind of masculine grace, nothing awkward, no effort wasted, as neat and as original as a Mozart concerto.

He was keeping something to himself. But then, so was she. For now, she let him putter, the only other sounds in the room the homely ticking of the case clock, the gas flame hissing under the kettle, a delivery van rolling by on the road, and a hint of her music floating up from below.

"Where's Sparrow?" Ben said.

Casual and ordinary as it was, the question took her by surprise.

"Ehm, the Blackhursts have new faeries..." She froze. "Puppies! They have new puppies. He's at Bobby's. I have to..."

The sentence had no finish. Bright pink flushed her throat, rising swiftly over her cheeks into her hairline. Mellis jumped from her chair and started into the parlour, then changed her mind and marched right back through the kitchen, skirting the table on the side away from Ben, and out the other end.

Ben turned off the tap, watched her disappear through the arch, marked her progress downstairs by the syncopated slap of her sandals. Half-consciously he counted off the even pace with the care of a metronome, marking the pauses in quarter rests.

Silence. The sound system cut out.

Creak. Snick. The window closed and locked.

Ding. Silver teaspoon rang on porcelain saucer.

Pause, two, three, four. Right on the beat, footsteps marching up the spiral stair—two, three, four—two steps again—one, two—and she reappeared, her morning tea things rattling on a tray—three, four, and stop. Heroically, he did not laugh.

When she halted, looking down at the tray without a word, Ben was wiping his hands calmly on a striped tea towel that read *Keep Calm and Make Music*.

"Really?" he asked, as if she'd never left the room. "What kind of faeries?"

"What?"

She shot up a look, the color draining from her face.

The tea tray dropped *bang* to the polished granite counter. Sugar cubes bounced out of the Blue Willow bowl into the sudden pool of congealing Devon cream. Lumps of cream leapt for Ben's glasses and made it, the stragglers settling on his original 1987 *Crest of a Knave* t-shirt.

Blinded, Ben cleared his throat theatrically, and put out a

hand.

"Bar towel."

"Oh!" Laughter lurking in the corners of her mouth, she put the damp cloth in his hand. "Oh, sweetheart, I'm so…"

Pointlessly, he dabbed at the shirt. The dainty, lady-like snort came from his wife. Mellis took the cloth and rubbed a little at his glasses, which, of course, only made it worse. The nervous smile began to break.

The hint of a chortle bubbled in her throat.

"Uhm, sorry. Hold still."

Straight faced, he let her lift the side wires over his ears and drag them gently off his face while her mouth tipped into a grin.

He crossed his eyes.

"Boo!"

"Eek!"

The tension gave way, she threw up her hands, and kept laughing, and they both cackled every time they looked at each other until their knees gave way and they collapsed to the painted floor, hanging on to each other and gasping for air. As soon as one of them had found space to breathe, their eyes met and they started all over again.

Warm with silliness and the steamy kitchen, Ben hardly noticed a damp chill blow through the room. Someone wasn't happy at the delay. All Ben cared about at the moment was the woman he loved. The ice had broken.

Somehow he prised his glasses out of her hand. And somehow he managed to struggle up and at least give them a good rinse while she sat on the floor still giggling.

In a moment, Ben caught her hands and lifted her up.

"Are you all right?"

"Yes, I just, no… It's just… Oh dear! It's so ridiculous."

In a moment he was holding her, and that was always a good thing. By the time they had calmed down, the coffee was ready, and Mellis installed in a chair at the sturdy kitchen table. He brought over the cafetière, cups, spoons, also brand new containers of sugar and milk.

He settled into the chair across from her, where he could

best appreciate the English rose of her face under her thatch of golden hair. It had been short and springy all summer, but she was letting it grow out, and lengthening curls made a Botticelli halo around her face. He reached over to twine a curl behind one ear.

Nerves settled somewhat by the customary rhythms, he began simply.

"So, you did ask me about Oberon last night, didn't you?"

Her glance darted about the sunny kitchen, then came to rest.

"I did, yes."

"And faeries, just now? "

"I know, isn't it ridiculous?" Her hands flew nervously. "I've had faeries on the brain lately, I don't know why."

The wonderful eyes nailed her, willing her to the truth as he took her hands.

"What do you remember about the year before last, that week in May?"

She squirmed in the painted chair, snatched her hands away, nervously scrubbing her hair back over her ears. Stared at her fingernails a moment, then looked up and met his eyes, as brown and damp as a puppy's. She folded her hands in front of her like a schoolgirl and willed them still.

"Whatever do you mean?"

That wasn't what she'd meant to say, and by his silence, she could tell he already knew better.

"All of it," she said steadily.

"All what? Tell me, love."

"Everything." Her face bleak with tension, she paused. "The last week of term. Dominic being stolen away, that horrible changeling." A shudder rocked her where she sat.

"And what else?"

She wanted to look away, but she didn't dare. He had asked, finally, and she wanted him to know how weary she was of carrying those memories alone.

So she drew back from the emotional, and gave her report sensibly, clearly, with an intellectual reserve she usually kept for the classroom, almost as if it had happened to someone else.

The words rattled out as if she could chase the images away by reciting as fast as possible. The threats to Sparrow, Titania's overt attack, the restoration of the dragon ring, even her own march through Faerie to release her son.

Ben didn't care how fast she talked, or even whether the narrative made sense, though it did in remarkable detail. He just needed Mellis to give him her story, ask her questions, and let her lay the burden of her fears on him, where they belonged. Because he knew it was his fault. If he'd accepted Oberon's mission the first time it was offered—before his own stupidity put his family in peril—she would never have been involved. Never been aware. And he'd still be keeping secrets from her.

When she stopped, Ben let out a breath like a silent whistle.

"And what else?"

She stared at him.

"Isn't that enough?"

"That's up to you, love," he said, knowing that the real issue still lay unspoken between them.

She thought about that.

"I wasn't supposed to see him again, your Oberon, was I? Even after all that. But I did. Dominic and I went home and you went off again, like nothing had happened."

Arms folded on the table top, feeling like a cad, Ben explained as well as he could.

"I tried to tell you once, sweetheart, don't you remember?"

Her golden brown eyes swung up to a corner of the ceiling, as if the memory lay there.

"As I recall, I seriously questioned your sobriety, not to mention your sanity. But you have to admit, you were a bit dazed and the idea was mad."

"Exactly. The truth is, people dismiss what they know can't be true, like Oberon or pixies or a boy who turns into a raven."

Her forehead creased at that one, but he pressed on.

"For that matter, only a few of us mortals can even see them if they don't mean to be seen. His Grace thought you would, well, wake up thinking it was all a dream. We agreed it was best to let you."

"The two of you…" she said, rolling her eyes. "Men! It was

a nightmare, Ben, the kind that wakes you up, and when you go back to sleep, starts over again. It might—just might, mind you—have gone away. But then other things kept happening. How was I supposed to explain Meg, I ask you?"

"Meg?"

"Brownie Meg? Ben, our housekeeper is a faerie! I almost never see her, except early in the morning, when the house smells like fresh bread baking. One morning I looked in and found Dominic with her, drinking cocoa."

"Oh, God." Ben leaned his face on his hand and started to laugh. He really had been an idiot. Aubrey'd sent Meg over during the changeling episode, and apparently never thought to take her back.

"I tried to pay her, once. She wouldn't even touch it. Told me ever so politely to put away my sil'er and she wouldn't take affront, but she'd have honey a bit, and a cup of fresh milk on Saturdays, if it was convenient, and I'd remember why soon enough. So I called my Gran. She knew. And she said to hang rowan in all the windows."

Mellis's family had been on the moor, right here in Iveston Vale, for five hundred years, maybe more. Her Gran was over ninety, and her memory touched others even older.

"I'm sorry," he said, quietly taking her hand across the table, but that seemed to make her cross. "I should have told you everything as soon as I got back from Cheltenham."

"All right." If her hands were trembling as she raised the coffee to her lips, they stilled soon enough. "You never answered my question."

"What question?"

"Where is Oberon sending you this time?"

He took a breath to answer, then stopped, considering. He hadn't really told her as much as she deserved, but now was not the time.

"It's complicated."

"Can I come?"

Jesus!

"No, you can't."

"Because it's dangerous?"

"Because I'm not having tea with Queen Victoria, sweetheart. Lives are at stake."

She frowned, torn between fear and something else.

"What if I asked you not to go?"

"I can't do that." The coffee mug clicked on the table, all smiles fled. "I've given my word."

There was no answering that, and she knew it. He was the man he had become as well as the man she had married. If he'd said anything else, she wouldn't have loved him.

She got up and came around the table. Draping her arms around his neck, she kissed him well and he kissed her back.

"Oh, you don't half love all this, don't you, haring off through space and time, righting wrongs. My own bloody hero."

And suddenly it was over.

So, how do you prepare to meet a god? Or a guardian spirit, or king of the river, or whatever? He'd met Odin a couple of times, and he was a jolly sort with little to do in these latter days. But the Thames was a force of nature.

Ben set the problem aside for now to run a comb through his hair and consider which of his *Imaginary Foundation* tees would make the best impression on Father Thames. Then he threw on a soft linen shirt on with his jeans instead, and rolled up the sleeves.

What else? If he was taking the king of Faerie's cittern, and he was, he'd need his leather satchel—a supple, much-used bag from the piney woods of Northern California. Back in college, he'd worked with Wes at Swadeshi for months on the design, throwing money on the account whenever he could until it was both perfect and paid for. Rich with layers of dark brown leather, the flaps lined with lambskin, it closed with latchets and bone buttons. The inside was fixed with straps and loops and drawstrings; extra pockets with pockets inside. When Sparrow was too small to say "Swadeshi" he'd called it the sushi bag. Ben did too, often as not.

At the moment it was serving as an auxiliary warehouse for

Sparrow's Legos. Once he'd hunted up a bag for those, he packed socks and t-shirts, just in case. Clothes were commonly the least of his concerns with Raven around, but clean underwear never hurt.

Mellis brought him a couple of sandwiches in zip-bags, so those went in too, and a packet of Mentos. The mobile phone went into its own padded pocket. It shouldn't work at all where he was going, but when Aubrey wanted him, it always did. Last of all, the cittern slipped in neatly, reclining at an angle so the top flap closed neatly leaving only the cherry-wood dog-head and the tuning pegs sticking out.

Throwing on the black leather jacket, he patted the diary in its inside pocket. Well, he said "diary" but it was more of a cross between a scrapbook, a gossip column, and *The Hitchhiker's Guide to the Galaxy*, with vulgar cartoons, some passable poetry, and terrible jokes in the most appalling handwriting. But along with the noise and nonsense came useful advice, maps, music, and details he might or might not need, all provided, somehow, by the timeless legions of Faerie.

All in all, it was the most valuable tool that Aubrey had given him in almost three years of service. So it found a pocket, too. But that song was starting to play through his head again, and a chilly damp was rising up from the floor. Better go before the drains started to back up.

"All right!" he muttered, throwing the satchel over his shoulder. "I'm coming!"

11
May 1593, Chelsea

There can be no hiding failure from a god who sees all things. How should Simon Carew's desperate longing ever rise to Heaven's notice if he had so little stomach for this great service? Even his nagging angels—he knew now that his voices were angels—even they were disgusted. Perhaps his fate was set after all, his parents' sins a doom visited upon their child. Was a man without a soul even capable of virtue?

A test, it must be a test. Heaven had noticed but was testing him. Aye, that way goes the game. Well, he would compound his effort, and prove his worth. The Atami would cease to trouble the world of men.

Atami. They were called Atami, the children of Ata'rathi — he had discovered that much from his bloody efforts—but none knew the name Oriana. Of the Mermaid Stair he could learn nothing.

So many months had passed, and still he had slaughtered so few in the name of Heaven—as many by accident as by design—watching them glimmer away on the moonlight before he could force them to render up their secrets with their pain. Creatures of pleasure, they had no tolerance for mistreatment and died so easily.

The Thames where it flowed past Chelsea, graciously accepting the wholesome waters of the Westbourne, was broad and pleasant, rich on either side with fields of barley and hazy rye waving tall and green under pewter skies. The river itself, the inconstant river flowing west or east at the whim of the tides, lapped its banks with a rippling, hollow sound. Simon Carew hated it, even while it called to him.

Still, he could use that inconstant flow to his advantage, easily sailing his little punt upriver with the westward flow. When he turned north up the Westbourne's stream, he trimmed his sail, tacking with skill back and forth leaving Chelsea village behind, feeling his heart swell with anticipation. Deceitful, inconstant, and pagan; in his silence he longed for it, too, drawn by the surging flow that echoed in his blood.

There was no escaping his birth. There might yet be revenge, and reparation.

His father, so the stories said, had fallen in love with a river nymph. Oh, not just any faery, the village gossips said, but the demon goddess of the Dart herself, from whose banks his father had cut a channel to his forge, and in whose waters he quenched the knife blades and horseshoes, pothooks and plowshares that came from his hands. No one knew what she was at the time, of course, nor how they met. Only that she had appeared one day in a blue kirtle, small and silent with eyes like a summer sky, and left the big, taciturn smith, Giles Carew, smitten to the heart as any schoolboy.

He called her Issa, and that were no name for a Christian woman, wherever it was she came from. She never would say. She also never came to church of a Sunday, which must have cost young Giles a pretty penny in fines to the parish warden.

"But is she even a Christian?" asked the frowning vicar when the warden quizzed the smith about her.

"She's wed to me," the smith answered shortly, "and tha' be Christian enough."

By way of punctuation, he slapped three gold sovereigns on the communion table—more wealth than any of them had ever seen—and stalked away without another word. The vicar, a practical man who had not survived in his post through every quirk of religion by being inflexible, pronounced an end to the matter.

This much Simon had learned in spits and spots, mainly from the vicar's wife who took those three gold coins and hid them in the church crypt, in case they were fairy gold.

*
**

Simon had met his mother once, though the memory of it pained him. It had been on a grey day in April when he was nine or ten years old, still just the blacksmith's boy in his Dartmoor village. While fishing on the banks of the Dart he met a lady in a blue kirtle, a little older than he but no taller, with a sweet smile and sky-blue eyes.

It was enough, then, that they walked along the river's edge, taking a new path where any new stream met them, until they had wandered far from any houses or farms and into a country he didn't know. They sat together on a broad rock in the middle of the river, and though the water was cold, the wood about them hummed with the warmth of a long summer morning.

She held his hands and touched his hair, though he tried to resist her blandishments. She told strange stories in her musical voice, about his birth and how much she had loved his father, and the pain of her leaving.

"Born in the river Dart itself," she said, while she patted the dark curls away from his face. "Aye, your mummy sat right down in the flowing water and leant back on your papa's chest, and pop! Out you came, swimming like a minnow! And oh, how your mummy and all your pretty aunties sang to greet you, my little love."

She taught him some words, with the promise that he would understand them, one day. She gave him a lucky charm, a talisman, she called it: a string of carnelian and gold with a carved disk of amber hanging in its middle.

"Tell no one of this," she said solemnly, kissing him. "Tell no one, especially not Giles."

She looked so sad when she said his father's name that

Maggie Secara

Simon agreed.

When he was hungry, she gave him white manchet bread and golden honey to eat, and he sipped the clear river water from her silver cup. When he gave in at last and wept, she laid his head on her knee, while the ache in his belly went away; and as he slept she sang over him, peculiar words in a low voice.

When he woke on a riverbank, three days had passed. He was cold, hungry, and far from home, being sniffed at by an otter. The only sign of her, the talisman tied around his neck. With a child's outrage, he had scraped a hole in the mud by the river and buried the pagan thing, stomping on the earth to stifle her lies. Then he stumbled home to his father's terrible but reliable anger.

She had never said her name or told him who she was. It was years before he understood, and then only because he had begun to find some of those strange words of hers in his books.

And now? Now there were nymphs lying asleep under a hawthorn tree, cloaked in a shimmer that betrayed them to his knowing eye. Three small nymphs like nubile girls, their sweetly rounded limbs twining together among the nodding flowers on the heath by the Westbourne's ancient spring.

He knew how to find them, yes, though each time still left him revolted. Weeks might pass, even months, before he could venture out again, and too often they had left the spring or pool when their protection of it failed, and men buried or built over or spoilt their homes. Where they went was still a mystery.

Though he had learned how to use them before they fell into madness or death, still he knew little more than he had at the start: mere random pieces, a handful of words that led to more questions.

His shoe pressed the grass. The dark eyes sprang open and one-two-three they leapt up to greet him as he knew they would, with fond kisses, words of praise for his beauty, his shape, the light of magic in his manly eye. Did they notice the disfigurement the fire had written on his limbs? He was never sure, for unlike human women they showed no fear, no horror at the swirled and glossy scars. No mocking laughter came.

Ever playful, ever trusting, they opened his many buttons and loosed the points that tied doublet to hose, drew off his horrid woolen suit, cast aside his linen until his skin grew flushed and prickled in the balmy air. For it was always balmy where they met together.

One would tease him to attention, twining flowers into his greying locks, garlanding his crown. When he whispered to the fairest, and there was little to choose between them, it would ride him like a Southwark whore, only singing out with pure unfeigned happiness while he pretended pleasure in her touch, and the taste and touch and scent of her sisters surrounded them until his dark purpose all but slipped away.

Frolicking through the long twilight, they teased him into their games, fed him honeycomb and sweet wine with giggling kisses and tickling caresses into the long summer's gloaming while sweet aires played all around them.

Finally exhausted, he slept, languid with pleasure, and in a while he woke in shame with the three of them curled about him like kittens. Shame quickly turned to loathing, and that to cold fury. His soul was at stake, and his mind, too. With the smell of them on his skin a sweet perfume, he bound them each, and began to ask his questions with the iron knife to prick them into honesty.

His master had gone to Huntingdon for the birth of his son. No one would be looking for Simon Carew; he could take his time. And so he would, for he would have his answers. If not from one soulless monster, then the next, or the next after that.

Maggie Secara

12
Iveston: "One's good, three's better."

Ben found Raven waiting in the sunshine on the wooden footbridge that crossed the Ravenbeck, the old mill stream that ran below the back garden and marked his property line. Beyond stood stone-crowned Raven Tor, which guarded a doorway to Faerie.

The boy leaned back against the guardrail with his face tilted up to the midday sun, dressed all in black and mischief. He had tamed his curls into a ponytail, tied back with a modest jewel the color of his eyes, but outside of that and his clothes, he had little of the human mask about him. Eyes and mouth, the sharp planes of his cheekbones, all spoke of Faerie to any who could see him at all. At the chunk of Ben's boots on the path, he straightened up, adjusting the fine silk jumper, pushing the sleeves back from his wrists.

"Ready?"

"Yep."

Ben strode down the path with his usual assurance, the TV presenter who was comfortable anywhere, the king of Faerie's sworn man. And yet, doubt hung around him like a cloud.

"So where are we going?"

"Hazarding a guess, here," said Raven, blinking. "River Thames, right? A bit north of here. Two hundred-odd miles long. Hard to miss."

"True," Ben corrected, "but wrong."

"Sorry?"

"The Thames—that's the water in the river. What we need is the man, or god, call it the entity who is the river. All the rivers of England. How do we find him?"

Head tilted, birdlike, quizzical, Raven said:

"But you can find anything, Ben Harper. I've watched you. It's remarkable. Come on, set us a song, we'll start walking and you'll sort it out as we go. You always do."

The raven-boy smiled an encouraging smile, and gestured him onward, but Ben held firm where he was, staring upstream to the high moor and the horizon, directionless. His gift, his imagination, the tug at his chest, the harp string hum that led him, lay cold and silent.

"At least it's stopped raining," he said irrelevantly.

Ben laid his arms on the old wooden railing, noting its want of maintenance, and stared down into the stream rushing over the rocks below, tracked its tree-lined path until it disappeared into Iveston Wood. He lifted his eyes to the horizon, the hazy purples and greys above the high moor. The little Ravenbeck rose a few miles above Iveston and tumbled south and east into another brook a few miles below, none connecting to the Thames in any way. That was no clue.

Beside him, perfectly still, the raven-boy waited.

Finally Ben sighed.

"What I find is things that are lost. Car keys, tax bills, the thread of the conversation. Or stuff I have a connection to, like I did with the dragon ring, or with you, even. For example. But I don't know how it works—or why it fails."

When it failed him, all he felt was a curiously hollow sensation, a distracting uncertainty.

"But the River Thames isn't lost. As you say, hard to miss. So I don't...sense it. Him. Whatever."

"Father Thames?" Raven asked. He joined his friend, shoulder to shoulder at the rail. "It's all right, you can say it out loud."

Ben made a face.

"His Grace says go, and we go, okay. But I can't sense a path. Y'know? There's no music. Or if there is, I can't hear it."

Without warning, a huge splash of water sailed over the rail and smacked him in the face.

"Hey!"

The chuckling below their feet was no longer merely water over stone.

Stupid, stupid, stupid!

Two or three delicate, girlish voices could hardly speak for giggling.

He's so stupid!

But he's very pretty! one objected.

Another splash followed. Ben hopped back but not in time.

Oh, come on!

Now he's wet, said a second.

And still stupid!

The third voice sang out with a last impudent, and much more thorough, spray. Swearing and soaked, Ben ripped off his glasses, futilely rubbing them on a shirttail as wet as the rest of him.

Is he wet enough yet?

How wet does he have to be to find our Father?

Raven was laughing too, and remarkably dry.

"Well? Are you going to ask them? They're longing to tell you."

"Ask who what?" Ben snapped, feeling oppressed. Also, soggy.

"Ha! Abandoned your gifts, have you, human child? Them, of course!" The lifted chin indicated the stream itself, or something in it. "Ravenbeck's naiads. Or pixies, being it's Devon. Don't tell me you haven't met them before."

Grumbling, Ben hunkered down and poked his head through the space abandoned by at least two of the supporting balusters, almost afraid to look. But there they were, three small, quite lovely adolescent girls—or so they appeared— paddling in the shallows. Perfectly made, with small breasts and slender faces. Each was wrapped or hung about with some kind of diaphanous draperies both wet and transparent that showed off all their girlish charms. Each had her ringlets bound up in ribbons like a goddess on a Grecian urn.

Even as his eyes widened, he knew at once that they were clearly and utterly inhuman. Not unpleasantly so, but still quite alien. And they were laughing at him.

Of course they were. Still, he knew how to behave, if anyone did.

"O most fair," he began, because it is always best to be polite to the faeries. Three pointed little faces beamed at him expectantly.

The angle was awkward, so he sat up, dangling his legs over the edge. Raven, the grinning bastard, was content to lean on his elbows and observe over the rail.

Ben began again.

"Fair ladies, will you say how we may find the Father of Rivers, the noble Tamesis? We seek him on Lord Oberon's command."

"Oh, you are good," Raven observed. "Kipling could have taken notes from you."

One of the girls raised up, balancing her slender pink feet on a mossy stone, and reached a tiny hand as dainty and as strange as a Brian Froud painting. When she touched his shoe he felt a slight, almost electric tingle, and realized what he must have known all along. The little Ravenbeck wasn't that deep—she was closer than he thought. In fact, she could be no more than two feet high, standing on her tiny toes.

She tapped his foot again, then held out a hand like a child asking for candy. Transparent moth-like wings, which could not possibly be meant for flying, fluttered with agitation.

Ben threw a quizzical glance at his partner, who lifted his hands and his eyebrows, totally useless.

Not to be ignored, the pixie frowned, hopped into the air with a boost from the little wings, and this time gave Ben's knee an irritated slap.

No one brings us offerings anymore!

The voice was small as a child's, not like the twittering little folk of the meadows and hedgerows, and unlike the moth-like flower faeries, she spoke real English.

That's right, said another with a precious pout.

It makes us sad, said the third, who sat on a rock leaning her elbows on her knees.

"What? Oh, hang on."

Smoothly, Ben swung the Swadeshi off his shoulder and blessed his own foresight and the craftsman's orderly mind that made everything in it easy to find. He pulled out the packet of rainbow Mentos and began neatly tearing away the paper.

A pink one for the pink-draped naiad at his knee; pale yellow for the little spiky-haired blonde; and a faintly purple one for the pixie with the violet eyes, which opened wide as soon as she touched the sweet, the size of a bread loaf in her exquisite little hands.

Oh! she cried, and inhaled deeply of the fruity smell. *Sweet!*

Her little wings beat like a hummingbird's, lifting her a few inches straight up, then softly let her down again.

Sweetness!

Lovely!

They all sighed like kittens, showing sharp little kitten teeth as they each took one lick, then twittered:

We like you, Ben Harper! We always did.

As dimpled and darling as kewpie dolls, they were adorable apart from the teeth. And like most of the other little fae, they had a hard time staying focused. That was half of the danger, Ben suspected. They might pop a man under a rock just for fun, then forget him completely and flit off to dance on a moonbeam. But for the moment, at least, he had some part of their attention.

"So, dear ladies, can you help me?" he asked as if for the first time.

Of course we can!

Now they were fluttering about him like the nymph in the painting. Any painting.

We love to help a handsome man!

"I need to meet with Father Thames. That is, my friend and I do."

Oh, we know Raven!

They giggled, and the lemony one swooned a little. The pink one planted a not-quite-chaste kiss on the raven-boy's cheek, and touched his lips. Still grinning, he took her little hand on the tip of one finger, and kissed it like a gentleman, then spun her back toward Ben.

Who blinked twice and asked again,

"Can you tell me where your father is now, and how to find him?"

Still clutching their candies, almost stoned on the sweet smells alone, they laughed and ducked under the bridge. When they popped up on the other side, Ben and Raven crossed over to see them pointing both up and down their little river, singing nonsense.

You're halfway there already! they chirped. The water knows, human child!

You'll find him!

Trust the water!

A last great splash rose up and hit Ben in the face, again, and he rolled back. When he opened his eyes, the nymphs were flittering off in the distance and Raven was roaring.

"Nicely done, Ben Harper!"

When he had stopped cackling, the boy slapped his hand in the harper's and hauled him to his feet. Without waiting to be asked, he also made sure his clothes were dry.

"Right," Ben said tightly, marching off the bridge to the relative safety of the opposite bank. When he sat down under the willow by the water's edge, boots among the leaf litter, the raven-boy handed him a cloth for his glasses, then stepped carefully along the stony bank.

"And what did we learn from today's exercise?"

Ben worked at his glasses again.

"Uhm, that naiads like Mentos?"

"Mark it, Horatio. Might be important."

"That their size is proportional to the size of their stream, like goldfish?"

"Perhaps. They are rather koi."

Ben ignored that to get to his point.

"And that they can't give a straight answer, any more than the rest of you can. So much for help."

"But they have given an answer," Raven added, slightly affronted, "in their own way. No, seriously. Look, my lord would probably tell you that all rivers are one river, and you do seem to have one right here at the bottom of your garden."

Ben considered, combing both hands back through his hair.

"Are we supposed to swim?"

"It's an option."

"Wet enough for one day, thanks. A boat might be useful. What option?"

The raven-boy was grinning again.

"Perhaps you should have asked sooner."

Ben stood up, batting the damp from the back of his jeans, his face scrinched up with doubt.

"Yeah?"

He picked a slippery way along the bank for a closer look. Raven, the soul of grace, followed along easily.

"It's a little primitive, yes, but it should do."

Bobbing like an eggshell in the shadow of the bridge was an oblong black…well, a sort of market basket, except it was seven feet long, the oiled hide of a vast black bull stretched over a wicker framework. No deck, no lining, just the knotted hazel rods underfoot like something out of the dawn of time, with two flat planks set across the middle to incidentally provide a seat, and a pair of short paddles that couldn't be much use. If they were very cozy, it might have room for them both, assuming it didn't capsize the first time they moved.

"Okay. What is it?"

"A coracle!" said Raven, and when Ben looked doubtful, he explained. "Traditional boats on the rivers of Britain and Ireland from time out of mind. Just the thing for a summer cruise."

Ben turned a dubious eye on his friend.

"That's fine for me. Where's yours?"

"Well," he said, and for a moment Ben saw the Raven ruffling sable feathers. "I do have alternatives. But come on, there's room for both of us. Magic, Ben, remember? It'll be fun."

They settled themselves in with varying degrees of grace. It floated light as a leaf, more on the water than in it. For a brief, slightly hysterical moment when he was stashing the satchel under the seat, Ben knew for sure it was going to tip over and throw them out. He could swim—what California boy couldn't? And he'd sailed before, sure, but he'd been challenged enough these past two days without them being swamped with every shift of his weight. Like now.

"Whoa!" He swore and grabbed for the gunwale but, magically, it held steady. Raven in his current madcap humour seemed slightly disappointed.

The harper let out a gathered breath.

"Ready?"

"Are you asking me or the river?" Raven said.

"Well, then."

He settled his thoughts, more or less, and began to whistle a bouncy country dance. The coracle trembled under them like a racehorse longing for a starting bell. Balanced so lightly, surely it should have simply drifted away, but it didn't move.

"I guess," Ben said, "Father Thames has sent a car for us, but not a driver."

"Is it stuck on something?"

A trill of birdsong reached them across the common. A breeze stirred the leaves of the trees and grasses that marked the stream's edge. Raven punched his shoulder, pointed out the slender chain, tenuous as a cobweb in the dappled sunlight, which tethered them loosely to the shading willow tree. At the raven-boy's nod, the knot slipped and unwound, the chain retracted slithering into his hand to the sound of a light chime. When he held it up for Ben to see, it was nothing but a notched and knotty hazel twig.

"Neat," he said. "And we're still not moving."

They each took a paddle, if that's what it was, and pushed out into the mid stream. Though clear water chuckled under their feet, and the coracle bobbed and rocked as gently as any cradle in the treetops, it failed to move with the flow.

Ben took a deep breath, then sat up straight and flung out a hand in something like a magical gesture.

"Home, James, and don't spare the horses!"

Raven snorted. "I don't think that's going to work."

"Open sesame!"

"That either." Laughing, the kid dabbled his fingers in the water. Maybe they would sink after all!

"Speak, friend, and enter?"

"What in all the worlds are you doing?"

"Looking for the start button, the key, the…" To the lifted eyebrow he said, the frustration clear on his face, "Look, I assume we've been given transport because I don't know where we're going."

"You only needed six good notes to get us out of Cheltenham, in the dark, bespelled, with the queen of Faerie throwing fire balls at you."

"Yeah, but all I had to do was get us home. I can get home from anywhere."

Girlish giggles reverberating under the pillars of the bridge made them turn around, carefully. Only wavering light and shadows rippled across the stones.

We told him what to do.

He's forgotten how, silly human child.

Ben shook his head in disgust. "Typical."

I said he was stupid.

But he gave an offering!

Their tinkling voices came from the water, from the reeds clattering at the bank, the leaves of the willow sketching runes on the surface of the stream, but the naiads were nowhere to be seen.

"Ladies?" Raven's honeyed voice carried sweetly into the mossy shadows.

They are very polite!

And there was the offering. No one ever gives us offerings.

And Father says we must help them.

Aye, me! Then they must trust the water.

That's what we said, trust the water.

Trust the water, pretty mortal!

Fare well!

Wherever they were, they began to sing, the harmonies unsettling but perfect. Catching the sense of it, Ben lifted the cittern to his knee. Put a quick twist on a tuning peg, a more considered one on another. Head cocked to listen, he began to pluck the melody from the strings.

Errors examined: A sharp where he expected a flat, a pause where he would have moved.

Lessons taken: Slide into a phrase this way, the silence is part of the sound.

Melody unlocked: At last, and with it sweet and strange, a current, a tingle, a longing in the harper's chest that drew him as it had drawn him to the Mermaid Stair. The touch of his gift, the harp string sounding the note he knew, in a different kind of chord.

"I should have realized," he murmured "I should have known it wouldn't be the same."

"Ah," said Raven kindly. "Better now, human child?"

In answer, Ben lifted his hands from the cittern and, instead of stilling the strings with a touch as he might have done, he let the vibration linger on the air.

"Thank you," he whispered to someone.

He began again, this time sure of his gift and his intention. The first notes rang out, lively and quick. The little boat leapt forward as the tune became a song under his hands, and the voices faded into water, air, and sun. It spun round a few times on the current as if searching for bearings, then at last caught the current and sailed free.

Raven waited for more, until finally he asked, "So, you do know where we're going?"

Bright-eyed, Ben gave a curt nod as the borderland of Faerie came up with the mist at his left hand. "Yes."

"And you know this thing can't be steered like this."

"That's all right." The American's mouth twitched into a knowing smile. He threw his friend a look. "Trust the water."

13
On the Rivers of Faerie

i

On Dartmoor, as every moor-man knows, Faerie is seldom more than a step away. Playing the naiads' song and following their advice, Ben Harper let the water lead them at its own pace into the Borderlands: a soft summer morning on the Faerie bank, England in golden autumn on the other side, touched with fire. The music took them into the brook below Iveston, and after a while a mossy wood embraced them as easily as a water ride at Disneyland, without the clanking gears or the singing bears. The banks receded and the current slowed as the river broadened, but the coracle slowed only when Ben asked it to.

Near Newton Abbot they could hear the faint echo of human traffic and chatter leaking through the faerie gates, a police whistle, the alternating wail of an ambulance. Orange, red and sere yellow leaves fluttered one by one into the boat, carpeted the water. Then a darkness opened and swallowed them into a tunnel.

Ben kept playing. The ringing music bounced and echoed back in a kind of counterpoint for a hundred yards or so, keeping them company in the dark passage.

When they emerged, expecting sun coins and black water, they found themselves instead in the center of a broad, blue stream as wide as the Thames at Big Ben, and filled with pleasure craft of all sizes.

"Is this right?"

Ben's hands lifted from the strings, the music died, and they slowed almost to a stop.

"Curious," Raven said under a lifted eyebrow. "This is the Dart. We're halfway to Dartmouth."

Music, chatter, adverts from competing radios tore the air like a particularly irritating battle of the bands as one of a pair of sailboats overtook the other. A tour boat putt-putted upstream on the opposite side. An orange-jacketed child waved at them and Raven waved back and pulled faces at it, but otherwise no one noticed their little coracle at all.

Ben shut out everything but the gurgle of the water, the breeze across his ears, the changing scents of moss and sedge, the interfering tang of diesel, and he listened.

"That's weird," he said softly. "Do you hear that?" He bent his thought to the sound, and sang the melancholy verse:

> Said the sailor to his sweetheart,
> We soon must sail away.
> And it's lovely on the waters
> For to hear the music play.

The world shimmered, the light changed. Both the heartline of Dartmoor and its namesake the Dart still bore them along, but they were much further from the sea, heading north again. Here they sat shadowed by slender trees almost barren of brittle leaves, spanned by the vaulting arches of an ancient stone bridge. The river here was swift and should have bounced them downstream, but the magic was holding them gently in place.

"Holne Bridge," Raven observed. He was humming the old tune, mind turned inward, feeling his own way through the worlds with the concentration peculiar to his race. Until the night-dark eyes turned suddenly to Ben.

"Did you hear that?" they said together.

Ben wanted to make the usual joke about timing, but the look on Raven's face warned all humour away. The sound was clearer than it had been, no longer on the edge of his awareness.

"A child?" he wondered.

"No."

"There!" Ben pointed suddenly and setting the boat rocking.

A shape glimmered on a rocky shelf beside the bridge, brightening and fading. A voice meandered as if lost, in search of a tune. And when he looked, really looked, he knew what it was.

On the Faerie bank, as if spring overlay the autumn world, a slender young woman knelt weeping in a cave fringed with green leaves, her face in her hands. Dark hair spilled over her plain violet gown to the earth.

"Isn't that the nymph from the Edgware Road?" he wondered.

"It can't be, no. That one was frightened, but there was no sorrow in her. I think she is the Dart herself."

"But why?"

"It is more than I can say, human child. I have never seen such a thing."

It seemed the weeping would never end. When she raised her head and saw them, she cried:

"Does my father send spies to me now? My river thrives. I do none harm. I have not abandoned my charge as some have done. Go, lord, for pity, and leave me to my pain!"

Her grief gave shape to the song, terrible to hear.

> *Four hundred years beside the waters*
> *My fear held him in thrall;*
> *If I could take it from my dear love,*
> *I would gladly spend it all.*

"We were meant to see this," said Raven "By whom, I wonder. And why?"

Then he changed the music, or pulled some faerie strings, and they slipped smoothly into a pool carpeted with yellow leaves and sun coins glinting in the water. Overhead, a hoary old oak reached a vast arm across the stream.

Answering a familiar prickling of his spine, Ben turned to look behind him. Bridge and lady were gone. He and Raven were no longer on the moor, no longer in Devon. And though it had been broad noontime when they set out, the sun was setting on their left and the landscape had changed again. Whatever had diverted them to the Dart, whatever the reason, they were back on course.

"Are we there yet?"

Ben's companion lifted a hand to signal quiet while he listened. Nothing but a nightingale warming up for evening. A few breaths, and a deep gaze into the gathering darkness, and the long-fingered hand came down again.

"I don't know why, but it feels like…" he said thoughtfully. "It doesn't feel like…"

"Kansas anymore?"

"Something like that. Faerie, and yet no place of Faerie that I know, and I have been everywhere in my lord's service. Or I thought I had." He was silent a long while, then said abruptly: "Forgive me, Ben, your fingers must be numb. I'll mind the music for a bit, you keep us on track."

Ben thought the boy looked curiously uncomfortable, and that always made him uneasy. If it had been anyone but Raven, he would have called it fidgety.

"You think we should be there already, don't you? You think Father Thames doesn't like my fingering?"

"He could only admire it."

"All right, then." The American brought his hand up, a gesture of grace simply tracing the shoreline. "That way."

The river took them.

The sky was more crowded with stars than he'd ever seen, as if the Milky Way danced across the whole bowl of the night. Where the river swept them past open pastureland or wheat fields cut to golden stubble, they could see the mounds of hills rising in purple shadow against a watercolor horizon.

Raven sang lightly, ancient tunes in ancient tongues, while keeping the naiad's song near the surface of his thought, until Ben said with a gentle nudge,

"We're wavering. English tunes for an English river, I think."

The raven-boy stopped and thought, then he smiled and clapped his hands.

"Very well…"

He tapped out a new beat, quickening the time.

> *There was a lofty ship, and they put her out to sea*
> *And the name of the ship was the Golden Vanity.*

"Much better!"

They picked up speed and Ben relaxed. That was all they needed. His gift might fail outright, but it never lied.

And then, it twisted.

"Wait!" Ben yelled.

The coracle stopped dead, throwing them both forward in the tiny space. The flat bow nodded so close to the surface it shipped water once, twice, again until they had restored their balance point. Ben caught his breath.

"We need to go ashore."

Asking no questions, the boy directed the little boat into a nest of roots under an old willow.

"Yes?"

Craning his head to get a clear view, Ben pointed through the trees where dim lights glimmered.

"See there?"

"Of course."

Raven's vision was as clear in darkness as in daylight. He nodded, then fetched the hazel twig and tossed it toward a place where rocks and willow roots formed a kind of stair. The silver chain paid out as it flew and locked under a root.

"A good stretch of the legs will do me good anyway."

ii

The light here was definitely brighter, the colors clearer. They went ashore and shortly found a path marked with a white stone every few paces. The two men exchanged a look, then set out to see whatever they were meant to see.

Shortly they came upon a poor hovel patched together of grey weathered boards and old plaster, shabby and run-down as a slum though it stood alone at the edge of a wood in the twilight realm. An old-fashioned stone well stood in front of it, with a pitched slate roof to keep the sun off, and a winding crank.

Under a broad hat that nearly covered his face a wee man in a coat as shabby as the house was walking away from the well gripping a rope tightly in his two fists. First he backed away for a while, then he turned and walked on with the rope over his shoulder. He took a few more steps then turned round, hauling on the rope again, whereafter he faced about once more and walked three paces forward with his shoulder taking the strain. He had been doing it so long that he had worn a smooth track in the earth.

He appeared to be hauling a bucket up from the well, but as they drew closer, the rope slipped from his grasp. The wee man yelled as it whipped out of his hands and slithered along the ground, snaking a trail in the dust while the bucket fell and fell. Two seconds later, or maybe three, a faint splash echoed from the bottom of the well. The rope stopped squiggling with the frayed end brushing the ground

Crestfallen, the little man began to trudge back to the well, muttering as he tripped over the tails of his coat.

"Can we help you, Little Father?" said Raven.

The wee fellow only muttered, glared briefly at them, then picked up the rope's end and began again. Clearly he was too short to see over the well's rim, or to attach the rope to the crank, or to wind the crank and pull up the bucket, even if it were attached.

Now, the curious thing was that right next to the well stood a hand pump which, had he used it, would have made fetching his water the easiest thing in the world.

"Tell me, grandsire," said Ben, following him as he trudged. "Surely it would be easier to get your water from the pump."

Without stopping or changing his habit of turn and turn about, the little man grumbled, "Broke, innit!"

Again the rope slipped away. Ben stopped then and watched the cycle begin all over again. When Raven joined him, they shared a look and a shrug. It was Faerie. They both knew the rules. Ben took off his jacket and rolled up his sleeves while Raven found a spade, a wrench, and some other tools behind the house. After a quarter-hour's work, they had dug away a good hole at the base, and found the problem. A great toad sat in the cool, damp space where the water should have been drawn up into the bronze pipe.

Freed, it gave a miserable croak.

"Nice work, ass-hats."

Then it lumbered towards the river and disappeared. Mortal and fae stared, then began to laugh so hard they sat right down on the dusty ground.

"I suppose you boys are thirsty," said the little man in the big coat. He was standing over them now, glaring over the long pointed nose that nearly met his long pointed chin. Clearly he was not a man at all, but a gnome.

"I beg your pardon," Ben said. "Don't I know you?"

"Nah," said the gnome. "You know my cousin Hedger. Grumpy fellow, no sense of humour. I'm Slider, me."

He waddled into the shabby old house while Ben and Raven threw back their heads and laughed some more, then got up and finished the job.

In short order, Ben had restored the pump to working order, and filled in the hole, while Raven drew the bucket up from the well on its long, long rope. He poured some water over the top of the pump to prime it, then placed it under the spout. With a few hard pulls, the water was gushing pure and clear and all was as it should be.

Slider came out of the house with a crystal pitcher and two brimming crystal goblets on a tray. Ben looked at the water pitcher, then at the well and pump, then back at the full pitcher. Then he raised his gaze to meet Raven's who had clearly done the same.

"If he had…"

"Then why…"

"Don't ask!"

They each took a glass, but the harper put his down, withdrew his hand, and stepped back.

"What's the matter?" the boy said.

It was Faerie. Ben knew the rules. At the doubtful expression, his friend chuckled.

"What, sir!" he said lightly. "Still so cautious. Has my lord not told you? You have the freedom of Faerie for all time, by his express command. And sure, he owes you far more than that since last Christmas. I'd be careful of the heather beer, but only because the hangovers are murder."

"Oh, like you've ever been hung over," Ben said, gratefully accepting the frosty glass at last.

"You see my point."

They touched glasses with an ethereal chime, toasted their host, and drank down the coldest, fairest water Ben had ever tasted. As he drank, the aches in all his muscles eased. Even his hands and fingers cooled, and his spirit lightened.

They refilled the glasses and drank again gratefully. And when they put their goblets down, the wee man gave a nod and disappeared in the twinkling of an eye, along with his house, the well, and the pesky pump, leaving a muddy patch and an adjustable spanner in the shadow of the wood. With a quick sparkle and a shiver of glass chimes, the wrench disappeared, too.

"Ah," said Raven. "Of course."

"I like a gnome who takes care of his tools."

"Look again."

Where the spanner had been, there now sat a gleaming silver flask, round as an apple, etched around and about with fancy scrollwork and the odd cherub. When Ben picked it up, he read his name in swirly characters engraved along its equator, and the words: *"King's Man."* When he snapped it open, the delicious fragrance of the sweet well water wafted up at once.

Knowing it's not good to have too much of a good thing, he quickly capped the flask and stashed it in the sushi bag, which he promptly shouldered.

"There'll be another good deed, I expect."

"You know there will. Any feeling about how we find it?"

"Or how we put ourselves in the way of being found by it? I hate to say it, but it's time to get back on the water."

"It's going to be a wet one, this adventure, isn't it, Ratty?" Raven said, as though he weren't already as dry and fresh as when they'd started.

"Come along, Mole," said Ben, "if you please."

*
**

The riverbank, when they got back to it, hummed with dragonfly fae and lilac-blossom faeries dive-bombing the coracle, filling the air with shrill whistles. Not the coracle alone, which the men discovered as soon as they came down the rocky stair and pressed aside the willow fronds. Hunkered down among the latticed hazel rods sat the uncouth toad, pocked with the litter of blown catkins and fallen leaves, while faeries gold and lavender flickered like lightning bugs around it. Over and over it shot out its long sticky tongue at one of them, and missed.

"Bugger," it belched, and lashed out again. "Bugger."

"Don't sulk," said Raven, smiling broadly. For Ben, he added, "The wee folk wink out the instant before he strikes, even though they're there when he does."

"What?" Ben was more concerned with how to get the thing out of the boat.

"Never mind. Pop off home, Rana, if you want a proper meal."

It glared at them, and snap! settled for an ordinary dragonfly.

"That's Bufo to you, doc," it croaked. Then it heaved itself over the side, followed by a substantial splash.

"If it breaks into *Hello, My Ragtime Gal*, I'm leaving."

Ben snorted and tossed his pack into the little boat, making it bobble and dance as he clambered in after it.

"Get in, kid. We're almost there."

iii

They gathered in the silver tether and pushed off, content to let the current catch them. A light breeze sprang up that chivvied them along, rattled the rushes, soughing in the reeds, soothing their cares.

Then the river hung a sharp left. The coracle banged into a floating branch.

"What?"

Ben's head jerked up. He stared about, heart slamming in his chest. Even Raven looked startled.

Their broad stream had narrowed and begun to race. The pitch grew steeper, and somewhere ahead of them the burbling stream was beginning to rumble like the drop of a roller coaster.

Ben raised his voice over the rising noise. "We're picking up speed."

Hands trembling in counterpoint, he collected his satchel and made sure of the cittern, snugged down the slide-locks. Then he slung the strap across his chest.

Raven got to his knees to get a better look ahead, taking a good grip on the coracle's frame.

"Trust the water, they said," he shouted, eyes alight with a kind of wild ecstasy.

"I trust the water! It's the rocks I'm worried about!" Ben yelled back. "Hang on!"

The banks had begun to close in on either side, rising to a series of bluffs where browsing deer surveyed the little craft as it bumped along, faster still. In seconds they were a stone skidding over the surface of rushing rapids; shooting over slips and dropping over rocks; leaping up and crashing through white water a coracle was never meant to meet. Too thrilled to be terrified, Ben whooped gleefully with every bang and splash.

One of the paddles flew up and vanished in the spume before Raven could even point a thought towards it. Moments later, the other one rocketed after it.

"No life jackets, no helmets, no paddles!" Ben hollered, as an eddy swirled them back upstream for a moment of near calm.

Raven just cackled.

"And a boat that only floats when it's right way up!"

"What could possibly go wrong?"

Catching the leaf-light coracle once more, the current flung them forward. A wave that should have sunk them outright crashed into the boat and splashed out again, knocking Ben back and leaving behind a wake of milky bubbles and an enormous trout. A string of Dartmoor pixies—the little ones Ben often heard but seldom saw—popped off its ridged back piping *hup-hup-ho!* in their chipmunk voices. Like a team of tiny acrobats, they doffed their green caps to the fae lord and gave a practised bow, oblivious to the bouncing of the boat. Then they turned and blew raspberries at Ben Harper. Another series of *hup!* and *ho!*, and they clambered on to their gasping mount. The next wave swamped the boat, and as it emptied, lifted fish, pixies, and attitude back into the river where they vanished into the spray.

Raven, dripping wet and staring after them open mouthed, hooted with laughter till the next wave caught him full in the mouth. While he sputtered and coughed, Ben hung on, laughing.

At last they shot round a curve into the center of a broad, blue stream, where they rocked again to seeming stillness, spinning slow pirouettes in a side pool formed in a half-moon shingle of splintered agate. The cliff above it glittered dark rose, pink and almond, Prussian blue and cobalt, lapis, and a thread of gold. Opposite, an open park sloped swiftly up and away into the arm of a lofty cliff face filled with some kind of thick white flowers, straight as soldiers, trumpeting from tall straight stems. Golden poppies spilled into the spaces at the base.

14
Passage

The water only seemed still; the canyon was so long that passing through it took the best part of a minute, but they had not stopped and were nowhere near the shore. Before Ben could wonder any further, Raven's head jerked around, alert and focused.

"Did you hear that?" he shouted over the ringing in his ears. Rapids, rushing wind, the flicker of bird song all registered in the fae lord's hearing, and something else. A voice? A lover's whisper?

Ben smacked his shoulder.

"I said, look!"

"Oak and ash!"

Less than a hundred paces ahead, and approaching way too fast, the river split around a rocky islet overgrown with shrubbery, spangled with purple flowers. From the wall of mist and the cream-pale crust of the moon hanging beyond, there was no mistaking the bone-rattling roar pounding over the brink of a cloud-hung cliff. This fairy-tale idyll had gone too far.

"I hate to say it, kid." The harper was laughing a little hysterically. "We're here!"

This was crazy. He could hardly hear his own words over the thunder, even in his head.

Raven knew he could have them out of there with a thought. Coolly, he said, "Touch my hand!"

"No, no, I'm fine!" Ben's face was a wide terrified grin as he took off his spattered glasses and tucked them under the Swadeshi's lid and pulled the string down hard. "I'm supposed to do this!"

"You're supposed to kill yourself?"

"I hope not." Ben shrugged. "But it's the next step!"

"Of course it is!" His rueful laugh became a raucous cough, and from the rocking edge of the impossible coracle, the King's Raven vaulted into the air, sable feathers rattling. "I'll find my own way down. Try not to drown!"

No one survived a waterfall without a barrel, Ben thought. And what did he have but a bit of leather and a few twigs. But then, he had done so many impossible things lately. Hell, the stupid boat should have tipped him out ages ago, except that someone wanted him whole. Whoever it was would have to take him as he came, then—soaking wet. He hoped there'd be lunch in it somewhere.

The islet rushed toward him; it was longer than it had appeared from behind. And now he was passing it, swift but unhurried. Just at the cusp of the waterfall, the slender finger of a tree limb lurking under the churning water snagged the coracle. It half spun in place, and stopped with Ben facing back the way he'd come. His heart in his mouth, he peered over his shoulder, but the mist occluded any view. He wondered how far it was to the bottom—as if it mattered.

He wrapped the satchel's strap around his hands and, as he reached for the magic that was waiting to reel him in, he steadied himself. A song. He needed a song. Then he laughed, and sang out:

> One misty moisty morning
> when cloudy was the weather,
> I met with an old man,
> a-clothèd all in leather.
> A-clothèd all in leather,
> with his cap beneath his chin—

The restraining branch snapped, gave way, released, let him go. The last thing he saw clearly was the black silhouette of the

Raven at the edge of the sky, and the boiling base of the falls.

Singin' how-d'ye-do and how-d'ye-do
And how-d'ye-do again!

Water folded him in its embrace, murmured in his ear, which tickled, but that was okay. Someone was kissing him, and that was okay, too. The hands at either side of his face held him, softly insistent. So did the sinuous leg wrapped around his thighs to brace him. Nice dream, he thought. His hands, free to wander, found a slender waist; exploring thumbs travelled smoothly up a ribcage to the fullness of a pair of perfect breasts that weren't his wife's.

Ben's eyes snapped open, staring into the lovely but inhuman face; the billowing sea-green hair; the tiny, multi-hued scales dusting the arch of a mermaid's cheekbones. The gasp that would have drowned him instead drew in air from the sensuous mouth clamped onto his. In a moment, she broke off, but laid a pair of webbed fingers over his lips. He got the picture and held his breath, no problem. She nodded. Then, unwrapping her shimmering tail from his legs, she took his hand and started undulating upwards through blue water towards a circle of light.

Riding the thermals in the fragrant airs of Faerie, Raven watched with a peculiar feeling of dismay as his all too mortal partner tipped singing over the verge. He had seen this view often enough from Oberon's study when the king was in the mood for grandeur: the long straight drop, the plume of mist, and supposed it to be Yosemite Falls plunging over its fifteen-hundred-foot cliff.

He circled, dropping as Ben dropped, feeling the wind, icy under his feathers, chill his soul as the coracle fell away seconds before Ben himself disappeared into the crystalline glitter at its base. The lower falls, another thousand feet of rock and death, showed only the glitter of rainbows. No sign of the harper, alive or dead.

Trust the water, everyone said. Fine. To do what? What was the point?

"Brilliant," thought the Raven, and swore coarsely, as only a corvid can swear.

The airs over the ratcheting falls were ragged, rowdy enough to buffet most normal birds into the cliff or slam them to the ground with ease. The King's Raven felt the forces flung against him by wind and water, driving him back, and he didn't care. It might not be his place to be the hero, but this was his own country, the harper was his charge, and he plain hated being left behind.

Mind grimly set, he swung up and called his name to the Moon's pale disk. Then, wings clapped tight to the night black body, Raven flung himself out of the air spiraling toward the pool at the bottom of the falls.

15
1594 Westminster

The long days of summer drew down toward autumn, the long blue nights becoming shorter and more melancholy. Three churches within hearing had just struck six, and where another man would have begun cleaning his pens, Simon Carew pulled a fresh sheet of foolscap from the drawer when his master's compact frame filed the narrow doorway to the cramped little office, a jovial burst of excitement and sanguinary humours. Barely contained in his arms was a travel-stained wooden crate, fairly reeking of the sea.

"What, still here!" cried Robert Cotton. "God's Death, master Silence! Still here?"

In the carefree way that admitted all mankind to his good will, young Robert Cotton gave pet names to anyone he thought required one. Simon had earned his more swiftly than most, having twice been locked in with the books at day's end for lack of any clue the man was still there: his working pen no more than the scratching of a mouse.

"God giveth us good work to do," Cotton went on, "and good wine to follow it. Put down the one, man, and take up the other."

Silence Carew. He'd been called that as a boy, and again at Cambridge. Silence, and Sullen, and Sorry. Even Robert Cecil, who was not given to familiarities, had called him so. From Cotton, at least, there was no malice. Instead of resenting the foolishness, Simon had come to appreciate it, to think of himself as re-baptized into his true calling.

Simon looked up slowly, reluctant to lose his place.

"I am well content, sir, if it please you to let me stay a while longer."

"Nonsense. I am no slave-driver. I'll not have you saying so among your cronies at your old boozing ken. What is it again? The Pope's Nose, eh?"

"Sir?"

At his look of horror, Cotton laughed again.

"Peace, peace, Silence, never mind. I do but jest, as well you know. Pray forgive me a merry heart."

His assistant's reformed habits were well known among his household, verging on the legendary. The man whose own drinking companions included scholars, poets, and players would never understand.

Nor should he, Carew thought with satisfaction, though his expression remained suitably meek.

"It is good for me to be reminded betimes, sir."

Ever helpful, he went to take the box from his master, who seemed to have forgotten it.

"Ah, yes, gramercy!" Cotton exclaimed. "New come in from Antwerp. Well, from Donato in Stamboul to start, but Antwerp had it last. Fetch an iron crow, man, and we'll have it open!"

Enthusiasm is contagious when two men share a deep and esoteric interest. Grinning like children, they swiftly cleared away the nearest flat surface and prised open the top, jumping at splinters, and wincing at the high-pitched creak and strain of iron nails drawn unwilling from swollen wood.

The captive air released sharp and sweet the fragrance of sandalwood and pepper, strange inks and foreign climes, tendrils of the mystic East come home to their grey island in the north of the world. Breathing it in, Carew's eyes closed in a kind of childish joy, imagining the scents of Paradise.

The top layer contained a long letter from a colleague attached to the Imperial embassy in the Sublime Port gloating a little about what he had kept back, then cheerfully listing what he had sent and calling on the Almighty to protect these pagan relics as they crossed rivers and mountains and through the hands of thieving Flemings, Turks, and Frenchmen, all of them his friends. Beneath that, they lifted aside the layers of dried palm fronds pleated like a lady's fan, to reveal the treasures one by one, checking each against the Venetian's list. Silence found a fresh quill and made notes as they went. Proper cataloging would come later.

Here were a few bound books: a translation of some obscure work of Plotinus, a genealogy of the Dukes of Artois, a richly colored book of hours bound in with a life of Charlemagne. Excellent but trivial stuff, inevitably useful if delivered to the right patron at the right time.

They lifted out unbound stacks of thick paper and parchment, folio and quarto and duodecimo, in a dozen languages and as many hands, clapped between boards or rolled together with a string, each tantalizingly anonymous but for a numbered tag. A handwritten notebook was filled with drawings, observations, notes in a hand that might, if shown to a mirror, be some sort of Italian. A dozen more loose sheets were shoved into the back cover.

Breathing heavily, Cotton said, "John Dee will want to see this. I may have to give it to him, you know. I haven't returned the last book I borrowed, but he will forgive me, I think, for this." He set it carefully aside.

"And do you mean to return the other book?"

The scholar was smiling, but not at the implication. He had both arms in the box again, buried to the elbows, pressing through the last rattling palm leaves to get at the very bottom. The sweet smell of the finest vellum rose up to wrinkle their noses. Cotton wrenched aside to sneeze.

"God spare you," said Silence out of habit.

"Oh aye, aye, if he will."

Ser Donato's notes identified it as the Ata'rathi Scroll: a trimmed roll of good vellum of about ten inches width and almost two Venetian ells in length, dating from first-century Rome. The curiosity was that it incorporated scraps of a much older papyrus document in Greek so old that no one alive could read it. Although the papyrus itself was falling apart, other ragged pieces pasted into the newer scroll provided illustration for the commentaries upon its supposed contents. Each fragment was surrounded by neat notes in Latin and Greek both classical and modern.

"Hmm." He handed it across to Carew, who took it with trembling hands.

"Does he say more of this? Anything?"

But it didn't matter. The magic reached out to the secretary, whipping his whisperers to a desultory mutter.

He didn't need invisible voices to tell him what he could feel in his bones. He had read about this scroll, stumbled over oblique references, a cryptic footnote. At one time, knowledge of it must have been common to every ploughman, familiar in pagan mouths as scripture to a bishop. So well-known that a brief mention, a few lines, even a paraphrase, was enough to make a point.

Now it had simply fallen into his hands. This would contain, it must contain the secrets that had eluded him these long months of study. The tool he needed to complete his task. The price, he thought as he cradled it in his arms, of his soul.

"The papyrus itself," Cotton carried on, translating his friend's Latin, "purports to be from Nineveh, though he does not believe it. The condition is very poor. He believes it to have little value save as a novelty, but 'I know thy weakness for any bauble so long as it be older than yourself.' He suggests we use it as fire starter to keep us warm in the fog!"

He tossed the letter aside with a laugh. "The old villain. As to that, aye, we shall see. Come, Silence, shall we each open one of these folios? The first few pages only, eh? As a reward for our long day."

For a while they pursued with almost childish glee what titles and lists of headings they could find. For all too brief a space, Carew rested from his terrible mission, the voices silenced as his excellent mind was caught up in the tangles of scholarship for its own sake. Though rest is relative. His awareness of the scroll tickled the edges of his thought, the enchantment a dry lump in his throat.

The bells of London had struck seven before Robert Cotton

stood up from the circle of lamplight, straightening his back and blinking against the gathered shadows. A Cambridge man, he had taken a Bachelor of Arts at the precocious age of fifteen. He was only twenty-four now, but serious study, however joyful, was already taking its toll. Like his secretary, he squinted in the failing daylight slanting across the desk.

"Enough!" he cried, and yawned. "Enough of this. God's truth, there're too few like us who love such study, eh. Come sup with me at Lady Lumley's tonight. Get out thy chair. Make yourself known to men of consequence who can do you some good. Make your way in the world, eh?"

The accents of home were never far from even the most educated tongue, and so it was with Rob Cotton. He revelled in the rhythms of its speech, let anyone laugh who would. Furthermore, it amused him that Carew had buried his muddy Devon mumble under the sharp clipped speech of a Londoner, but never mind. A man does what he must.

"Nay, I cannot, sir," the secretary replied, thin smile fading. "For Silence in company is never merry."

"A jest? Silence, was that a jest?"

"Nay, master, not I. But you must go or else be late. Go and be merry with your noble friends. Only give me leave to stay and read awhile."

"Well, if needs must, I'll not force you to serve your own interests, though the company and the discourse would suit you well."

Ah well, the truth was, at Carew's age and circumstance, there was probably little to be done for his advancement, but Rob Cotton was young and eager, and thought all men must be so as well.

"Give me your word, then, that you will do no more work on my account today."

Standing to do him reverence, Carew answered:

"Marry, sir, you have it."

"And that you'll touch no more of these new texts without me!" He indicated the piles of papers, books, and shattered palm fronds.

"Nay, sir, I will not. Upon my name. And that is Silence."

"Another jest, i'faith! And faith, I must away before thou break'st my heart." Cotton turned to go, waving a hand about his hat. "Then for the sake of a loving Christ, Silence, have Randall trim the wicks in those lamps, eh! And built up that fire, too. Black as Plato's Cave in here, and you a leapin' shadow on the wall!"

"So please you, Master Cotton."

"Oh!" The antiquary spun round, patting down his doublet with the distracted look of an over-worked professor. "I nearly forgot to show thee. Look here!" Reaching between the panes of his trunk hose, he dragged a pocket inside out, and from a fold of silk, produced a sort of jewel, a necklace maybe. When he held it up, a golden disk dangled from a strand of beads.

"This was lurking at the very bottom of the box. I found it when you went to piss awhile since. Donato doesn't mention it. What think you?"

What did he think? A long string of cloudy red beads, probably carnelian, strung between polished lumps of gold. A red-gold disk of carved amber hung by twisted cords in the midst of all. Silence almost snatched it from him, ignoring the charge that ran though his hand and up his arm, the rush of memory. Trembling with unseemly passion, he held it to the light,

On one side, some sort of wedged markings had been pressed or cut around the edge of the disk, spiraling into the center like dancing arrowheads. On the reverse, he already knew what he would find: *morven*, the old writers called it, a grotesque figure like a faceless woman with hair and limbs of writhing, intertwining serpents. A mermaid, they called it, too. His palm was sweating when he handed it back, while the voices clamored at him to destroy the heathen thing, pitch it in the fire. Except for one soft voice that said *Study, learn, make it a weapon against them.*

"I think it must be very old," he said tightly, and handed it back.

"Look through all this tomorrow. There should be notes, some provenance or other. It must be a talisman of some kind, think'st thou? One of your mermaids, eh? Or some pagan god."

"Perhaps, sir." Oh, yes. It was that.

"That will be your task, I think, tracing its meaning and application, if it can be found. If not, well, perhaps John Dee can make somethin' of it."

Carew only murmured absently,

"Yes, perhaps."

"Well enough, good night, and if you are too late, use your room here, aye? I'll speak to Eliza, to have it made up. Save you pitching into Fleet Ditch in the dark and drowning in the mire, eh?"

The man was still talking into the next room and the next until he reached the stair, flinging back instructions and last thoughts. His young wife would, when she caught him, make him put on the new doublet first, then send him off to spend the evening boasting to his fellow antiquaries.

Silence Carew sat down again, almost too dizzy to think. Perhaps he would go down and beg some bread or cheese, and a mug of small beer from Mistress Cotton. Yes, surely he should. He got to his feet, paced to the door, turned about, then went to poke up the fire.

The talisman had almost sung to him when it touched his hand. He had thrown it away once; he would not do such a childish thing again. The ancient scroll radiated potential. And a whole long night lay ahead of him, bright with promise.

16
Monday: Tam of Tam Hall

i

Time had become as fluid for Ben Harper as the featureless, almost frictionless medium through which he moved. Water, yes, he knew that, but neither cold nor warm. The light he saw came not from the surface, wherever it might be, but from globes suspended on immense stalks anchored so far below they disappeared into the abyss. Other more fleeting lights turned out to be creatures so bizarre he thought they must be from another planet.

More extraordinary yet was the sound. He had expected silence or at most, the gurgle of water in his ears. Instead, a haunting music enveloped him, subtly alien. It came, he thought, from voices far away, encountering one another almost by chance to create a song so achingly beautiful it sang in his bones, resonated in his blood. It called him to join his voice to the moving chord, his body to the chorus of the deep world. All would be well, all doubts resolved, dissolved, dispelled. The music swelled to fill him, caressing, promising.

Ben felt his body answering, his mouth open to sing. Dreamily he watched the air in his lungs leaving him drop by drop, each silver bubble breaking with a new note. He reached out with his free hand to touch them, and would have chased after them.

"No!" The mermaid squealed a harsh high note that scored across the perfection of the song, the needle scraped across the record. Furious, she jerked at the hand she held. "You must not do that."

"Let me go!" Ben cried, hating her. He kicked out, struggling, desperate to escape, to become the song.

All the air in him rushed out, bubbling into the water in a weird cacophony that sounded, almost, like mocking laughter. Then darkness.

Water was rushing over his eyes, through his hair. Ben could feel his skin again, tickled by a swarm of fingerling perch in the chilly river. The pressure over his chest altered, turned into pain; the loudest sound, the banging of his heart and the crackling burn in his lungs.

Silvery darts pattering just out of reach showed him where the surface was. Desperate for air, he pulled his aching arms down, kicked, and surged toward the rippling light. His ears popped, and the instant before he could bear it no longer, his reaching hands broke through, then eyes, nose, and mouth. And he was gasping, coughing, and drawing in sweet autumn air—lead-enriched, tangy with ozone, twenty-first century air. Oh God, and it was raining too.

"Okay, I'm here!" he sputtered as he flung dripping hair back from his face. "Anybody? Crap."

Weary arms and legs worked to keep him treading water not far from a green-smelling, overgrown riverbank heavy with foliage but offering little in the way of a landing place. The leather jacket floated like a blanket of seaweed off his shoulders, bound down by the weight of the sushi bag. From the looks of things, he was somewhere below Teddington Lock, coughing up Thames—the tidal transition tasted greenly of salt. No angry mermaid. No insidious music. No clue. Just his favorite question:

"Where the hell is Raven?"

As if in answer, a rush of water and the clever face broke the surface practically at Ben's right hand.

"Man, you're all wet!" Raven laughed.

"Well, it is raining. How did you get here?" Ben demanded, still gasping.

"No idea. Where are we?"

Before he could take a breath to answer, a huge river otter popped up between them, all round black eyes and whiskered muzzle. It chittered at Raven and patted his shoulder with a long-nailed paw. They turned to watch as it dived and struck out for the opposite bank toward an enormous blue houseboat docked in the shade under a stand of willows and ancient elms. Above the upper level a whimsically lettered sign bore the name *Gates of Dawn* on a carved and painted ribbon supported by busty mermaids. Alternately hidden and revealed by the lapping waters at the bow end rode the mermaid badge Aubrey had called a *morven*.

"Are we here? Oh please say we're here."

Waiting for them, hearty as Father Christmas, stood the man Ben had last seen—it felt like days ago—from the deck of the *Darling Girl*. The old guy was beaming as the otter humped up a long boat ramp to the deck and rocked up on its hind legs, staring back at them.

Ben swung up an arm and waved, calling,

"Ahoy, *Gates of Dawn!*"

"He may show what outward courage he will," declaimed the old guy, a river god if ever there was one. He sent the otter away with a pat and gestured them in. "But I believe, as cold a night as 'tis, he could wish himself in Thames up to the neck; and so I would he were, and I by him."

Raven had already struck out after the otter in a strong crawl. Ben shook his head, took a deep breath and followed with a touch less speed.

"Henry the Fifth," Ben said, hauling himself up, sheeting water from every plane of his body. "Act IV, Scene 1."

At least the rain had stopped.

He turned to haul Raven up, who right now looked more like a heron pulled from an oil slick than the king of Faerie's principal gentleman. Gripping his wrist, Ben could almost share the impulse to change shape and take flight.

When he had his feet, the boy folded one long-fingered hand to his breast and bowed slightly.

"My lord, if I may?" he said.

The old fellow nodded graciously. Raven gave his reverence in return and, careless of any watchers, leapt into the air, black-winged and raucous. For a few seconds the King's Raven perched on the rail of an overhanging gallery, the water coming off the ruffled feathers like an autumn rain. With a double croak and the flashing sapphire eye, he took off and winged quickly out of sight.

"Impulsive lad," said Tamesis, turning to watch him go.

"He'll be back," Ben said, paying more attention to his host than to his friend's flight, much as he envied him.

A trim, well-apportioned gentleman apparently in his sixties, the lord of the rivers and waterways of England stood taller than Ben expected, rather a bit over six feet. The long hair teased up by the breeze in which Ben was shivering lay on broad shoulders in shades of brown and even a hint, in the shadows, of blue or green. His slender face where it showed above the flowing beard and moustache was creased with laughter, sorrow, and long years out of doors; bright hazel eyes sparkled silver in the twilight.

Ben slicked back his hair and stuck out his hand.

"Ben Harper, sir."

"Well met," said Tamesis, taking it. The grip was firm and warm, a solid handshake with power leashed under the pleasantry. "Come in, come in, young man. Been expecting you since yesterday."

"There were a few distractions along the way, sir. But thanks. Oh, uh…"

Speaking of distractions, 'sushi' had never been a better name for the Swadeshi bag sagging heavily against Ben's hip. "I should probably do something about this."

It was designed to be proof against rain and storm, but not against being dragged through the watery underworlds of Faerie. It squelched as it hit the deck and laid over. A striped white fish squirmed out and flopped over the side. Kneeling, Ben popped the buckles and loosened the drawstring so he could fetch out his glasses. More carefully, he pulled out the king's cittern by its snarling dog-carved neck. The water beading on the varnish sparkled like diamonds even in the sultry air. He turned it over, shook it; water gushed through the pierced rose in the middle sounding a metallic thrill from the four pairs of strings.

"Oh, God," he murmured, shaking his head.

"Tam will do," said the river god, cordially.

Ben smiled, not listening.

"His Grace is going to kill me." He set down the instrument and started pulling his bits and bobs out of their neat holders. The sandwiches Mellis had packed for him were a dead loss. "What made us think… Sorry, what was that, sir?"

"Call me Tam. The folk along the river call me Father Tam. They think I'm a retired clergyman. Which in a way I suppose I am. Stop fussing, boy. Would I damage Oberon's toys?"

It wasn't clear whether he meant the cittern or Ben himself. Father Tam called into the house, "Llyea!"

A handsome young woman with a familiar scowl appeared from the shadows under a shock of green-blonde hair. A very cropped top revealed iridescent scales glittering green and gold where the shadows of her hip bones curved into the low-slung jeans.

"Well, look what the mer-cat dragged in."

"That's enough," Tamesis said pleasantly, but the deck rocked briefly under foot.

Llyea looked penitent, but not very. She nodded.

"My lord."

"See all this is tidied up, eh, before it rains again? Get Luther, he won't mind. Come in and be welcome, Ben Harper."

Within, the air was cool and pleasant, the air tasting of tidewater and lemon, salt and sweet with a kind of formless energy humming pleasantly across his skin. Both deeper and wider than he expected from outside, panelled in dark woods and crowded bookshelves, the sitting room merged at one end into a kitchen and dining area. At the other end, sleek modern furniture, fat cushions, and a fireplace, which currently contained a flat-screen TV at the perfect height for watchers in a kind of pit—Ben thought he heard a splash—set into the Moroccan tiled floor.

"Cricket?" Ben asked, his eye drawn by the screen.

The old man smiled.

"They can watch it for days, don't ask me why."

Well, being immortal, more or less, they had plenty of time for it.

Beyond this, another wall of glass showed a foggy rural landscape that might have been unchanged for a thousand years, apart from the deck chairs and the smoking barbeque on the dock. In the sparsely lighted room, half a dozen boys and girls, all trim and adorable, lounged about reading or watching the match. They looked up when Ben came in, tracking his movement briefly, then lost interest. All but one unsmiling boy, a little older perhaps than the rest, whose glance Ben felt with the snap of a static charge. Before he could blink twice, the boy had vanished leaving nothing but a memory of—and this was very odd—was it a color, or a sunset—or a sound like the sea?

"My dears, this is the harper I promised you," Tam announced without preamble. Waving generally about the room, he added, "Young Benedict, this is everyone. Sit you down, catch your breath. I'll be back in a minute."

His Worship proceeded to disappear up a steep stair into the upper reaches of the houseboat. The deep voice boomed.

"Somebody get that man a cuppa, will you. What sort of hospitality is this?"

At least his clothes were drying quickly, Ben thought, feeling conspicuous and kind of middle-aged as well as damp among all this aggressive youth. And with that thought, rather than testing the upholstery next to a nymph with a knowing smile, he chose a tall barrel chair where a service bar divided the kitchen from the parlour, happy enough to be ignored. He'd had his fill of watery tarts for a while, and Mellis would never understand.

On his own, he let out a breath so heavy it came out like a sigh. Thoughts raced while his heart slowed to normal. He peeled off his jacket and hung it over the back of the chair beside him. He didn't want to think about the diary right now, so he went after the phone instead. When he flipped it open, water gushed onto the terracotta floor.

What the hell. He shrugged. Everything here must be waterproof, or water-loving. And sure enough, the tile had soaked it up before he could even think of getting a towel.

The mobile couldn't possibly be working. But then, it shouldn't work at all. What was the area code for Faerie, anyway? He hit Aubrey's speed dial.

"Yes?" said the king of Faerie at once, a bit testily. "Done already?"

Biting back a sharp reply, Ben said, "Just checking in, sir. We had a few delays, and we're a bit wetter than we expected to be."

"Ah, you're fine then."

Ben made his report, endured a certain amount of friendly condescension, and forbore to say anything about his last conversation with Mellis. When he rang off, he found a cup of tea waiting for him, hot and fragrant in a translucent beaker he thought might be alabaster. Well, he could marvel at that later. For now he wrapped grateful fingers around the heat and leaned over the neglected diary.

Amazingly, though the cover was warped—well, it always had been, really—the pages themselves were unharmed, if a bit damp at the outer edges. Ben grinned with relief.

"I love magic!" he said, and not for the first time.

He turned in the chair and opened out the little book on the counter in front of him. As expected, there were a few new pages, including some he really should have looked at before leaving the house: the names of the Mentos-loving nymphs under Ravenbeck bridge, for a start. Admittedly they were buried among some very naughty drawings and bawdy jokes, and a riddle he was definitely not going to share with Sparrow. Still, it might have helped.

The next page or two included some scholarly remarks about the nature of Atami music in the Icthylean mode, with the scale written out for his edification. When he pressed a finger to the staff, the scale played lightly for his hearing alone—a somewhat bubbly sound as if played under water.

"Does that make it a wav file?" he snorted.

Their adventure so far was narrated in the usual ridiculous

style and crazed handwriting, with snide comments in the footnotes. In the margins: a primitive sketch of what might be a woman in a fish-suit, and the many names of Ata'rathi: Tirgata, Derceto, Atargatis, even Aphrodite. Finally the words TRUST THE WATER floated up as if from underwater to the surface of the page, circled over and over in red, with spiking arrows and the words *Get it, harp-boy!?!?!?!* in scratchy letters.

"Yeah, yeah, fine, I get it," Ben muttered, and turned the page.

Beyond that, the book remained blank; it had given him what someone thought he needed for now, and that was plenty. There would be more if they chose to tell him, whoever they were. All he had to do was pay attention.

Well, good. Okay. Homework done. He sipped at his tea again, tasting oranges, honey, and cinnamon, energy and resolve. But apparently the book wasn't quite done with him.

When he started to close the cover, it gave a little hop and flipped open again. All the new pages fluttered back to where a folded slip of rough paper had been used as a bookmark. All right, he knew a hint when he tripped over it.

The page he'd marked was to do with Elizabethan England: exchange rates, some useful if vulgar slang, and the street map of 1590s London. Though laid out like a centerfold, the map was smaller than he remembered but, he was happy to see, it still worked. He had only to touch a spot to have the detail expand, showing the names of streets, shops, houses, and inns. And that could only mean one thing: time to set the mental way-back machine again for the period of history he knew best. There was something in Old London he needed, or someone he needed to talk to.

Ben scanned it all over, grinning with pleasure, and finally got to the folded paper that had marked the place.

"Oh yes!" he thought, glowing with a sudden flush of pride. As he smoothed it out, the thick texture of the paper and the brown-black ink of the neat italic script almost vibrated under his fingers. "How could I have forgotten about this?"

Signed by the gaudily dressed Sir Thomas Weston, an agent of the Revels Office, it was a pass into Richmond Palace to play before the Queen. He'd had to pass up that opportunity, of course. Too many other things going on.

Wonder if they missed me.

"Anything good?" said Raven, just over his shoulder.

Ben refused to jump, startled or not. He simply swung the chair around and said, "I give it an eight. It's got a great beat but you can't dance to it." When Raven snorted, he added, "The real question is, if they know so much, why do they need me?"

"Best not to ask."

"That's what I thought. You're looking happier."

"And so I am. Ravens are not great swimmers. The otter helped. Where's his Worship got to?"

"Upstairs. Above. Aloft, or…" Ben flipped a hand generally toward the stair. "What about the music? Did you get sucked into the music?'

"What music?"

On cue, the big otter trotted in from a shadowed passageway with his whiskered head poked through the shortened strap of the sushi bag. He shook it off and sat back on his haunches, tall as a mastiff. The black eyes blinked; he rose up sparkling into a handsome, broad-chested, athletic young man with liquid brown eyes and a neat chestnut beard and moustache. Gold chains draped across the curling hair on his chest.

"Good to see you again, milord."

Raven brightened with recognition.

"I thought so! Ben Harper, this is Lutra. A colleague, you might say. He guided me in."

"They call me Luther here." He reached to shake hands. "Well met, sir."

He might look like a surfer boy, but the accent marked him as a Londoner. A slight glow marked him, as it did Raven, as one of the Great Fae, though he was clearly not a courtier. He shrugged, rippling his tan.

"By the way, Mr Harper, there was some samwiches in your pack?"

"My wife thinks I never eat," Ben agreed, wondering when Luther was going to notice that apart from the gold chains he had no clothes on.

"Hope you don't mind. They was a mite soggy, and I was starvin', weren't I, after all that!"

"Then that's probably why they were there."

"You're gettin' it. He's gettin' it, ain't he, milord?" Luther said to Raven, and nodded in something like a bow.

The fae lord had the grace to accept the courtesy, even while waving it off.

"I'd say so. Where's your gov'nor?"

"On his way. Oh, and here's your bag. Swadeshi, innit? They're brill." He handed it over—dry now, well oiled, and good as new with none of its character harmed. "Fab workmanship. The stringed thing, the cittern? It's craik. But— well, there's this bit."

He held out the Ata'rathi fragment, dry but almost entirely blank, except for a faint smear of ancient lampblack and walnut juice.

"I was going to bin it, but Llyea said it might be important."

Raven accepted the papyrus. Ben took the bag with thanks by the padded straps, but suppressed a smile.

"I think it got us where it was supposed to."

"Right. I'll get dressed now. I wanted to get this back to you 'fore we forgot. Everything's dry and back where it belongs. Except the samwiches, like I said. Be seeing you!"

Both men almost broke into schoolboy giggles as Luther sauntered away, his golden flanks flexing at every step. Raven snorted, most genteelly.

"Custom of the country, and all that…"

ii

"Well met, lusty gentlemen!"

The lord Tamesis entered the room like the force of nature that he was, and it was down to business.

He waved Ben back to his seat, and Raven into the one next to it. He put a bottle of good beer in front of each of them and cleared away the mugs, then proceeded to potter around the kitchen, pulling bright red tomatoes, onions and mushrooms from a pantry. There would be a meal of some sort, Ben guessed, and was grateful. He couldn't remember when he'd eaten last. Mr Wong's seemed a very long time ago.

"Oberon speaks well of you, Ben Harper, but it was useful to see you in action."

"Is that why we couldn't just take the bus?"

Tamesis laughed again, a chuckle really but without apology, all the while milling a huge chef's knife, small in his massive hands, through a bunch of onions.

"Slider likes you by the way. Said you were very respectful. Bufo the toad, on the other hand…"

"Can't please everyone, sir," said Raven dryly.

"Hunh, true. You two acquitted yourselves well."

"So it was you that sent for us?" Ben asked. That at least was some kind of explanation.

"I?" Tam looked up from seeding a tomato. "No, it was Herself, though I would have done, if she had not."

"What is it you need of us, my lord?" said Raven. "You and the Most Gracious?"

Tomatoes were seeded, diced, and set aside. Bell peppers, aubergines, garlic, all prepped while the river god talked, wielding the knife like a baton to make his points.

His sister Fleet, Tamesis said, had fallen asleep some little while ago—understanding that for him a thousand years or two was only a little while. Her river was controlled in these controlling times, mostly hidden, partly used as a sewer to cleanse the city. Better than in centuries past, he noted generously, when it had been used as a toilet. Her spring on Hampstead Heath was clear, and protected by conservationists, and he was grateful for that. But her voice, the Fleet's own dear song, was silent. None could say why. And there was more.

The Atami of the rivers, he said—some of them, too many—were disappearing. To be sure, most of their springs and wells had long since fallen to the modern world: poisoned, neglected, buried and built over; others had dried up as the world changed. When that happened, Ata'rathi's children retired to the Mermaid Stair or simply faded to their long sleep.

"That is the natural course of the world," said Tam, his

hands and body now quite still, only his eyes alive as a storm. "What is not natural is slashed faces and hacked limbs."

"My lord?" Raven sat up, the long hands curling into a gesture of warding.

"My children are being tortured!"

Ben's jaw had dropped, then clicked shut. He swallowed.

"Sir," he almost whispered. "Who would do such a thing? Why?"

Anchored as it was in the mantle of the earth, the anger of the river held steady, not subject to distraction.

"Our people do not kill their own, not for sport nor at random. That is a human failing. But no one knows."

Someone was out there, someone human, as vicious as Jack the Ripper and as twisted, but far more terrible. He left his victims either shocked into a state which Tamesis could not penetrate, or with souls so damaged they melted away on the unfeeling air; the rare witness too dazed to speak of it or of anything again, their songs turned to one mindless quavering note.

Worse—if anything could be worse—this serial murder had happened, was happening, not only here and now, but down through the time stream, its source buried somewhere in the past. One day not long ago, he said—and by this he meant a fortnight or two, not centuries—one of his own present household had vanished without a word.

Father Tam's awareness, both flexible and deep, had sought for her and found only an insupportable conundrum. She had come to him after a German bomb destroyed her Kentish spring in 1939. But she had just as certainly left the world almost five hundred years ago, while the waters of that spring still bubbled up under a hazel branch as they had since time out of mind.

"Cynegyth, she was called."

Raven almost came out of his chair.

"No!" He fell back, his face behind his hands until he had collected himself. "That is, I knew her. Nice girl."

Tam put a massive hand to the raven-boy's shoulder.

"She was that."

"Maidens used to tie ribbons into her hazel tree, hoping she would whisper to them of good husbands. She always did," he breathed through a thin smile, remembering. "Even when they couldn't hear her."

In a heavy enameled pot, fat slices of button mushrooms hit butter and bright green olive oil with a tantalizing sizzle, then garlic, and the onions. Outside the windows fogged with steam, the sky had cleared to moon-filled twilight. Ben's mouth began to water, even though his appetite had fled. Raven only balanced his chin on his hands, his thoughts contained.

Considering, Ben asked, "How many, sir?"

"Does it matter?" the river god rumbled. "If it were only one or two, or five, or twenty, would you call that an acceptable loss? We are already too few."

"Of course not, sir. But if it is only one or two, we can hope he's only got started. We might even catch him in time to prevent wholesale slaughter. If it's fifty or a hundred…"

Tam made a disgusted noise, then granted it was a sensible question.

"We don't really know. We lose them one by one, seemingly at random and months apart. Mainly within my valley and along what men call my tributaries, especially around London."

Tight-jawed, he stripped fresh herbs from the planters in the window—oregano, thyme, basil—and added them to the pot.

"So he is walking through time?" said Raven with a birdlike tilt of his head.

Father Tam shrugged eloquently. "What else explains Cynegyth? Unless he is immortal himself, which I doubt. When I listen, I can feel the echoes of his song rising and falling with the tides of the worlds, but no more."

"There's a lot of time between these… events?"

"We can't be sure, but I think so, or I might have understood sooner. Perhaps something constrains him from being more thorough."

"A shred of conscience, maybe," Ben suggested, thinking out loud.

"Doubtful," said Raven.

"Maybe he has to recover afterwards. Or maybe he can't travel easily or often… I'm sorry, sir. I'm not a detective, just a musician with a knack for putting things in order."

"Isn't that what's needed?"

"They lend grace to the world," Raven murmured, almost to himself. "They harm none. This is human work, but how, if no human can see them? And what's the point? What reason?" He glanced to Ben who was staring at his interlaced hands, processing. To Tam, he said, "Y'know, we met one of your nymphs the other day."

"Oh?"

Raven told that story swiftly and without ornament. Knowing it too well, Ben winced and flung his glasses on the counter to rub tired eyes with the heels of his hands. The image of a wild-eyed man on a bus step crossed his mind; he wondered what it meant. A few more questions came and went, most without satisfactory answers, then there was no more to say.

Ben scrubbed his face with his hands, combed fingers through hair stiff with travel in unknown places, and wondered idly if he was going to get a shower at all.

"So," he said, "you want us to find a serial killer. One man, with unknown motive, who could be anywhere in time."

Tam said somberly,

"I want you to find this thief of grace, this murderer, and stop him. Or give me the means to stop him." Damp-eyed, he added almost as an afterthought, "And if he has not killed her too, find my sister of the Fleet. If you can, bring her home."

He gave a last taste to the stew, put the lid over it and clicked the flame down, then turned to the boys.

Ben passed the papyrus across the counter, the ancient fragment awkwardly out of place in the ultra-modern galley.

"I was given this the other day," said Ben. "His Grace says it's very old. Would it be of any use?"

The heads nearest the kitchen began to turn his way. Someone made an arch remark. Another voice hissed. The old man lifted a shaggy brow, but otherwise ignored them..

"How did you come by this?"

The boy told him, adding, "Still a mystery, sir."

"Hmm." Tam glanced at it, then pushed it back. "Hold on to it, please."

The ratatouille was simmering nicely. Father Tam's sober stare rested on them both for a moment, then he added a splash of red wine to the pot and adjusted the flame. He lifted the lid on the stockpot next to it and fluffed up a vast mountain of rice. Two handsome boys came in from the deck with a cauldron of clams and mussels that had been steaming down on the shore, and hauled it onto the serving counter.

With a few efficient moves, the master of the hall plated up two big bowls of food, and set them on the counter, then pulled garlic bread out of a warmer and moved Ben, Raven, and everything else to the dining nook off to the side. Gesturing for them to begin, he stepped out into the living room and, putting two fingers to his lips, blew a melodious whistle.

"Tea, everyone!"

They came in by twos and threes, handsome and insubstantial as the *corps de ballet* of *Les Sylphides* costumed for modern dress: bathing suits or jewelled G-strings; cut-offs and jeans; sundresses, t-shirts or no shirts at all; halter tops (favored by nereids with little wings); crew boys, nymphs, and staff and friends all appearing out of who knows where. A few like Llyea sported iridescent scales in interesting places.

Giggling in the chilly air, they queued up on the deck for portions of halibut and sausages from the grill, according to their tastes, then shuffled lightly through the kitchen for ratatouille, rice and shellfish, chattering and laughing. A bright brown girl was late with a big tray of sushi. Slamming it on the counter, she accepted good-natured teasing as her due, and collected a lingering kiss from Luther.

Their voices bubbled and clattered like a babbling brook, rising and falling with greetings and exclamations, jokes, teasing, and snatches of song. In the same twos and threes, they sorted themselves into the living room, up the risers of the stairs, or out onto the decks to watch the stars come out as the rain clouds drifted off shredded by the evening winds.

Ben ate because he knew he must, but he had set his plate aside before the last of them were finished serving themselves. Knowing the world he had entered, he knew better than to ask where they all came from or how it was done. Magic, of course, but it wasn't important. He had lost a day, maybe more, and the magic wouldn't give that back. He also knew how ill-prepared he was to look for clues, stop a killer, and incidentally find a lost nymph, even with the magical tools at his disposal. And he had always known how to deal with that.

While the party swirled around him, he set a process running in a corner of his orderly mind, creating a kind of filing system for sorting and assembling and separating known from unknown, identifying options, discarding irrelevancies. With enough input, eventually it would all make sense.

At the same time, he tuned in to the ebb and flow of energies in the room, the current of conversation, the strange music that lay beneath all of it. The free-floating air of tragedy was undeniable, but it was not in the Atami nature, apparently, to dwell long on heartache. Innocent, they would be constantly surprised by sorrow. And yet the woman on the Dart had been overwhelmed with grief.

That, too, he set aside to find a place in the pattern. Anyway, patterns were Raven's specialty.

"This is some establishment you have here, sir," Ben said, shifting to a more sustainable tone.

Raven's glance turned to him slowly, the slight lift of an eyebrow asking what the hell he was thinking.

Tamesis, replete and relaxed, leaned back in his chair, lacing his fingers together behind his head.

"I can't keep a great Court as I used to. The world below the river has become too crowded. Too filled with noise. It no longer hears me as it once did. But this vessel suits me and answers to my whim. It is as adaptable as your king's great house, I think."

"And all these people?

"They keep me company in this world of concrete and metal, and I…" His voice caught in his throat. The arms came down to the table. He cleared his throat. "I care for them. Show me that bit of papyrus now, if you will."

Ben had tucked it into the diary along with the pass from Sir Thomas Weston. Where it should have gone to begin with, dammit.

"As I said, the water got to it."

Tam nodded slightly, accepting the fault. For a long minute or two, he held it between his big hands and scowled at it, as if seeing the words that should have been there, imagining the whole document new and fresh from the scribe's hand. When he handed it back, the lost inks had in some part re-assembled, or been drawn together, though the newer Greek message was gone. With a blunt finger he pointed to the *morven* in the corner, looped in the loops of her hair.

"You know what this is, yes?" he said at last. "This symbol?"

Ben nodded.

"Yes, sir."

"Of course, the pet shop in the Edgware Road. Well then, I have no other spells or talismans to send with you, but where you see this at the water's edge, you can look for aid from the Atami or those who love us. Trace the design with your hand or even with your eyes, and say these words here, and a door to the Stair will open. I think you already know to take nothing with you that is made of iron."

He paused, collecting their agreement. Well, Ben nodded. Raven gave a shudder that shook him to the pin feathers, and got up from the table. During dinner he had pulled the silver jewel out of his ponytail to let his hair dry in the soft air. Now he paced a short course into the sitting room, stood for a moment while he combed long fingers through the curls, and gave them a shake. Some of the girls noticed and smiled, as did a couple of the boys, but his attention was elsewhere.

"Sir," he wondered as he returned. "The Atami Stair is accessible from all times, yes? If a man knew that, or if he guessed it... Could he step onto it in one time, then step out again into another?"

Before Tam could answer, someone turned up the sound on the cricket match again.

Voices chorused, "Turn it down!"

At once, the volume dropped to nothing. Eavesdropping needs silence. Someone whined, "For our mothers' pity, at least put up the captioning!"

Cushions were thrown.

"Perhaps," Tam allowed after some thought. "That would explain part of it. Though what mortal man could find his way there without help? "

Raven shook his head soberly, but it was Ben Harper who spoke.

"So, sir, about the scroll."

Now every voice in the room, upstairs, or out on the deck went silent, anticipation hovering like a cloud. Perfectly aware, Tam said, "The scroll?"

"What is it? We have nowhere else to start."

"For godssake, Father, tell the story!" shouted Luther, all bronze and boyish on the staircase. "You know you want to!"

Laughter broke the tension along with a hail of cushions flying towards Luther, who promptly dropped into his otter shape and scuttled up the stairs.

"Music first!" the old man roared, and rumbling with laughter of his own, the river god got up and led the whole party up to the playroom.

iii

Up here, there was nothing but the river and the willows, the shadows of elms. On an ordinary night so close to central London, only the toughest stars should have made it through the urban glow, especially in the eastern sky. But this was the Borderland, and the Milky Way spread out overhead like a vast river, outmatched for brilliance only by a butter-yellow moon.

With all that for a backdrop, and while the others settled all around, Ben took the cittern out to the open balcony that ringed the upper floor. He settled at the cushioned edge of a wicker chaise, testing the pegs and plinking each string. Oh, it needed no tuning, being Oberon's, but he fiddled with it anyway to settle his nerves and focus his mind. Besides, he expected any Atami music would fall outside his usual playlist, and he wanted to be sure of changing modes smoothly.

"Comfortable?" said Tam, taking up a position on the guardrail, bamboo neatly reinforced with steel and magic.

Ben made an agreeable noise.

"Neighbors?"

"None near enough to matter. The rest of them work for me. Or for the king."

The balcony stretched the full length of the upper storey, opening off a general-purpose playroom, with billiard table and table tennis. Furniture could be shoved into any configuration, cushions stacked or flung about, and everything could be battened down or shoved aside for dancing, depending on the master's whim.

On three sides, glass doors could be slid open, louvers folded away, to open the space to the air. One panel was hung with antique weapons: tritons armed with walrus tusk, coral-tipped spears, and a curved damascened sword that might have been cut from a giant scallop shell, fiercely honed.

In a corner behind a club chair, trunks, and cubby-holes held musical instruments old, new, and mythical. And a harp somewhat like his own Moytura, but shaped of ivory or the bones of whales, carved like a leaping dolphin.

"Oh, my lord." Gently he ran a hand along the satiny curve of the dolphin neck. "May I, sir?"

Smiling broadly Father Tam nodded.

"Her name is Baleen."

Raven rescued the abandoned cittern before it could hit the floor, then slipped a better chair behind his friend.

"I'll need a minute or two," said Ben Harper. He touched a string and then another, adjusted a couple of tuning pins, listened, tried another. "There's a tune I need to play for you. Something I heard the other day. I've worked it out on the cittern, with some help. Only it's meant for the harp. Maybe you can tell me what it means."

"I suppose so," said Tam, puzzled.

Ben flexed his hands, cracked his knuckles.

"I should warm up first. Maybe while I do that you could tell us about the scroll?"

At that, the rest started clamoring like a hyperactive

kindergarten, "Stor-y! Stor-y!"

"It's all right, sir," Raven assured the river god. "He can play while you talk. And listen too."

Ben sat back, bringing Baleen into his shoulder. The first notes struck tentatively—not silvery, like the king's harp Dariole, but a bronze as smooth as caramel. As he became more comfortable with the touch and tension under his hands, the music came.

*
**

"Very long ago and very far from here, as all know," Tamesis said, "Ata'rathi's temple was built partly in the sea, where the lady of the stars was attended by both mortal and immortal men and maidens. The charms at first were graved in the nacreous walls and floor of the sanctuary. Any of her followers who wished to could see and use them, if they dared. In the course of the changing world, Ata'rathi commanded the charms to be written out for the use of all those who honored her, and to preserve them when her temple fell at last."

Curious, Ben lifted his hands from the strings to say,

"Forgive me, sir, what charms?"

In that brief pause, every pair of eyes fair, dark, or rainbow hued and nictitating, stared at Ben in startled disbelief. Then Llyea laughed, and whispered something to her neighbor, who giggled, making the crystal shells chime that dangled from her ears.

Tam cleared his throat, meaningfully, and went on while the harper played.

"The goddess gave her children three charms. The first allows a mermaid to walk in mortal lands on her own feet and dance with her friends on the land."

"We love to dance!" The mermaid girls cheered and hugged each other and their riverine cousins. From the look on Raven's face, he was dazzled.

"I suppose," Ben asked, "that it's all walking on knives, and their voices…"

"No!" snapped the old man, and the waters beneath them heaved with a sudden swell. "Stupid story. Don't get me started."

"Father? Everything all right?" From the staircase, Luther's head popped into view with an expression of alarm. He touched his forelock in salute, then he grinned at Ben as the houseboat settled. "That film, you mean? We turn down the sound and make up new words. Except for the songs. The songs are excellent."

Tamesis, ever changeable, changed again and laughed as Ben picked up the cue and Luther retreated, rocking to the calypso beat.

Father Tam took up where he had left off.

"As I was saying, the effect lasts until the charm is sung again or when the goddess calls—usually at sunrise. The second charm grants a mermaid's tail to a mortal man or maid, though for no more than the space of an hour."

This time the same sea maids giggled, a thin line short of mockery. Ben felt no need to ask why.

"The third charm is the most perilous, because it allows an Atami to fall in love."

Ben stopped again, grinning.

"But aren't they always falling in love, mermaids?"

"Well," Llyea snapped, "not with you."

Father Tam's solemn look softened a little, and he went on.

"They are amused by humans, and by sex, as much as by dancing and song. But their hearts are shallow... Take no offense, ladies, you know it is true. And their blood is cold. They pull their lovers into the deep and forget to put them back."

Llyea clucked and looked away.

"We can't help it, you know."

"I know, dear. But this last charm will give you a heart such as mortals have: a heart that can break. And for a year and a day you may walk and live with your beloved on the land."

"As if!"

"On that last day," Tam continued, "when the year has ended, they must return to Ata'rathi's realm for all time."

"Father! Isn't there one more?"

"Some say that Ata'rathi provided a way of reversing the

third charm, should the beloved mortal die or prove faithless. Whether that is true, I cannot say."

"Father! Father!" the clamor went up with questions. "Was it dangerous? Was it safe? What happened to the scroll?"

Of course, he assured them. All the charms were safe for the Atami. But for the human child who reveled in the mermaids' dance, the result could be a terrible addiction. The hours between grew endless, their lives often fading into fantasy and neglect. And for the human lover abandoned at year's end, the price was often a lifetime of despair, anger, and reproach.

But the world changes, and the gods with it. The temple had long ago fallen into the sea, and finally the scroll had come to rest in the great library at Alexandria.

"And," Tam concluded, "we all know what happened to that."

"Fire," said Ben. "Earthquake. Religious riots. I just know it's gone."

"The library, yes, but not every book. Some, like this one, were in other hands at the time, to be copied, translated, studied. Some eventually resurfaced as the founding documents of the Renaissance, collected, broken up, dispersed, or lost again. That a scrap of any copy survived to bring you to me is remarkable."

"So we need to find it."

Tamesis shrugged.

"The fragment came to you for a reason. It may lead to the killer, or to a weapon, or simply to another clue. That is part of your quest, I think."

"And that," said Raven with quiet delight, "will be task number three. Balance in the universe."

"Now, about this tune of yours, Mr Harper."

Flushed with unaccustomed nerves, and grateful for the warm-up, Ben again set his fingers to the strings.

It began with a slow and plaintive verse, a slightly quicker repeat. A rippling chorus led to a sprightly variation, and the chorus again, then a key change still in the minor shading, the curious syncopation the Atami favored. Feeling encouragement on the air, Ben started again from the top, this time singing along in a wordless descant, ornamenting where it felt right, holding back when it didn't. On the third pass, he returned to a simpler, more basic line even than the first, returning to earth with a final spill of notes, and no more.

He lifted his hands to let the sound reverberate to stillness on its own, and waited, hardly daring to breathe. The only sound was the plop of a fish in the stream far below, and a sudden clatter of dishes coming up from the galley. Half afraid to look, Ben raised his eyes, and in that moment, he knew beyond all doubt that Tamesis was the river and always had been, by whatever magic of the world gave flowing water a living consciousness and will.

The old man nodded, finally, and cleared his throat.

"You astonish me, human child. That's the song you were given?"

"Over and over, sir, yes."

"And you have no idea what that tune belongs to?"

"How could I?"

"Ben," said Raven, raising his head. "I thought you knew. That's very old. Older than I am."

"It may be older than me," said Tamesis. "They say it came from the sky with Ata'rathi. It would seem that now she has given it to you. Well done."

Voices all around began to chime in, agreeing in their lilting voices, and when he looked, Ben realized why it had been so quiet. Half the household seemed to be leaning back on the rail, or sprawled across cushions on the deck, or in a window, most with dreamy looks on their pointed faerie features. In the light flickering on the dock below, there were upturned faces with their long hair shining on their shoulders, and their glittering tails tucked up around them. Yet again he had docked in the Borderlands where while he played and sang it seemed that time stood still—and perhaps it did.

And as on other occasions, he had started something both strange and wonderful, quite without meaning to. Flutes and flageolets came off the wall, and things with strings, and even Raven picked up a fiddle. Hopefully he would choose to restrain himself tonight. His fiddle tended to make people want to dance, and if he kept playing, they sometimes forgot to rest, or eat, or to stop dancing at all. More than a few pairs of dancing slippers had been worn to rags on his watch. And more than a few dancers.

But for the most part Atami music is made with voices, and on this full-moon night they took their cue from the most ancient of their songs. So it was the oldest aires that came out, as it was the oldest tales that made them smile. Raven on his borrowed fiddle took their songs and their stories and even their jokes, absorbed and returned them in his own way while, leaning back in the padded chaise, Ben fell asleep to the singing.

"By pavèd fountain, or by rushy brook, or in the beachèd margent of the sea," says a faint silvery voice. *It is a little, just a little, like the ring of a violin.*

Ben turns his glance from where the setting moon's face smiles on the rippling stream, but there is nothing to see. Only the voice.

"In the meads upon the heath my fleet-foot daughter lies and dreams alone, unknown. She sleeps, mortal child. Wake her. Bring her home."

"My lady?"

The great river flows on, breathing in the silence, mists dancing from its living surface as shapes of pale transparency. Cold candle flames, they whisper, flutter with light laughter. They sing. Ben follows. A little boat waits for him at the riverbank—a proper boat this time—and he gets in. Invisible boatmen guide him into the stream under the moonlight, past ruined castles, past darkened towns ringed with timber palisades, past men singing around a hunting camp among the youthful oaks and beeches; the herds of elephants.

The river grows narrower, more shallow, carpeted with water lilies. Suns rise and set; glaciers move, advance, retreat; marshes and meadows form and pass away to grassland and forest and circles of stone, ditched forts and marble temples; and still the river flows. Here even the fae have no names and little substance, alive only in the spirit of the land, the river and the sea. But some wave to him from the shore and he gives them their names: Kennet, Loden, Coln, and Leach; Windrush, Efra, Churn. The family of Thames, Tamesis, Tam, from the ash tree to the sea's grey, star-sparkled arms, to the breast of Ata'rathi.

A star falls, streaking across the dawn sky. The song ends, but now he knows it all.

Part Two
London, April 1595

All our Creeks seek one River, all our Rivers run to one Port, all our Ports join to one Town, all our Towns make but one City, and all our Cities and Suburbs to one vast unwieldy and disorderly Babel of buildings which the world calls London.
—Thomas Miles. 1604

17
Lambeth Marsh

The sun, a white hard-edged disk, rode towards noon behind a muggy haze that blurred sharp boundaries, seeped into shop fronts, warped books and characters. Beneath it, the Thames swept along bearing the world's goods to London in its wealth and its sins, in lighters and cogs and wherries; trading vessels with swearing crews; wherrymen giving quarrelsome way to noblemen's gilded galleys, their oars rising and falling in time with the Queen's whim, or Cecil's.

On the opposite shore, the marshes of Lambeth lay shrouded in a thick fog that reached up from Surrey and stopped at the Thames' south bank, leaving a grey pall from the Archbishop of Canterbury's palace in its manicured park all the way back to the Bridge. Having spent too much of the morning waiting on Sir Robert Cecil in the airless corridors for a five-minute interview and a small commission, Silence Carew turned his back on Westminster with relief and crossed the river.

Grumbling, the boatman turned aside from the Archbishop's landing wide and fair to let his single brooding passenger off at the ill-kept marsh stairs, barely visible in the murk, muttering some babble about ghosts and witches and strange lights.

"God spare ye, master!" the man muttered, and shot away without lingering for a return passenger—not that there would be one.

In short order Carew found the punt he had pushed into the reeds, and traded his best suit of clothes for the stained, almost rotting garments he kept bundled under the seat. Taking up the classic punter's stance on the flat till, he lifted the pole into position as easily as he had done in his Cambridge days. These outings, for all their violence, had put the strength back into chest and arms made slack with long hours hunched over a desk. A deep breath, and he traded the stinks of London for the honest rot of the marsh, the purity of his true goal. Another, and he felt the tightness ease from around his throat.

He set the punt in motion, choosing his path through the many channels of dark water, penetrating deep into Lambeth Marsh through the grey-green mist into the waiting quiet. The stream opened to him as it always did, drawing him in. A fool might call it a legacy of his mother, this ease upon the water, but he rejected the notion.

The tide was in, the river especially high. Though a low wall for the most part held back the water at the bankside, still it seeped in and cleansed the stagnant channels, altered the shifting islands; every now and then a path opened to a black pool over-hung with straggling willow and stuck about with alder. Reeds clattering, insects humming, the stench of vegetation in perpetual decay clogged his nose, but it hardly mattered. Nearby, a crane on one long leg bent its sinuous neck and snapped up a frog. Carew spoke three words clearly aloud.

"*Rabbatu atiratu yammi*," he said, repeating the words that began each charm. An invocation to the sea goddess, so the old scholars said. Utter blasphemy, of course, but what is sin to a man with no soul, if it will open the way to virtue?

"I say again, *Rabbatu atiratu yammi!*"

Into the stillness, the sudden sound of drumming wafted over the sedge, and the piping of some sort of flute, twisting the key in the way he had realized must be the Icthylean mode named in the scroll. They were out there, in their filthy revels. When a course opened in that direction, he took it, poling calmly, masking his growing excitement as he had learned to do as a child.

A minute or more passed as he navigated the winding

stream of the marsh, turning back on itself while the mist clung to the muddy earth. A minute more, another recitation of the invocation, and with catlike delicacy the swirling feet of the fog began to lift showing two yards, three yards of shapes and shadows ahead, meadow grasses below.

It was time to move inland, he thought, just as the square prow slammed into the shore, riding up over the mossy verge, and flung him ashore on his face. As well here as anywhere.

As he struggled up from the muck, a salamander slithered over his hand, or a spider, but he no longer cared.

Collecting himself, he secured the boat to a bush, and thrust the pole firmly into the muddy bottom to mark the place for afterwards. At his first step away, he stumbled over a low grey stone, and continued on. A moment later he stopped, frowning.

"How now?"

When he glanced back, the mist obscured whatever he had almost seen in the corner of his antiquary's eye. The music called him, his voices urged him onward. Death was waiting! Curiosity won him over.

Two easy strides brought him back to the stone. Flat-faced like a Roman milestone, it had once been shaped and finished, now it was racked and worn. He had to kneel again in the moss to see, and yes... There had been carving once, though the long years and the changing land had almost destroyed it. That figure again!

His heart jumped. His breath, already quick, nearly left him. Faded and blurred with time, still the faint trace remained of the familiar loops and curls, the top of the morven figure now green with lichen, the rest sunk into the earth.

"Oh, God!" The words rasped out of him. "I cannot stay! I cannot!"

Shaking with excitement, he fetched a rag from the clutter in the boat and tied it around the stone like a flag.

"I will return, do you understand? Upon my oath, I will return when I know what it means."

Then he hurried away, throwing anxious looks back over his shoulder until the carved stone disappeared, swallowed up in the mist. He must focus his whole mind on the task at hand or the meaning wouldn't matter.

Recalled to his task, Silence Carew spoke the words again. With each repetition they became heavier, more fraught with consequence. A kind of path or animal track appeared at his feet. The music had faded, but the path would prove true as it had before. Now sweating, now shivering as if with fever, moving quickly through the moss, he hardly felt the brackish water sucking at his shoes. Every few feet he paused to peer above the broom and bracken, aware of a heat rising in him, a terrible joy.

In the hazy distance a flickering blue light flared about the sedge: the *fata morgana*, the lamp of the faeries pale against the thinning fog marked his goal. The city men, these practical men, Cecil and his ilk, dismissed such things as folk tales and fancy, but he knew. He knew it was a flame erupting from the depths of hell.

Carew spat away the spittle foaming at his lip and tried to look past the dancing light, but his mortal eyes ached with the effort. Something must be there, he could feel it.

"Show yourselves, damn you!"

His quest was here. He had only to make it visible. Another few yards should do it.

In his haste, he missed the ledge of lichenous rock jutting out of the waters. It thrust up under his foot and threw him to his knees, the oozy damp seeping through the linen shirt, the plain kersey hose already mud-colored. With an oath, he reached into his jerkin and drew out a scrap of wrinkled paper, already disintegrating in the muggy air.

He got to his feet and cleared his throat again, and this time sang the words in what he hoped would do for their music.

"*Rabbatu! Atiratu! Yammi!*"

A clearing in the mist appeared before him; that was encouraging. So he went on, chanting the words of his own devising.

> *Neither sun nor moon,*
> *Neither morn nor noon*
> *Nor watered dawn, nor dimpsy dusk*
> *Nor proper time of day*

Come when I call!
Atami Atiratu!

Finally! The air opened to him. The voices came to him clear and bright. Silence could hear their singing, their chattering, mincing voices as vain and light-minded as babes.

His gaunt face froze as he lowered himself to the spongy ground, until he came to rest on his belly in the muck behind an alder. Before him, a circle of fog had lifted over a low outcropping of stone at the edge of a grey-green pool. Then parting the bush, he saw them at last.

Naiads, and others too, frolicked like lascivious harlots in a ring of young bay trees as slender as they. Some danced on the green moss, some played in the stream, while a few leering, goat-footed boys, vulgar satyrs, beat a drum or blew the syrinx, beloved of the demon Pan.

He wanted to vomit, but dared not, not yet. Swallowing bile, he stretched his thin lips into the simulacrum of a smile and stood up. He took a step forward. Before he could take another, a silver voice rang out.

"You called, and I am here!"

At once, the music stopped. The little moth-winged nymphs left off their play and began to run light-footed over the moss, though not to him. He turned his gaze to follow theirs, and snatched one quick intake of breath.

Poised at the edge of a dark pool fringed with wild roses sat a mermaid of the sea, as perfectly made as the rest but proportioned for the wide ocean, with strength in the graceful shoulders and arms. He could hardly bear to watch her, a creature of his nightmares. The smirking face, the goggle eyes too round and wide, the luxuriant breasts above a dainty waist that swelled to a woman's hips. There the creamy skin grew armour, fine scales in every shade of green and bronze, a grotesque fish's tail glistening like sunlight over deep water. Preening in a silver mirror, she teased curls into her long sea-green hair, decked herself in strands of pearl and coral. The very model and picture, Carew thought, of vanity.

Disgusted, aroused, heart racing, he knew his luck had changed, his goal stood before him. For surely a proper mermaid could tell him what he needed to know about the Mermaid Stair. To overpower her would take more than stealth, but after all, what was she but a woman?

While he considered, a gaggle of what might be golden-haired children exploded out the water's edge like salmon leaping up a weir, to land shrieking and giggling on the moss with long fluttering tails silver, green, and gold, swirling the water behind them. Children! Say demons, rather. Mermaids like this great one made small.

"Meropë! Meropë is here!" the water babies shrilled like piping chicks new-hatched. Their little pink and gold faces beamed, their little pink and gold arms waved, the flukes of the gossamer tails splashed droplets of foul marsh water in his face even where he stood.

Carew spat out his disgust as his eyes hardened. Their childish shape would not sway him.

"Meropë!" The gauze-draped nymphs gathered round with curtsies and kisses. "Dance with us!"

Dance? He would make her dance, indeed.

"Nay, nay, my dears!" Meropë laughed. "First I must have my feet about me, and so must you all. Sing first, then dance. But oh!" She frowned, and glanced pointedly at the long tail draped behind her. "Alas, what shall I do?"

Even the wrinkling of her nose was very pretty, for a monster. The satyr musicians all threw down their instruments and ran to her aid. The tail must have been three yards in length, tapering from her broad hips to the size of a man's wrist, topped with flukes that floated like silk on the water. It took four of the goat-boys to bring up the whole length and pile it beside her with a stream of earthy jokes that made her laugh. At the same time, the nymphs went to help the smaller ones who also, it appeared, required to be completely on dry land before they could begin.

When all were well-arrayed, Meropë began to croon in a voice like the moan of the tide.

Rabbatu atiratu yammi!

The others echoed this, then together they sang:

From Ascalon to far Urhaal,
my feet to walk, my voice to talk,
mine eyes to blink, my mortal soul
to drink the air until my mothers call!

Oh, God! It was the first of the charms in the scroll, and he a mortal man present to witness it! The scholar warred with the zealot, the cool brain with the obsession.

It didn't matter. What mattered was his great task. Later, when he was clothed in the soul he had earned, he could turn his mind to matters of intellect, of philosophy, but not now. The scroll had given him tools for this purpose, and he would use them.

The air within the green glade glittered as they sang, and when they were done each shining tail had become two shapely legs, though touched still in scales from the navel to their feet. Meropë leapt up lightly and smoothed web-fingered hands along her body. Voluptuous as a queen of Egypt, the creature laughed and flung up her arms.

"Music, now, my cousins!" she cried joyously. "Say who will dance with me!"

That was his cue.

"I will," said Silence Carew with false cheer, stepping into the glade as an actor onto the stage.

As every time before, these mindless creatures swarmed about to greet him with kisses, drew off his clothes so the damp breeze cooled his naked skin even while the fever in him rose and hardened along with his *membrum virile.* Then Meropë, finding a partner so tall and to her eyes so comely, claimed him for her own. She was, however, for all her stature no more mindful than her daintier cousins.

"Now tell me, sweeting," Silence said while they lay at last together under a bay tree apart from the others. "Know you one of our Atami cousins called Oriana?"

She shook her head, making all the little shells and jewels tied into her hair swing and chime.

"Nay, I do not."

They never did; that name was as false as the bitch who wore it. Meropë kissed him again expertly, folding him into her arms, but that game was done.

"What is the Mermaid Stair?"

Thwarted of her desire, the mermaid raised up on one elbow to stare at him owlishly.

"It is our home, of course, though only mortals call it so. Our half-kin say Atami Stair when they do speak of it, but we say this."

Some whistles, chirps, and nonsense set the air to shimmering.

His mouth went dry, breath caught in his chest. In his eagerness his hands clenched her wrists. When she looked alarmed, he drew them together and kissed her hands, willing himself to calm reason.

"Of course, poppet. Then…"

"Ah!" She giggled—she had been giggling all day—and exclaimed, "A game! Oh, excellent! Ask another!"

If it had not already taken so long to get to this point, he would have said it was too easy. He must have been asking the wrong question all along.

"Not a game, darling girl. And where is the Atami Stair?"

A rippling shrug shifted her breasts against him, but he would not be distracted.

"That is no question. It is where it is, at the Stair. The water falls from every height, rivers all rush down to the sea, the water is sweet and lilies grow. We play or rest or sleep, and none can harm us there. It is always summer."

"And how do I get there?"

Meropë touched the amulet handing round his neck.

"You wear the suns and lions."

"And what does that mean?"

"You are very stupid." She shook her head. "This is a terrible game. Let me ask one."

Hours ago, he had scratched a shallow hole in the soft earth here and hidden the iron knife. Slowly he reached for it, fingers closing loosely around the blackthorn hilt. The time would come soon enough, when he would have his answer no matter what tool he used to get it. And she would die no matter what she told him.

"Very well, ask."

Twining an errant curl around a finger, she said, "My question is, why do you not know how to find the Stair?"

Silence tried to look sad.

"My mother told me once, but she went away and I cannot find her. I have forgot the way." He met her childish frown as if he were as simple as she. "I am lost."

So she told him. Lisping and laughing, distracted by a passing zephyr, she described the morven badge, the marker on the stone, and how to use it.

"Gramercy," he said, eyes bright.

In a single fluid movement, he rose up to his knees and pushed her down, but when she reach playfully for him, he raised his arm and thrust the knife deep into her chest. She gasped, then as he pulled it out she screamed, and he struck again before the others could react. But Carew feared nothing any longer. Even his accusing angels clapped their wings in praise. He would buy his soul with her death, her and all her filthy kind.

Meropë wept with the breath bubbling through blood from her lips that had given him shameful pleasure. Holding that thought, tied up with self-reproach, Carew made no sound except for the harsh, hot breathing from the bellows of his nose and mouth. Deaf to her shrill whimper, he dragged the blade down the pale white belly till it stalled against the armour of scales at hip and thigh. The iron, anathema to all her kind, burned at the edges of each wound, melting the flesh, sending up a silvery kind of smoke. Unsatisfied, he withdrew the blade and thrust it in again, this time across the vulgar bosom, marking her with the cross of his vengeance. As her eyes rolled up he drew the razor edge across her throat. This time, the blood gushed black as tarnished silver as the life spilled away.

A strange awful keening vibrated the air, filling his ears, his mind, the paths of his nerves with the lightning of her pain. A silvery wisp of spirit rose from the corpse like steam, paused a moment to look at him sadly, then a breath of air took her and she was gone.

Everywhere, the air grew shrill with noise as every Atami,

every fae creature fled the place in horror. Silence cried out too, and clapped his hands over his ears. Then Meropë was still, the eyes blank and staring. Alone in the empty glade, he crouched over her, panting with the expense of passion, revolted even while he revelled in the sight, taking strength from the death.

At last, unsteady but not overborne, he got to his feet. Anxious as he was to be away, Carew had one last gesture of his hatred to impose. He punched the iron knife to the sky, and shouted his own invocation, culled from old books and perverted to his needs.

> *Feet and fins*
> *Blood that burns*
> *Voice be still*
> *By God's will*
> *From earthly strands be gone!*
> *In the name of Jesus Christ.*
> *Amen!*

While he watched, jaw set in a grim rictus, the light rippled around the ruined body, the bloodied legs drew together, the grotesque returned to its true form even as it began to dissolve. He didn't bother to wait. On fire with need, he turned and ran for the place he had tied up his boat, for the *morven* stone, the Stair, his hope of heaven and his fear of hell.

The path opened to him, the way clear. He fairly flew, until someone called his name.

"Simon!"

At once, the air around him changed, charged with light and glittering color, sunshine on ice, the smell of snow. A solid force slammed into him made of perfect cold. It kicked his feet from the path, sent him tumbling, flying in truth until he fetched up choking and coughing in the reeds of the creek bed. Mud and muck, the roots of marsh grass, the bones of a dead weasel broke his fall, but he was not in Lambeth marsh. Not any more.

"Simon!" Issa shouted over the sound of rushing waters. Anger and sorrow, fire and ice filled the sound of his name. "Oh, Simon, what have you done!"

18
Cheapside: At the Mermaid

Souls of Poets dead and gone,
What Elysium have ye known,
Happy field or mossy cavern,
Choicer than the Mermaid Tavern?
—John Keats

i

Leaded windows glowing with lamplight through the rain, the tavern in Friday Street was, if anything, bigger on the inside than what showed from the street, but even that was deceptive. The Mermaid, as everyone knew, filled the lane along Cheapside all the way to Bread Street: ordinary, inn, and hostelry all sharing a red-brick courtyard.

Big as it was, it had still taken most of the morning to find, given they didn't really know where they were going. For some reason, the old city had a mind of its own where Ben's gift was concerned, periodically leading him a merry chase or cutting out altogether. When the rain that had dogged them all morning finally crashed over their heads, they dived for the first available shelter suitable for men and horses both. Did "trust the water" apply to rain, too?

They reined in the horses, staring at the sign swinging over the door: a buxom two-tailed siren, rather better rendered than the usual mermaid, with curling hair and a lubricious smile.

More to the point, a round stone sunk into the earth near the gate, almost lost in a clutch of drowning dandelions, bore the mermaid badge worn with the years but still clear. Something or someone here would be able to give them aid and information, though the river was streets away.

Timber-frame, plaster, and brick, the Mermaid Tavern rose three stories to its roof of slate and thatch. It rented rooms by the night or month, and in some cases by the hour, though all in all it was an honest enough establishment. Open galleries ran around the upper floors. Not so long ago, before anyone thought to build a playhouse for its own sake, the Mermaid had hosted interludes and ballad singers, French farce and good English moral plays in that courtyard. Still did, sometimes, when a travelling company passed through, though there would be issues with the Master of the Revels if the texts were not approved.

Ben Harper pounded his saddle bow with excitement and practically danced where he sat, until he checked the year with Raven. The boy took a deep breath, tasting the soggy air like a wine snob, and quietly pronounced it to be 1595. Probably mid April. On a...yes, a Saturday. In Lent.

Ben's good cheer collapsed. The Mermaid Tavern, famed in song and story, wouldn't host the most brilliant minds of the English theatre for, oh, another decade or so, if in fact it ever had. Beaumont, Fletcher, and several of the others were still in the nursery in '95. Ben Jonson had yet to stage a play, though doubtless he was honing his skills doing piecework: mending old ones and acting in them, too. As a hired man he'd be learning twenty roles in a season, brawling in pubs, and otherwise aggravating the authorities. Kit Marlowe was dead these what, two, three years?

Of that legendary circle, only Will Shakespeare was even likely to be here, and honestly, how likely was that? Legends are ten a penny, and whatever the truth, it would probably not be proved today.

The chestnut gelding was growing restive under him, dancing a little on the bricks, and twitching its ears. Ben Harper stared, gobsmacked, breathing steam and ignoring the rain, trying not to look like a tourist.

"Heaven and earth, Francis!" Raven laughed, riding at Ben's knee. "Wake you, sweet ass."

He snatched off his sodden cap to smack the American's shoulder with it. Water sprang away in all directions, unnoticed among the raindrops.

The familiar persona of Sir Francis Browne took over, soaking wet and cranky under the gorgeous green livery cloak. Well, it had been gorgeous when they set out. At least Lord Aubrey's oak leaves, so finely pricked out in gold on the shoulder, would take no harm.

He swore back roundly, and for good measure added,

"Thou knave thou! By God, I'll…"

He raised a gloved fist for show, but Sir Rafael Fitzroy raised only a flaring brow and failed to look impressed.

"If you'd be pleased to come in out of the rain, O captain my captain, you may find a fire and good company withal. And if you've the wit God gave an oyster, you'll see there's a boy here to take poor Flaminius from you. Stand in the rain as long you will, but have pity on the beast."

Thunder rolled, and the sky opened up for real. By the look of glee splashed across his face, you'd have thought the weather was his idea. And maybe it was.

While Ben glared, the boy dashed lightly across the puddles for the tavern door. At the step he turned to shout over the din of raindrops pounding on stone.

"Mind you, his lordship sets great store by that cittern!"

Bugger. The cittern was in the sushi bag, which at present appeared to be a neatly packed saddle bag with a dog-faced rosewood neck and finger board sticking out the top into the rain. How many soakings, he wondered, was Oberon's magic good for?

By the time he had dealt with the ostler's boy, and flipped him an extra penny for the good oats, Raven had long since disappeared into the dim, fire-warmed ordinary. Standing in the scant protection of the stable door and staring out through the curtain of rain, Ben thought about waiting for it to stop. Well, that was not bloody likely, and he knew it. He pulled his collar up and dragged his sodden cap down around his ears, as if it would do any good, and started across the courtyard, trying to avoid the worst puddles. With one hand he held the sushi bag tight around the back, tucked under the edge of the good green livery cloak.

Was it wetter than at home, this rain? It seemed always either raining or snowing in London. Or someone was trying to kill him. Otherwise, he thought as he put squelchy boots across the threshold, he could enjoy himself.

ii

Say, what abridgement have you for this evening?
What masque? What music? How shall we beguile
The lazy time, if not with some delight?

—*A Midsummer Night's Dream*, Act V Sc. 1

Out of a wall of water, Sir Francis Browne stepped into a wall of heat and friendly laughter loud and coarse, and the rich smells of beef and gravy, and old floorboards richly fragrant with years of ale and wine. Lighted tapers and fires of two hearths, one at either end of the room, pushed back the dreary shadows. A familiar figure was telling a story—a very long, very shaggy story—to the whistles and calls of a dozen or so men around a trestle by the fire.

Ben, taking the part of the elder, more responsible of his lordship's gentlemen, went first to the hostess to negotiate service. Smiling and plump, the ample bosom powdered but not too much on display, she turned out to be a good deal tougher than she looked. Dimpled chin or no, it was quickly made clear that the only thing not firmly under her control were the golden curls escaping her cap in all directions to frame her apple-cheeked face in a hazy glow.

He put down five silver shillings when she asked for ten against the eventual reckoning. The bill would be totted up before they left, and any owing returned, barring damages, and there was no chance of her missing so much as an egg.

"That's your friend, then." She beamed in Rafe's direction as the boy warmed to his theme.

Whatever it was involved multiple characters and a high-pitched woman's voice.

"Thou must chafe it a little at the fire!"

"Marry," she chortled, "he doth it as like one of those harlotry players as ever I did see!"

"Harlotry's his second name, that boy," Ben said.

At least when traveling with a lord of the fae he was never short of funds. Who knew where the money came from, but Raven swore it was legal tender and wouldn't turn to dead leaves after they left. Fair enough. When he'd haggled sufficiently and let the woman put a pint of something in front of him that he hoped was beer, he leaned back against the bar, watching his friend work the room.

"So he saith, Woman, didst thou not feel the hand under thy skirt? And she said, in a wicked small voice, Ow yes, Oi felt it, but Oi did never think 'e were after me purse!"

"Well done! Well spoke!" cried more than one of a dozen or so men all pounding the table or stomping boots on the wooden floor.

All in their twenties or thirties. Not at work, but too decently dressed for casual layabouts who'd missed a morning's hire. Hiding from their wives? Players, then, from the Theatre and the Curtain, both closed for the penitential season, and the rain. Odd though, for Curtain Lane was a good walk north of here, with who knows how many ale sellers, taverns, and inns more convenient.

"'Tis true enough," shouted another. "I know, for it was my hand!"

Rafe snapped, "I thought it looked familiar. Now, I need a drink. Hostess!"

He's not Puck, he's Peter Pan, Ben thought, watching the boy trading quips from the table top like a pirate pacing his quarterdeck. As if he'd heard the thought, Rafe threw a grin over his shoulder. All Ben could do was grin back. It might not be a subtle entrance, but it was memorable.

"Good hostess!" the boy called. "A round again!"

The woman, plump and sweet-faced, looked up from the bar

with an expression that said she had survived any number of poets, players, and fractious boys and was so not impressed. The dainty rose-pink mouth opened with a roar.

"A round is it, Rafe Silver? Such an idle knave. A wicked boy! Th'art so round with me, I could use thee as a football!"

Silver? That was new. Just keep laughing, Ben.

Two lithe steps and the kid had bounded off the table, flipped in the air and landed with a flourish at her side. Stuck the landing. The hostess shrieked like a kittiwake as his arms went around her, with him counting down till she stopped, three, two, one, and as soon as she paused to breathe, he kissed her full and heartily to a further round of whistles and applause.

After that, he stood with his arm draped over her shoulder while she simpered like a schoolgirl, rosy from her hairline to the lush mounds of her bosom where his long fingers dandled in idle caress.

"And is this sober, agèd fellow your father then, Nan?" he said, blinking owlishly at Ben. "How now, good master tapster! Ha! Do ye hear it? Master-tapster? A rhyme in time. View halloo!" Throwing a look over his shoulder: "You could use that, Will. I could be in your next play!"

A broad-shouldered fellow by him snorted,

"Have a care, Silver, or you will be!"

Raven waved him off with a petulant hand.

"Go chafe your wax, Jonson."

"Oh Jesu!" the hostess shrieked and smacked his dandling fingers. "Go to, ye rogue. I've no time to dally with the likes of thee! I'm an honest woman, I am!" She punched his shoulder, too, and dove for the kitchen.

Appreciatively, they watched her go, then Raven leaned over the bar and snagged Ben's jack of ale. He finished it off and called for two more, and slapped hard cash ostentatiously on the bar.

Close enough for Ben to see him properly, the sharp features framed in black curls were Raven's own, yes, yet oddly different. From somewhere, a jaunty scar had puckered close to one sparkling eye, and he'd pointed a beard onto his chin, giving him a more dangerous, far less boyish look than usual. In these rough times, doubtless a good thing.

"And do you know yet, Francis, why we are here? More than to shelter from the rain, methinks."

"Nothing so far. It hardly seems the time to ask, with you clowning."

He waited. Raven waited, grinning like an idiot, clearly determined to make him ask.

"All right, shatter me. Who is…"

"Who dost thou think, lack-wit, if not thy hero, the bard of bards, swan of swans, or swan of Avon anyway?" Raven said, waiting for the impact. But Ben had already slammed into that wall and recovered, thank you very much.

"Nay, brother, I mean who art thou?" He dropped his voice even further. "Who the hell is Rafe Silver?"

"Ha! Know you not?" Raven hissed back in his best stage whisper. "Before Lord Aubrey took me up, I was their fencing master! Now these idle fellows must traipse all down here to Blackfriars to be *stocattoed, affondoed, botta-in-tempoed* by that Italian, that Bonetti, or Spaghetti, or Salmonelli, I care not."

Every immortal boy needs a hobby. Idly, Ben wondered who else waited on Aubrey in this time, then. Where he lived, what the Queen knew. Not that it mattered. Raven was on a roll.

"Now it is thy turn, Sweet William."

Rafe Silver sauntered back to Will when the drinks had been delivered. Half sitting, hip cocked, on the edge of the table in his shirtsleeves to face a man who turned his easy smile to meet Rafe's glittering blue eye. "I have paid my forfeit, long owed. Now you must tell a tale that I shall chose. Nay you must compose one, and we shall enact it."

Mysterious as a gypsy with a gold ring in his ear and a knowing smile above the somewhat scruffy beard and moustache, the man leaned forward into the light. Darkly auburn hair just beginning to show a silver thread was making up for the retreating hairline by waving pleasantly to his collar.

A bit longer than was modish, but common enough among poets.

"Comical, classical, or lyrical?" he asked, full of restrained laughter.

Rafe appeared to be thinking.

"All at once?"

The man Will tipped back his tankard, draining it, then slapped it to the table.

"And the matter?"

"I shall tell you. A band of rude mechanicals have gathered to perform a play."

Will turned a gimlet eye on his mad friend, then opened a wood-framed book and started making notes not on paper but with a stylus on a hard-waxed surface.

"Comical, aye."

"In the forest beside Athens, wherein two, nay, three pairs of glovers also lurk, for reasons you may settle as you will."

"Three pair of glovers, I see."

"Lovers, young William. I said lovers!"

"Certes you did, and so classical enough. Though this begins to sound familiar. And lyrical?"

Rafe Silver looked to his left, and to his right, as if he might be overheard. He bent double and peered between his legs, and around to squint under the table, and into Will's ale pot, and under the fruit bowl. The stone wainscoting on the sturdy walls gave back no sound as they all fell silent, watching him skulk about the room peering into pockets, poking up the fire.

"Ah ha, a spy! Aroint thee, Salamander!"

A single red flame leapt from the fire and scuttled like a lizard across the rush-strewn floor, leaving a sizzling line of sparks before slapping with a hiss against the damp stone wall. Most of them, Ben noticed, heard no noise at all but the rain crashing in the courtyard, and the dripping gutters, and the creak of the Mermaid sign on iron hinges.

At last, Rafe fell into a crouch in front of Will, sitting by the fire with amusement twitching the corners of the expressive mouth. Then he rose to his knees so they were nearly eye to eye.

"Well?" said the poet. "And for the third part?"

"Faeries!" A great groan passed among the company, shuddering into the rafters. "And I, Robin Goodfellow shall seem to be! For I do wander here and there, and I do serve the fairy king."

"Queen!" The others roared their correction. "Fairy queen!"

Will snapped his tablet shut and tossed it down with clatter and a sour face, though his eyes were jolly.

"Marry, my madcap, mumpsimus, maiden, misery-guts, if you came to hear a play now and then, you would know already. We gave it last year for my old lady Southampton when she wed the Vice-Chancellor. And a dozen or fourteen times since then."

Startled by that piece of news, Ben coughed on his drink. Of all the questions he would never be able to ask, the first playing of *A Midsummer Night's Dream* was not among the highest on his list, but here it was anyway being handed to him.

Will glanced briefly to where the new man had stopped in his tracks.

"I shall pay thee out, recreant, in some other coin some other time. Meantime, go and sin no more, and let us meet thy friend."

"Frank!" the boy called.

"Who's that?" It was a perfectly good by-name for Francis; he'd just never used it. "Sir Francis, and it please you, boy."

Ben sauntered to join them, but Raven was running this gig.

"Gentlemen, this is my ancient grandsire. Have pity on him, he's a bit deaf." He put a hand to Ben's shoulder and shouted solicitously in his ear. "Shall I beg an ale posset for you, sir? Nice soft egg beaten in, sir? For your aging bones? Sir?"

Even in the low light, the mischief sparkled out of the midnight eyes. When the laughs came, he broke off and spun away, accepting their applause.

Sir Francis greeted the company all around as he hung his sodden cloak on a peg, at last, and thrust the saddle bag and cittern under a bench. Then he threw a leg over it and slipped Rafe's tankard out from under his hand.

"Gramercy, infant!" he said heartily and knocked it back. It was only fair, and the wine, warmed with ginger and a red-hot poker, was strong.

When Raven started to swear with color and invention, Ben said mildly,

"Peace, boy. Get another to cool thy temper, and be quiet."

So Ben got a few laughs of his own, which made up a little for knowing he could ask no questions, not yet.

iii

They were young men, for the most part, though not all quite as young as he had thought. The first to take his hand was a dark-haired youth with that sensitive poetic air. When he looked up, Ben's heart almost stopped.

"Jack Donne is my name," the youth said so softly that Francis Browne, his ears still ringing, almost asked him to say it again. John Donne, reluctant law student, intense and complex, and what Mellis would have called terminally romantic, looked exactly like the portrait at the National Gallery, right down to the full lips and the flat lace collar.

Then came Richard Carew, an antiquary, and Richard Martin, a lawyer, and one or two others whose names Ben was relieved not to recognize. Holding onto the illusion of being a worldly fellow who met extraordinary men every day had become a serious challenge. Remembering these men were all meant to be strangers to him only made it harder.

Then the curly hair and sandy beard, big hands and pugnacious air gave his name as Jonson, and felt it was enough. Ben Jonson, it had to be, in his early twenties. The harper was suddenly glad he carried some other name in this persona.

At last, the most notable of Rafe's friends held out his hand. He was a little older than the rest, easier in his skin. Already celebrated, already comfortable with it, he nodded, saying in his surprisingly rich voice:

"And I am Will Shakespeare."

"We came to hear a play of yours last summer, Will," said Rafe Silver. "Which was it, Francis? One with a king."

"A king is it?" said Will, laughing as he reached across the table to grasp Francis Brown's arm in greeting. "Then surely, it must be a play of mine!"

Jonson said something vile and got up to find the jakes, but Browne hardly noticed, except that it was a kind of blessing not to have both of them at the table together.

"That would be your tragedy of Richard the Third." He stopped just short of calling him "sir". He was only a player after all.

So was Raven.

"We had a free afternoon. Took up nearly all of it."

An actor playing an idiot.

"As my lord was with us," Sir Francis Browne said dryly, "I can't say it was completely free."

"As you say, though thou and I stood with the groundlings—"

"And the orange girls."

"Whilst his lordship had his seat upon the stage. Q, as they say, E.D."

The boy thumped back onto the bench, followed by a buxom tavern wench of the giggling sort laying fresh drinks and a dish of oysters in front of them. It was nearly noon, after all, and breakfast was long ago and very far away.

He would have to go more carefully than usual, Ben thought, spoon in hand. Remember not to mention Hamlet or Macbeth, still to come.

"So," said Will. He smiled tolerantly at Silver but addressed Francis Browne. "Liked you the play at all?"

"I did, aye! 'Now is the winter of our discontent made glorious summer by this sun of York,'" he declaimed around a hunk of manchet bread. "A subtle line, and a mighty one, the first of many. As full of excellent conceit as an egg is full of meat. Moreover, my lord agreed."

"He better liked the one with the faeries," Rafe said with a twitch of mischief.

Will beamed modestly and shoved Jonson, who had returned still sullen and now a good deal wetter.

"There, you see. Lord Aubrey likes it, and his discerning eye is well renowned."

"'Tis a fair enough work, Will," Ben Jonson grumbled, "but

vast! Too vast! What of the unities? Why, in my plays…"

"The one's you've yet to stage?"

Jonson's face flushed red at once, but Will put up a conciliatory hand. "Faith, lad, I know. Thou'lt show me yet how 'tis done, I'm sure. And I'll play in it for you, too."

"Aye, you can be the clown."

"Yet the picture and history of such a villain as Richard Plantagenet can hardly be compassed in a single day or a single place." He broke off with a chuckle. "Forgive us, Sir Francis. 'Tis an old wrangle, though our Ben is such a fresh wit as he thinks it new each time. Pray let it go, and tell me what beside the tempest brings you to the Mermaid after so long?"

There were so many things Ben wanted to say, wanted to ask, that had nothing to do with why he was here! Some of them so personal even a friend wouldn't mention. Who was the Dark Lady? Or Mr WH? Why the second-best bed?

Even meeting John Dee had not left him so constrained. On the other hand, if he had all the answers to four hundred years of scholarly speculation, what could he do with them? Publish? Better to enjoy his luck and let the rest go.

So he did, contenting himself with whiling a rainy afternoon in the best company he could have imagined. Player, scholar, or lawyer, they challenged each other in couplets, quatrains, and epithets, satires, sonnets, songs. Even Raven, to his credit, improvised on the spot lines both witty and mainly graceful. Then he pointed out, as someone always does, the cittern in Francis Browne's kit, a rather better one than the old beater hanging on the wall warping in the soggy air. And then there was nothing for it but he would have to play. So he did.

More ale went round, the conversation sharpened, even got a bit strident, especially on the subject of poesy and its purpose, while avoiding the shoal waters of politics. Raven had many opinions and engaged them all, betraying the subtle mind working behind the antic mask. Other patrons came and went, but for one thick-set fellow sitting against the far wall nursing a cup of wine, forgotten almost as soon as they had seen him.

The rain slowed, stammered, and stopped. The players started thinking perhaps they should take up some responsible

Maggie Secara

occupation. It was Lent, after all. And Ben started to panic. He still didn't know why he was here. The gift of True Finding was not in the habit of simply shuffling him in out of the rain for the sake of a party. But aside from the *morven* at the door sill, and the tavern's own name, not one thing today had borne on his mission.

Now he stood in the dripping doorway, watching delivery men hauling sodden layers of canvas down from a wagon filled with wine casks and brandy barrels, rolling them across the courtyard into storage. When he heard a throat cleared behind him, he expected Raven, then knew it couldn't be. Raven never gave warning.

"You never answered my question," said Will Shakespeare.

When Ben half turned a quizzical look on him, the poet joined him at the door. Two idle men watching others work; some things never change.

"Is it a secret, this burden of yours?"

"What burden is that? Only my master's business, as ever."

The slight, knowing smile flitted across Will's face again, lighting the hazel eyes.

"Your master is at Court. The Court is at Richmond. I know, for we played there last night, and I spoke with him, but saw neither you nor your waggish friend."

It always surprised Ben how visible Aubrey's place in this time was, yet somehow avoided the historians' gaze as neatly as he did the cameras in 1922..

"Did you indeed?"

"Very. So why come you to London and the Mermaid? Seek'st thou me?"

"Nay, Will, not knowingly."

Relieved, but still cautious, Will asked, "Should I guess your meaning?"

And then it occurred to Ben that there might be something in this question after all. His wayward gift was jangling again, without sending him anywhere. He was meant to be here. Now. In this conversation. Pay attention.

"Better not," he said. "But let me show thee somewhat. Pray sit here by the window, and I'll fetch it."

Regaining their seats where the others were pulling on their coats and bemoaning ruined feathers, Ben pulled out the diary, relieved to see its glamour in action, as always. The cover, though still swollen and battered, was a good one of leather stretched over boards, raised bands on the spine like any well-bound book. The paper, apparently well-made and well-trimmed.

He pulled the papyrus scrap from between two closely written pages, and was relieved to see that this time it had been saved a soaking. Whatever Father Tam had done to restore it must have carried a virtue to keep such damage from happening again. It was a damp enough adventure already.

"Marry, what's this?" Will asked, frowning over it. "I know this mark. The rest is nonsense, for all that I can tell." He picked up the fragment, and suddenly dropped it with a hiss, shaking his fingers as if—well, wasn't that curious? Almost as if he'd felt a spark from a brass doorknob on a windy day. The poet glared at it like a misbehaving child, and picked it up again, this time with no reaction.

"What are you?" he muttered, with a glance at Francis Browne who was trying not to notice.

"Can you tell me about it, or do you know someone who can?" said Ben, aching with excitement.

"A figure of a mermaid, or so it's called, though 'tis not much like one, is it. Stay awhile, though. Mine is not the head you seek. As Jonson never tires of reminding me, I have some Latin left from my school days, but little Greek. But these university men, they're as good as books themselves. No need to know all when all know something. Ben Jonson!" he called, and Ben Harper twitched in spite of himself.

"I am he, as you see me!" Jonson declaimed. It was his turn to stand in the doorway, checking the weather and shrugging into his cloak and hat. "And you see me as I am away. Gadding longer with thee will do me no credit with the Lord Admiral's men."

"Stay a moment. Bring Dick Carew as well. Sir Francis has a puzzle for us."

The paper passed among them all, each taking a turn to hold

it up to the light, frowning and scratching their heads. All agreed the text was Greek, most of it, but broken as it was, none could give it meaning. To Ben's relief, of them all only Shakespeare had any physical reaction to the weathered papyrus.

"Neither rhyme nor reason," Will said with a twinkle.

Watching from a different angle, Raven gently slipped the diary from under Shakespeare's questing eye and hand. Perhaps he could read it, perhaps not. It wasn't time to find out.

Jonson handed the fragment back to Francis Browne with a shrug.

"The man you want for this is Rob Cotton."

"Who?"

"Robert Cotton. He's an antiquary like Martin, here."

"Not," said Martin the lawyer with a corrective sniff. "Not, I say, like Martin at all. Robert Cotton is the man for oddities, that is certain. No mere classics will content Rob. He would have your Hebrew and Assyrian, and all the dialects of Timbuktu. Latin and Greek are the stuff of mere lawyers to him, the barber-surgeons of his Academy. There's too little of those here to sort out a meaning. As to these other scratchings, Rob's your man."

Richard Carew, a dark little Cornishman, added,

"His clerk is a sort of twice-turned cousin of mine. Odd fellow, melancholy as an owl, but good with ciphers, so Rob tells us."

"I have heard of Robert Cotton," Raven said, handing the diary back to its proper caretaker with a merry look. "He hath a notable library, so they say."

He and Ben Harper hadn't blown it up, exactly. Not all by themselves. Not yet.

"The very man for an ancient text," Will agreed. "And he loveth a mystery."

This was it, Ben thought. This was why they were here. Had they not spent the day together and earned their good will, he might never have had the chance to ask.

"How do we find this excellent antiquary? And will he see us?"

"His house is in the passage out of Westminster Hall as you come into the New Palace Yard, a little beyond the stairs going up to St. Stephen's Chapel."

"Built all of brick it is, hard by The Apple Tree."

"If you fall into the river, you've gone too far!"

"A new house to house his old books and coins and such like. That's where you'll find him if he's at home."

"Give him my compliments," Will added. "Tell him you have a puzzle for him, he won't wait for more recommendation."

"Gramercy, gentlemen," Ben Harper breathed with true relief. "Now, I have kept you all long enough, and the rain is done."

And so they made their farewells, shook hands once again, and bundled themselves out the door. Suddenly Ben and Raven were alone but for the hostess. And Shakespeare, leaning against the windowsill and looking thoughtful, with the glow of the leaded glass a watery reflection across his face.

"There, Will," said Ben. He had the next clue. He was ready to move on, boyhood idol or not. In gratitude and good cheer, he offered his hand, and said, "Is that answer enough?"

"He means to say he's honored to meet you," Raven said, leaning into the corner of a tall settle.

"Me? For a single play? An afternoon's idleness?"

"For all of it, sir. Aye, in very sooth." Then he added in a less playful voice. "Sir Francis, our merry bard can see me, as thou dost."

"I suspected as much."

"How now? Sure I can see you well, Rafe Silver. And hear you, too." If they had expected him to react with fear, they had reckoned without the country boyhood. "I always have, since I was a boy. Did you think I would forget, even though you be bearded like a leopard, now, and swearing a soldier's oaths?"

"I have wondered if you did."

"What's this?" said Ben.

"Many a summer afternoon, many a day I should have bent

over a kidskin in my father's shop, or droning Latin pronouns at school, I spent in the wood or out on the hills and often in your company."

"Faery-haunted woods," Raven said softly. "So everyone said."

Will laughed.

"Aye, so they said. And so they were. So many adventures, eh, playing at being kings or knights, lovers and lions, enacting every foolish notion. You nearly got me killed once, falling from a tree."

"And then he discovered girls!"

"Ha! Yes, and the rest of life's cares."

"Not for the ages but for all time," Ben said. He sat down, shaking his head. "Now we know why. Will, you hear the bells of Elfland."

Shakespeare looked away thoughtfully, then back at Ben.

"As do you, Sir Francis Browne."

"As do I."

"And your master, the good Lord Aubrey? I have noted something of the same thing in him as in you, Silver, at certain times. A faery light, as they say."

"My lord and I are of the same kind, aye, though he is much the greater."

"You said…" He repeated Raven's earlier delivery not only in word but in voice and manner, a gifted mimic with a perfect ear. "You misquoted the play, but I think you knew it. What is he, truly? And whence…"

"Peace, Will." Raven waved off the query in a gesture almost like a benediction.

"That's more than anyone can say, Will," said Ben. "But you have aided us, which does him service in some degree. Don't worry, there is no evil in it."

The broad forehead creased, but not with worry.

"I should be pleased to be in such service, I think, had I not other obligations."

Ben thought of Mellis and said nothing.

"Write your plays," Raven said with a courtier's smile. "That is service enough."

19
Westminster, Cotton House

i

The streets were mucky; the air spat at them. The people of London surged around them with their usual vulgar enthusiasm, paying no more mind to the weather or each other than any Londoner in any year. By the time they had slogged through the oozy kennel of the unpaved streets, Ben was wishing for mud flaps. On a Land Rover.

"And that would be the River Fleet," Raven said, gesturing as the horses picked a careful way down the slope of Ludgate Hill.

"As nasty as reported."

"And they wonder why the goddess abandoned it. Replaced they say by a hag so horrible her very breath is toxic."

There was no sign of a hag either, nor of anyone else besides small boys throwing stones at a white stick, or maybe it was a bone, sticking out of the greasy water.

"Maybe she hasn't moved in yet."

Nevertheless, before they crossed Fleet Bridge, they wrapped scarves over their mouths against the stink. Ben would as soon have crossed as quickly as the crowd allowed, but he braved the smells to rein Flaminius aside for a minute and listen, really listen for any hint of Fleet's nymph or her song in the noisome ditch that bore her name.

He said her name clearly in his mind, then spoke it aloud

just once, but Cyfla gave no answer. The city, its foundation clay undercut with streams and springs, had a song of its own made of those gurgles and splashes, the rattle of commerce and religion, the crackle of fire. He could sense faint echoes of the medieval city and, fainter still, the revenant dreams of the Roman town.

Flaminius, Faerie-bred as he was, snorted and sneezed, and looked back over his shoulder at Ben with something like reproach.

"There's nothing, is there," Raven said, more a statement than a question.

Dull-eyed with the effort, Ben shook his head. They turned away, heading at last down Fleet Street towards the Strand, which was paved, at least.

"No, nothing that matters. Not even a hag. I keep almost seeing blonde hair, and the tail of a pale blue dress in the corner of my eye. But no. Nothing." Barely the echo of the memory of a sigh.

"Sad, but city rivers are nearly all like this, you know. The Seine is no better where it runs through Paris. Even Father Thames is drowsy in this age, and keeps his state far upriver under an ash tree."

"Mm-hm, so why is this one stream so important to Ata'rathi? Other rivers' nymphs have gone missing, some have died. And if we're here, this must be the center of it all. We need to find the killer, not some little goddess. Why is this one so special?"

Raven shrugged.

"Ours not to reason why, I suppose."

The break in the weather had brought the populace back to the streets, eager to complete their day's errands before the storm closed in again. Sir Francis and Sir Rafael, superbly mounted on Faerie-bred horses that took nothing from nobody, had a serious advantage over most of them. They rose with purpose and the grim expression of a nobleman's retainers on serious business. That and some creative swearing got most people out of their way with little more than grumbling and a touched cap. Between the mud and the crowds, however, speed was not an option, even after passing Temple Bar where the road widened into the well-paved Strand.

The houses of great lords lined the street: Burghley and Bacon, the Earls of Arundel and Bedford. Leicester had lived here, Ben recalled, in the grand manner worthy of a queen's favorite and, who knows, maybe more. The mansion before them had passed to Leicester's stepson, the earl of Essex. From one end to the other, every gate in the Strand hosted a throng coming and going, queuing up to beg a moment of the great man's time.

Ben started to laugh.

"It's like someone sold a map to the stars' homes! Do they even know who lives there, or are they hoping it's someone important?"

"Oh, they know," Raven said, his voice more in Ben's mind than on the air. "They'll have studied carefully."

Without warning, Raven drew aside for a thick, badly shaven fellow in a black cassock and biggen cap who, taking advantage of the assemblage at Essex House, had stepped up on a wooden box and begun to preach, thumping his fist on an English testament. After a moment, the fae lord caught his eye, and nodded slightly under a lifted brow. The fellow quickly looked away.

Raven smiled a little.

"Cecil's man," he said quietly. "He was at the Mermaid, did you see him? I do believe we're being watched."

"I wonder why?"

"Oh, we are dangerous men, Francis Browne, did you not know?"

"Ah, of course."

Dangerous. He'd never been dangerous before, except to recalcitrant hoarders. Ben sat up a little straighter in the saddle.

And on and on, one broad frontage after another with the same crowds and smells, even the same dung heaps as ordinary householders though at a greater distance from the front doors. But at Charing Cross, in front of the royal mews where the streets joined into a processional way at Whitehall, two loaded wagons had evidently barreled out of opposing lanes at speed and decided to argue about the right of way, to the despite of all other traffic foreign and domestic jamming around them. With the passage blocked by rolling cabbages and leaking wine barrels, and eager folk with buckets and baskets clear to the Holbein Gate, and rain spitting at them again, even Raven lost his good humor.

It took no more than a shared glance, a shrug and a nod, and between one heartbeat and the next they were trotting into New Palace Yard and tying up their horses at the Apple Tree Inn right opposite a laid-brick mansion as handsome as any gentleman on the rise could want.

Master Cotton was in. Sir Rafe gave their names and mentioned Shakespeare's, and they were admitted at once, asked to wait, which gave them a chance—Ben, at least—to straighten rucked clothing and discover, gratefully, a discreetly accessible chamber pot. Now, still somewhat bedraggled, Ben stood lightly steaming in the anteroom taking in domestic details in front of a hearth fire that wanted poking up.

The house wasn't entirely new, but the latest linen-fold wainscoting gleamed under good plasterwork, and the comfortably high ceiling had been lightened with coffering. Access to the rest of the house was evidently through a pair of flat-arched doorways with scrolling vines carved in the spandrels, of which one bore the date 1547. From sounds in the distance, one red-and-white-tiled passage must lead to kitchen, scullery, stillroom, garden. Through the other he could just see the corners of a boxy staircase. That would be the public rooms above, and perhaps a dining parlour.

Between the doorways stood a massive court cupboard he knew Mellis would faint over, even without the gleaming display of pewter plate that filled its shelves from side to side. It was, of course, the first thing any visitor saw coming into the house, and a point of pride for Mistress Cotton.

A servingman came in, sketched a bow, and fetched a pitcher from the collection, then touched his cap again. Sir Francis nodded in acknowledgement, recalling his own serving days at that faire they used to have in Marin, and especially at Farthingale Hall. In both places, a gentleman had to learn his trade from the ground up. In fact, he thought to say something, a word of camaraderie, but the fellow had already sped away toward the scullery.

Aloud, he observed, "Nice house."

Raven chuckled, nodding agreement from a mullioned window by the door. Leaded with surprisingly good glass, the Cotton shield of arms had been set gleaming in the middle, all its quarterings faithfully rendered. The raven-boy's attention, however, was not on the décor but on the yard. It was Westminster, Whitehall, the seat of government, which never stopped for rain, and thus as busy as on any day.

"You going to keep that scar?" Ben wondered. His eyes flicked to the damned thing every time he glanced at his friend.

"Don't you like it?" Satisfied with what he saw, or didn't see, Raven turned back into the room. "I think it gives me an air of mystery."

"It does make you look like a street thug, if that's the mystery you're going for."

The fae nodded, considering the concept with a rakish grin. "Girls love scars."

"A gentleman scholar might think of putting you out the door."

"Ah, but he'd think twice about it, wouldn't he?"

"Yes, Watson, I suppose he might. Next question. Now that we're here…"

"Gentlemen?" a courteous voice inquired from the doorway that was not the kitchen. "My name is Simon Carew. I am Master Cotton's secretary. Will it please you to come with me?"

Watching them each for agreement and finding it, he turned and took them through the second passage.

Ben saw at first only a thin, long-faced fellow in his early forties, pale with too much time indoors. From under a modest frill at the wrist, the top of the man's left hand hanging loose at his side showed not the ropey veins of a man under constant stress, as he surely was, but a polished mound of keloidal scars, threaded here and there with red and blue, the obvious souvenir of an intense fire that had melted flesh without burning it. He'd known a girl in college with something similar, and the court-awarded trust fund to go with it. This man would not have been so fortunate.

Following him up the staircase, noting the slightest awkwardness in Carew's gait, it was easy to guess the hand was not the only limb affected. Lank hair fell over the ruffed collar band, but Ben could spy a tendril of the same keloid reaching up the fellow's throat to curl around the ear.

Even climbing stairs, his posture betrayed bitterness. It must be terrible to live with, cursed forever to be some other man's clerk—a lesser man, as he supposed— and kept forever out of the way of advancement by a grotesque scar. Folk supposed the outside reflected the inner man, and would avoid him. The Queen would never receive such a man. That much anyone could see.

But when Ben applied his other gift and looked more closely, the image shifted and a deeper truth made him stumble and clutch at the bannister. Raven's hand caught his other arm before he could fall. Two steps above, Carew stopped and looked back with concern.

"Sir, are you well?"

"Yes!" said Sir Francis Browne. He stared up into the sallow face, haunted and hollow-eyed, into an image of fire, and thoughts of blood. Gasping, he shook off the True Sight and straightened, steadied himself. "Yes, all's well. Prithee, pay it no mind. Press on."

He could have lived a long time without that vision, content to see only the mask of the disappointed servant, the cliché; but the man was cloaked in smouldering resentment, anger, and some other, deeper horror. The lines around the lips pressed thin hinted at lighter moments, laughter, perhaps even outright pleasure, though not in wholesome things. It was not his career that he hated, but something else.

Ben's glance flicked to Raven as they proceeded, but the fae lord's expression had frozen almost the second the secretary entered the room. Best to watch them both, then. Fae emotions were always hard to read, but he knew this one. The evil streaming off Simon Carew, complex and layered, must have rolled over the raven-boy like a breaking wave. Withdrawal was his rejection and defense against nothing so mild as mere disapproval.

Clearing his mind, Ben let his observing eye wander as they progressed through a series of small rooms, each one leading into another. In the last one, an old man sat frowning over some letters through a pair of spectacles: thick glass lenses cased in leather and held on by cords looped over his ears. That was not the master of the house, no.

The door beside him led into a long gallery some eight or nine yards long, well endowed with paned glass windows and overlooking a garden. On a sunny day, the room would be flooded with light. Today they only amplified the murky grey.

Most people used such a room to display portraits of their noble ancestors, heroic tapestries or murals documenting their lineage back to Alfred the Great, Charlemagne, or Adam and Eve; after supper perhaps filling it with candlelight for dancing and games.

Not Robert Cotton. Against the inner wall and running the length of the room stood half a dozen massive book presses, the shelves still loosely filled with books and manuscripts with plenty of room for more. Simon Carew led them more slowly through here, his standing orders being to let anyone gawp and admire at their leisure.

In a niche above each case sat the bust of some classical figure, an emperor or queen. Trembling, Ben slapped Raven's arm and pointed from one to the next, whispering.

"Look! Nero, Vespasian, Claudius…" "That's his only filing system: under which emperor, on which shelf. I wonder if the Beowulf is here yet. Where's Vitellius?"

"Down, sirrah," Raven said tightly.

"Beowulf was filed under Vitellius, see."

At last Carew showed them into an office carved out of the

gallery's end, where he offered them chairs under more leaded windows. He brought canary wine down from a cupboard, and silver cups, then bowed, and left them alone.

The instant the man had disappeared, Ben let out a shaky breath, giving in at last to a shudder that shook him to his toes.

"Bloody hell."

"And what did you see?" asked Raven smoothly.

But there was no time.

"How now, how now, gentlemen! Well met!"

Wreathed in smiles, a small neat man with a small neat beard and fine eyes entered with open arms. His dress was good brown serge, edged and welted with rows of black passmentarie braid, but otherwise as plain and serviceable as their own. He looked, if anything, more like the classic image of Shakespeare than Will Shakespeare did, but decidedly less relaxed.

ii

The bells of St Margaret's across the yard were striking four as Robert Cotton of Connington in Huntingdonshire hurried to his private closet, both pleased and slightly alarmed to find messengers from Lord Aubrey waiting for him. One of them he knew, by sight at least. The dark one, Fitzroy. The menacing scar under the eye always gave him a start, especially when the man smiled, as if he had been laughing when some villain's sword had scored across his youthful beauty. The fellow did smile to excess, he thought, for a gentleman.

It always made him uneasy, though surely without reason. Lord Aubrey had always been his friend. And he, Cotton, was discreet, conformable, and useful to the Queen. He had no reason to fear, that he knew of. But who knew anything, these days? And today, not one man at his door but two, and with no warning.

He was fretful, and he knew it, so he paused outside the gallery to collect himself. Ready, he made his entrance like a player entering a scene, radiating his native good humor and bonhomie.

They pulled off their caps to give reverence and remained

standing, politely bare-headed.

"Master Cotton," said the one he had not met before, a fair-haired Saxon type with a golden beard. "My name is Sir Francis Browne; this doughty fellow here, Sir Rafael Fitzroy."

"So it is, so it is! Sit down, I pray you, and say what I may do for Lord Aubrey. Pray tell me he is well!"

"Most assuredly he is well, sir. And will be pleased to know that you are the same."

And so on and so on. The usual courtesies were exchanged, wishes from Lord Aubrey for the antiquary's health and that of his young wife, pregnant again. Good wishes and assurance of continuing service were pressed upon them to Lord Aubrey.

Servants appeared with candles against the grey afternoon, just in time for the westering sun to break through the clouds. For a quarter of an hour Rob Cotton rattled on about his work, the collections, the latest acquisition. Did the gentlemen know he was writing a history of Huntingdonshire? Did they know the county at all? They did not, and he began to wonder why they were letting him ramble.

"But that is enough of my affairs. You must have come to me with some purpose?"

So far Browne had done most of the nodding and agreeing, while Fitzroy had sat still as a stone. Suddenly the villain sat forward. Rob sat back with a start.

"So please you, Master Cotton, we know time is precious to you, as it is to our master."

Fitzroy reached down by his chair and pulled up a sort of leather portfolio, blazoned with Lord Aubrey's arms.

As if the wind had changed, the scholar's mind spun round, slowed, found harbour, gave all his attention. Whatever had come in such covers he knew was no warrant, no request for a loan to the Crown, no demand he surrender half his best serving men to the army to fight in Ireland. He swallowed. What on earth did Aubrey want in exchange?

"I had nearly forgot," said Sir Francis Browne, chagrined. "Marry, but I do grow old!"

"As you say." Fitzroy twisted up a small smile, making that scar dance.

Cotton, sweeping aside stacked books and curling scrolls, could pretend not to see it.

Browne held the case while Fitzroy drew from it a small folder, just two plain boards with leather hinges, which he placed on the table between them.

"What is it?" Rob Cotton whispered, looking to Browne. He rather liked Browne; the man's face was as open as a flower, and as blank.

"I have no idea," Browne said.

Whatever it was, it must be extraordinary. Rob could feel it, smell it: old ink, old parchment, a peculiar hint of—what was it—violets. He put his fingers to the edges and began to lift them apart, then stopped.

No, he should have his own man here as well, to be sure. A witness. And besides, Carew would appreciate whatever he found far more than either of these martial fellows.

His hands sprang suddenly away from the boards.

"Not yet," he said, and went to the door, shaking with excitement.

"Fetch Carew to me, " he croaked to the man in the outer room. "Be quick!"

Soon there were footsteps, and the secretary stalked into the room, clearly expecting to see the visitors out, and not a moment too soon.

"Excellent, here's Silence, at last. You've met Simon Carew. I call him Silence, betimes, for that's your nature, eh? Well, well."

Cotton ventured a short laugh, to which the grim fellow replied with a nod and a twisting of the lips that was nothing like a smile. Lord Aubrey's men exchanged glances he couldn't read, though Browne had got abruptly to his feet.

"Look, Silence, look here," said Rob Cotton, the collector's passion making his voice hoarse. "Lord Aubrey has sent me…ah, well, I know not what, eh. Let us see."

With care he turned back the cover and lifted out the first sheet. There were but two. Just two loose folio pages, written on one side in an angular, antique hand. Some slight water damage, yes. Ink smeared here and there; discoloration, only to be expected.

Dazed, Cotton looked up with glowing amazement on his narrow face. His man Silence muttered something, which he dismissed.

"Unimportant. Of course, some damage, think of the age. But for all that, look! It is nearly perfect. Do you know what this is, eh? Unless I quite mistake me, it is a poem, of sorts, in the runic script of the Saxon tongue some call Old English."

A thought crashed through his racing mind. He gasped and looked up.

"Does John Jocelyn know about this? Jocelyn, down in Kent?"

Browne looked doubtful. "I know not, sir. Is it important?"

"Is it valuable, then?" the other man asked, all innocence.

"Ha!" Cotton nearly crowed. "Ha! I have a copy of Jocelyn's commentaries, but no one has seen the poem itself but him, or so he says. And this is that poem. Ah ha!"

By God's Grace and Blood and every other Holy Part, of course the two men knew its value. No gift from a great man was ever free of obligation, and this had taken not one man but two to bring it. How could it be? Aubrey would have told his henchmen that much at least, and more.

He should not have revealed himself so overcome, but dear God! Better to collect his manners, if it were not already too late. The greater his desire for it, the greater the favour owed.

"Indeed, indeed. That is, eh—" His hands were too damp to trust them to the paper itself. He only waved limp fingers over them. "The letters are clear, the lines are faded somewhat, as we should expect, but goodly made. And, God's mercy, it must be above five hundred years old, by all accounts! And, and…"

At this point his knees gave out. He had to sit down. Silence quickly poured a cup of wine and put it in his hand, still without speaking, bless him.

When Rob had caught his breath, he saw that his visitors were both standing, and when he had calmed a bit, and Silence, dry-fingered, had put the pages again into their folder for safekeeping, he waved them to their chairs once more.

"Gentlemen, I am touched by your master's care and

honored more than I can say. I would ask how this came to him, but likely you do not know." As both shook their heads, he added, "But say now, gentlemen, what service can I do Lord Aubrey for so great a kindness?"

"A simple query which he hopes that you can answer easily, but fears may be otherwise," said Browne. "Mermaids. His interest is in mermaids."

The sharp intake of breath came from Silence, still hovering just within sight. The stubbled jaw tightened, a nerve ticked under one eye. The burned hand, ink-stained to the swollen knuckles, went to his collar, as if touching a relic against evil.

Thoughtful, Cotton's brows drew together not into a frown, not exactly. Not that he disapproved, but…

"Mermaids, Sir Francis?"

"Say demons, rather," Carew muttered. "Lewd, wanton, cruel—"

"Say'st thou?" Sir Rafael glanced up sharply.

No reply came but a baleful stare.

Brown went on. "Aye, mermaids, nymphs, naiads, or what you will. Old tales even, such as country folk tell, as well as any ancient texts."

How curious. Lord Aubrey was known to be, oh, a trifle eccentric, but mermaids?

"Ehm, eh, how may I ask this without seeming to pry, good Sir Francis? Is his interest new? That is to say, if I knew what books he has already, I could…"

"My lord wishes to learn of any documents, however old, in Latin or Greek perhaps, or even older tongues, where the word 'Atami' appears."

Again, Carew reacted as if he'd been burnt.

"Or anything of the sea goddesses of old. The most antique of course, would suit him the better. Even in a language or text indecipherable, if this figure be upon it."

With that, he withdrew the papyrus scrap from his purse and unfolded it for him.

Carew let out a cry, quickly stifled as all the color left his face.

"I have seen this!" Cotton muttered, handling the fragment

delicately. "A *morven*, it is called by some scholars, others merely 'the mermaid badge'. But where…? I have it! There is a stone set into the pier at Richmond Palace that has this sign upon it, above the high water mark. Queer, you know, because the figure is an old one, and pagan without doubt, yet the palace was built in the time of the Queen's grandfather. How such a thing came to be put there is a mystery."

"There is another on the foundation stone of the Mermaid tavern," said the younger and clearly more dangerous of Lord Aubrey's henchmen.

"Is there?" said the antiquary. "Is there indeed? Curious, eh, Silence?"

Through the glazed windows the westering sun, the clouds having at last slunk away northwards, threw a sunset glare over the faces of Cotton and his man. At the same time, the slanting light cast the visitors into deep silhouette, with only a faint haze glinting off the gold threads of their livery badges.

Carew blinked, staring at Sir Rafael as if he had appeared from nowhere.

"What art thou!" he hissed in a voice like broken glass.

"How now, what's that, eh?" said Robert Cotton, unaccountably flustered. It would not do to offend either of these men, no matter how unsettling they might be.

"Nothing, sir," Silence said tightly. "I cry your pardon."

"Be as thy name, man, and listen, for I know the very thing will please his lordship. Go fetch me the scroll, ah… Know'st thou the one I mean? That scroll Donato sent from Stamboul, last year, eh, or the year before. Aye, you know the one I mean. Do you…?"

But Silence was already gone, leaving Robert Cotton alone with his increasingly uncomfortable guests.

"I am sure he will find it. It's not like Silence to let me forget something of such interest. A pity, for I might have translated it for his lordship."

He turned to the gentlemen, and stopped, startled.

Against the window, both men in their handsome livery seemed haloed like angels in the golden light. Then Browne leaned on his elbow, and was only a man, after all. The pleasant

     Maggie Secara

face and golden beard resolved once again to ordinary lines. There was nothing the least mysterious or strange about either man or their errand. Still there was no denying, the moment felt uncanny. But no matter.

Minutes passed.

He offered them more wine, which they declined with courtesy. He offered a tour of the library; they had already been impressed, but evinced no deep interest. Running out of ideas, he asked if they might like to dine with him. They could not, they thanked him kindly, being stayed for elsewhere. The fair one's eyes seemed to drift closed; was he humming? The fingers worked in the air like a conjuror's until a word from his friend made him stop.

Unnerved, Cotton sipped some wine, pushed paper around the desk, straightened some books. Thought about sharpening a quill, but no, not that; he dared not handle the knife. He sat back, hands clasped over his belt, trying to appear at ease. One finger drummed another, *tap-tap-tap*, *tap-tap-tap*.

"Master Cotton?" said Sir Francis Browne, making him jump.

"Where can he have got to, I wonder?" Robert said, more a moan than a question. "The portrait of a good servant is our Silence, most times."

"Forgive me, Master Cotton," Browne said again, "I must ask you about this good servant of yours."

"No!"

"What's that?"

"I mean, of course, but rather, let me send after him."

He started to call for the old clerk, but Sir Rafael also gained his feet. Like a blithe spirit of menace, he seemed to caress the sword hilt at his side.

"Sh— Shall I find him for you?" Rob said, still no closer to understanding what was going on.

"Let me come with you," said Sir Francis, more pleasantly, but only a little. Even he, with his plain honest face, seemed grim.

"Gentlemen, please!"

"We mean no harm, sir, on my oath. I only wished to know

whether you have noticed anything unusual about this Simon Carew, perhaps in recent months, or even days?"

"Or since you came upon this scroll you mentioned?"

"What?"

Before Cotton was quite aware of it, they were moving all together down the gallery, the two swordsmen almost shepherding the scholar through his own house.

"I am sure he is discreet,' said Brown, "but mayhap he has been more than usually secretive?"

"He keeps to himself, but he always has."

"Has he changed in any way? Perhaps taken up a new pastime? Fishing, or anything that keeps him on the river?"

"Nay, nothing like. But what curious questions you do ask. He has neither friends nor diversions that I know of."

"The stews?" Fitzroy asked sharply. "Women?"

An uncomfortable question. He'd given his word.

"No," he said, perhaps a bit too quickly. "He... No. But why, what has he done?"

So far every room was empty of the man, and the house was filled with noises. The baby was crying, dishes clattered being laid for supper, a maidservant ran past them weeping. Cotton was not accustomed to being quizzed over the doings of his servants, and meant to take offense, once they came upon him. But where was the man?

Abruptly he halted at the foot of a staircase, the newel post charmingly carved in the likeness of a mermaid. No, a dolphin. Why had he thought it a mermaid?

"Yes?"

"We keep a chamber here for his use. Often he stays quite late, caught up in his work, you know. The streets are so dangerous at night. I let him stay here rather than...and risk...or be tempted, you know."

"And where is that room, sir?" said Browne, gently, though Cotton had a feeling that, in some uncanny way, the man already knew.

They stood at the landing to the third floor. He glanced up to the attics, wary of footsteps coming down.

"At the top of this stair. Here, what's this? Is that Martin?"

"Master!"

One of the younger grooms, not yet grown into his grey-marbled livery, sat weeping on the top step with his hand over one eye.

"Martin, come down at once, boy. What is the matter?"

The boy got up reluctantly and started down the stairs, until Francis Browne caught him up and set him down again with a father's skill. When his feet hit the ground, the boy wrenched himself free and snatched off his cap.

"Master! He knocked me down again, sir, I swear it on my mother's name. You said we was to tell you, sir, if anyone did the like. I didn't do nothing. He just hit me in the eye and made off."

Ordinarily, Robert would have cared a great deal. He would not have bad blood or violence among his servants. For now, already jumping out of his skin, he had only one question.

He snapped, "Martin, have you seen Mr Carew?"

"That's him," the boy sputtered. "That Carew. He swore at me, master, in most terrible words. He 'most killed me! I think he's gone mad!"

Under the fringe of his hair, the wide eyes were crimson and damp, and the left one was closing over a growing bruise. He knuckled away a tear and straightened up, mustering his anger.

"He come tearing out of his room, master, with a face like the devil's bunghole."

"Mind thy language, imp!" Cotton blustered, but Sir Francis Browne put up a calming hand.

"Sir, if I may?" More easily than most such men, Browne took the child aside and went on one knee to look him in the eye. "How old art thou, Martin?"

"I shall be ten come Easter, sir."

Sir Francis nodded with manly approval.

"Well now, Martin, I've a son near thine age, and I know a good lad when I see one." He also clearly knew the way to a boy's heart. He reached into his pouch and pulled out a shiny silver sixpence and held it up. "This is for thee, if thou'lt tell me what I need to know."

The boy's eyes went wide, the tears vanished. Sixpence was his whole week's wages

"Aye, sir, what e'er you will."

"Before he swore at you, when you came upon him, what was he doing, do you know?"

Martin didn't even have to think.

"He was putting his clothes in a horse pannier, like when Master sends him traveling to foreign parts."

"Packing, excellent. Did he have anything else, or pack anything more than his clothes?"

"Money, aye. Silver, and some o' them old coins of yours, too, master. From the cabinet. And gold ones, too!"

"No!" Rob stammered in horror. "No, he would never... Those are Roman coins, two thousand years old."

Oh, he had to sit down. He couldn't sit down. Powerless, he could only pace up and down while Sir Francis pressed the child further.

"Any books, or papers, perhaps?"

"Oh aye, they too, sir! He had one of master's books, the rolled up ones, laid out on the bed. But 'e didn't pack it. 'E were ripping it apart!"

"God's Death!" Cotton roared with fury that made his whole house fall silent below. "Oh, the traitor! God's Death, how am I betrayed by him. Call up the Watch! Call up the Watch!"

Fitzroy was already on the stair, climbing quickly while Browne kept at the groom.

"And did he say anything else?"

"He never stopped talking, sir. Like he was speaking to the bishop, all humble and all, except then he'd start talking wild."

"Wild? How so?"

"He were stark mad, sir!" Martin said. "Mad as Bedlam. He said he had all he needed now, and sure the Lord would give him a soul."

"Give him... You mean save his soul?"

"Nay, sir! He said it twice." With an earnest air he scrunched up his eyes, remembering. "*The Lord will not deny me. I shall have earned a soul at last.* That's what he said."

"Francis!" Fitzroy's voice rang out from under the rafters. "Master Cotton! Up here!"

iii

In a cramped closet of a room at the top of the house, surrounded by a clutter so deep it made Ben Harper's orderly soul twitch in response, they found Raven bending over a radiant brazier on a tripod, staring grimly at a few shattered bits of ash. A curling scrap of papyrus between his fingers still flickered red-gold at the edge. He had pushed open a shuttered window, or possibly created one, in the hope of clearing the oppressive heat in exchange for some air to breathe.

"Is that it?" Ben asked.

"I think it must be."

"Oh God!" Cotton gasped. "All of it? To escape the library at Alexandria only to come to this!"

Before the truth of it could crack the scholar's heart completely, Ben grabbed Cotton and sat him down on a battered joint stool.

Raven was still talking.

"Or rather, it's only the papyrus bits. Sacred or not, they must have caught at once." He glanced at the wretched antiquary. "I'm sorry, sir. He's been gone for some minutes now."

The last thread of fire flared and ate the last of it out of his hand. He brought up the other, holding a fat, loosely rolled parchment scorched as if it had lain under a lens on a summer day. The stains of spills and discoloration at the edges were probably much older.

"This was on top, but it was too big and too damp, thank fortune. Had it caught, it would have fired the thatch."

"Jesu spare us," Cotton was moaning. "My library. My house. My family!"

"We'll find him, never fear," Ben assured him, but the man was barely listening.

Raven, meantime, had spread the scorched scroll out on the narrow bed to its modest length.

"Damn it, look at this."

Neat columns of Latin and Greek defined five or maybe six islands of negative space, stuck with horse glue and vegetable matter thousands of years old. Around them and in the margins, crawling along the edges, later hands had added more, commenting on the comments, analyzing. But worse still, another fiercer hand had scored across the small neat letters. Vile curses, terrible oaths, in every language Carew knew, damned the Atami to destruction.

Both shocked to stillness at the sacrilege, compounded by the knowledge of what it had led to, Aubrey's men stood quite still. Oddly, it was Robert Cotton's strained voice that broke the silence.

"It was sadly incomplete, or so I believe. We spent—or rather, I spent, God forgive me—only a little time with it when it first came to me. So much to do here, you know. Councillors ever at my door. Always some new thing. Mr Carew appears to have given it a great deal of attention all this while. Now it is gone."

A deep emotion rattled his voice, subsided. He pointed to the notes there, and there.

"This was largely a Latin gloss upon a few patches of text in a curious script, which is now lost to us. I had hoped one day to see the script itself deciphered, using the Latin as a guide."

"The harm is worse than you think, sir," said Francis Browne, his own voice shaking.

"How so? What could be worse?"

"Young women have died," Sir Rafael croaked. "Something in this text, and whatever else he has read whilst studying, has moved him to kill."

"But…nay," said Rob, blank with shock. "Simon Carew? That is impossible."

"Can you tell us where he lives, or where he might have gone?"

"Nay, nay, he said little enough at all times, most nothing about himself. A Devon man, I know that much from his speech, though he tried to hide it. I was told…"

"What were you told, Master Cotton?" Ben prompted.

Wringing his hands, pink with embarrassment, Rob looked

up at the two strangers, each focused now on him.

"I should not say. I promised Master Cecil I never would."

"Sir Robert Cecil?"

"Oh. Fie on't, I ought not to have said that either. Well, as well hanged for a sheep as a lamb, eh, and what harm can it do now? It was confided to me, when I took the man on, something of his history. If he has gone to ground, you may seek out his old haunts."

"Devon?" Raven snapped, and his look was murderous. "If so, he is already a dead man."

"Oh, nay! Nay, not so, not at all. He would not go there, I am sure, though I never heard the story of it. Nay, you might not think it, but at one time, between drink and the pox, he near killed himself. They say a drunkard never reforms, you know. And the pox, well," he shrugged helplessly, "some men never learn, do they? Southwark, gentlemen. You must look for him in Southwark."

Overwhelmed, deeply embarrassed, and a wrapped package of apologies, Cotton first called for a servant to show them out, then personally conducted them back through the tiled and rush-carpeted labyrinth of his house to the front door. When he closed it on them at last and threw the lock, he collapsed in exhaustion, and practically wept. In one day, to be humiliated before a great and noble patron and bereft of a competent servant! It was too much, simply too much for a man of sensitivity to bear.

When his young wife, gravid with child, found him—the maids had called for her in some distress—he was sitting on the herb-strewn floor with his back to the door, as if holding it against barbarians. And perhaps, all in all, he was.

iv

They stood at the top of Westminster stairs, each with a hand resting on his sword hilt, contemplating the sunset colors on the river. The stiff breeze made them both grab their hats. It would keep the fog off, at least, but Ben was glad of his cloak.

"He's the guy, then," he said. "This Simon Carew."

"Oh yes. If I had understood it sooner, we'd be home by now making music at the Star. There was something very curious about him, did you notice. Almost—"

"I saw more than I wanted to. Believe me, that was enough."

"Never mind."

"This is about to get more complicated, isn't it, Watson?"

"Or much simpler."

"We have to catch him first."

A passing stevedore caught their voices in a corner of his ear and glared.

"Foreigners," he muttered, and stalked on.

"We do have a lead, of a sort," said Raven, staring longingly into the sky storm-streaked with purple and gold as the sun drew toward the horizon. "Southwark."

"Rough neighborhood."

"They know me there."

"Of course they do," Ben said. "Then there's the Cecil connection. I mean, Sir Robert Cecil got him this job. What do you want to bet he—"

"Employs him in other ways? It would only surprise me if he didn't. You don't want to talk to him, though."

"Also his Grace is with the Court, so Shakespeare said."

The fae said nothing to that, still engrossed in thought.

"Flip for it?"

"Oi! You lads goin' anywhere, or just gettin' romantic?"

A waterman balancing his boat at the foot of the stair had plastered a smile of sorts over his customary scowl. At least, his teeth were bared, what teeth he had.

"What, man, you've only got one hand!" Raven scoffed. Because it was true—from below the elbow, the scrofulous fellow's left hand was carved of wood in a shape that might control an oar, and strapped in some eccentric way to his arm.

"Sacrificed in her Majesty's service in the Low Countries! Don't expect a bargain rate for all that! All fares is set by the Council and the blessed Queen, God save her."

"Oh God, the comic relief," Ben muttered. "Why can't we ride to Richmond?"

"Better to go back to the Mermaid and spend the night you paid for than ride that road in the dark."

"I suppose that's—"

"Out of the question, aye. I've already sent the horses back. Now then, Southwark's across the river no matter how far it is. It's take this old bugger and his boat, or else make a way back to the Bridge, and get across before the gates close."

There was only the one bridge, and city wardens closed the gates at nightfall, which was sweeping in at a breathtaking pace.

"He's already got a lead on us, if he did run to Southwark, even more if he's taken— You there!" he called down to the squidgy wherry man with one arm and a desperate squint. "What's the passage to Richmond?"

"Eight pence, good master, tide comin' in, tide goin' out, Council says, and likewise from Richmond right back 'ere to Whitehall stair. As ye've the look of gentlemen in yer fine livery and all, yer honors won't mark the cost, I've no doubt."

Raven turned back to Ben.

"What does your gift tell you now?"

"Pfft. It says: Of course, some people do go both ways."

Any icy stare from the raven-boy.

"Someone has to go to Southwark, Scarecrow."

"Mm-hmm, and you're the one who doesn't need a boat."

"And you could phone my lord and ask him to look around the palace," Raven said with a shrug. "Assuming he's still there. You know how he is."

Ben exhaled with some force and definite meaning.

"Give me twenty crowns to keep my state, and we'll stop talking about it."

"It's already in your purse. Lucky at tables, that's you. Now go on, if you really trust this old fustilugs."

"What choice have I got?"

"I 'eard that!"

"I trust the water," said Ben. "I think."

"Meet again by midnight, or sooner, with luck," Raven said. "If you find him, or there's any trouble, give a shout. I'll come."

Their eyes met, honest mortal and glittering fae, and their

hands clasped, and Ben trotted with care down the steps to the wherry.

20
Raven at Southwark

On the old maps, Southwark looks positively suburban all the way to Lambeth: blocks of flats, shops, two tall round arenas, and a theatre with flags bravely flying, braced by a great cathedral at one end and a bishop's palace at the other. Gardens and fish ponds flourish among the warehouses. Even a street called Dead Man's Place seems a broad avenue lined with trees and so perhaps it must have been, in the artist's eye. On a good clean print, it looks much like a good clean place. It also looks dead flat and easy to navigate.

Maps lie.

To a man on foot, even a lithe, immortal fae who can see in the dark better than in daylight, it was a dense warren of alleys, cock-pits, open fires in alleyways, and brothels that hugged the river, all largely without the control of the Lord Mayor of London. The lone theatre on this side of the river, the aging Rose, was dark, as were the bear- and bull-baiting arenas, having rained out as thoroughly as the Curtain and the Theatre up in Shoreditch. Passers-by might be aware of some drama within, voices declaiming, arguing, brawling, or the occasional clash of steel—maybe a fight scene rehearsed at half-speed with blunted blades, and maybe sharpened steel drawn in anger. Welcome to the Bankside.

Resigned as Raven was to ducking in and out of unwholesome places and buying a round for whatever unsavory company he found there, he wasn't looking forward to it. Not that he hadn't on other days done exactly that for its own sake, and enjoyed whatever came of it. But that was merry-making and mischief, dropping his h's and lifting skirts, shouting out scurrilous songs and occasionally delivering a crude justice of his own on ill-tempered pimps and bawds. It was not in his nature to be the clean-cut hero but, sensibilities of the Great Fae being what they are, he managed to be heroic now and then anyway.

This was different. Greater things were at stake than his own amusement or levelling a few mortal egos.

He had more than one mask for this side of the river, just as he had on the other. Tonight he chose Rankin Foy, disgraced schoolmaster, the ink-stained scrivener and part-time jackman. His specialty, that is, among the illiterati of the district was creating licenses to beg, trade, or travel. Rankin could draw you up a paper for anything: travelling papers good all the way to Scotland, or an army discharge; a passport to France or anything you please, writ perfect as the Queen's own hand. His fees were modest, and he even provided the seal.

In exchange for a drink, with his long legs stretched out under the only table in the house—any house—that didn't wobble, he'd scratch out a chapbook sonnet for a love-sick youth; for two drinks and half a crown, he'd pen in a neat, sober italic hand a contrite letter home after the same youth had spent all his allowance at the Bell and the Cardinal's Hat. Rankin didn't even mind knocking out the odd threatening letter, fraught with menace when he read it out, though the venture seldom turned out exactly as expected.

It was a pose that let him talk to anyone, high and low, in a shugging house or at the archbishop's kitchen door, and led to adventures, if that was his mood. Everyone's friend, everyone's gossip, affable Rankin with the thinning ginger hair, fit neatly in wherever he went south of the river.

The question first was where to begin. His faerie talents were many and powerful, but he lacked Ben's gift for finding. Pity he hadn't thought to leave some mark on the bastard, but there you are. Another tick against the villain's account. Instead, he would try to see what Ben would see, if Ben knew what Rankin knew about such places.

From hole to ringing smoke-clogged hole, Rankin went questing ever westward from the Bridge, thanking the powers that made him for his ability to 'drink and no be drunken, fight and no be slain.' Between drinks he sucked on countless little clay pipes, harsh with tobacco and henbane. The cramped, stifling ale houses, the sweating common rooms in the houses showing blind Cupid over the door, the greasy cookshops reeking of tallow, all hazed into blue around him while he talked, and talked—all without asking a direct question.

Curiosity never worked, but the fae have other ways. Applying his powers of invention, he built the image of a man, better than life, in the minds of anyone around him. Some twitched a little, some stopped to scratch their heads, but no one—no one at all—came to him with any tale of a damned hypocritical puritan bastard called Silence Carew.

Moving on, he tried again, this time introducing the name idly into the story, the joke, the shred of half-remembered Court gossip that confirmed everyone's opinion of the damned nobles, or the old Queen. Should have thought of it sooner.

He told a tale at the Bull and a joke at the Lion, each time about a mad fellow called Carew, didn't they remember? At the Bell he made two copies of a letter to a lawyer but subscribed the customer's X on one of them as Simon Carew instead of Silas Clough, at which he swore roundly, apologized, and gave tuppence back from the fee to make up for it, as well as rewriting the letter.

And as he did so, the fellow said, "Marry, now I mind me. There was a Carew about betimes, some whiles ago."

Or maybe a few of them. Others agreed, now they heard the name repeated twice or three times. It was common enough down in Cornwall and Devon, and West Country men came to London like everyone else, and all of them were canting, sheep-swiving bastards. But no, no, they thought, not here. Not lately.

Lately?

"Well, not as you'd say 'of late'," said the fading rose playing hostess tonight at the Bishop of Rome.

The Bishop fancied itself the up-scale establishment south of the river, and so leaned to the Classical. Her name, this year, was Drusilla. Five-and-twenty, she must have been near to the end of her career: all bad skin, sharp bones and frizzed yellow hair, brown at the roots. The voice was shrill but merry, in its way.

"There was a man used to come here, just as you say, my love. Terrible scar he had all down the one side. We reckoned him a penny more for bringing that thing in here. Nearly scared my quim into fits."

Rankin laughed easily, feeling a jolt of relief he was sure could be felt in the depths of Faerie. He hadn't mentioned the scar. To encourage her, he filled her cup with the wine he'd brought himself. Put a silver angel on the table, too, and nudged it slightly towards her. So she sat down on the bench and put a hand on his thigh. Just to be pleasant. Like you do.

He could ignore the paste of white lead and antimony she applied to appear elegantly made-up and to plaster over scars from the pox. With a stick of blue chalk, she'd sketched veins over the whitely powdered bosom, aping the ladies of the Court with their transparent complexions. Maybe she had seen a few of them once, coming out of the Rose after a play, fanning themselves with their stiff paper masks. The illusion was easy enough to maintain in the gloom of the brothel's common room.

"Not now, dear Drusilla," he said pleasantly. Lifting her hand from his leg, he gave it a kiss by way of a promise for another time. "Tell me more about this fellow Carew. I have some news for him, see."

Disappointed, she shrugged, but took his coin. No telling when she'd seen as much as ten shillings all at once. Then she put it in her mouth and brought it out wet, and slapped it on her bosom like a beauty patch.

Yes, well.

The story was simple enough, all in all. Young Simon Carew, freshly down from Cambridge, would end a few days every week drinking himself stupid, then shamble through the stews. Fell in through the Bishop's door, often as not. If he had the chinks, he'd take one of the girls and get it over with, all the whiles weeping and praying. The girls would go along with it, unless the swearing started, and the blows.

"Give our Portia a black eye, he did," said a simpering olive-skinned girl of about fifteen. She bent over the table, with one hand on Drusilla's shoulder, to put her cleavage at handsome Rankin's convenience. The older woman snarled and pushed back.

"Calpurnia, thou drab, break off!"

But the wench hadn't finished.

"Broke my arm, too, and me but a wee maid new come from the country. I never heard such swearing since my grand-dad died, God rot 'im. But I got him back. Poxed him, I did."

Already chuckling, Rankin nearly choked on his wine as she stuck her tongue out at Drusilla and flounced off.

"Ha! Oh, bloody gods below! Ha!"

"Then our Dickon," Drusilla went on. "You remember Wee Dickon, aye, 'course y'do—he'd roll him out the door. Or if he got sick all over everything, or pissed hisself, then we'd turn out his pockets first. Terrible thieves in this street, you know. Poor mad thing." She sighed, glancing heavenward, or possibly at the ceiling. "Never was 'ardly a groat on him by that time."

She'd gotten a bit of a faraway look, spoiled by the sidelong glance to see if he'd realized his ten-shilling sweetener was about used up. He had, but so, very likely, was her information. Rankin, never one to scrimp, pulled half a crown out of the woman's ear, and held it up bright and shining between his fingertips.

"Now, love, what can you tell me that will help me find him? Where might he go, if he could not go home?"

The eyes might be dulled with drink and long hours, lips chapped, hair coarse with bleaching, but the coin had her attention entirely. Then she looked away, as if it didn't matter. The one on her breast dropped into the shallow well of her bodice.

"Well, love, who can say in these terrible times? It happened some fine-looking fellows, they'd come for him. Said they was from the Palace, aye. Oh la, we all said, to have such friends as that!"

"The palace? The Queen's palace? What did they do with him?"

"God knoweth, not I, my dear. They tooken him away. He always come back, though, till that last time. Ain't seen him since."

"When was that, eh?" he asked with supernal calm. A sleepy smile lingered around his mouth even while he drained his wine.

Drusilla nodded, her eye still on the coin till he let her snatch it away to join the other one.

"Three years? Four? Ain't seen him in oh, a long time, your Simon Carew. Can't say we miss him."

And that was all there was to it, apparently, and little enough help. He was at the door, the woman already forgotten, when a screech turned him round again.

"Wait!" There stood Calpurnia, small and worldly.

"Wherefore?" Rankin asked under a lifted eyebrow. Down-at-heel boots, threadbare cuffs, a doublet that was old before the girl was born, still some things about him never altered.

She slunk into his shadow, one little hand brushing at the worn mockado over his chest, or maybe it was the silver buttons.

"No token for little Calpurnia?"

Both brows shot up, the unshaven chin tilted, bird-like.

"Hast something I want, love?" he said softly, though the noise in the place was fearsome. A quick breath lifted the impressive bosom, but his finger went up as a warning. "Something I can use to find this Carew?"

"Might be." She was already too old to be kittenish, not old enough yet to be clever. "No," she admitted, looking oddly troubled. "Just a thing he used to go on about. And mayhap, you being a man of reading and all, belike you'll know what it means. Never had no one to ask before."

An ordinary man, the men she was used to, would have struck her out of pure annoyance. Kindness ruled the faery prince tonight. He nodded, disarming her.

"Go on, love."

"You ever hear of a man with no soul?"

He frowned.

"Many a man hath lost his soul, girl, or plain given it away."

"Not lost 'is soul," she insisted, "nor not sold it like the man in that play. Never had one, see! Who ever heard of God makin' a man with no soul? It's what made him weep so. What's it mean, then, eh?"

Rankin touched her ravaged cheek, and put a shilling in her hand.

"Not a thing, sweeting. Not a thing."

Fleeing the Bishop of Rome, Raven took his bearings then sauntered along the bankside trying to balance his anger against cheerful thoughts of mayhem.

No soul. Young Martin had said the same thing. The man believed he had no soul. If he had no soul—which Raven was all too happy to credit—he couldn't sin according to the notions under which this age lived. That would explain the debauchery, and in some way, the murders. Sad, perhaps, but no less horrible.

Raven's own soul after the fruitless hours felt polluted with bad airs, unsavoury smells, grotesque colors all swirling through the muck of twisted thoughts and tawdry deeds. He wanted to dive into Faerie and bathe in fire and music. Even more he wanted to get Simon Carew under his hands, but he would settle for the sweet song of steel slithering out of his scabbard and a rousing punch up. Aye, he would.

Naturally, when he wanted a fight there was none to be found, not even in what was supposed to be the worst district in the city. At Paris Gardens he turned down the road, hopped a hedge into someone's orchard, and clambered into a pear tree, leaves and limbs still dripping from the day's rain. Not even a dog noticed.

Barely a shadow, he climbed higher into the sweet-smelling branches until he came nearly weightless to the very top, no more than a silver glimmer as the moon shook free of clouds.

His mind open, he let the airs flow and shift around him, as sweet for a few minutes as if they came from Faerie.

Refreshed, the Raven leapt above the trees on night-black wings, climbing, soaring to the clear air above the smokes and stinks that had assailed him all day. Gliding on currents of night, the wind streaming through rattling feathers, he could breathe again. The evil taste in his mouth and mind would not be sweetened until Carew had been taken care of, but he could breathe.

He crossed the river to perch for a while on the topmost spire of the Tower and exchange gossip with the local ravens that gathered there, wings as yet unclipped. Quickly bored with their domestic chatter, he moved on steeple by steeple to the damaged tower of St Paul's, the largest, highest building in London. It too provided no view of any use to him, and no news from the dim-witted pigeons. There was, in fact, no more news in the air than on the ground of a wicked man tormenting river girls.

Raven set out on one last flight surveying both banks; always a chance the monster might be skulking in some hole or creeping in among the night-soil men. If he came up empty, he would head over to Richmond to see how Ben was getting on.

As he expected, strafing the dung heaps showed him not a thing that shed so much as a flickering rush light on his mission, unless...

He caught a column of cooler air and rode it down a little south and west. That glow in Lambeth marsh might just mean something.

21
Ben on the River

After a briefly glorious flare of exuberance, the sun disappeared into the dismal cloud wrack still fringing the Thames Valley. Church bells tolled out the hour. Darkness closed in. London shut its gates.

Settling into the *Mary Ann's* stern end, Ben Harper arranged his sword alongside him, making sure the draw was clear and wouldn't tangle him in God-knows-what if he needed it. He had done this enough now that the movements came as easily as pulling over the seat belt in his Austin. Weary yet watchful, he slumped against the low back of the passenger's bench. The long strap of the sushi bag lay snug across his chest.

The tide outward bound, the wind onshore, the man through some invention of his own set up the wherry's lateen sail to ease their going, then bent to his oars, striving with little grunts against the current. Curious as to how it was managed, Ben didn't care quite enough to ask.

Westminster slipped behind them. The river swallowed up its noises, leaving only the creak of oars, the slap of water at the gunwales as the boat rose and fell in the tidal chop. The trip would be a long one in rough water till the tide changed.

Traffic plying upstream and down kept the river crowded for a good way with folk travelling home to families in Chelsea or Putney; gadding out to supper by torchlight; messengers sent with invitations or regrets; thieves, rogues, and cozeners whose day was just beginning. Swords rode light in scabbards, easy to hand for those moments when the slightest word became a mortal challenge.

With the Queen at Richmond, only the most essential services remained at Whitehall, including the unending job of scouring and cleansing a royal residence after its denizens in their hundreds withdrew. Most but not nearly all of its many windows had already gone dark. On the marshy south bank, a few lights bumped along, then those too extinguished.

Had an hour passed? Two hours? The further they got from the metropolis, the more they were surrounded by a curling, insinuating fog in which the passage of anything at all, the time or the shore, seemed to halt. The monotony had Ben drifting toward sleep, but mistrust kept him wakeful. He didn't quite trust the waterman—Wickit, the name was—to keep his purse and his throat uncut. Not that the man wasn't friendly enough, though he muttered a good deal.

Thinking music might pass the time, Ben fetched out the cittern, but the April chill had already worked into his fingers, and Wickit showed no interest. He put it away.

Ben shook himself and threw one edge of his cloak across the opposite shoulder while Wickit relentlessly rolled the oars in their locks. He seemed to be rowing through cloud, as if they had run aground on a foggy mountain top and teetered at the peak, even though the steady, hypnotic pull never ceased.

"How much longer?" Ben asked, to break the trance.

Eyes half glazed, the man replied without missing a beat.

"Till we're there, sir, by God's grace. Aye, not a minute afore nor a minute after."

"Soon enough, then, eh?"

With a grunt, a nod, and a gesture involving shoulder and chin, the man let Ben understand he should lend a hand and drop the sail and tie off the boom. Cold fingers and all, pierced by cold and damp, he fumbled through the procedures. To Wicket's satisfaction, apparently. Whether they sped along any faster was more than Ben knew.

On a whim, he fetched out the diary. There was a moon up

there somewhere, and a lantern bobbing on a rod behind him gave off a hazy glow, but nothing a man could read by. However, the diary being what it was, the words became clearer as he turned through the pages, as if they were drawing light out of the air. Wickit didn't seem to notice, tranced in a rowing world of his own, maybe.

On the first of the new pages, the day's adventures had been written up in a small, spikey hand, with the usual bizarre sense of humor and childish illustrations. One showed Ben swooning over Billy the Shake, Pop Idle. It was hard to tell if the goblins or whatever spirits were responsible actually understood a pointless play on words, or if their spelling was just that bad.

Damn, he was tired. All right, read that later. Next page.

The boat he rode in now was called a wherry, and was 22 feet long by... Was this really important now? Next!

In big block capitals in the middle of the next page, the three strange words from the Ata'rathi fragment: *RABBATU ATIRATU YAMMI.* As he watched, an unseen hand circled the words with a dark red line, round and round, then paused and added *! ! !* He could almost hear the sharp dot of the marker at the bottom of each one.

Okay, maybe he should pay attention to that. Ben rubbed his eyes and looked up.

Something had changed. The fog might be thinning, or they were riding closer to the shoreline. On his right, a dark line had appeared though still at a distance. The ride, though, was getting choppier, bumpier, the water slapping and splashing up the sides. The shore had begun to reappear, dotted with bobbing lanterns. A few lighted windows swam hazily in the misty distance. Ben searched the fog for nymphs, a friendly grin at the ready, but as none appeared he turned back to the book.

He read up on the current political scene from reproduced handbills, song sheets, and obscure excerpts from the Calendar of State Papers Domestic. Lord Burghley, Sir Robert Cecil, the rebellious earl of Essex; religion, faction, war in Ireland; yes, yes, he knew all that. Where was any mention of Silence Carew, or Lord Aubrey, or a map to the Mermaid Stair?

The fact that the lesson was included, though, gave him some pause. Cecil's paranoid government was not much like the Merrie England presented by even the most history-loving Renaissance re-enactments, but he had known that already. He didn't expect to fall afoul of the law in any way, so why should it matter? At the bottom of the page, new words appeared:

Don't ask, mortal boy, just learn!

A wavelet slapped hard against the side of the *Mary Ann*, rocking it beyond the usual.

"We've passed Kew, milord," said Wickit. "Richmond after. It's a big place, Richmond. Where shall I set your Worship down, then, eh?"

"Oh!"

Where indeed? As he started to snap the diary shut, a folded paper popped up from the back cover. Right! The pass from Sir Thomas Weston. Perfect.

"Palace stairs, of course."

"Of course, sir." But when he rested the oars, raising his head to meet Ben's eye, the withered face paled. "I'll take my fare now, sir, if it please you."

Another slap, and the boat rocking more radically.

"Jesu, master!" Wickit stammered. "What devilry is this?"

"What are you talking about?"

"There's light on yer face. Aye, and yer hands, too? And…" He was shuddering and backing away, through there was nowhere to go but over the side. "Who are you, then?"

No time to decipher the waterman's hysterics. Three gnarled, sucker-tipped fingers wrapped over the gunwale, green and black and dripping. Then another next to it, dragging the edge down to the water, slopping the river over the side.

"Christ save me! Jesu, help me! I'm bewitched!"

Two goggle eyes peeped over the gunwale, yellow bright as two moons, and a smiler's mouth full of pointed teeth.

"What the hell?" Ben cried, and snapped, "Hold!"

The thing froze grinning at him out of a wide face, and the waterman gasped. When the tapering end of a thick black tail flipped up over the thing's hands, Wicket's eyes rolled up in his head.

So did Ben's, though he didn't faint.

Now what?

He had no magic of his own, but he knew where to find some. Reaching out through the veils that divide the worlds, into a corner of the twilight realm, silently he called on favors owed him there, and felt a reply.

"Well?" The creature blinked froggy eyes. "What now, king's man?"

Three words rapped out of Ben's mouth before he knew they were there.

"*Rabbatu. Atiratu. Yammi!*"

The thing flinched but held fast, and its laughter was the dry rasp of broken glass.

"Those words not yours to use, human child."

"What are you? What do you want?"

It made no move towards him, though a pair of leathery wings erupted from its shoulder blades, beating counter to the rocking of the boat, keeping it balanced. The grotesque head bobbed in a kind of bow.

"*Llamhigyn* is me. The *Gwragedd Annwn* say come."

"The what?"

"The Lore Mothers of the Atami! You are called to council, king's man."

"What— You mean now?"

"Do what you must. Come when you may." It tipped a nod towards Wickit. "This mortal wakes."

Apprehensive but a deal more annoyed, Ben stood up and in one fluid motion drew his sword, finding his balance more easily than he expected. He hovered the rapier's point over the bulbous eyes. Time to get medieval, he thought with a smirk, just as Wickit leapt to consciousness, shrieking.

"Kill it, master! A' God's name, kill it!"

The monster seemed to shrug with the leathery wings, as if to say the show must go on.

"In Ata'rathi's name I say be gone. *Rabbatu atiratu yammi!*"

This time it worked, a bit. A white spark flashed from Ben's hand and travelled shimmering down the blade, faint but enough to make his point. With a crack, he brought it down across the thing's webbed fingers.

A strangled cry, and the *llamhigyn* fell away, snapping out the stinging tail like a whip as it uncoiled. It twisted in the air. The broad wings unfurled to their full span, and it flapped into the fog. The crackle of its laughter lent nothing to Ben's peace of mind, nor did the curious expression he would have sworn was a wink. Could a frog wink? But then it wasn't a frog, was it?

"'Swounds!" gasped Wickit, his swearing self again. "God's five bleeding wounds, man, art thou a witch or a priest? Or some cunning man?"

"What?"

Suddenly aware of the somewhat tippy nature of his heroic stance, Ben put away his sword and sat down hard, feeling drained. He had no time for the wherryman and his fears.

"Peace, man, 'twas naught. Words from a play I heard did but wake me from a dream. Say how much longer?"

Pale and shaking, Wickit scrambled to take up the oars again. A few hard pulls thrust them up and forward, gliding swiftly toward the fanciful, sparkling wedding cake that was Richmond Palace as it grew ever larger in their view.

Torches lined a long wooden dock, and stone pillars by the stair, lighting up a royal barge and other long boats draped in bunting diced in black and white. From the smell of gunpowder and ozone, there had there had been an attempt at fireworks on the opposite bank, spoiled by the mist. Wisps of smoke tailing into the light hovered like old campfires. Sure enough, a team in royal livery, specialists snapping at their apprentices and servants, were bundling up their pyromantic kit and staging them for orderly removal back to Blackfriars. Between the rain earlier, and the fog, and who knew what other fancy might have taken the Court's iron whim, they didn't look happy, and nor did the halberdiers in royal red and gold who lined the quay.

Another mighty pull or two from Wickit, as though he single-handed rowed a dragonship filled with Vikings, and the landing thrust out to meet them.

"Whoreson idiot madman!" Ben shouted. "Mind the stair!"

The man worked mightily to veer off, but it was too late. At the dock edge, three stout men with sturdy poles did their best to divert the prow. In seconds they were scrambling out of the way as the *Mary Ann* shoved its nose up and over the first two or three steps with a grating squeal and crunch. Wickit yelled, gloved hands pushed back, the boat's wooden bottom stuck fast across the granite.

"Master!" Wickit moaned one last time. "What was that thing?"

In the hands of half a dozen Yeomen of the Guard, a half-dozen silver ceremonial halberds had dropped into position, pointing right at them, eager to repel intruders.

Ceremonial? Well, they were gilded. And there was a lot of fringe.

Mildly, Sir Francis Browne asked, "What thing?"

22
Raven on Lambeth Marsh

There had been lights on the marsh where no lights ought to be. Now they were gone. The Raven banked, circled, rode the air until the lights appeared again, an undulant line as if in procession, hazy in the mist that hovered in the wetlands.

Another slow pass showed him something he had never imagined in a life long with joys and sorrows: nymphs in mourning—lissome girls and lithe, tow-headed boys, their faces normally lighted with laughter and careless song. They were accustomed to going about in the artless nudity of their nature, decorating themselves only if they chose in wisps of color and ribbons of mist, coroneted with lilies and wildflowers.

Now a train of naiads and nereids, some tall, some small as the silly girls of the Ravenbeck, with their lovers and brothers and goat-footed playmates, attended by moth-like flower faeries, had cloaked themselves in shadow, their weeping faces covered. They wore wreaths of pungent rosemary sprigged with dog roses, and carried branches of blossoming myrtle in their hands, so that they seemed a part of the marshland itself dancing a grim pavane. In the moonlight they glimmered, ghostlike.

Within the procession threading through the watered paths, a slim white body tarnished with silvery wounds shone palely under the crescent moon. It was covered with white flowers, and its hair like gold thread was knotted amongst the blossoms.

The Raven chose the path of his approach with care, alighting with a bird's hop and a man's step towards the leaders. Clad now, as they, in mourning to befit his rank and station, Raven stepped forward, a silver circlet like a new moon on his brow. The plaintive wailing of flutes in the ancient mode of the Atami floated on the air, and the irregular tapping of a drum. He held out his hand to beg their pardon, and the procession shuddered to a halt.

"Hail, lady," he said softly. "I am the King's Raven."

As one, the bearers stepped back into a graceful kind of reverence and rose again with downcast eyes; the bier they carried still rode level in their milk-white hands.

"Sadly met, my lord." The tallest nymph stepped out, almost as tall as he, a goddess on an antique vase. She followed the bier as chief mourner, a delicate creature with parchment roses in her cheeks. "I am Teifi, a sister to Tamesis. You honor us, but how come you here?"

"As I passed overhead on my lord's business, I saw you on this terrible journey. May I come with you? May I speak with you afterwards?"

She nodded gravely, and offered him a place beside her, which he took and paced along with them, leaving no prints in the grass. At last they came to a secluded pool of clear water deep in the marsh. The procession parted, the bearers moved through them and passed the bier to six others who stood up to their waists in the water. Without pause, they walked further in, until the still water closed over their burden, where they let it go, then bowed, resting their faces in their hands.

At Raven's thought, a tiny flame of the *fata morgana* burst from the water at the place where the tiny figure had disappeared, then arced out to tip the surrounding reeds with watery flame. One by one, the mourners' moth-like wings lifted and took them low over the marsh where they vanished into the mist, each with a little spark of light in farewell. Only a few remained: her sisters, and the tall river goddess in her reed pale gown.

"Pray tell me, noble lady, who you are and how this happened?" Raven said at last.

With a gesture, a tapestry woven with the image of the Three Graces carpeted the ground at their feet, and cushions for their comfort. The sound of plaintive music wound through the grasses, though that was not of his doing. He sat with them, and never minded as they wept, only wondering as he waited how Ben Harper fared.

"I am the Walbrook," said Teifi, naming the ancient stream that was her home and her especial charge, now bridged and vaulted over these hundred years or so. "But I come here to sing with my daughters."

The others broke off to give their names, little nymphs of boundaries, wells, and pools that met the great river or its tributaries here in the marsh.

He greeted them all and asked his question again. Nymphs, as he knew too well, are not given to sustained conversation at the best of times. Only patience would get anything sensible from them.

"Go on," he said, as gently as he could. "If you will. How come you to such mourning?"

"Oh, alas!" they all cried. "Alas for our sister!"

"A monster!"

"A demon!"

"A man," said Teifi, eldest and most focused of them all. "A man of the City came. He has come before, beset with demons of his own, troubled in his mind. He comes to do harm, though it makes no sense!"

"Why does it make no sense?"

"Because he has Atami blood himself! We do not make war upon our own kind, yet he is at war with us!"

It was rare that the Raven had no words, but it happened now, as clarity spilled through his mind, drawing together everything he had sensed but not understood since they'd arrived.

"Has he a name, this man?"

"All men have names, and so must he, but we do not know it. He says he is Silence," said Teifi.

"Yes," Raven hissed.

"His mother was Issa, our cousin in the south, whom men call the Dart."

Though he had heard the words and nodded, it was a long moment before they penetrated to his mind. And then they rocked him back as if he had taken a blow to the heart.

"Gods below!"

Silence Carew, a Dartmoor man with faerie blood. No wonder the Dart had wept! Raven's senses lurched as if he had touched cold iron. He swallowed hard to catch hold of the anger flooding his spirit and tarnishing the very blood in his veins with fire.

"Is there aught else you can tell me?" he asked.

Again the nymphs trilled their answers.

"He comes among us with a sweet voice and old spells!"

"And a poisoned knife! An iron knife, my lord!"

"An iron knife?" Oh, excellent. Tam had warned them.

"A monster!"

"A monster!"

"Ata'rathi protect us!"

Fresh tears flowed at her name.

"And what of his mother? And do you ever see her on the Atami Stair?"

"She goes there only to mourn for the son she lost, though she will not be comforted. The Lore Mothers do not understand her grief. Ata'rathi's charm is meant to last no more than a year and a day. She should have been free of it long ago. Perhaps…"

"What?"

"I think perhaps the child had already stolen her happiness. Ata'rathi gave us that charm for joy, but I think she should not have. No good has ever come of it that I know of."

As with any longer answer, the smaller nymphs listened and nodded at first, but quickly lost interest. Their eyes wandered, they whispered and giggled, exchanged kisses. They braided each other's hair with night flowers and colored stones, or twirled it through their fingers, their attention as brief as a mayfly's.

He hated to pose the next question, fearing the answers would be buried in new wailing.

"Tell me, what happens when he comes among you?"

Again he had to wait. It was simple really, and horrible to hear.

"He is a monster! He brings death to us all!"

"To us all!" The youngest one echoed, and hiccupped. Raven would have smiled at that, had the tale not been so horrific.

It took ages, but he eventually managed to pick out the whole story from the moans and tears and endless repetition. The man might come on them everywhere, it seemed. Not only here, but up and down Thames as far as a man could travel in a night and return by dawn. Sometimes even farther. At first, he waited to be spoken to, and answered politely, then paddled off in his little boat. He might find them again another time, and join their games. And if now and then one of the girls disappeared, no one suspected him. There are other wicked creatures in the dark places.

Now, said Teifi, he had changed. Ever more sure of himself, he lured the Atami girls to sport with him, singing their songs. Though some could tell he was hard, hard as a stone, and ran away, yet others would stay, curious as kittens And when they did, he caught them and bound them, and pricked them with his horrible knife and his hatred. And while they wept, he would laugh and curse them, raping away what they had offered him freely.

Broken, their little spirits flew to the Mermaid Stair where they walked for a time until, losing interest even in play, they let the fragrant breezes rising from the stream catch them, and at last they dissipated into the waters of Faerie. More often now the man unleashed a ferocity the Atami had no name for, and their sisters left the world outright.

So it was not just savage serial murder. It had become bloody torture, rape, and living death. Monster was the only word for this man. On a deep breath, Raven bit back the oath that would only frighten gentle Teifi and accomplish nothing.

Not much more to know. Carew had no power to travel in Faerie, nor any magic of his own, and he so far knew nothing of the Mermaid Stair. But he would know it soon, if he once stayed his hand long enough to listen.

"Listen? Does he ask you questions?"

"Two questions, and neither has an answer. They tell me, those who survive him, that he asks for someone called Oriana. It's quite ridiculous. That is a name I called my sister Cyfla long ago, for her golden hair. But none else would know it, and I would not tell it, so it cannot be she he seeks."

Raven smiled a little.

"It is a name they give the mortal queen in her golden palace, as well."

"Is it?" Tcifi brightened, her loveliness as suddenly restored as if the sun had risen on it. "She must be very beautiful!"

Raven thought of the aging Elizabeth, never pretty, though once handsome enough, living now on flattery and fear. He nodded.

"She is a queen. What is the other thing?"

She turned a look on him even more puzzled than before.

"He asks for the Mermaid Stair, but that also has no answer, for we never call it so. We say—" She warbled through a series of whistles and tones, then smiled again. "It is better under the water, of course."

"Of course. No one has told him this?"

The full lips trembled.

"Some say Issa came for him, very sad and very angry, when he killed our cousin Meropë. Perhaps she took him there. I only know that he has found his way there now."

"What day was that, my lady? How long ago!"

"I do not know, my lord!" she cried. "A day, many days? The moon may know but I do not!"

His hands reached for the starlit shoulders, but he wanted as much to shake her as to comfort her. So much time was already lost, so much life wasted. But it wasn't her fault, and she had given him so much already. And how should she know? What was a day or a passing year to a goddess whose life was as old as the earth? Instead he pulled her into his arms and held her while she wept.

⁎⁎⁎

Brooding in a patch of moonlight, Raven sat cross-legged on the tapestry until it melted for lack of notice into the grassy slope. After a very short time, since he seemed to have stopped asking them anything, the moth-winged nymphs fluttered up one by one and kissed him sweetly each on one cheek, and went away, already singing. A series of neat plops marked their return to the water, then only the frogs and a hunting fox, the sounds of the night.

Teifi stayed, still kneeling by him, and watched him for a while, admiring the handsome face creased in thought, charmed by his interest. By and by she took from her own neck a carcanet of plaited sea-green threads and bearing a disk of carnelian. On either side gleamed three golden beads of fluted amber so carved that they caught the light like small suns, and next to each one the face, exquisitely formed, of a sleeping lion. She looped it over his head and slipped the knots that closed it. Then she touched her fingers to his hair and pushed the long black curls back behind his ears.

When he looked into her eyes, he saw at once the flicker of intelligence that sets a guardian goddess apart from the self-involved mermaids and giddy water fae.

"Help us?" she whispered.

As she bent forward to kiss him, the fabric of her dress, of no more substance than moonbeams and starlight, opened across his skin like the finest silk, like nothing at all, yielding the satin curve of her breasts into his hands.

He kissed her firmly in return, surprising them both with a spark that neither expected. Almost shyly, when they parted, he pulled a dog rose out of somewhere and placed it in her palm, folding the fingers lightly over it.

His own eyes full of fire, "Lady, I will," he said.

Then it was time to go. Stars were swirling above the reeds that had nothing to do with the goddess. Ben was calling. He might have been calling for a while.

Maggie Secara

23
Ben at Richmond

Six quite competent-looking Yeomen guards glared down the shafts of their perfectly functional halberds, all pointed at Ben's chest. The shining steel heads delicately etched with floral tracery gleamed, he noticed with sudden clarity, razor sharp in the torchlight.

Their sergeant noted the livery badge on Ben's chest, finally, and asked his business with courtesy just as sharply honed.

"Uhm," said Ben. Another first. No one ever seemed to ask awkward questions when Raven was around. Whose idea was this again? He got to his feet a touch unsteadily. "I'm Lord Aubrey's man."

"I can see that."

Almost reluctantly, the sergeant gestured the guards to lift their weapons, which they did but otherwise maintained their watch on him. In annoyance, he waved two of them back to position at the gate.

"May I know your name and your business at the Palace tonight, sir? I was not advised of your coming."

"Were you not? I am Sir Francis Browne," he said and for the first time in his life, stammered a little as he said it. "I've been asked to play for the Queen's Grace at her supper. You see?" He hitched a finger around the satchel strap and hauled it up so they could see the cittern's dog-faced fingerboard sticking out of the corner like a bunch of celery.

"Is that so, sir?" said the sergeant, as polite as a cop at the side of the road and just about as sincere. "And pray, by whose authority?"

The question came with a gesture to abandon the broken *Mary Ann* and come up the stairs to the dock, which Ben did, cautiously.

"Authority! Ah, indeed, I have a paper from Sir Thomas Weston, if I may show it."

The sergeant, whose name turned out to be John Decker, examined the much-folded pass and invited Ben to come within the guardroom, where someone took it away presumably for verification. They also took his sword and hanger, his dagger, eating knife, and the purse chinking merrily with twenty silver crowns in half-crowns, shillings and testons. To discourage his wandering off, the man said. Decker even wrote him a receipt for the goods, including the purse, though not the money. Then he left him alone with only a man at the door.

Men came and went, but not with Francis Browne's name in their mouths. The sergeant left him for whatever it is sergeants of the guard do, setting a grim sort of man, the experienced sort, to keep an eye on him.

Apprehensive, too edgy to be bored, Ben rocked, clip-clop, on the wobbling three-legged stool they'd sat him on, and looked around. Plain stone walls, patched with damp; some stacked barrels, a table and a few chairs; a bench. Against the wall nearest him, a rack for pikes and halberds, including some less decorative, more merely serviceable items than those in current use with the Queen in residence. The one nearest him seemed to carry the brown stains of old blood caught in the braided scarlet collar, and a twisted strand of the fringe was blackened and flat with it. Ben looked away, cleared his throat, hummed a little.

The cittern on the table jangled every time anyone marched in or out, and once or twice on its own. He knew that sound, and allowed himself a small smile. The magic, reminding him it was there. Holding his breath, he took hold of the dog's-head and pulled it toward him. No one seemed to mind. A pretense of tuning, then some modest noodling about, mellow and melancholy, as suited the serious trouble he was in. No bawdy catch nor none of your frivolous dance tunes.

> *Time, cruel Time, canst thou subdue that brow*
> *That conquers all but thee, and thee too stays:*
> *As if she were exempt from scythe or bow*
> *From Love and years unsubject to decay?*

There were three more verses but he let them go, improvising for a while until gradually and in the wrong key it became the Atami tune, wordless but for the odd *fa-la-la*. Eventually, having made whatever impression on the universe it might, he modulated into something else, singing softly.

> *There were three ravens sat on a tree,*
> *down a down, hay down a-down*
> *There were three ravens sat on a tree,*
> *with a down.*
> *There were three ravens sat on a tree,*
> *They were as black as they might be.*
> *With a down, derry derry derry*
> *down, down.*

Outside, the guards chattered as men at an idle post do near the end of their duty. He could play and mind their conversations at the same time, but not sing while he was doing it, so again he left off. Over the last mouthful of sour humour, though, something in their tone changed, a mirthless laugh and a name grabbed Ben's ear.

"You've a rare voice, sir," said the sergeant, leaning in the door.

Ben raised his head.

"Gramercy, good sergeant," he said, and played a little more.

All at once he stopped and asked, as if it had just occurred to him:

"Look you, Sergeant. I have just come from Master Robert Cotton's house. He would speak for me. Is he known to you?"

"Aye, he is, and that beetling fellow his clerk, as well."

Perfect.

"Carew, isn't it? Aye, a frowning puritan by his looks."

A shudder seemed to grab Decker and shake him. He came all the way in to the room and opened a cupboard for a beaker and two battered cups. When he had poured them each a good drink of bad wine, he went on.

"Aye, faith, he's that and worse."

"And worse? How do you mean?"

The sergeant grunted and filled their cups again, meeting his guest's eyes as if he might read something there. Ben kept his expression cautiously interested. Huddled in the dark, the low mutter of flaring torches, the men grumbling at their posts, it felt like a night for confessions.

"He has some little business with the Court, this Carew. His master's business, I suppose. Letters and books and the like."

Ben had already marked him for a Londoner; the dropped h's and g's fairly littered the floor.

"As have I," said Francis Browne, shifting his own speech slightly to match without mocking. "And 'tis common enough."

"For most men." Decker squirmed a bit. "But other times we see him out on the river, a wee skiff and a sail, all alone. In all sorts of weathers. When he passes by in the fog, he's like a ghost, silent as the grave. But he returns, he might be singing and laughing like a drunkard, or else muttering, or wailing like as he'd been pinched by the faeries!"

"Faeries?"

"Well," said Decker. He leant forward with an air of intimate conspiracy. "Some of the men, they've heard voices with him. Sighing and moaning, too, or weeping betimes, as maybe a child or a woman were by him, yet when he come into sight, all alone he was."

"You've not heard any of this yourself, sir?"

"Not I!" the fellow snapped, and went to stir up the dying fire. "They're country lads, see. I've seen service in Flanders, I have, and fought a whiles in the Germanies when I was their age. I've seen enough true horrors not to conjure 'em out of river mist and beer."

Which meant, of course, that he had.

"What else do you know about this Carew?"

"Not a bloody thing, save he's unchancey. The lads all mislike him, the grey-faced, flap-ear'd knave. And that scar all down his left side, as he might have been touched by the Devil himself."

"Makes you wonder, doesn't it."

More wine poured out for them both, though Ben ignored his. Decker took a deep draught.

"Best not to wonder, sir. If he's doing aught on the river by day or by night, an it be not for Master Cotton nor the Devil, then it will be Sir Robert Cecil's work, and that's not for me to wonder at. But this Carew, he's no friend to you, Sir Francis Browne."

Ben's eyebrows shot up.

"Is he not? I have known him no more than half an hour in all the world. Not long enough to know his right side from his wrong one."

"He spoke your name to me when he came!"

"What? When was this?"

"When he came here not an hour before you. Said if you turned up, I should keep you and send word. And if he said that, then belike Cecil will be saying it too, for he is one of the Pygmy's informers. And so— And so, till my watch is ended, so you bide with me here till I know more."

"Am I under arrest?" The bright seam of panic edging Ben's voice was not all feigned. In a moment he was on his feet. "By God, that will not do. I serve a great man, his name protects me. By my life, Master Decker, how is it this miserable clerk speaks and his one word holds me here against my interest and my master's? Has he such power, this, this scribbler, this prating ass? Lord Aubrey put me forward, for his sake as well as mine! This should have been the making of me, don't you see? A post at Court, it might have meant."

Decker remained still, watching him more soberly than you'd think.

"Send for my lord. He will assure me to you! Or where is Sir Thomas Weston? Did you not send for him?"

The sergeant turned a wary eye in Browne's direction.

"Would that I could, sir. Would that I could, for he was a merry man."

Was? Uh-oh...

"But see'st thou, Sir Thomas Weston's dead."

"Dead!"

"Aye, a tavern brawl down in Kew. An accident, they say, as he was not much given to quarreling. If he writ that pass for you in June, he done it from his grave!"

"What, no! Nay, nay, nay, that cannot be. Not he! Then I have been cozened and lied to! For I swear to you, a man gave me that name and that paper in June..." He hiccupped on the memory, and sat down again, stunned.

Yes, it had been in June—in 1592. Three years ago. Before he could finish the thought, a light, reedy voice said, "Is this the fellow?"

A small man with huge black eyes, a pointed black beard, and an ebony walking stick had appeared in the guard house doorway, a sour expression on his narrow face. One shoulder surely was higher than the other, but the gossip had exaggerated, as usual. Hunchback was a strong word, maybe, for Sir Robert Cecil. Crooked, maybe not.

Decker was on his feet at once, with a kick at Ben to do the same.

"It is, Master Secretary. Sir Francis Browne, he says he is."

"And so I am. Sir."

"And a witch he is as well, milord!" came a screech from outside. Still babbling, Wickit the waterman flailed the wooden arm as he launched himself into the room.

"He's a witch, I say, 'tis true! I did see him read from a magical book right before my very eyes. He could read in the dark, he did, and that book, it made its own light, so it did. Then spoke some spell or other and called up a demon into my boat, and it grabbed for me, though I say my prayers and hear the sermon twice every Sunday."

Cecil glared at him, to no effect.

"Three times, sir! Three times of a Sunday, aye. Oh, a monster such as you have ne'er seen, sir! Like a vast toad it was, size of a mastiff! And it spoke, it spoke to him in some demon tongue!"

"You lie!" Browne snarled.

"An' then, then he banished it with a wave, like. A wave of 'is hand! And, and, and... Abracadabra, he said, like in the stories!"

"Oh, now you're just making things up," Browne said with disgust.

"Hark at him, Oh, let him not speak to you, my lords! It were witchcraft, sir, upon my very soul, foul witchcraft, that is Christ's own truth!"

"Get him out of here."

They dragged Wickit out, still testifying.

Well, that would explain the delay, the more than ordinary duty gossip, the men who came and went without explanation. The personal attention of the sergeant. On the report of not one mad man but two, word had gone all the way to the Queen's spymaster, her Secretary of State, in fact, who had finally found a moment to come down in person.

Ben snatched off his cap and gave a calculated reverence, clutching it in his hand as he rose.

"Recover yourself," said Cecil peremptorily. "Sit down."

So he did. It allowed the man, who was just about as small as history reported, to stand over him and look down on his prisoner, though clearly he would have mastered the room sitting or standing.

"Now," Robert Cecil said, leaning a little on his stick. "Do you know who I am?"

Browne gulped and controlled his trembling.

"I do."

Of course he did, as Cecil's expression seemed to say.

"And I know your name. But what are you?"

He hadn't had stage fright in years. All he could do was stay in character and hope to channel Errol Flynn.

"I'm Lord Aubrey's man, sir, as I told this fellow, the sergeant."

Clearly, the little man had severe doubts.

"I have never seen you among his gentlemen. No, you're a Browne of Sussex, I think. One of young Viscount Montague's countless—and Catholic—relations?"

Well, on most days, yes. But today...

"Catholic! Not I, sir, never a day since I was born. Why, the world is full of Brownes, and I..."

"Be quiet. And what are you to Lord Aubrey, if indeed you are anything to him at all?"

"I am a gentleman in his service, sir. Messenger, henchman, gentleman waiter, singing monkey. His musician, in other words." He gestured toward the cittern.

"Musicians have been traitors before now. Are you one?"

"Sir, I am not!" Francis Browne huffed with indignation. "As my lord will assure you. Send for Lord Aubrey, sir, and he will soon set it right."

"The right noble Lord Aubrey left Richmond at midday after the hunting was spoiled. A pity you did not know that. Your other supposed champion, Weston, lately died. If you are a spy or a traitor, I may say you are a very poor one."

Cecil nodded toward the confiscated satchel. "What's this trash?"

"Necessaries, sir," Decker snapped, not looking at Francis Browne. "Common cittern, that's clean enough, no papers inside or messages scratched on the back. Aye, I know that story, as do all true men. Some paper, pen and ink in a scrivener's case, fire steels, nothing much."

"And twenty crowns," Ben muttered bitterly.

That got Cecil's interest. Twenty crowns was a year's wages for some people, and a goodly amount for an honest nonentity to be carrying around.

"Have you so? Stand him up! And find this famous book." The Queen's secretary paced away while his bidding was done.

In seconds they had Browne slammed up against the granite wall with the breath and all the irony knocked out of him. The grit of the stone followed the pain into his scalp. Sweat trickled down his spine.

Well, he thought giddily, pat-down hasn't changed much in four hundred years, has it. Apart from the violence. He wondered what they'd find. There were always odd things in

Ben's pockets that came and went with him in various guises through Faerie and through time.

When they reached the diary, he gasped, then snapped his mouth shut, trying not to betray too much concern. It had managed its own camouflage in the past. The thug-at-arms, who was enjoying his job a little too much, snatched it from the doublet and handed it to his chief, who handed it to Cecil without even looking at it. The other guard went on shaking the contents of the neatly constructed Swadeshi all over the wine-stained table.

"Oi! Mind that!" Ben yelled, and got a fist in the gut for his pains.

Shoved to one side, the king of Faerie's cittern spun disregarded on its round belly and wobbled, till it walked itself off the table and crashed to the floor, jangling and twanging. It wouldn't be harmed, of course, but Ben winced all the same. Cecil didn't even glance up.

"No ear for music, I see," Ben wheezed. "Look you, those are Lord Aubrey's things that are in my charge. And, and mine own, too. Say if I am under arrest or no."

"Just assisting with our enquiries," Decker said with a thin smile that must have echoed down a few centuries.

With fastidious fingers, the Queen's secretary picked through the essential detritus of a life he knew nothing about and which, looking at it across the room, Ben wasn't sure he did either. He remembered matches, Mentos, the phone, socks and a shirt.

Robert Cecil found a flint and steel fire kit, as promised. A fuzzy thrum cap, a woolen scarf and a spare pair of nether stocks, and a linen shirt already worn and soiled in the damp creases. A packet of tobacco and a clay pipe.

You could watch the annoyance grow. No pamphlets, no rosary. Nothing seditious nor irreligious. Nothing in a vial or a paper that might be a poison, nor gloves or scarf where a poison might lurk. Nothing in short, that would give them any reason to hold Francis Browne longer. Not that they needed a reason. The witchcraft business would do as a last resort, but why bother?

Vexed, Cecil finally picked up the diary. With a quick gesture, he called for Wickit to be brought back in. This time, the man came cringing but furious as a beaten dog.

"Is this the book?"

"Eh, that wee thing? Nay, sir, nay, it were huge, a proper book, big as the Bible at St Paul's it were."

"So you have never seen this before?"

"Never before in all my life, yer worship, so Christ save me."

"Enough. Decker, give him something for his pains, and send him on his way."

"What about my boat?"

Cecil nodded curtly to another man who went out after them, then he returned his attention to the handsome, well-knit idiot in his custody. Francis Browne had been allowed to slump against the wall, but not to sit or, giving them credit, to fall. It was almost not worth pursuing, and other more pressing affairs awaited him. Doubt and native resentment niggled at him, though.

"This is what you were reading while Wicket rowed you up from London, is that correct?"

Surly and sick, Ben gave half a shrug, gritting his teeth. This had gotten way out of hand. It got worse when Cecil nodded his impatience, and the same enthusiastic thug threw the back of a gloved hand across Ben's jaw, rocking his head over the cold stone. The pain shot through his head and neck, locked the shoulders, radiated to hands that clenched and were still.

"Give his lordship a proper answer."

"Aye, your Honour, it is," gasped Francis Browne. What on earth was the man seeing in those pages? It couldn't possibly be what was really there.

"I would not have taken you for a man of such devotion."

Ben knew better than to react, he really did. It didn't help.

"What meaneth your Honour? You pick through my things like a raven, like a Raven I say, and expect me to know your mind?"

The hand that had grazed his mouth before was a closed fist this time, and Ben's head cracked against the wall. Stars filled his vision, pinpointing the pain.

Stars surrounding Mellis's face that swam into his vision.

Mellis's face smiling at him out of a mirror.

No, not a mirror— a damp patch like her silhouette on the opposite wall.

He shook his head and even the damp patch disappeared; no more than a crack in the stone.

All but three of the stars disappeared finally, and those darted here and there like hummingbirds, or dragonflies. Or like the tiniest faerie intelligencers he had ever seen. One by one, even they winked out. From somewhere, as always, came a hint of tiny laughter.

Then he knew what they had done, his wee helpers, and he almost laughed. They'd wrapped a clue into his concussion. Terrific. And if he was right about that, even if Raven didn't come when he was called, he might actually avoid arrest. Oh, surely Aubrey wouldn't let him die here. Would he?

Cecil was waiting.

God his head hurt. Where was I, he thought with a rueful shake of the head. Bad idea. His brain felt like it had come loose.

He winced, eyes closed, and said, "I cannot deny it. But what man likes to admit he is devoted to his own wife? People point at him in the streets. His friends laugh."

The beefy fist clenched where he could see it.

"For godsake, it is naught, only foolish verses. Bad sonnets and dog Latin, as surely your Honour can see. Pity my poor lass, she can't even read."

In the silence that followed, Ben wondered if he had guessed wrong, and counted the seconds the king's bloody Raven took in coming. Cecil flipped another page, and sneered.

"No man writes such drivel to his wife," he said. "I dare say you have a mistress among the… No, not among the Queen's ladies, or I would know of it. A kitchen maid, more like."

He fingered another page, and another. "Unless there are messages encoded here, of course. Or…" He managed a sharp bark meant to be a laugh. "Perhaps it is spells and cantrips, as the boatman says, hmm? Hidden in bad hexameters as an alchemist hides in metaphor."

The aching shoulders lifted expressively.

"Oh, prithee, not that tune again, your Honour. Had I drunk so much as that scurvy jack, that barnacle, I might have seen monsters, too."

Robert Cecil just stared at him out of those anthracite eyes, turning over this story in his mind. Clever, fine-featured men, straight-backed men, would be the death of him, unless he was theirs first.

So he turned from the wretched musician. He threw a glance at the captain of the guard he had brought with him.

"Take him."

Francis Browne howled as they laid hold of his arms.

"Nay, my lord! Do but send for Lord Aubrey. Aubrey, do you hear? Bloody Ravens, jacks, and daws! Fie, for bloody shame, now would be a good time!"

One of the three tiny lights reappeared with a tiny pop, and a half-heard sound of crystal chimes.

A guard shoved all his things back into the satchel to bring it along, and tripped over the cittern, then kicked it out of the way in irritation. The straight line of Cecil's mouth almost quirked into a smile. It probably was his smile.

"Enough!"

There was someone at the door.

The guardsmen fell back, hard hands still circling Ben's arms like steel bands. The tall figure, his white beard long and thin with great age, stepped firmly into the light. Ben Harper caught his breath, staring at another face he knew only from portraits.

William Cecil, Lord Burghley, it had to be. With his nightcap on and fur-lined dressing gown wrapped about him, he took in the scene: the wretched musician in custody with his livery coat half unbuttoned, the smug face of his favorite son doing the job he'd taught him. With another step it was clear whose arm he was leaning on—a broad-shouldered vision all in sober black edged with silver and pearl under a short furred gown.

Ben nearly fainted.

"Francis!"

Oberon's beautiful voice conveyed only sharp reproof, but warmth flowed from him like a wave.

"Let him go." That was Burghley, whose thin old voice still carried an undeniable command.

"Get up, by God. You shame me! Fitzroy, see to him."

The vice grips on Browne's arms suddenly loosed, but before he could fall, Raven was there to catch him with apologies in his sapphire eyes.

As the blood rushed into compressed tissues, Ben almost gasped, but caught himself. He concentrated instead on standing upright and looking contrite, smoothing back his hair, straightening his clothes. Touched away the trickle of blood under the bruised mouth and cheek.

"My lord!" Robert Cecil protested, caught off guard. His father didn't often over-rule or even question his activities, though he sometimes intruded with advice. This would seem to be all three come together.

Cecil was trying not to sputter while his father hushed him with a paternal wave.

"Indulge me, sir, an thou wilt. What stand you accused of, Master Browne?"

The hunchback glared over his crooked shoulder at the subject in question.

"Answer his lordship, sirrah!"

Ben caught his breath and a mental nudge from Aubrey.

"A-God's name, my lord, I know not! I was told to come and play for the Queen, as you know well, for I did crave your leave. I gave my pass. I must have forgot the date it was given me, but it did happen as I said it, on my oath!"

All true so far.

A lifted eyebrow, an arch look.

"Go on."

"And then a mad boatman befuddled in his drink tells these honest soldiers that I am a witch, mumbling spells like some old monk, though in sooth I never saw a monk in my life but once, and that at the end of my sword and he no monk at all but..."

"Be still," said Lord Burghley.

Ben gulped and stared at his hands.

"My lord Aubrey," the old man said slowly, so all would hear and understand him. "I do not know this man of yours, this Francis Browne."

"Sir, uhm, Francis Browne," Ben chirped, before his lordship could reply.

"Quiet, sirrah," Aubrey barked.

"No more do I, my lords," said Cecil, a bit stiffly. He glared briefly at Raven, whom it appeared he did know, then focussed on his parent alone. "Word came to me—"

Lord Aubrey was no more to be interrupted than Burghley, and his voice was stronger besides.

"He is a sound fellow, my lord, with an excellent voice and from time to time a merry wit, although today—" He lifted an open hand as if to say how hard it was to get good servants these days. "I shall have to find some fit employment for him, since he hath so little to do."

Busy enough, Raven was at his lordship's quiet direction gathering up Ben's things, the cittern and the satchel, and Ben's hat, locating his sword belt and dagger. And, oh yes, the diary.

"I'll have that." Lord Aubrey held out his hand.

Cecil found his opening, though clearly he hated explaining himself in to anyone, especially his father.

"I have examined it somewhat, my lord. It looks to be naught but a few bad sonnets, some songs writ out. But there is Latin there of a strange sort, and some other script, perhaps a cipher when used together. I had thought to send it to Doctor Dee, who I suspect will find more there than some doxy's trembling thighs."

"Oi! Those are my wife's trembling thighs!"

A pinch from the supporting hand on his elbow reminded him the gig was winding down. Let it go.

"No matter," he grumbled into his beard.

But no one marked him. Aubrey was paging through the book, a broad grin lighting the aquiline features.

"Latin, is it? Aye, you might call it that. Schoolroom jests and some vulgar turns of phrase passing for wit! Oh, Francis, such a shame, all that education drunken clean away."

His thumb holding the page, he handed the diary to Burghley, pointing out a couplet. The old statesman read it under his breath, and actually chuckled. Apart from the spymaster, pale with fury, the whole room relaxed.

The Lord Treasurer closed the little volume, remarked briefly on the nicety of its binding, and tossed it to Rafe Fitzroy. Sir Rafael Fitzroy, of course.

And it was over.

24
On the Stair

From Richmond Palace stairs, they clambered, stepped, or in Ben's case more or less fell into Lord Aubrey's waiting barge and pushed off. When his lordship touched the *morven* badge at the dock, no one marked it or would have cared if they had. Many thought it was a lucky charm, and often enough it was. As the barge with its faerie crew passed under the next bridge, Thames' flood took them straight to the river of Faerie.

The king took them to a rustic landing and a cabin with a pitched roof above and a broad porch in front, well supplied within. He stayed awhile, too, to hear their news, have a drink, and offer first aid. Aubrey remarked with some humour on the bruises even while his cool fingers soothed them away, along with the concussion, and anchored a loosened tooth. Whatever other harm Cecil's bully-boy had done went with them.

Leaving an admonition not to dawdle, his Grace reclaimed the cittern and left them alone. The whole story of how he had managed to get 75-year-old Lord Burghley out of bed and down to the scene in person would have to wait.

Hours later, clean and somewhat rested, and wearing his own clothes and name, Ben sat on the railed porch at a polished redwood table, breathing the sweet air, putting things in order. He'd already emptied his pockets. Holding his breath, he upended the Swadeshi bag and tipped out the contents, spreading it all out in front of him. And let go the breath. Even in haste, Raven had managed to gather up everything. Socks, matches, the silver flask, everything was here and in its proper shape. Ben the Organizer started again, repacking and reordering both his stuff and his thoughts.

Raven, who had gone out to walk under the dawn stars, sat on the porch step, looking refreshed but less than cheerful.

"Y'know," Ben began tentatively.

"Many things," said Raven. "For example, the London you love so much hath an awful stink."

The harper snorted a little and swore out of habit.

"You really are Robin Goodfellow, aren't you?"

"Nah, he's a story. I'm another shrewd and knavish sprite altogether."

And to prove the point, he scrambled to his feet, ran into the clearing and dived into the air, all broad black wings and bright blue eyes.

With something approaching envy, Ben watched his friend spiraling up and up into the blue air between the reaching tops of the redwoods, and wished that leaning his head back didn't stress the ache in his jaw so much. He still had grit in his scalp and thumbprints in his biceps that felt like they'd never go away, even after Aubrey's soothing. Being manhandled in a cold stone room was now high on his list of things never to do again.

Nevertheless, he thought, tying down the latchet on his bag with a firm jerk, he was glad to be back, however briefly, in jeans with a zipper and a jacket with snaps. And the king's efforts had eased the worst of his hurts. He could give the kid a break. The air was fragrant with growing things, balmy and...

But, it wasn't, really. A slight frown put a crease between his brows.

Something was wrong. When he listened, really listened, to the sounds around him, he flinched; the enchanted summer was becoming a brittle, discontented autumn. In fact, it was all decidedly seedy.

Some of the pines seemed almost smog-bitten, yellow-tipped and grey. Not many, but one or two might even be dead or dying. And though the water still hissed like flowing sugar across the granite planes of the creek bed, the level was shockingly low, the music discordant. If this really were the mountains above Santa Cruz in a drought year, that would make sense. But not here, not in any corner of Faerie.

While Raven took the air, Ben fried up bacon and scrambled some eggs from the cabin's well-stocked larder and got real food inside him for the first time in… Well, he didn't like to think about it. Back on the porch, he stabbed at the eggs while he rifled through the diary, hoping for something useful to jump out of all the nonsense. No new pages usually meant there was nothing new to say, and there were no new pages.

"Come on, come on, what's the point?" he muttered finally, throwing the fork down with a clatter. "How are we supposed to catch this guy? What am I missing?"

The book took a little hop.

From somewhere, tiny laughter exploded like shattering wine glasses. Just like at home.

"Very helpful."

Read! Read! Read! the voices exhorted.

It made him smile though. He pushed aside his empty plate, opened the book out flat on the table. Then he sat back, pretending patience. One by one the pages began to curl and flop over, as if turned by some unseen teacher for a particularly dull student. When they stopped on the picture of the amulet known as Three Suns and Three Lions, and again in the middle of the text of the third Atami charm, it was clear he had not been paying attention.

"D'oh!" To the utter tumble-in-the-grass delight of his wee friends, wherever they were, he dropped his forehead to the book's stitched spine.

The charms were there. In English. With the whole sorry text of the scroll, right in front him, each charm with an introduction and commentary from, by the heading, an English translation of the Latin transcription of the original Urgic-Akkadian, as rendered into Homeric Greek by the Author, 1916, from a damaged copy in the Cotton Library. It read:

The Last Charm

That a child of the Atami may love truly and with a full heart as do mortals, bind on a talisman of three suns and three lions, having employed the first charm if required, and sing these words in the Icthylean mode only. To use it otherwise is to invite great danger and even death.

And below that:

> *RABBATU ATIRATU YAMMI*
> *Be blood for burning,*
> *Soul for yearning,*
> *Home forsaking,*
> *Touched by lightning,*
> *Leave off sighing,*
> *Heart delighting.*
> *ATARGATIS ATA'RATHI ASHARA!*

Ben winced, but read it again, and the directions, too. Good verse or bad, the tune itself was of no matter, only the mode. Sing it in the wrong key, or for the wrong reason, and unspecified horrors await.

Eagerly he turned the page to find just five more words:

Contrary to the last, these

Raven found him still bent over the diary, making notes in the margins and talking to himself.

"No. No. Yes! Okay!"

When a booted foot creaked on the step, Ben sat back, the wire-frame glasses precariously poised at the very tip of his nose, the eyes behind them alight with intellectual delight.

"You don't look half pleased with yourself," Raven said. "Are you going to tell me what you've discovered, or are you content to be insufferable?"

"There's a fourth charm," Ben said with a certain smug flair.

"Insufferable, I see." The boy moseyed inside and came back out with a pair of ice cold Cokes from the fridge. Taking the other cane-bottom chair, he added. "You're joking."

"I might as well be, but I do have an idea."

"Ben, the scroll is gone."

"No, no, nothing to do with the scroll." The American waved that away. "We only need the scroll now because Carew has it, most of it, and wants the rest. What if there's another way to find him? Let me see that necklace a minute, the one Teifi gave you."

Raven's hand went to his throat, his expression unreadable. A heartbeat's hesitation, then it was over his head and in Ben's hand.

"Of course. Why?"

"What if like follows like?"

The medallion tingled like a mild electrical charge. He could already feel the tug of direction building in his chest as he explained what he'd read.

"Carew has one of these. I saw it on him at Cotton's house."

"Yes, so?"

"So…what if they resonate together in some way?"

The boy nodded, following his thought.

"Through time, though?"

"It's magic, Raven," he grinned.

"Indeed." Ageless, the fae still sported the mocking scar that floated under his eye. It stretched now as a slightly bitter smile creased his face. "But you have a date with the *Gwragedd Annwn*, remember?"

"Oh, that." Absently, Ben whipped off his glasses, cleaning them on his t-shirt. "Lore Mothers, you said. And who are they when they're at home?"

Waving one graceful hand generally, Raven said, "The old ones of the Atami, you could say. Sort of a high council. All female, not all friendly."

"I test very well with a female demographic," Ben said dryly. Glasses on again, he hefted the talisman, feeling a way opening tentatively in front of him. Thoughtful, he handed it back and got up to clear his plate and empty Coke bottles into the cottage.

"Do we recycle?" he called.

Raven snorted a laugh. "Naturally!"

Water ran, glass bottles clanked, and Ben reappeared,

flinging on the battered leather jacket. He touched the breast pocket to be sure of the diary, then shouldered the sushi bag and trotted down the steps.

"Old Ones," said Ben. "Just what I need. Do we know what they want?"

"I shudder to think."

"Or how to get there?"

"I'm pretty sure water is involved," the fae said wryly as he fell in beside his friend.

Ben was already striding not toward the river's edge but up the shady hill behind them. They pressed through ferns and Queen Anne's lace, painted their knees with goldenrod. Wild anise flung up licorice pollen to make him sneeze, but he didn't care. A songbird trilled overhead, cutting off as they approached.

Ben stopped.

"Did you hear that? Nearly everything is kind of, I don't know, off key. Listen!"

Raven listened, lifted an eyebrow, nodded.

"Yes. Although—"

"Exactly." Ben launched forward again, following the chatter of running water. "So there's got to be a…"

With firm hands, he pushed aside a screen of pale green shafts, and there it was: a low waterfall sheeting over a single shelf of stone into a shallow pool. Here the music of the Stair rang unmistakably true.

"That's better." Ben turned to find Raven, hip cocked, head tilted with bright-eyed interest.

"And now?"

"Water. Mothers. Answers. This is an invitation, right, not a command?"

The boy shrugged. "If you like."

Gingerly, Ben put one foot on a submerged stone, felt icy water rock it under his shoe, then dared to advance the other.

"All right. In the water. What next?"

"Me? I'd start with giving a close friend my kit bag."

Grinning, Ben handed over the Swadeshi.

"And then?"

"And then I would go back to Thames and start there."

"But why, my lord?" a flowery voice enquired. A glaistig rose up out of the base of the waterfall, all silver raindrop hair and pale blue gown forming out of the droplets like a film of diamonds. "Why, when you have a friend to guide you?"

Ben peered at the creature— a challenge when its mostly transparent form altered with every moment. Even its eyes and mouth were an illusion, an accident of the flowers and foliage seen through leaping water.

"Friends, lady?" he said politely.

"Oh, Ben!" She giggled like a starlet, and seemed to toy with her hair. "I'm crushed you don't remember. There was a revel. I was sent to bring you by way of a maze. You made such wonderful music that night, you and the Lord Oberon and all your friends. You played Greensleeves for me."

Standing in the water he squinted at the changeable nymph, or demon, or whatever she was.

"Gaezel?"

That made her laugh with tinkling delight, and step out of the mist into a somewhat more substantial form. Her gown, like her hair, puddled in silver blue bubbles at her feet where she stood among the stargazers.

"Sweetheart," said Raven wryly. "We have no time for reminiscence."

"You," she sniffed, "I am not so fond of. However, I can help you and I will. The nymphs are my sisters, too, you know."

"Are they?" the boy said under a sharply arched brow.

She ignored him.

"You will need the mermaid's girdle, Ben Harper, if you mean to talk to the Mothers. They cannot come to you."

"And what is that?"

She shrugged with the pout Ben remembered, and leaned toward him in the provocative sort of Jessica Rabbit way he also recalled. Then she reached in among the lily pads and brought out, dripping with water and moss, a long plait of fresh green reeds or grasses starred with yellow flowers, and hung with reddish pods and green berries. She held it out to him, letting it dangle from the ends of her fingers as graceful as a smile.

Oddly, this gesture did not make him more trusting.

"Very pretty," Ben said doubtfully. "And what will that do?"

"In theory," Raven said, not to be left out, "it will allow you to bide under the water for a time, breathing and talking, even walking as if in the open air. But only for a time."

Gaezel scowled, annoyed with his lordship, but she turned only a sunny smile on Ben.

"Exactly," she said.

When she said nothing more, Raven drawled,

"Ask her for how long."

Ben asked her.

Simpering just a little, she said, "Is it called an hour? I think so. Oh, what do I know of your passing time!"

If she could have stamped her little foot, she surely would have.

"And after that," said Raven, "you will drown, human child, so do not let them keep you."

"You're silly. What does a Raven know? As if the Mothers would do such a thing!"

"Sweet girl, half your people are good and lovely guardians of lakes and streams and bridges. The other half drag children under those bridges and drown them for their sport."

"How different from your Dartmoor pixies, then?"

"All will be well, so long as you wrap this about your waist and let none untie the knot."

The glaistig knelt to bind the braided vines around his middle, tying it off with a weedy bow. She finished by rising up to press cold lips to his mouth. Gently but firmly he pushed her away, remembering sharp teeth.

"An hour only, Ben Harper," Raven said around a grim smile. "And remember your manners."

"What do you mean?" Ben said,

"I said, remember…"

The girl's hands slipped from his neck, touched his forehead.

With a shout that nearly gagged him he fell, and swiftly dropped through swirling waters as though through open air.

It was a shallow creek, he thought. How deep could it be? Or was that a foolish question? Unlike the journey to the *Gates of Dawn*, he had no escort. The music that surrounded him drew him on with no sense of bliss or seduction, only a gentle command in a voice like his mother's, the song as familiar as a lullaby.

Words slipping past his mind resolved themselves at last, and whether it were wise or no, he began first to hum along, and then to sing:

> *Full fathom five thy Father lies,*
> *Of his bones are coral made:*
> *Those are pearls that were his eyes,*
> *Nothing of him that doth fade,*
> *But doth suffer a sea-change*
> *Into something rich & strange:*

Then he realized he wasn't so much singing as holding his breath and thinking about singing, and it was making him giddy.

> *Sea-Nymphs hourly ring his knell.*
> *Hark now I hear them, ding-dong-bell.*

25

Lyonesse

So he breathed. Yes, that worked, though it was like falling through the stairwell of the university music building, a jangling concert of instruments running scales, singers vocalizing, jazz band and Django Reinhart jamming in a set over a basso continuo line of monkish chant. Like that, and not like that at all.

His head was spinning again.

For a while he passed through a space where all was dark, and Ben's sense of time, already distorted, completely abandoned him. Panic followed. He only had an hour. How was he supposed to know when his time was up? It already felt as if that much time had passed. Was he drowning already? Had he been tricked? Raven wouldn't have let that happen, but the boy had little experience of the Atami. And the glaistig was not known to be the most gentle of her kind. In fact, weren't the glaistig among those who tempted young men under bridges and drowned them for their sport?

Remember to breathe, human child, Raven's voice murmured in his head. *I am with you.*

Sure, okay.

Trust the water, and trust me.

Then gently, light began to grow. Not sunlight, but sparkles first then bobbing lanterns and glowing jewels revealed a cavern walled in pearl, creamy pink and white and shadowed in mottled grey, roofed in vaulted green as if abalone of impossible size had given their shells to build a palace. And within those halls, he began to see the outlines of a city like those of men, timber-framed houses with their chimney pots streaming, and slate-roofed shops, winding streets, and behind them all, the square tower of a church. He imagined he could smell flowers and mown grass in the pasture beyond.

His feet alighted at last in a cobbled square into which, though it seemed a long blue twilight in summer, the folk who came to watch him swam in and out the windows. Men and maids both on great blue-green tails. As in every village in Europe, at the center of the square a tall obelisk noted the fall of soldiers in wars long past. Raven's voice whispering in his ear told him so, for the carved words were long lost.

This is a village of Lyonesse. It was taken by the sea long ago.

How are you even here? What are you seeing?

My lord bade me come with you, and so I have. Look about you, I can see what you see, and I will hear what you say and hear.

Oh. Good. I'm a camera. Where are you?

With Father Tam, on the houseboat. I can only see what you look at directly, so do try to stay focused. I will be here, but there is little I can do.

You can stay in sight of a clock, mate. How much time do I have?

You have been gone no more than a few minutes, so Tamesis says. Never fear, he is aware of all that passes in the waters. Hush now, and keep your wits about you.

He had company, in other words, but he was on his own. The lofty diction alone told him that. So he waited by the obelisk with the old Atami melody once again running through his mind. Atami of all sorts seemed to be playing, marketing and gossiping, mimicking in some way the lives of the land folk who had once populated this village. A very young mermaid with a dainty trident herded a shoal of—were they fish?—past the obelisk like a family of ducks going to market. Others looked towards him but without curiosity.

"Ben Harper!" said a clicking, gentle sort of voice, and a

shape began to resolve in front of him out of the dim jewel light. Not a mermaid, this one, but a fair lady like a Roman goddess in a mosaic. Skirted in silken draperies in the classical style, her bosom was hung with ropes of pearls, her hair dressed with woven braids drifting above her shoulders, and knotted with flowers. Her name came to him in Raven's thought: *Amphitrite, Poseidon's consort.*

Without faerie glamour to provide otherwise, Ben's clothes here were his own, but even so, he kissed his hand to her and gave a reverence as if he were dressed for Court with a rapier at his side. She nodded, seeming to approve.

"You are welcome to our halls, king's man," she said. "We have been longing to speak with you."

Behind her he began to see a half-circle of chairs, thrones really, of shell and pearl and coral. And in each one, a figure: light or dark, nobly made or grotesquely patched and colored by the deep seas, and no telling which meant him well or ill.

The Lore Mothers.

Ben wondered what it must be like on Raven's end. Had Father Tam rigged the television so he could watch too? Magic is a funny thing in the modern world. Anything was possible.

For pity's sake, pay attention!

Amphitrite was watching him, assessing his quality.

"We are Ata'rathi's daughters, that some call Gwragedd Annwn," she said, gesturing to the figures enthroned behind her.

She gave them no names, but Raven did where he could: Mermaid, River Sprite, and Undine; a Selkie with her sealskin loose around her waist like a wetsuit. There were nymphs of clear waters and dark ones as well: Nixie and Lorelei, long-nosed Kelpie shaking out her straight black mane, Uriskean of the lonely pool, and a green-eyed Merrow whose smile opened over needle teeth. When the old charms called on the mothers of the Atami, these were the spirits they meant.

Ben bowed again.

"You are known to us, human child," said the goddess, her deep green eyes dull with sorrow. "And we know your mission.

A monster is loose among us, and our children are dying."

He waited, lifting his chin to show he was listening.

"He comes upon them by guile, and we are powerless."

"Not all of us!" the Merrow cried with what might have been glee. "Let him come to me or mine, that will be the last of him!"

The shabby creature behind her cackled aloud, displaying a maw slick with green moss.

Jenny Greenteeth?

Hm?

Later.

More voices chimed in, the darkest being the loudest. What was the big deal, they wondered. A few silly girls, useless at best. And in the meantime, the dark places could protect their own.

The Mermaid, distracted from her mirror, shrieked in reply, chittering like a dolphin. Raven declined to translate except in the most general way, and eventually the arguments fell away.

The goddess went on.

"He carries death with him in his anger and the iron weapon that burns and tears apart even an immortal's soul! What magic do you bring that we have not?"

In the ringing silence that followed, Ben Harper spread his hands and answered plainly.

"I find things, lady, if they can be found. I can hear their songs."

Muttering and fluttering from the Mothers, and a Lorelei's bark of laughter for punctuation. Then Amphitrite raised her hand for silence and got it, sudden and stark.

"The Star of the Sea asked you to find Cyfla, her daughter, whom your people call the Fleet."

"Yes, ma'am," he said, pushing up his glasses with irritation. Did she think they had been lounging around drinking beer all week? "I know that."

She nodded with queenly tolerance.

"We thought perhaps you had forgotten."

"I—"

Manners!

Maggie Secara

Reining in his temper, Ben cleared his throat and began again.

"Madam, we have been chasing a murderer."

"And you have not found him."

"No," he answered stiffly, "but we have a trail to follow."

"Follow, but never catch."

"Lady, I have a wife at home to scold me."

Ancient eyes flashed, the haughty chin came up. The goddess spun on her heel and strode to the empty chair in the midst of the others, stirring up a train of lights in the wake of her silken hem: darting fishes, spiral shells, the sparkling sands of the chamber floor.

Nice move.

"The guardian of one lost river," Ben went on, "can't be more important than finding the man who's killing them all."

She paused at the top of the dais, her figure misted as if in the finest silk.

"And you believe this man is the key?"

"I'm sorry?"

"Are you?"

"Madam!"

Seriously?

A flock of bright yellow fish, too tropical for an English river, swarmed between them like a cloud of mosquitos. Something was nudging him from behind, nibbling the flowered cords at his waist. He waited impatiently for the one, and smacked away the other. Scaly fingers smacked him back. Fingers?

Ben sputtered, "We know he is the killer. What other key is there?"

"You have had dreams," the Mermaid trilled.

"And a song!" barked the Selkie mother.

The shy Uriskean stood up to agree out of the spikey tangle of her hair, but shrank back in aprehension. The air, if it was air, grew grey with spangled clouds as tempers flared, their voices a tuneless shrill of whistles and pops, strange words that seemed to draw the air from his lungs.

He heard, or saw, a Highland voice sing out, "You have our

talisman, the suns and lions!"

Startled, he stepped back and slipped on an oyster shell, stumbled on an unexpected drift, and tumbled into shadow, a darkness that snatched at his breath as it drove Ben down. He went to his knees with a sense of deep oceans and bone crushing pressure. A shape even darker shimmered within it, a hollow voice intoned,

"And no hope."

No!

A flare of power true as an arrow flew through his mind on a single bell-like note. The darkness flared, collapsed, and withdrew.

Head pounding but breathing more easily, Ben scrambled to his feet. He could feel the girdle's grasses sharp-edged, almost brittle when one hand brushed across it. The glowing hall between the nacreous walls seemed to have grown dull, the lanterns flickered as if the music that made them had slipped out of tune. All wavered while their songs and their snarling laughter, their anger and placid arrogance tore at the air and whatever Ben Harper had left of patience and courtesy.

Why are they wasting time?

Because they're immortal?

You're not!

I am quite aware. Time?

Is of the essence, yes.

No kidding. How much time?

Hurry.

Badgered, terrorized, and heartsick, Ben had been weary when they started. Now he had a raging headache from being the target of one kind of hard magic and the impromptu vector for another. Maybe the attack and the raven-boy's swift response had left him especially sensitive to the enchantments all around him. Maybe it was only his innate sense of order being violated.

Whatever, a vibration had begun to thrum under his feet like the rumble of a ship's engine, not so sharp as a tremor, but not a comfortable feeling to a man brought up in earthquake country. The Lore Mothers had raised this hall over the drowned village, and they would bring it down unless they left off tangling the magic with their quarrel. And not one of them appeared to notice.

What can I do?

What you always do.

Heart pounding, he wanted to shout, to tell them to shut up and look to their handiwork before the walls fell, but he knew they would never listen. Hell, they would never even hear him. Unless…

He began to sing, refitting their own words to the old tune.

> *Hark now, harken now*
> *To the waters of the sea*
> *where all hearts return,*
> *the first home, the deep unknown.*
> *O peace, let there be peace*
> *With the Atami in their home.*

And when he felt that begin to distract a heart or two, adapting others. Ben could feel the warmth of Raven's pleasure and approval, lending what support he could, content to let Ben direct the magic as he found it.

The music welled up in him and through him, and somehow, his pleasant baritone wound and looped through the hollows of the Mothers' wrangling, reaching onto the dais and into the hall.

> *Rest sweet nymphs, let golden sleep*
> *Charm your star bright eyes*
> *While my lute the watch doth keep*
> *With pleasing sympathies.*
> *Sleep sweetly, sleep sweetly, let nothing affright ye*
> *In calm contentments lie.*

Threads of melody touched up the glow, brightened the air until gradually the flickering forces steadied along with those primordial tempers, bracing the vaults of the ceiling. Shortly it came to him that even the gilded floor had stilled, the golden sands settled. Startled, a sloe-eyed face popped up to stare at him through the spangled mist, and then another.

When he stopped at last and the echoes died, a dozen pairs of eyes, jewelled or scaled, melancholy, fierce, or simply mocking, were blinking at him. Astonished, he guessed, to find him in their living room, their music in his mouth, with something too much like magic at his mortal command. He hoped they wouldn't ask him to explain it.

In their midst sat Amphitrite, sunken down and looking grim, beringed hands draped over the sea-lion arms of her chair. As the air between them cleared, she raised her head and met his eyes at last.

"What do you want from us, human child?" she said, more coolly than he had expected.

"My lady, you sent for me," he said, returning the attitude. "Why?"

"To answer your questions. That is one."

"Out of three, of course."

Great, the usual faerie games.

"Very well," he said, then paused, and cleared his throat. The air, spangled or still, felt thinner than before, and his breath more labored than it had while singing. Raven could not breathe for him. Precision was his only hope now.

"First, the man, Carew. The killer. We know he is Issa's son by a human blacksmith."

The suppressed response, including the tittering, indicated it had not been common knowledge, though Amphitrite nodded slightly. She raised that commanding hand again, and they quieted.

"We know."

"Is Carew immortal? Or rather, can we kill him, or must we find some other way to stop him?"

Good one!

A chill set in as she considered, and with it, the gathering sense of a wave drawn back, suspended like Hokusai's over the sea of her thought. Behind her, some of the Mothers nodded. Others shrugged. One, the Riverine Nymph, shook her head emphatically.

Watching them, Ben sensed a prying hand at the Atami

girdle and batted it away. Shattered flower petals drifted to the sand as lightly as through water.

At last, Amphitrite said, "I know this much. Issa bound him as a child with three suns and three lions and sang the third charm over him. She hoped, I believe, to spare him the pangs of love and loss. It only hardened his heart, to her, to our world, even to his own. His father taught him resentment, and his priests taught him fear."

"He believes that because he is half-Atami, he has no soul," said Ben.

The grey eyes widened, almost crinkling at the corners in what might have been humour, until Ben went on. Biting back the growing cold, he pushed the next words out in his best podium voice.

"He believes that killing you all—all—will make his god give him a soul as a reward. Madam, can we kill him, or does his Atami nature prevent it?"

Tight-lipped, all humour fled, Amphitrite flung herself from the chair and marched to him, tall and naked in her power and her anger.

"He denies his Atami nature," she said harshly, "and so do we. Kill him."

Finally! Quick as you can.

They were shouting again but, weak with relief, Ben didn't mind. In the seconds before the goddess brought them to heel, he could gather his thoughts, form the right question, breathe. When she did, he was ready.

"For the last, we know that Carew has somehow learned of the Atami Stair."

At this news, even hooded eyes flashed, but none looked away.

"And he is using it to travel into both past and future. I believe he is seeking Ata'rathi's scroll in a time when it was new, or nearly so—new and not a copy. He thinks it contains spells for your destruction. If he keeps on tearing at the Stair in this way, he could be right."

That pulled gasps even from the most arrogant of the Mothers. However little they cared about the murders, some things were sacred even to the darkest.

"It is true!" said the Kelpie, her voice the mutter of galloping horses. "The stair is breaking."

Amphitrite said, "You must stop him."

Start wrapping it up, Holmes. Ready or not.

"My lady, we can't keep chasing him on his own terms. You said it yourself. We can follow him, but not predict his movements. We find nothing but disaster."

"Then you must get ahead of him, human child. Outwit him."

"Yes!" he said, hoping not to sound hysterical. "He wants the scroll. If I knew where it was, or is, or the first place in time when it came into in England…"

Tam says three minutes.

It took longer than that to get here!

"Yes," said Amphitrite. "You must draw him to you, yes."

"Lady, of your grace, tell me how."

She turned away and strode into the circle of her sisters, talking or singing or something.

Ben's breath came quick and short; a growing pressure beat at his ears and his heart. Beyond the precincts of the hall, the drowned village had grown dark and empty, unless his eyes were failing too. The only light radiated from the opalescent walls.

When he felt the interfering hand at his waist, he grabbed the wrist and whipped round to meet mossy green teeth in a face like a shrunken head: the Merrow's weird attendant. With a cry of disgust, he flung her off. Bubbles trailed behind her as she flew back cackling with fragments of the seaweed girdle disintegrating in her wake. His heart stumbled in his chest.

Hurry!

I can barely breathe. How do I get out of here?

When you feel my hand, take it.

The sea goddess, Poseidon's consort, turned back to him, looking slightly more sly than she had before.

"Find Cyfla."

"My lady, that's no answer!"

Did she want him to fail?

He watched her expression change to one of alarm, and felt the sea assert itself, the wave release, reclaiming Lyonesse.

"Go to the Roman city!" he heard her cry as if from far off. "Find Cyfla."

Ben! Now!

A long-fingered grip wrapped his wrist. Ben latched on, and gulped the last mouthful of bitter air.

And the walls fell.

26
Wednesday: Gates of Dawn

The trip back was quicker than the descent, and Ben wasn't sure whether he closed his eyes or blacked out. Either way, a white-hot pain pierced his head like a ten-penny nail as he broke the surface and cried out, gasping.

And then he was awake, face half-buried in a pillow. The smell of pure linen hit him first, rich and sweet as a rainy day; then the cool, crisp slide of sheets over his skin. Groaning he rolled over into a cave—no, a painted box—under a wavering light so grey he thought at first he was still under the water.

He felt around for his glasses. Found them hooked through a tasseled lamp cord on the wall. Slid them on, and blinked. Evidently he'd been put to bed in a kind of cupboard: the wood panelled walls washed with lime, the arched ceiling dotted with six-pointed stars like an Egyptian tomb. Thankfully, one long side was open, though curtained with lengths of colored silk, stitched with crystals and tiny bells that chimed faintly as they swayed.

The light, however, hinted strongly at England, as did the persistent patter on the roof. A gentle rocking suggested, to Ben's relief, that he was on top of the water after all. Nearby, a mellow music worked at the pain in his head, rolled it up and stuffed it in a corner taming the residual effects of channeling so much magic.

Pushing up on his elbows, he squinted through the ribbons, then swept them aside. A few feet away, perched cross-legged on a low, padded bench, Raven bent over a guitar as if he had just left off playing.

"Welcome back," he said.

"Uhm, have I been doing magic?"

Raven smiled slightly, and pushed an errant curl behind an ear.

"Have you?"

Shaking his head in confusion, Ben sat up and swung his feet to the floor.

"Okay, fine," he tried to say, then cleared his throat and tried again. "We really have to work on our exits."

"I don't know. I think we're getting better."

"Hm."

A pile of clothes, clean, dry and thoroughly mundane, waited for him on a fold-down shelf. He reached for the jeans.

"So, where are we?"

"*Gates of Dawn.*"

A swift glance took in the slanted upper walls, the folding doors, the electric fire in the corner of the narrow room.

"This is a canal boat."

"Well spotted," Raven agreed with a slight nod. "Coffee?"

No good saying that it was near to hand. Everything was. Paddy Casey's narrowboat had been the same.

"Yes." Ben wrapped his fingers through the handle, sipping gratefully, daring the headache to come back. "How long have I been out?"

"An hour, maybe."

Buttoning the 501s, Ben thought about that and a few other things.

"What's a nymphaeum?"

"A temple, like. More of a chapel really. To the nymphs of a spring or a river. Why?"

"I'm not sure—something I heard in the background, I think. And the Roman city?"

"Well, we start with Rome, see, and…"

At Ben's look of alarm, Raven snorted and picked up his own mug of whatever he was drinking.

"Do you know how many cities there are in the Roman Empire?"

In answer, a pulse like a tropical wave rolled the deck under them and pressed into the room, and took shape as a deep, glad voice intoned,

"Londinium."

"Sir?" said Ben. He grabbed a t-shirt as he hopped down.

"It is the only sensible answer," said Tamesis, filling the doorway. "There is no nymphaeum in your modern city."

"Amphitrite couldn't have just said that?"

The river god's shrug was fluid and eloquent.

"The Ladies are inclined to be obscure. You handled them well, Mr Harper, in spite of their games. The young king's opinion of you is well founded."

Ben nodded, modestly pleased. He wondered what that meant exactly, but decided to let it go.

"What next?"

"You must relax, make some music, practise your Latin."

"Excuse me?" The American managed to put the coffee down without spilling much. "Latin?"

"The Romans occupied Britain for four hundred years. Our Raven, I'm told, gives you all manner of English when you travel together, but you will want some practice for a time where no trace of that tongue yet exists in this island."

"More wasted time," Ben grumbled into his coffee.

Raven laughed.

"Then don't tarry. Work to do." He disappeared, snickering, "The young king!"

Arms over his head, half-in half-out of a faded Born in the USA t-shirt, Ben stopped and let out a whoop.

"Damn! Shakespeare!"

Latin. They ran vocabulary drills after breakfast, and afterwards bellowed out Goliard songs for practice while Tamesis manoeuvred *Gates of Dawn* through time in his own timeless way.

With Raven's grudging permission and Father Tam's help, Ben restrung the Atami talisman so he could bind it around his left arm. The pendant amulet now lay hidden under a sleeve, comfortably flat against the pulse of his wrist.

The diary had said the form of the suns and lions made no difference. He hoped that was true, because he had only one idea to work with. If he could tune his gift to the amulet, and the amulet to its goal, it might reach out to Carew's jewel and home in on the exact right time and place. Raven could help him focus, but the burden was on Ben to make it work. So far, the carnelian disk had warmed, tingled, even hummed, but otherwise told him nothing sure.

He could track their progress through an endless twilight as the canal boat altered from power to tow-path to sail, at last to a kind of galley rowed by rough-looking men while the Thames itself grew broader, slower. With their passage, a tinkling music like a gentle breeze passing through wind chimes kept them company, tuneless and constantly changing. He was missing something, but what?

Wearing the generic tunics and leggings that had served common men for a thousand years, Raven fished over the side, while Ben, sitting cross-legged on the captain's deck, laid the diary on his knee, scowling. His little helpers, whoever they were, had written up the latest pages in what he hoped was decent Latin. Well, decent meaning as vulgar as ever, scrawled over the pages like Roman graffiti. Which it probably was. At least the Latin that Raven had been pouring into him was coming easily now, and he could tell a bad joke from useful information.

That wasn't the problem. Even the persistent pain in his head was tolerable, if annoying. No, the problem was that for the first time, magic or not, the map they'd made for him was utterly useless. It described a place he did not know. For all its detail, there was nothing familiar in it, no sense of the modern city he knew.

Lost rivers and streams flowed blue through the contours of the land, open to the sky. The dark line of the Walbrook snaked between two low hills, dividing the settlement in half. Eastward to a brick-red line—probably the city wall—the land looked to be as crowded with buildings as the East End. To the west, beyond another red line, a tributary marked Pistrinum opened wide-mouthed into the Thames. That would be the Fleet, which meant its eastern bank touched the Thames at Blackfriars.

Houses, shops, and open fields, roads, marshes and pastures, four hundred years of Roman occupation lay jumbled together in one unfolded sheet of paper, as if every bathhouse and temple, every wharf and potter's kiln had sprung up all at once and remained together the whole time. A vague bridge extended to the south across the river, but led to nothing but marshy islands and a few round, thatched houses that might be a village or a barracks, swathed in fog.

"How is this supposed to help?" he grumbled.

Familiar laughter broke the air as if the little folk had heard him. Of course, they had. With no grass or flowers to hide in on shipboard, they were sitting by him like naughty schoolchildren giggling and poking each other, and now and then bursting into silly songs.

Look away!

Seize the day!

Find a way!

Oy vey!

"Yeah?" he said doubtfully. They always meant something, even if it sounded ridiculous.

He picked up the book and held it out flat, tilting it this way and that to catch the fitful light.

Look away, they said again.

All right, he would do as he was told. Raising his eyes to the horizon, he tried to empty his mind. Along the creamy surface of the book and below his vision, as on the distant riverbank, colorless images formed and reformed in the shifting mists. The creak of ropes, the groan and thud of long oars in their locks, all retreated. The pressure in his chest grew lighter, even as the white pin-point of pain he had been fighting all day grew again.

Seize the day, find a way?

No, no! Let go!

He let go. At once, a silvery chord sounded in the air like

three pure notes struck from the king's harp, setting a kind of counterpoint to the music of their movement through time. He looked down at the jewel exposed on his wrist, and caught his breath.

Out of the twilight of the Borderland, a white light broke through each bead of the talisman, raking scarlet, rose and gold across the open map. Superimposed over the flat drawing, he could make out the lines of the modern city—the Tower, the Houses of Parliament, St Paul's—so he could get his bearings. He tilted it another way, the silver lines lifted into wire-frame layers, and he could see what he was meant to see. Skipping the intervening centuries, the generations of Roman London showed themselves to him in stepped layers while he watched in awe, fading in and fading out, built, burnt, ploughed up, rebuilt through blood and fire.

Swiftly, the images came together again in his well-ordered mind, sorting and organizing: an amphitheatre under the Guildhall; a fort full of soldiers in the bent arm of Cripplegate; a temple of Mithras under an office building, and more and more. Then the movement stopped and held where the line of the Wall, nearly finished, became a constant ribbon. Here the images were strongest. The mithraeum half-finished, the forum gleaming and new, the governor's palace already showing some age. Even a cargo ship actually sailing up the Fleet. No, the Pistrinum. The Museum of London would love to know all of this; too bad he could never tell them.

A chill breeze ruffled his hair. The wind had changed.

"Mr Harper!"

When Ben looked up again, it was there in front of him, the ship sketched on the map tacking up Fleet's clean and swift running stream. He could imagine a spring beyond the smudgy horizon, and apple trees among the oak and beech.

"Aye, my lord!" he called back, his heart suddenly racing.

"Are we there yet?"

The carnelian disk on his wrist had gone very warm, his fingers tingling as if he had struck the notes from the harp with his own hand. This was new: not a single vibration but a pure chord pulling at his heart.

"I'm not sure," he said finally. How could he be sure?

Closing his eyes, Ben let his thought reach out, just enough to lean against the first veil it came to, nudge a gate, and felt the intensity fade. It wasn't much of a compass, but it was all he had. This was going to take getting used to.

Find the Fleet, he thought. Carew will find us if we find her.

A hand touched his shoulder, and his eyes flew open.

"Don't wander off," Raven said gently. "Tam asks how much further, if you know."

Ben swallowed and felt a tremor run through him lifting every hair,. That was new.

"We're here," he said.

Part Three
Londinium

In the consular year of L. Calpurnius Proculus Piso
and P. Salvius Julianus
Under the hand of the Governor Q. Antistius Adventus
Marcus Aurelius Caesar being emperor

Otherwise, the year of grace, 175 CE

27
Kalends of May

i

By Ben's calculation, he had been wet in whole or in part every day for a week, and today—whenever it was—promised more of the same. The smell of rain hung heavily on the air, as well as the layered stinks of the waterfront, waxed canvas and hempen rope, strange spices and local fish. Above all a rich green fragrance as if the whole island were a garden. Masses of clouds in a slatey sky streamed overhead, being kneaded by the upper airs into galleys and galleons, building them into black-bottomed towers moored against the horizon. Even the blue that remained hovered behind a misty film, though the sun rode high and warm behind it.

None of which dulled Raven's spirits in the slightest as they came ashore.

"*Bene venutis Britanniae!*" he declaimed expansively. "Welcome to Britannia—the tarnished fringe on the cloak of Imperial Rome." Sporting an optic white toga with a narrow violet band over a tunic embroidered with exotic birds, he added, "Come along, Festus!"

"*Magister reverendissime et illustrissime.* I hear and obey, O most excellent."

Dutifully, Ben tugged a sandy forelock and followed him down the springing boards of the gangway. He resisted the urge to shuffle crabwise like Igor.

Then a voice shouted in alarm,

"You there! Look out!"

"Move!"

"Oi!"

A flying tackle slammed him in the middle and pitched him to the ground just as a netted load of amphorae swung from a crane through the air where his head had been. The burley workman who had tackled him heaved Ben up and set him on his feet.

"Thanks!" Ben said with feeling.

The man nodded without smiling and went back to his work muttering, "Tourist."

Billingsgate never changes.

As if nothing had happened, Raven waited with an air of princely detachment he hadn't indulged since this expedition began.

A whole week, Ben thought, vainly plucking the muck from his dull green tunic. It must be killing him.

It wasn't bad enough to be stuck in the role and clothing of a humble freedman, an ex-slave, bobbing along in his former master's dazzling wake, the dingy behind his yacht. There was only room for one noble gentleman in this scenario, and it was Raven's turn. And if Festus was a ridiculous name, it was a serious improvement on the others his friend had proposed— Manlius, Furius, Curius—all authentic, all guaranteed to make one or the other of them burst into unmanly giggles at some inopportune moment. But as it began with F, the quondam Francis Browne would probably answer to it, even if he was stuck in these terrible clothes. At least the native breeches had been roughly the colour of clay to begin with.

"All right," he asked when he was nearly presentable, "where to?"

"The question of the hour," said the fae lord. "You said we're here, and here we are. Now what?"

Within sight of Teifi's free-running stream, Ben placed two fingers over the amulet and closed his eyes seeking the pin-point of light where the curious new sensibility had anchored itself. It came more easily this time—a swirling center, a jewel of opal light, the core of a star not quite formed, and less certain than it had been. Then the colors steadied, images resolved, but not much. London was having its way with him, as usual.

Blinking, he found they had removed from the riverfront to the peaked roof of a temple built almost on the bank of the Walbrook, which the practical Romans called Dimidia for the simple reason that it cut the settlement in half. Londinium ranged about them, green fields alternating with bustling town streets, dotted with neat squares red-tiled or thatched—the Roman colonial grid in full play, unexpectedly softened by a flowery burst of color on every door.

Ben waved generally north.

"Up there," he said, squinting into the haze. "And a little west. Clerkenwell, maybe. No, further than that. Primrose Hill?"

"It's not much to go on."

"It's all I'm sure of."

The fae lord drew a deep breath, tasting the air like a fine wine. With a look of pleasure he let it out again, smiling.

"I know people here. Let me look into this," said Raven.

"And I get to hold your toga?"

"Don't be ridiculous. Look, see up there?"

He pointed to the north and east a bit where Cornhill swelled to its modest height, crowned by a massive building, a dull ivory wall under a red tile roof. The market spilled from the gate down the road almost back to the river, a maze of wicker stalls and brightly painted canvas.

The map had showed him this. Ben nodded, connecting the map to the territory.

"The forum?"

"Mmm, and today is market day. Also a holiday!"

"I had no idea ancient Britain was so festive," Ben said dryly. "What's going on?"

"It is, in the modern counting," said Raven, declaiming again, "the year of grace one hundred and seventy-five. My clever friend Marcus Aurelius Caesar is Emperor. And rain or shine, today is what the Romans from here to Alexandria call the Floralia. The festival of Flora, goddess of flowers. A market and fair today, rustic games and chariot races tomorrow. Rejoice, my dear. It's May Day!"

Without trauma or discernible transition, they stood in the road before the temple of Isis, an imposing structure whose roof, Ben suspected, they had just profaned. No matter. Raven slapped his friend's shoulder amiably, a good master giving his man a half-day out.

"All those banners and such are the Floralia fair spilling out of the gate and into the town. There's money in your purse and a song in your heart, and you... You do remember what to do at a May fair, I hope."

The sly smile on Ben's face was probably older than he was.

"Aye, sir. Eat junk food. Drink cheap wine. Steer clear of morris dancers."

Raven snorted aristocratically.

"And avoid anything in a red crested helmet. This is an occupied country, and the bastards are bloody everywhere."

"What about you?"

"I will be making my own enquiries."

ii

So Ben went to the fair. The snapping breeze that had nudged away the morning rain swirled through the market place where it set the flower-decked stalls to swaying lightly, rippling the brightly colored linen of the walls and sunshades. Rain or no, they had set up in the pre-dawn chill to be ready for the day. Looped strings of brass hawk bells clashed and jangled where they hung over piles of local produce to scare away the birds. The same bright air mingled the scents of cooking meats and exotic spices, perfumes and wet sheep, and other smells less savory.

Like the fairs of his youth, the place was a hodge-podge of wicker stalls hanging off the wattle-and-daub backs of shops, or perched on temple steps, or free-standing lean-tos lurching against each other for support. And like those fairs, it offered everything, as the Romans said, from eggs to apples. Jugglers, rope-walkers, and garland-sellers clogged the pathways with gawking idlers. Fine gold work gleamed on trays next to the man selling pigeons for the table or the altar, take your pick.

Cartloads of turnips jostled for space with sacks of jewel-like spices from the ends of empire and sacks of almonds; baskets of cheap wooden trenchers and bowls cheek-by-jowl with the best red Samian dinner ware. Browsing, a man could nibble at grilled meat on a stick or pickled oysters wrapped in a burdock leaf, or slurp down overpriced wine or heather beer, and return the cup later for the deposit. Security was a bit more formidable than in his faire days, being provided by the off-duty legionaries from the local garrison: mainly Italians and their Swabian auxiliaries.

Ben would have appreciated it a good deal more, however, if it hadn't been for the nagging sense of impending crisis. Not long to wait.

A rattle and clank, and a beefy arm landed heavily across his chest.

"Watch it, you!"

Sure enough, he was nose to nose with his own reflection in the polished bronze of a centurion's moulded breastplate. The snarling face immediately above it, lacking any neck to speak of, glared with more casual menace than he'd seen on anything human, even Robert Cecil. And this one's sausage-like fingers twisted into the fabric of Ben Harper's tunic, hot eyes glaring.

"Mind yer manners, sunshine. Clear the road!"

Before Ben could summon the breath to object, the legionary flung him aside like a bad bargain and moved on, repeating the gesture and the sentiment every few feet, as did a counterpart across the way. Shaking with relief Ben realized it wasn't personal. Crowd control, that's all. Or not quite all. His left wrist itched under the heavy amulet. Something fae was going on.

Some kind of commotion was stirring, drawing everyone's attention down the slope where a cloud of dust and flying gouts of mud marked the progress of whatever it was. A manic ululation rose above the shouts of anger and surprise like a band of wild Indians, or wild Celts, chasing down their enemies.

Folk shrieked and crushed out of the way, opening a path

like the Red Sea. A little boy fell, to be snatched out of the way with only an instant to spare. Across the lane, a tall man in a dark Roman toga and a haunted look turned around, and Ben's stomach gave a lurch. The unmistakably scarred face of Simon Carew stared back at him, wild-eyed.

Lightning exploded in Ben's head like the mother of all migraines, swamping his senses, filling his mouth and nose with burnt sugar, mildew, apple pie, leaf mould. Hooves at the gallop roared in his ears, and the drone of a hurdy-gurdy, the tinkling bell of his mother's flower shop.

He never knew when his knees hit the dirt, but another part of his brain thrust a hand out to catch himself. Fingers touched the vibrating earth, and he felt himself washed in ancient waters, bathed in sun and rain, lifted into the sky on the swaying limbs of an apple tree.

His eyes flew open just in time to watch a light British war chariot thunder toward him behind two white horses driven by a woman, bared-armed, whip-hand in the air. Golden curls rippled back from the long eyes, the wild face framed by savage joy. Long fingerling braids tossed Medusa-like behind her.

Laughing eyes flashed and for a moment met Ben's. She winked at him, he thought, but nothing slowed her. Red lips drawn back in exultant laughter, apple-cheeked with passion, she drove like a goddess pursued by furies, while in her dust, catching up with an expression more fierce than hers, a second chariot swung round the curve behind her, the driver crouched low on the bouncing wicker floor with one foot braced on the churning haunches of his horse

"—you, Oriana! I will have you!" Ben heard him shout. "You'll never beat me!"

The driver never noticed one staring freedman or anything else around him, only the girl. Only ever the girl. And she responded with a ferocious war cry that chilled the blood of the oldest in the crowd, so that they turned and ran as if from Boudicca herself.

The chariots pounded up the hill toward the basilica, flinging gouts of earth to every side, heading for a timber gate already closed against them. They never got there.

Maggie Secara

Shouts went up, even the guards flung themselves to either side. But where there should have been a heedless, horrendous crash and hideous death, the drivers, horses, chariots and all simply grew smaller, still galloping, swerving through rooster-tails of dust until they dwindled into a point in the vista of another world. To most they simply vanished in a plume of gilded dust, which collapsed on a hoot of triumph and a mad cackle. Mocking laughter trailed behind them like a banner.

Finally on his feet again, Ben scanned the crowd in vain for any sign of Carew. Stunned and shaking their heads, the crowd broke up whinging about other people's children, and spoilt young nobles with nothing better to do but ruin an honest man's livelihood. Ride roughshod over a perfectly good holiday. And look at all these flowers, spoiled!

But even the muttering didn't last long. In an hour's time, no one could say what exactly they had seen. A whirlwind, some said. No, no, said a few others, it was a waterspout that spun up from the river, couldn't you hear the water nymphs laughing? The more sensible remembered clearly it was dogs tussling in the street, or hard boys rioting out of the wine bar, or an unbroken horse got free of its owner. Well, you could see why, they said. A horse like that.

Or it was something else.

Or nothing.

The fire in Ben's head cooled and banked, though the afterimages remained clear, both his visions and the racing drivers seen through a haze of blue and green, or through the wall of a wave. Memory and moment tumbled together and finally clicked.

"I know you," he whispered in something like awe.

That same noble lady who had forced his meeting with Jack Greengage when the ploughman plucked him out of the way. And wasn't it she that day outside Richmond, before meeting with John Dee that first time? In the halls of memory he heard a whip crack, felt his hand go up to touch his cap for the glittering cavalcade of some great lady, who threw him the same dazzling smile as she passed. He could smell the dust of their passing when a chilly breeze made him shiver, the same again on a different day in Victorian London.

As the muggy Roman day imposed itself again, one last trailing impression joined the others: Raven tight with disapproval at a kissing couple in a Lambeth park.

Even as the migraine died, a shadow of the pain remained. Vile tastes lingered sour in his mouth as real as if he'd swallowed each one. A few rough coughs hacked the dust out of his lungs, and he'd have given good money for some of that cheap wine right now. Or cider. Why cider?

"There's water in that bag of yours," said a voice at his elbow. "Ain't there, me 'andsome?"

"There is," he said, swinging his head over his shoulder, "but how can you know that?"

Reeling with enchantment as he was, Ben was not quite surprised to find a crabbed old woman sitting on a joint-stool among shattered baskets of fragrant apples, plums, and pears. Half her wares had been spilled over a mud-colored blanket, tumbled and trodden by the panicky crowd.

When he stared down at her, she blinked her one good eye, and hacked a wet sort of stage cough, *kheh-heh*.

Grinning, Ben Harper flipped open his bag and reached in without looking. The etched silver bottle came into his hand at once. *King's Man*, said the scrolling letters in plain English.

Oblivious of the surrounding market, the shifting light as clouds moved aside and sunshine streaked the day, he popped the cork and hunkered down to offer it.

"Would you like some water, Grandmother?" he said with genial courtesy.

The old woman snatched the bottle from him and drank thirstily until the last drop fell onto her coated tongue. Then smacked her withered lips, and handed it back.

"You know," she drawled in a thoughtful, if sarcastic sort of way, "that Caesar—not the one what now is with all the wise sayings, but the real one, that Julius—he'd 'ave paid for these apples when he'd knocked 'em all about."

The harper lifted an eyebrow as he put the empty bottle away. Now what? he wondered, listening for tiny giggles.

"Well, he would have," the woman went on. "Caesar." One foot nudged an empty basket towards him. "And he might even have learned something to his advantage."

The grin deepened, twitched. The collected absurdities of the morning bubbled up, broke out in a bark of sardonic laughter. Standing, he tugged the money pouch from under his tunic, drew open the strings, and shook it out.

"Yes, Grandmother, I believe he would have!"

A shower of silver coins rained over the woman's palsied, uplifted hand, collected in the spread skirt of the gown between her knees, decorated the checkered blanket. She picked one from her skirt and bit the edge.

"Flora bless you, sir!" she rasped merrily, tossing him a withered crab apple. "Trust the water."

Then she winked, and vanished—apples, silver and all. In her place, there seemed to be a dealer in talismans, love charms, and mass-produced figurines meant to occupy a household shrine. In fact, he looked to have been there all day going by the picked-over counter trays and hanging ribbons that earlier had hung with poppets of clay or bronze or woven corn straw.

Despite himself, Ben jumped.

"Say, wasn't there a old woman here, an apple seller?"

"Too early for apples, boss," said the man behind the counter. "Dried ones, maybe. My gran might have some cherries left, though. Next row over. Anna Bronwen, she'll be there."

"Ehr, thanks," Ben said, and rubbed his eyes. Then he stopped.

iii

After an hour's sober consultation with the procurator, and thirty or forty chatty minutes with Flavia Paulina, the procurator's stylish wife, Raven had picked up most of the gossip available in a busy garrison town, or at least the high points. And among the maddening trivia, he had learned that the negotiatore Hilarion Gallio's wife was a creature of enthusiasms and causes.

Oh yes, Flavia had said, bless her heart. Her friend Valeria

Lucila had some new cause every year—war orphans, civic improvement, patronizing the arts, sirens, as the Romans called mermaids. And of course, the latest obsession with her British ancestors.

Valeria had even flirted briefly with some mystery religion, and tried to involve her friends as well. But the prophet or whatever he was had turned out to be a charlatan who'd left a trail of broken marriages and empty bank accounts from Eboracum to Venta Belgarum.

"Of course, Quintus, that's my husband, clapped his sorry arse in irons and sent him off to the tin mines."

She tittered over the vulgarity and pushed back the curls falling out of her coiffure. The soul of grace, she permitted her handsome guest with the beautiful eyes to pour them each another cup of wine.

"Sirens?" Young Atius Corax gave a conspiratorial smile.

"Oh, yes indeed," she trilled. Since the Saturnalia, at least, Valeria Lucila had conceived a passionate devotion to the nymphs of every river, stream and well she tripped over—which in Londinium could happen every few yards. Most of the little waters feeding into the larger rivers didn't even have names, not that anyone knew, yet the ridiculous woman could be found tying silk ribbons into an overhanging tree or dropping a coin into the water at every crossing!

She had confided to Flavia— "And you must never say a word of this to anyone. She swore me to the deepest secrecy" —that the nymphs had told her their names themselves!

"I expect it comes from living out there in the countryside with no one to talk to all day. A woman may very well start to hear things, voices and things. Don't you think?"

"Very possibly, yes."

"No one can fault a pious impulse, I suppose, but still. Hilarion Gallio indulges her frightfully. Probably to make up for, well you know, his own enthusiasms."

"What sort of indulgence?"

"You mean apart from not beating her and insisting she stick to her loom like a virtuous Roman matron?" Flavia glared for an instant, until a hiccup burst her composure. Cackling with unalloyed delight, she swayed provocatively towards Corax.

Grinning, he caught her, cool hands firm on her shoulders.

"Nothing so old-fashioned, I'm sure," he said. "What sort of indulgence?"

And, giddy as she was, when her gaze met those sapphire eyes, she fell right into them.

"Why, my dear, he's building a nymphaeum in the back garden!"

iv

"Here, citizen, you going to buy that or not?"

Shorter than Ben, and stocky, with a daisy chain around his brow, the man should have been packing up—the meaningful sighs of the weary-looking woman behind him said as much— but he knew a tourist when he saw one.

"Five sesterces, legate. Good price that, seeing as market's closing."

"Uhm, what?"

"That one you're holding. The finest bronze, that is. Lasts forever. Take it home to the missus, eh? Tickle her fancy? Put it up in a doorway. Brings good luck, know what I mean?"

From the shadows, the woman said, "Cratius, let the man go and bring in the trays!"

Ben stared, then looked down at his cupped hand and the molded figure of a winged phallus, a good luck charm from Parthia to Gaul. Or was it? The round ball end was shaped, he thought, more like an apple than it probably should be; the shaft thin and pointed, like an arrow shot threw it. Crude wings on the side might be the arrow's fletching, in a way, if you looked at it right. He started to laugh, shaking his head. Winged apple, winged dick, flying fickle finger of Fate, he half-expected it to flutter and fly away. It had been that kind of day.

"No, wait now. I misspoke. For you, citizen, it's only four *sesterces*, no, three and a half," Cratius said, sensing a sale about to walk away, tourist or not. "Throw in a leather cord any color you want, free of charge, you can wear it home."

Ben hardly heard him. From the light in the sky, from the

smells on the air, from nowhere at all, answers came to him. A few, anyway. Not everything, but something—names, images, a direction. Clues, like little birds resting on his shoulders. Chuckling, he put the charm on the counter and started to walk away.

"No, thanks," he said. He had to find Raven.

"Go on, break my heart. Three *sesterces* and that's the best I can do, on the heads of my children!"

He sounded awfully desperate, but the thing was probably brass anyway, stamped and sold in the hundreds.

"Sorry, man," Ben waved him off, grinning. "My old one still works fine."

"Wait, wait!" The voice was fading behind him. "What was I thinking? Did I say *sesterces*? I meant *ases*. Just three!"

"No, really, it's okay!" he called back, and took a quick right turn between a garland-seller and a curtained area which, by the aroma and the sound of trickling water, housed sanitary facilities. The canvas walls were hung with rosemary to sweeten the air.

Privies, he thought, taking a minute to try them out. Good old Romans. Good old faire.

When he emerged a minute later, the market was disassembling around him. Ben stopped to survey the maze of leaning poles and wicker walls, looking for an easy path down the hill. He'd settle for a drink and a place to sit down for a spell, and he'd have laid odds the wine bar would be the last stall standing. So it was, if he didn't mind threading through the maze of collapsing wicker and piled baskets to get to it, and he didn't. But there was no way to do that without being distracted, not for an old faire brat like Ben Harper.

When a support pole started to skew towards his head on its way to the ground, Ben jumped to catch it, automatically asking, "Need help?"

In a moment he was bracing two poles with a canvas curtain sagging between them, while the tunics pinned to it were hastily taken down instead of falling to the trampled earth.

"My boy was meant to help me out," the owner said. "Trust him to run off when there's work to be done. Kids, eh?"

Since his hands were obviously needed, Ben hung around to help Senua finish folding and strapping and tying up. Once the errant boy turned up, it didn't take long.

"Many hands make light work, as my dad used to say."

When they were done, Senua thrust a tunic into Ben's hands for thanks before he could say no. Then he hefted the poles of a travois-like sled and lurched away.

Well, okay, Ben thought with a laugh, why not? A good madder red, the garment was a bit smudged from the day's handling and the braid had seen a better day, but worth keeping if fortune allowed. Never hurts to have a change of clothes.

"Mother of the Wood, where did you get to?"

Already forgotten, the charm-seller, Cratius, suddenly appeared in front of him, red-faced and panting, nearly frantic. The tattered circlet of flowers had fallen over one ear.

He must have seen something in the harper's face or in his bearing, or maybe a touch of the fae glow that John Dee had seen once. Maybe it was Teifi's amulet still strapped around his wrist. Whatever it was, the coarse voice strained, he snapped,

"Look, just take it, won't you! No charge."

Cratius pressed the golden charm into Ben's startled hands, earnestly watching to make sure he didn't drop the thing or fling it away.

"Uhm, okay. Thanks."

"Right. Fortune on you, then."

He turned and trudged back to his impatient wife.

Mouth open, Ben stared after him, then down at the peculiar charm strung now on a leather cord. To tell the truth it looked more than ever like an apple and an arrow than cock and balls, but still unmistakable. Newly made, it had no story to tell him even when he listened properly, but there was, yes, a hint of music in it. *Fecit in Londinium*, maybe. Maybe nothing. And maybe the city was trying to tell him something.

He dropped the thing over his head and let it shimmy down behind his tunic. For luck.

"You all right?" said a familiar voice about two feet behind him.

"It has been the strangest afternoon," Ben answered, without jumping even a little. "But yeah, I'm good. Spent all your money, though."

Raven didn't care. "There's always more. Come on, we've got a dinner invitation!"

28
Villa Hilarion, the same afternoon

i

Hilarion Gallio loved his country home, a modest villa halfway up the bubbling upper reaches of the river Fleet, which the Romans called Pistrinum, the mill stream. Villa Hilarion was near the spring, but not too near, in the stretch some called the river of wells. There was always clean fresh water to be had without being flooded out every spring. The pastureland was good without being too wet for the herd beasts, or so his native cattleman assured him. Even wrapped in boiled wool against the island's endless damp, Hilarion felt the comfortable glow of prosperity wash over him every time he crested the hill leaving Londinium's busy life behind. The land was good, his slaves were numerous, and both were for the most part well ordered. Not bad for a wild boy from northern Gaul.

"Things are looking up," he liked to say. "We are building again!"

And so he was, expanding the earlier, more modest house, replacing the timber with stone, in parts. He considered facing it with pink marble on the approaches, if it wasn't too dear. It would please Valeria, his wife, who remained the chief of his treasures, though no longer in the first or even the second bloom of her youth. Well, what woman is, who has given her husband three children alive, and two of them sons? And if Valeria Lucila was sometimes a bit more strong-willed than the ideal Roman matron, well, she was a redhead and native British besides.

All in all, through his skills as a negotiatore, buying and selling, moving the luxury goods of the Empire through the ports of Gaul and Britain, he had acquired a life as civilized as a man could hope for anywhere in the Empire. Rome meant peace and good order, and Britannia was Rome. The thought pleased him as he paused to look down into his valley.

To be sure, life had not always been so secure out here in the shadow of the hawthorn and the holly. There had been trouble with the tribes in the region, of course. That's what conquest means. But the last time was more than a hundred years ago.

True, the stories said the Icenian revolt had been horrific— the city in flames, human heads flying everywhere, terrible things—but you know how historians exaggerate. The fact remained that the Iceni had been put down, and the Brigantes pacified, and doves cooed in their cots. Whatever little dark people muttered far away in the north, the legions would sort them out soon enough. A man would have to be irrationally fearful to suppose such days would ever come again. So why live crouched behind the walls of the city?

Thus it was that he rode feeling secure and at peace with his life, into his little valley escorted by a small unit of hired and heavily armed Frisians, retired from the Auxiliaries and still deadly. He was confident, not stupid.

Part of civilized life, Hilarion reflected on riding through his gate, was dealing with surprises from time to time. He'd had one already today, that really ought to be enough. Well, the procurator would owe him a favor for the last-minute holiday entertainment and lodging of the visiting young sprig of a great house. The sprig's father was an old acquaintance, as the procurator had reminded him. Some business with horses, or dogs, or something. But never mind.

All in all, it had been a profitable day in both long and short term, spent mainly at the warehouse, partly at the docks.

Commerce had pursued him even to the baths where, he was happy to say, he did as much negotiating as he did in the forum. But when a man came into his own garden of an afternoon, he came there looking for a little peace, and why shouldn't he?

Yet here was Valeria Lucila, some sort of pink blossoms in her hair, walking in the flowery colonnade chatting with modest animation to some visitor still out of sight, and being aggressively British with that blue checkered *stola* over her long-sleeved yellow gown. Or was it the fashion? He had no idea. Thankfully, the graceful drape of the *palla* covered most of it. His particular concern was that when she was in this native mood she preferred to be called by the uncouth tribal name of Veloriga. A considerate husband, he was content to indulge her in this, when he remembered to. He usually remembered too late.

As he dismounted and sent away the escort, and someone barred the garden gate, his faithful steward Barates came forward with a welcoming cup of the soft sweet beer the locals made. Gallio took it and spilled a little on the herm under the grape arbour for luck. He gulped a deep draught himself for patience, then handed it back, still watching his wife through the leafy screen.

What an excellent wife she was. An ornament to his house, and so good even with difficult people like… Who was she talking to, he wondered with a touch of heat that couldn't possibly be jealousy. And then she walked into the open.

Oh, Mercury, not today.

That Dumnonian, whatshisname. Awkward, uncomfortable man. Livid scars all down one side; they seemed almost polished. He could feel the day turn unlucky just glancing at them, and then they trapped his gaze, try as he might to turn away.

Gallio crossed his fingers at the inauspicious thought. Perhaps if Valeria were not so kind the blasted fellow wouldn't keep coming back. He would have to speak to her about that. And here she was.

"Husband!" Valeria Lucila—Veloriga—swept forward, all smiles, to greet him with her usual soft hand to his chest and a kiss for each cheek, then signaled the servants to bring chairs to the portico, but no wine. Oh good, she hadn't asked the man to stay. This wouldn't take long.

"He's here again? Name?"

"It is Septimius Placidus, my dear," she cued him quietly. "He came one day last week."

"Did my messenger reach you about an extra guest?"

"Of course, dear. For the Floralia, never a problem."

Beaming, she stepped aside to let him work.

"Septimius Placidus!" the merchant boomed in hearty bonhomie. "Of course! It is good to see you, my dear fellow. Foolish of me to have forgotten we had an…" A discreet glance at Barates, who shook his head. "Not an appointment, no. Well, never mind."

Masking his reluctance, he gripped the fellow's wrist in the usual way, and noted again the thick weals snaking up the arm, a permanent memento of some terrible fire. And no jewellery of any kind, Gallio noted out of habit. Not even the iron ring of a freedman. Only an amulet hanging under the neckline of his tunic. Certainly the toga sat on him as if he'd never worn it before.

He gestured Placidus to sit. Two of the slaves arranged the furniture to his liking. Another set a pitcher of water and two small beakers on a low table between them, but he waved them away. They bent their heads, touched their shoulders in salute, and left silently. That gesture, when he noticed it, always pleased him, but apparently it made his guest uneasy. Tall, gaunt, all sharp angles, the man reminded him of those ascetics one heard about, living on roots and bog water. Some religious order or something.

Oh, he hoped not. Religion always made such a hash of things, especially trade. Still, it was only good sense to be polite, maintain the courtesies.

"I must be getting old, Placidus. Remind me, if you will, why I have the pleasure of your company again today?

The man calling himself Septimius Placidus cleared his throat and spoke in that oddly formal way he had, as if he had learned his Latin from a book.

"We spoke some, some days before. I asked concerning of an old papyrus. Very old."

From a book with a tone-deaf teacher. Was that really the accent of Isca Dumnoniorum?

"Of course, yes! A text from Babylonia, was it, or the Indus Valley?"

"Mesopotamia," Placidus said carefully, hesitating over the inflection. "Or so I was told. Possibly Syria. From the temple of…of Ata'rathi, or if that name is not familiar, possibly Atargatis or…"

Oh ye gods below, it was religion after all. No wonder it had slipped his mind.

With his usual infectious smile, Hilarion waved a hand more or less towards the city and nameless places further on.

"The Mystic East, eh? Of course, of course. I remember now. Something to do with sirens, naiads, dryads, nimrods, or whatever, eh? Barates, you dog! Oh yes, there you are. out that box that came in yesterday, and we'll have a good look, shall we?"

He wanted his dinner, he wanted good wine and a quick thrust with a slave girl, but he had holiday guests coming—he had at least remembered to send word ahead and saved himself one headache—and he had no intention of inviting this peculiar fellow to join them. Best to get rid of him as quickly as he could. Which he could, and shortly did.

ii

Reclining at the cushioned head of Gallio's new *stibadium*, the horseshoe-shaped dining couch, Antonius Atius Corax leaned on his left elbow remarking knowledgably on the frescos decorating the *triclinium* walls. Here Arion rode a wave rescued by the dolphins; there Orpheus sang on a riverbank to enraptured nymphs and priapic satyrs in some hazy paradise; and most elaborate of all, Neptune arm-in-arm with Amphitrite, attended by frolicking tritons and sirens and sea life of all kinds. The tile floor under their feet depicted a sort of siren, though it might be a chubby Venus, surrounded by nymphs. The procurator's wife had been right: Valeria collected mermaids.

With his right hand he could easily reach for the dishes as they were presented, lift his glass for a refill, or gesture theatrically. As little as he enjoyed this mode of dining, the last point was something he could appreciate. Though hunger was not among his usual appetites, being immortal, he graciously tasted everything, made an appropriate remark, appreciated the unremarkable wines. He was always and everywhere a charming guest.

On his right Hilarion Gallio, similarly posed, chatted and told stories of his successful enterprises, or his rivals' foolish ones, especially if he had gotten the advantage. Always generous in victory, he invariably offered thanks in the form of expensive sacrifices to Mercury, god of trade, even while applauding his own cleverness. And he loved most of all someone to impress. Young Atius Corax, a genuine patrician from Rome itself, suited him quite nicely. The pampered scion of an ancient family only lately come to commerce was longing to be taken seriously, or so the Governor had said. And unmarried, too. A happy chance for a man with a marriageable daughter.

"In fact, you may be interested in this, young man," Hilarion popped a honeyed dormouse into his mouth before launching the next story. "Have you spent much time in Narbo Martius, in Southern Gaul? I was considering a trade in horses, just a flutter you understand—Castor remembers, don't you— we went down last summer for the horse fair. Came home with a shipload of lavender honey!"

Raven set a part of his mind to listening while he continued scanning his fellow diners, feeling for the pattern. A lesser thought wondered how Ben was getting along with his own assignment, but it could wait.

On his other side, Marina, passionately fourteen, had clearly decided that her handsome prince had arrived at last. When he flashed his adorable grin, she nearly expired on the spot. All dark curls and moist black eyes, infatuation radiated from her in waves. Well, of course it did. She could see in Corax a charming, obviously wealthy, possibly important man, young enough to please her and old enough to satisfy her father. And he was obviously eligible or Mater would never have placed her so close.

On this holiday evening the painted panels that divided the room had been withdrawn, and extra tables brought in to accommodate guests and clients as well as family. Two sleek, middle-aged men—business associates, apparently, with their simpering wives all draped in holiday flower—filled out the company. Crowded as it was beyond the customary dinner party, there was enough space for the servants to move about easily. It was almost a dance, invisibly directed from the opposite couch where Valeria Lucila reclined between some female relative and Titus, the eldest son.

Eldest, Raven thought, but not first. She'd lost a child, but not in childbed or to terrifying, unexplained infant fevers, as so often happened. He'd seen that in many times, but this felt different. Her song was different.

The invocation of the household gods accomplished, the meal proceeded efficiently, the staff responding like a good cavalry horse to a small gesture, a nod. At the same time Valeria appeared to be attending to her husband's stories, nodding and smiling, adding a murmur of agreement, a cluck of dismay. But something was wrong here. Out of tune. The lady gave no outward sign of distress, yet discomfort vibrated through the villa like a harp string stretched to its limit.

In Valeria—whom he had pledged to call Veloriga when presented to her, though Hilarion rolled his eyes—Raven observed a careful woman, not much above thirty, taller than most, and slim despite four children, sharp-featured, and controlled. Some might even have said she was too thin; the elbows, wrists, shoulders too angular. Such attributes anyone might notice and believe they knew her.

But the fae princeling could see what others could not: the darting eyes, the tight corners that framed her smile, and how her festival garland vibrated even when she was most still. Well-dressed, well-jewelled—was the heavy golden torque that burdened her neck meant as mute rebellion against the

Roman identity that had claimed her British life? Or was it the relic of what Flavia Paulina had dismissed as enthusiasm?

From *entheos*, he noted: possessed by the gods.

She didn't seem mad or obsessed, but even while she kept a constant covert hand on the meal and service, she was the awkward piece in the pattern. Harbouring a secret, he thought. Was she plotting rebellion with native dissidents to throw off the yoke of Rome? Hiding Christians in the cellar? Running away to join the circus? There had to be something more to the mermaid obsession than a bored housewife longing for romance, or else why was he here?

Well, all right, there was the one thing. The wee folk of the house delighted in taunting her, plucking at her hem, untying her sandals, nudging the flowers out of the elaborate coiffure. Her hand came up to bat them away, but with no sign that she could see them. They were probably responsible when a slave tripped on a broken sandal strap and flung the dish of mussels in wine sauce across Amphitrite's painted court. Entertaining, perhaps, but also distracting. While Veloriga gave barely visible orders to have it cleaned up, Raven did the same. It was a small effort to slide into Faerie between the moments of human time and stop his little friends before further mayhem could erupt.

It's all right, boss!

She likes it!

It's fun!

The King's Raven of Faerie disagreed and offered an alternative suggestion. Delighted, they tossed their caps, spun on the spot, and disappeared. The raven-boy inserted himself into time again. Marina blinked owlishly. He gave her a conspiratorial wink, good for all occasions, just in case.

It had stopped raining, but the sound of dripping water was everywhere, raising the noise level in what should have been a peaceful room. Maybe that was all.

Hilarion was saying heartily,

"You know the oddest fellow came to see me today. (Corax, you'll enjoy this.) A sort of scholar, I suppose, called Placidus.

Septimius Placidus, he's called, that's it. Very intense, as all these Christians are. Oh, yes, I've met him before. I thought at first he'd come to beg a position, or a loan. His Latin was so awkward, almost childish, I swear to you I nearly took him for one of the native farmers. Terrible scar, he has, all down one side." He shivered melodramatically. "He was looking to buy an old scroll to do with sirens! Can you imagine?"

As he bit into another honeyed date, Raven nearly choked as the sweetness turned to acid in his mouth. Placidus, the man called himself. Silence.

Gallio paused in his narrative to dip a wing of partridge into the raisin sauce and bring it to his mouth.

"Sirens!" Corax let the cough mask his reaction. "And did you have it?"

"Eh, in a manner of speaking," said Hilarion. "More or less." Though he met his guest's eyes frankly, Corax saw more than perhaps he was meant to: the sharp dealer and the touch of larceny. "The scroll he wanted contained short hymns or poems, ancient ones, he said, and I seldom deal in antiques."

"So the customer had to be disappointed?"

"Ah, no, my boy. I had such a scroll, indeed. I never disappoint a customer, and you shall learn the wisdom of that if you will be taught by me."

"I live to learn, Hilarion Gallio, especially from you."

A telling glance flashed between the *negotiatore* and his wife, who shared a knowing smile with her daughter. Marina only blushed.

"Tell me if this is not true, my friends." He gathered agreement from his other guests. "If you don't have what a man wants, you must find a way to make him want what you have."

"And how do you do that, sir?" said Atius Corax, while the other guests nodded and nudged one another.

"The most telling points, you see, were the antiquity of the document, its antiquity, and of course the price. Once those were settled, the rest..." He shrugged as if it were the most elementary skill in the nursery.

But the boy was persistent.

"The price? If it was authentic, surely, it was priceless!"

"Almost, but not quite," Hilarion beamed, and held out a chased silver beaker for more wine. "For payment he had a purse-full of peculiar coins, silver and gold both. No idea where some of them came from. But the weight was good and you know what the poet says!"

"All that glitters is not gold?" Corax suggested.

"Ha! Ah-ha, very good! But no, no, not that at all. It was gold, all right. No, I was thinking of Juvenal: 'Coin smells good no matter the source'."

"But can it have been authentic, do you think?" said one of the guests, a rough-looking sort.

"As to that, it was quite ancient, to be sure. The papyrus was in very poor condition. Some might even have called it worthless. I offered to have it copied out for him in a fair hand, at a reasonable fee, but no, he would have only that one. Sacred, you'd have thought it was. But he was a Christian, you know, and they hold nothing sacred, those people."

He sniffed and nibbled at the partridge.

"So it was the real thing, then?" Corax persisted.

"No idea," said Gallio carelessly. "I couldn't make head nor tail of it, but in truth, neither could he, this Septimius Placidus. He said as much himself, though he claimed to have found a translation somewhere, with annotations. But it was complete, you see. He wanted four brief verses in an antique language with certain marks about them. I found him four verses. And…" he added slyly, "certain marks."

"Forgive me, four? But surely that is not a magical number."

"He said—let me see, yes—most authorities say there are three, but he had discovered the existence of a fourth."

The next question came carefully.

"But sirens, sir. If no one could read it, how could anyone know what it was about? It might as easily be a laundry list, or directions from Babylon to Eboracum."

"It might," Hilarion agreed cheerily. "Indeed it might!" His colleagues chortled with him, knowing his style and approving it. "But those 'certain marks', you see; those persuaded him. And his own desire for it to be true! And who knows, eh? Perhaps it was."

"I see, sir," Corax asked with careful humility. "One unreadable papyrus is much like another."

"Alas, can we ever really know?"

"Written by sirens!" snorted the rougher-looking of Hilarion's friends. "Jupiter, how authentic can it be?"

"I know olive oil and I know wines," the *negotiatore* said, "dressed hides and hunting dogs. Ancient mysteries I leave to women and idle aristocrats, begging your pardon, Atius Corax."

Raven indicated his tolerance with a nod. "Not too idle, I hope."

"Just so, just so. For me, I honour our household gods as all men must, and do my duty to the Imperial cult, of course! I give what I owe to the Fates, and I seek my fortune in the stars, but mostly in my own wits." He tapped his skull to indicate his excellent brains. "Sirens? Ha!"

Participating at last, sixteen-year-old Titus belched up the attitudes of his age and gender.

"All tits and no arse!"

"Ha! Ha!" Hilarion barked. "Well said, well said! The boy is right! What good's a siren, all tail and no place for a man to put his cock in, eh?"

"And yet they are thought of as tempting creatures," Corax mused with Roman sophistication when the coarse laughter began to fade. "Perhaps a case where your lesson applies, Gallio?"

"What's that, lad?"

"The sirens. If you don't have what a man wants, make him want what you have!"

When his host roared his approval, and his guests as well. Corax sat back with a less than innocent satisfaction.

"Gallio!" Veloriga was not amused.

"*Dulcissa!*" Gallio gasped, wiping his eyes. "*Carissa!* Dearest girl, forgive his youth, I beg you."

But he was still chuckling as he took refuge in a fresh beaker of wine.

"Do forgive me, Valeria Lucila," Corax said, chastised. "A vulgar jest. I did not mean to offend your piety."

Not easily mollified on this point, she found him hard to resist.

"First of all, dear Corax, you did promise to call me Veloriga."

He nodded.

"So I did, lady. Again, will you forgive me?"

"You are not at fault," she said. She had all the skill to respond to his charm while throwing an arch look to everyone else. "My honored husband and all our friends are aware of my devotion to the sirens, but you could not know of it."

The unavoidable theme of the room notwithstanding.

"It is not I who am offended, but my nymphs."

Ah, here it comes at last.

"Your nymphs, Veloriga?"

"Oh, yes! My mother's family…"

"Juno!" Marina moaned. Before her rolling eyes, the happy marriage fantasies were devolving on one of her father's far less attractive business acquaintance. At a smouldering glance from her hero, however, she sniffed back the annoyance and smiled.

Smoothly, as if the wretched girl hadn't spoken, Veloriga went on.

"My mother's family are descended from a sea-goddess, you know. The nymphs of our river come sometimes in the night and sing to me, begging me to join them! I sometimes think…"

Now that was too much for Marina. Mortified beyond bearing, the girl threw herself from the couch crying.

"Mater, no! You'll ruin everything!"

The quick slap of her sandals echoed her pain as she ran weeping from the room. At Veloriga's cool nod, the female relation rose and followed.

Restored at last, Hilarion lowered his trim figure to the couch, muttering,

"Wives and daughters, eh. Mercurius Andescocus, what can a man do? Dolphins, *carissima*," he corrected, adding a pinch of spices to the wine. "We agreed they were only river dolphins. And a rather large otter."

"Some of them, yes," she admitted coolly, then lowered her

eyes to the silver cup taking prints from her hand. "But you know what I think, that you are very foolish to slight the nymphs."

"Slighting them, am I, wife?" he said, wounded. "Am I not building them a nymphaeum to protect their spring? And at no small expense, I might add."

Finally!

"A nymphaeum?" said Corax, rocked in the emotional blast from Veloriga, clouding the air. At the mention of her pet project, instead of pleasure, she seemed on the verge of tears.

"Exactly so," Gallio said. "There's still finishing to do, mainly on the interior. A bit of paint for the statues, give them a bit of life. A few holes to fill in, you know the sort of thing. But this awful weather keeps getting in the way."

"Excellent, sir. And then the river Pistrinum will bring the pilgrims to the temple by the score. It will become a showplace…"

"It will not," Valeria said darkly.

"Ah, no." Gallio replied smoothly. "A nymphaeum for private devotions only, as my dear wife desires. The road and temple will be closed to pilgrims, and there's an end to it. I've no hope of my seeing so much as a *solidus* in return. Am I not the most benevolent of husbands?"

Sending his most sympathetic expression to his hostess, Raven agreed.

"I hope that one day I shall match you in benevolence to so good a lady as yours. *Arglwyddes*," he said, addressing her, and noted how the native honorific made her light up. "I hope you will you take me to see your nymphaeum. Perhaps tomorrow?"

Twice-flattered, Veloriga drew breath to speak, then cried out as the howl of a furious cat was drowned out by an enormous crash that roared into the triclinium followed by an angry chorus of shouts, a squeal, clattering pots, crashing boxes, baskets tumbling, muddled with the clash bang of bouncing iron and copper. And overall, a wild laughter that Raven knew too well.

And dogs, he realized with delight. Oh, lots of dogs.

The Floralia had not noticeably touched the kitchen on Primrose Hill. Oh, there were flowers and fruit at every door and in every room, and the younger children had made garlands for everyone in the house, but as far as the kitchen staff were concerned, a holiday just meant more work.

Ben had imagined dutifully waiting on his patron through dinner, slyly picking tidbits off the trays as they passed. He might even be expected to sing a festive song, of which he knew exactly none suitable to the occasion, but that had never stopped him before. Properly played, he could be sent on an errand and take his time coming back by way of Gallio's office and library. If the scroll was here, and he knew it was, he'd find it and they could move on.

Yes, and what is it again that happens to the best-laid plans?

The household dined the old Roman way, waited on by a dozen slaves. There was no need for him to serve, and he wasn't a guest. When they packed him off to the kitchen, he fancied sitting around on a counter top, licking the frosting from the bowl, and fending off passionate kitchen maids while waiting for the time to pass until called for. He was a personal body servant, after all, valued for his singing voice—the only instrument he'd packed. He could sing for his supper.

It was a brilliant notion, and might have worked if the pastry cook hadn't chosen this morning to take to the heather, leaving the kitchen short-handed. Ben was no cook, and he had failed to practise his Romano-British scullery terms. More to the point, Eporedorix, the big chef with the drooping Gaulish mustachios, was sweet on Milia the kitchen maid. So Milia got promoted to pounding fruit pastes and stirring up glazes that had to be tasted every few minutes on the end of a long wooden spoon. The pot boy was brevetted to assisting Perfidius, the scowling little undercook, and setting up the serving trays. That left Festus with the funny accent, whom nobody knew and who didn't seem too bright, to do the scrubbing, chopping, and carrying out the scraps.

As a freedman, Ben knew he should object, stand on his rights not to be made to work with slaves. On the other hand, no one was threatening to beat him up for the good of the state today. Not so far. He could live with that. And who knows, he might learn something. If you want to know what's what, someone had said, work in the kitchen. And when you can't stand the heat, at least the scullion occasionally gets out of the kitchen, if only to tote the kitchen waste out to the pigs and the midden heap.

The sullen resentment of the staff, combined with the stifling heat of a steaming *culina*, made bursting out into the mizzling half-light a joy. Even though it had been raining off and on all afternoon, and the baskets leaked pig's blood and fish guts all over his tunic, and his buskins were soaked through and caked with mud, at least he could breathe. And while he was out, he was spared watching the goofy love-play of Milia and the thuggish Eporedorix.

On his second expedition to the midden heap by way of the pigsty, he was actually grateful for the duty. The tinkling faerie laughter in the wildflowers as he trudged back and forth was almost comforting, the sounds of home.

A nameless brooklet pattered along beside the path on its way to the Fleet. Best of all, it appeared to have a nymph all its own. As Ben scrambled back up the steep slope with his baskets, he could make out the trill of her singing: more tuneful than birdsong and more wistful, suited to the weather. He tried to approach silently, but slipped on the muddy track, again. The song broke off abruptly, and he forced himself to go back indoors.

The next time, he had a plan. The leisurely holiday meal was more than half over. Picking his steps more carefully this time, he managed to keep his boots on the springy grass between the path and the brook. At the grey stone corner of the house, he stopped. If he turned here, anyone who glanced out the window would see him idling. If he stayed out of sight, they'd never even miss him.

The rivulet's source must be somewhere further up the hill, but right here the stream had split around a sapling may tree leaving a shaded islet. On the near side, a pool had formed, dashed with the fallen petals of the may tree, framed by a few grey stones. Ben got the idea that someone left offerings from time to time. Lucky nymph, he thought with a smile. So he squatted there by the water's edge, humming a tune while he made up an offering of his own.

The Mentos were gone, but Eporedorix had stuffed dates with whole almonds rolled in cinnamon and baked them in honey. He'd also made a pile of rosemary honey cakes, round and desperately sweet. Hungry, and missing out on the serving man's customary prerogatives at table, Ben had lifted a few of each in passing. Now he placed one of the cakes on a flat stone and topped it with a date. Standing with his back to the wall, still humming, he felt the carnelian disk on his wrist grow warm.

Hopefully, this wouldn't take very long. The scullery heat had worn off, and a sky full of rain hovered over the low hills just waiting for a cue. The mist beading on his face made him glad of the hooded woolen tunic and checkered trousers, pig's blood or no.

There. A faint glow moved among the close growing bracken. Was that a giggle? When he heard excited whispering, he resisted the urge to tell them to hush. Instead, he half-sang,

"You're not helping."

Oh yes we aa-are!

We have orders!

The young lord said we could!

The whispers folded into wild laughter, then wandered off. In the stream, a spear of lilies bent to an invisible touch. The glow intensified, moving closer. It was like playing peekaboo with a baby, but eventually a pointed, doll-like face peeped out, blinking and wide-eyed.

"*Oh!*" she giggled, and snatched away the stuffed date. "*I love these!*"

Two seconds later, and a touch more slowly, she stepped delicately out of the reedy cover, pink and white and every inch of two feet high with a pair of moon-pale moth wings fluttering at her shoulders. Big eyes stared up at him from under sable curls tied up with a silver ribbon.

"*Salve, domina,*" said Ben, choosing the Latin automatically.

She sprang back, the little wings lifting her.

"*You can see me!*"

"I can."

He nodded, and hunkered down to talk with her as he would to a small child.

It took a while, as such conversations always do, while the day grew dark except for the circle of light she brought with her. She made him laugh, and sang her favorite song, the one to make the flowers grow in summer, and little buds sprang into the long grasses and burst into stars around her.

Delicately, Ben asked if her sisters all were well, that she knew of. No monsters troubled them, or her? A puzzled frown, followed by tinkling laughter; she had no idea what he was talking about. Who would trouble her?

And Cyfla? What of her?

The top half of the kitchen door banged outward and slammed against the stone wall. Ben jumped. The nymph vanished, and the world darkened except for the light pouring out of the kitchen door along with the steam. Someone snarled.

"Out there. In the rain! Sodding idiot."

A male voice kicked into falsetto to say, "Sipping dewdrops with the little men?"

"Damn it!"

The reluctant freedman grabbed his greasy baskets and shot a look back over his shoulder. The rosemary cake had disappeared. Shaking his head, barely aware how wet he'd gotten, Ben shoved open the half-door. The heat slammed into him with the mingled odours of sweating bodies, cooked meats and unfamiliar spices in odd combinations.

"What now?" he snapped.

iv

The cook, the kitchen maid, even the little pot boy were laughing, but not, apparently, at him. It was one of the serving men, better dressed than the others for waiting on the guests. Collapsed on a stool, he was sitting back against the lime-washed wall while the kitchen maid poured a beaker of water for him.

"What's the joke?" said Festus, stashing the baskets under the table where they had come from. The staff all stopped and stared at him for a moment, then burst out laughing again.

"My mistress. She's rattling on about the spirits again! You know, the little ones only she can see."

Ben's brows shot up.

"Oi! My old mum had the Sight. They talked to her, the wee folk."

We heard that!

He might have to apologize later. The ones he could see were shaking their heads and heaving huge dramatic sighs.

"Yeah, well, madam sees them everywhere, Festus. Dancing under the table, hopping on the chair, frolicking in the brook!"

"Swimming in the soup bowl!"

Bloody hell.

"She's mad, then."

"Might be," said Milia, pouting but trying to stay in the conversation. She was supposed to be beating breadcrumbs and cumin into a sauce for the leeks. "Her maid, that snooty Egyptian, says she sees 'em in the bath, and in the water jars."

"Wine jars, more like," Eporedorix said over his shoulder while slicing veal into collops.

"Don't be daft!" The girl again, swatting him with a dishcloth. "She goes down on the river stairs at night. Sits right down in the water, talking to herself. Or maybe to one of her sirens. And who do you think has to wash the muck outta that gown? Not that snooty Egyptian, I can tell ya."

"Sirens?" said Festus carefully.

"Not them!"

"Say, you're some kind of a German, aren't you?" said the waiter.

They'd all stared at the stranger's hair when he came in, sandy where theirs was dark brown or auburn, as well as falling in his eyes. And, as usual, he was taller than all but the cook.

He nodded, improvising.

"Batavian. So?"

"So, all your women are witches, ain't they? What that on your wrist? Good luck charm?"

But before the curious waiter could repeat whatever slander he'd heard, Barates the steward marched in behind an expression more thunderous than the storm outside. In the sudden silence, they came to their feet, and the pot boy started to hyperventilate.

"Cauna took a tumble with the fish, and it's everywhere. No, he's not all right, that's not your concern. Dafy!" he snapped at the trembling pot boy. "You and Brutius get a water bowl and an armload of towels and get in there, now! Clean it up, and no dawdling. Hardalio, get off your ass and finish that tray, damn you. Then take it out, and get in position. Pay attention! She'll waggle her finger. And you!"

The man turned his hot-eyed gaze pointedly on Festus, who was leaning insouciantly against the wall by the scullery door, catching the cool air while the dogs, returned from explorations, whined to be let in among the third course.

"You! *Novus*. What's your name again?" Barates snapped.

Ben-the-new-guy's head came up, startled.

"Me?"

"Are you simple, man? What. Is. Your. Name?"

While the others stared, he pushed away from the door, and sat down on a hamper full of linens.

"Festus," he drawled, mentally shooting his cuffs. "Antonius Atius Festus."

"Ooh la, three names! A proper citizen!" the steward sneered. "Well, citizen, your patron's turned his nose up at everything, and the mistress is going quietly mad, as he's a friend of the Governor and all. She wants to know is he sick? Or is it some religious thing? Doesn't he know it's a holiday?"

"Holiday?" Milia cackled, as if nothing had ever been so ridiculous.

"Shut it," Barates snapped, "or you'll be back on the market by breakfast."

Ben dropped his eyes, thinking. Raven had probably tried a polite taste of everything and let the rest pass. But "my patron doesn't eat" would hardly do for an answer.

Festus looked up apologetically to find everyone staring at him, especially Eporedorix with his arms crossed over his massive chest clutching a big knife in one hand.

"Ehm, he does have a dodgy stomach. No offense, big guy— the pepper celery sauce was pretty rich. Tell me, *promus*[1], did he taste anything at all?"

"A bit of this and that. A couple of the coriander mushrooms. And most of the cinnamon-honey dates. And he's fond enough of the master's Falernian."

"Ah," said Festus, as if that explained everything, which it sort of did. The pricey wine was potent even watered and spiced. Of course Raven was knocking it back with abandon. Some stories about the fae are true. "Bread and honey is what he wants."

Big knife. Big slam on chopping block. Chef Eporedorix not happy.

"What!" he roared as if he still led a thousand barbarian warriors from his chariot.

Outside, the dogs were getting louder and more insistent, scratching at the door to get in. Tiny giggles in between the yelps meant something was egging them on.

"Are you saying my food's no good?"

"No!" Oh, God, he really was a French chef. "Not that, uhm, wait. You're right. It's a religious thing. He, uhm…" He scanned the room frantically for a clue. "He can't eat fish pickle on—what day is it?"

Eporedorix's frown deepened, bunching the moustaches.

"How should I know?"

Sour as the salad course, Barates sneered, "It's Wednesday, why?"

"That's it!" Festus slapped his brow. "He can't eat fish pickle on Wednesdays and Saturdays! Strictly forbidden. An oath made on Jupiter's altar when we, ah, when we left Rome, see."

---

[1] steward or butler

"You're joking," Barates said flatly. Fists clenched, he clearly wasn't buying it. Any reservations he should have had against calling a free man a liar were quickly dispatched. "He'd starve. What sort of Roman would make such an oath?"

"A very pious one?"

Festus held his pose and his breath, but he wasn't the problem. The dogs whining at the door had started leaping at it, banging at the hinges and barking wildly, mad to get inside. The man's face twisted from red-faced annoyance to choking fury.

"Here now, shut up, you! Go on, you bastards, get down"

Milia screamed, "It's the cat!"

"We don't have a cat!" Barates snarled, and cuffed the girl aside on the way to the door. "Mistress hates cats. You, Festus! Did you bring in a cat?"

"It's up there!" the pot boy yelled, waving an arm.

Shouting at the dogs to get away, he reached outside to grab the leather strap and pull the top door closed. Bad idea. A little whippety thing, the smallest of them, lurched at him, teeth first, and nearly scrambled over the top, but Barates flung him off and fell back, swearing.

"It bit me! I'll feed the perishing cat to it. Where is it?"

"Cat?" Festus coughed, trying not to laugh.

A dog bite isn't funny. Of course it's not. But as far as he could tell, there was no cat in the room, not on window, door, or table, though the dogs outside were plainly in howling hysterics, and it was catching. "What cat?"

"Right in front of you, moron! Lapping up the fish sauce!"

"Hey!" Eporedorix shouted, throwing the cleaver with the skill of a battle-hardened warrior. The wooden bowl exploded, flinging *garum* all over the walls, the stove, and the last tray of stuffed dates. Still no cat.

And that is why you lost the Gallic Wars, Ben thought, with a smirk he couldn't hide.

He also imagined this might be a good time to slip out, maybe explore the rest of the house, maybe take a nap if he could get into the hallway before the dogs broke through. But too late. The latch slipped, the lower door burst open, and two shaggy ponies disguised as dogs galumphed into the kitchen, muddy claws scrabbling on the tiles, with some sort of hound close behind. Once in, they looked around, confused and started sniffing the floor, growling over who would get the spilled sauce and who would get the boiled kid.

You know that pause when everyone stops to breathe at once? And one person says something appalling into the silence? That pause opened, and into that silence, unmistakably, a cat yowled, spat, and hissed.

"There's another one! A black one!"

The fragile peace unravelled with a bang.

The cook, the steward, the waiter and the pot boy stumbled after dogs snapping after cats that seemed to be multiplying over the tables and under the chairs, thundering into the pantry and howling across the shelves on little cat feet while neatly avoiding the iron stove. In their wake, baskets tipped, boxes tumbled, pot herbs in their jars crashed to the tiles, with ladles and strainers and mortars, oh my; and absolutely everything squealed.

Ben sat on his hamper, grinning quietly in the midst of the maelstrom. This was better than the Three Stooges. It also had a familiarly manic feel. And when he looked, really looked, he started to snicker, and then to giggle like a little girl, until he burst out laughing so hard he couldn't stop. Hell, he could barely breathe. The Bremen Town Musicians had taken over the kitchen, principal among them, hobgoblins: the little folk whose sense of *lèse-majesté* is unmatched in Faerie. Whatever their reasons, they had picked this kitchen to party in, this kitchen crew to punish for who knew what.

Multiplying "cats" were running a caucus race with the dogs round and around and under and over the work table, shrieking and thumbing their noses. The more pneumatic of them chose to float through the air like Samhain apples in a water barrel, caroming lightly off the walls and ceilings, the shelves and floors, free-falling into the dogs and everyone's hair, popping in and out of cooking jars. When they came to rest, it wasn't long before someone nosed or elbowed or drop-kicked them into play again.

Pointed noses poked, spindly fingers splashed the sauces, made handprints in the gelatin. One of the dogs, as tall at the shoulder as the table itself, found the platter of boiled lobster and was slurping merrily when he nosed it to the floor. Three very small goblins, hanging on like limpets, managed to braid the chef's mustachios together.

Hey! Hey! Hey! Hup-ho!

Ben swung around, but he had to stand up to see. A tiny team in the farthest corner were pushing hard at the base of a tall amphora, one of five, free-standing on its ridiculous pointed end. Pandemonium was leaning inexorably towards chaos.

He started to say something, but no one would have heard him in the din. A floating one was sailing his way. Cackling, Ben turned to let it bounce off his red plaid behind. Milia saw a mouse flying out of his butt, screamed, and ran out the door into the rain.

Movement drew his eye to the farthest corner. All but helpless with laughter, he turned to watch. Relentlessly, unalterably, slowly but picking up speed as it went, the destabilized *amphorae*, surrendering at last to gravity, had begun a fatal slide along the wall. Wine, olive oil, fish pickle, whatever, the first one slammed to the floor and cracked like an egg, belching a tidal wave of sweet oil over the floor. The next one, red wine.

"Oh, good," Ben wheezed. "We can have a salad."

He never did find out what the third amphora held, or any of the others that slithered and clattered and cracked on the tiles.

Long before Raven could get there, his festive freedman had slipped in a lake of finest Baetican olive oil, stepped in the boiled lobster, fallen backwards over a dog, and banged his head on the table before collapsing to the tiles in an avalanche of oysters. The cat, if there ever was a cat, was gone.

29

Villa Hilarion by night

"I can't leave you alone for two hours, can I?" Corax said, closing the door finally on the last well-wisher.

They'd cut Festus out of the ruined clothes which, when they were thrown on the fire, burned with a merry enthusiasm. Heavy-handed Auntie Bilitis, the children's nurse, had applied a poultice to his nose and dosed him with willow bark, and shoved the new red tunic over his head. She trusted him to put his own arms through the sleeves, as she wasn't coddling a grown man with no manners, not today.

Young Marina, demonstrating her proto-wifely skills, had helped a little with the bandaging, even though her heart's desire was not there to watch. Then they propped the patient up on the reading couch in his patron's guest room and bustled away, embarrassed about the whole thing.

Through it all, Ben suffered manfully, hoping they'd finish before infection or actual brain damage set in. Every joint ached, and the willow bark tea only helped while he was actually drinking it. Thankfully, one of the advantages of having a friend among the Great Fae is that a few minor disasters needn't ruin the whole day.

Raven flipped Ben's feet off the reading couch.

"Sit up so I can take care of this properly for you. Report, please."

"They made me take out the garbage," Ben grumbled. "You can't tell Mellis!"

Raven snorted.

"I won't even tell her about the broken nose. Relax, it's taken care of. And what else?"

Beside him the raven-boy sat with one hand on Ben's shoulder, the other against his brow. Under the warmth Ben half expected to feel the pooling blood sucked away from his bruised brain and the bones knitting up, but the magic didn't seem to work that way. He only knew the ten-penny nail in his head had been withdrawn, and his sinuses had opened. And he could sit comfortably in a pair of checked homespun British breeks, which was more than he deserved.

He took a deep breath and began:

"When we last left our hero…"

By the time the kitchen story was done they were both laughing lightly.

Raven said, "I think the lads may have taken my suggestion a little further than I intended."

"You sent them?"

"Y'know, I believe I did."

"One of them did say they had orders. But you know how they are."

"They still can't lie, human child," said Raven, frowning. "They told me that she calls them, that she likes their attention, but it can't be a conscious…"

"The staff say she talks to the little men, and to mermaids," Ben chuckled. "They also say she drinks a little."

"It may be her desire that calls them. Hobs like these will torment a poor housekeeper for their own amusement, but she runs her household as well, and as invisibly, as a cavalry dressage."

Ben watched his friend thinking, glad that one of them was still up to it.

"The rain's stopped," the boy said suddenly.

He stood and went to the narrow double doors, throwing them open to a garden washed with gold in the last light of the day. The fresh air surged into the room, smelling of ozone and damp earth spiked with gillyflower, thyme, and marigold.

Hands clasped at his back, a tall, slender figure in classical dress, he had laid aside the heavy toga. Hardly more than an austere silhouette, Ben thought he looked like a knight in an Aubrey Beardsley bookplate, touched with the eldritch light that was his marker to those who could see it.

"She could feel them touching her." He raised a hand to his ear as she had done, brushing them away. "I couldn't tell if she was pretending not to notice, or really did not know what was ruffling her hair. She gave no sign that she saw me as myself."

"And what else?"

"Her husband values her but does not love her. But even that, I think, is not the real source of the strain in this house. She is hiding something from him, from everyone."

"And what else? You've got something, don't you?"

Swiftly the boy told him what he had learned at dinner.

"If the nymphaeum is at the spring, it's only a mile or so from here."

"What do we expect to find there? And how will it stop Carew?"

Raven's shrug was eloquent even across the shadowed room.

"I'm just following you."

When he turned back to Ben, the oil in the lamps on the table and in the niches around the room burst into flickering life. Someone had left a ewer of mulsum in the room, a mixture of watered wine and honey. He filled the cup beside it and sipped at it experimentally.

In a similar spirit of scientific discovery, Ben shook his head and was immediately sorry. The ten-penny nail had gone, but he still felt as if his brain had come loose.

"This makes no sense. We've been led here, but why? If Cyfla is lost, we can't expect to find her at home."

"No."

"But we're in the right place."

"And so," Raven said lightly, "is Silence Carew. He was here in this house this afternoon."

"And at the fair as well."

"So it's about the scroll after all! Finish that report, if you please, Sergeant."

That took some explaining, as well as more wine, and in the end they still weren't sure exactly what Carew had bought and what Gallio had done.

"This does get more interesting, sir." Raven said, and passed him the wine cup ("No, it's good for you, take some.")

This time Ben told over his morning, chariot race, visions, and divine intervention. Showed off the winged phallus pressed on him by a stranger, which got a laugh out of the raven-boy. Then there was the moment when Teifi's amulet had resonated with Carew's and, Ben had thought at the time, nearly killed him. Now he wasn't so sure.

"Fraught with myth and magic, your day, wasn't it?"

The headache was making Ben impatient.

"More than usual. I've seen that woman before. It never meant anything, but what if…"

Raven waited for the thought to settle, to take shape in his friend's mind. He'd known as soon as Ben described the fair-haired girl. In fact, he must have known days ago, but hadn't pieced it all together. Hadn't understood he was looking at parts of a puzzle until it was too late to be useful.

"No, it's crazy," Ben said, waving off a thought. "Even if time is a Möbius strip, it makes no sense."

"You think it's her, don't you? The goddess."

Ben blew out an annoyed breath.

"But it can't be. I mean, if she's missing, how can she be here? Or, if she's here, how is she missing? And what the hell is at the nymphaeum?"

"Aye, that's the puzzle, isn't it?"

"No, the puzzle is that god-forgot scroll. Does Carew have the one he wants or not? And if he does, then what? I've read that benighted text over and over, but it goes nowhere. Even with a fourth spell, I mean, so what?"

"What does the amulet tell you?"

"Never to get involved with old gods?" The American shrugged, then put two fingers lightly to the carnelian disk, focusing his thought to reach for the light within. It woke, pale and wavering as a rush light. "Useless. Either it's broken or he's hiding in the closet. Did you check the closets?"

"You're the man who finds things, Ben."

Ben the Finder rubbed a hand across his forehead, willing the ache away so he could listen, really listen for the scroll or whatever was calling him instead of this clattering noise. Clattering? He stopped massaging his head and stared, eyes crossed. The cords that bound the amulet tight against his wrist had come loose so the disk swung against his arm, the suns and lion beads tap-tapping to the beat of his pulse. Suddenly anxious to be rid of it, he slipped the knots and pulled it off.

"Here."

He tossed the thing across to Raven, who grinned and put it around his neck where Teifi had placed it.

"You're sure?"

"It's done with me, I think." He also handed back the wine. "Remember King Alfred's dragon ring? When I try to find a thing, especially magical things, I hear its song. Once I have it my hands, I can tell you the whole story of its journey through time, how it came to each person who owned it or used it. That story kind of reaches out to me, and it's like it plucks a harp string, and I'm the sounding board."

"And can you hear it now, the scroll?"

"Yes, well… Yes, and it's nearby, I'm sure of that. But then there's another voice. Voices, maybe, of every place there's a piece of it. This feels like the harp string has a dozen anchors, in a dozen times. It's like the scroll is being touched in another room—in another country. Or no, it's like…" He threw up his hands in frustration. "If I could think what it was like maybe I would know what to do next. But people keep hitting me on the head! You don't think my gift could go away, do you? I mean, for good?"

Raven moved forward into the light and crouched in front of his friend, looking intently into the mild brown eyes. Ben could detect the lifted brow that went with hesitation.

"No," the boy said finally. "No, it's more than a trick of human physiology. A blow to the head can't knock it out. You always have trouble in London."

"Within the line of the old wall. Or the new wall, as it is

right now. It's all those layers of history past and future stacked up tight in one little space. But out here? It shouldn't…"

"All right," said the raven-boy. He got up wearing a different tunic than he had sat down in; ankle length and deep green this time, the Greek-key borders embroidered in silver thread. "I am obliged by the ancient laws of my race to go and challenge the master of the hall to a game of chess. Or win one. I can never remember. As long as I don't have to grant any wishes. You can lie here a while and contemplate the mystery of history whilst munching slivered almonds, if you like. Unless, of course, you feel up to slouching about in shadows to search for that perishing scroll."

"Sure, I…" Without warning a hot wire drove from one temple to the other. "Ah…sure."

There was no hiding the pain this time.

"Oak and ash, Ben!" Raven hissed with alarm. "Why didn't you say something? Come on, sit up and close your eyes, now."

Swiftly the boy cupped gentle hands around his friend's skull and, leaning forward, breathed across his hair.

In the moment, Ben thought he had walked into Faerie. A summer morning green with life and soft with music. His wife's strong hands holding his, the fingers lithe and promising. Her voice a pleasant murmur in his ear. His son's cheerful narration of a picture he'd drawn.

Then the light changed again, and the music faded along with Mellis, and the headache with it. When he looked for Raven to thank him, the boy had already gone.

30
Veloriga

Beltane. The wheel turned. In the break between storms, coals would be brought from every hearth to set the hills ablaze. Out in the ploughed fields, under the forest's edge, over the cliffs of the sea, the tribes would be dancing and getting drunk to the thudding drums while the women sang the summer in. The young men who would have been warriors not so long ago would leap the summer fires to encourage the sun as they had for a thousand years and a thousand more, from time out of mind.

The king horse in the person of a powerful, laughing young man would take his summer queen with rampant pleasure in the sun house, so the year would be a good one. And when the sun came up, as Veloriga knew, the cattle and the horses would be herded between the dying embers on the way to the summer pastures.

Here below the ridge, within a spear's throw of Boudicca's last battleground, the night drew down in silence as one by one the lamps in their hallway niches flickered, flared, and went out, dimming the frescoed walls. Lighted cressets marking the outer walls burned lower too, though a slave would refresh them before the Frisians made their rounds, jiggling the outer doors, testing the locks. All the guests had taken their midnight possets, or their pick of bedmates, or their prayers, and settled for the night, peace restored. Someone had already swept up the bruised and broken garlands.

Hilarion Gallio had built his house a good distance up the slope from the river of wells and filled the walled space between with a leafy pergola and a terraced garden. He had also dredged out the channel for larger boats, and put in a landing and a stair down to the water for deliveries and his own pleasure. His and Veloriga's with their young family.

On Beltane nights in times past, when they were young and understood one another, though too civilized for primitive rituals, they would have torches to light the landing, and braziers to hold back the mists. They would sit on cushions under a bruised sky, dining on apples, walnuts and raisins, and getting tipsy on heather beer. The children—there were only two then—ran in the grass or poked through the reeds for frogs and squiggly salamanders. Such little children, giggling at the world, babbling in their nursery argot, part Latin, part British, partly the language of the birds.

And then a scream, too far up the river.

And then silence. So much silence.

Sometimes still, when the weather held fair for an hour or so, and no crisis loomed, the lady of the house would venture alone to the river's edge. Tonight, for instance. Sitting alone on the steps, dabbling her feet in the stream, watching for nymphs. Being watched from a shadow.

Voices floated out to her from the house, rising and falling, stopping and starting: slave girls' harsh foreign voices quarreling. She imagined them as a skein of homing geese. Stared up at the moon and down at its reflection rippling in the River Pistrinum, and there they were, two long unbroken wedges crossing the moon like a black M.

M for Marcus, two years old.

A swish of her sandaled foot scrambled the image. The voices disappeared with their noise taunting her melancholy. A fish plopped in the water, but no nymphs came, and no Marcus.

She took a breath, listening for intrusions. She could hear the Frisians down at the front gate exchanging passwords and changing the guard. No other voices. Even the frogs seemed to be waiting for her.

"*Anat, Ashtart, Ata'r,*" she declaimed. "Let my tail rise, open my eyes, let my soul drink the waters. Ata'rathi, call me to the waters!"

Veloriga waited, heart pounding, her white arms raised over the waters of the river. She could almost feel a kind of stirring, but it might have been the wind.

Nothing happened.

Had she pronounced the old words wrong, or in the wrong order?

To be sure, she shifted a little on the cushion she had brought to the cold stone step, and reached for the scroll in its painted box. With care, she unrolled and squinted at it, hoping for enough light to read by.

"Some things are meant to be read by moonlight," said a pleasant voice just a little behind her shoulder.

Veloriga gasped and twisted about from where she sat.

"Corax?"

"Forgive me, *arglwyddes,*" he said, "I could not sleep. May I join you?"

She nodded and pulled aside the girdled folds of her tunic, ever the perfect hostess. The long limbs folded easily, though even sitting cross-legged, his head was still higher than hers.

"Shall I fetch you a sleeping draught?" she replied, hoping to be rid of him.

"No, no, I thank you. It's my man, Festus. He snores most abominably."

Her smile, the professional matron's smile, softened at this. His voice was deeper than it had been at dinner, a man's voice. Why had everyone thought he was so young?

"I should think," he said, when the silence had grown, "that even nymphs have to sleep, don't they?"

"Oh no!" she said, too quickly. "They love the starlight. On clear nights they sit in the shallows over there, and sing and comb their golden hair."

"Yours is red, I believe."

"It will be white soon enough. And then…"

A heavy sigh said her misery was too complicated to explain.

"Then what?"

"Then I will be too old for them."

She stopped, sniffed back tears, and looked away, expecting his scorn.

Atius Corax neither laughed nor turned away. Instead he said gently, "Will you show me what you were reading?"

He could feel the difference as soon as his fingers closed around the scroll. Rob Cotton's document was fresh from the scribe's pen compared to this, though the ancient papyrus was more supple, the ink darker and the lines immeasurably cleaner. Even the *morven* figures that separated the three charms and decorated the corners seemed to have been fresh drawn this morning, but he knew they had not. When he reeled it out to a torn right edge, it was clear that Latin had indeed been scrawled in the margins, but only a quick translation key to each charm before understanding failed, not the pages of commentary Carew had studied.

An unaccustomed excitement touched his mind, and he nearly laughed out loud. He had found it—and there was still a piece missing. It might have been missing for centuries.

Raven let the scroll snap back together in his hands, then said, "Tell me why you wish to be a siren."

Caught off balance, her reasons flew unguarded.

"To find my little boy." One hand went to her blushing cheek. "Oh, Isis, I never meant to say."

He had been prepared to put his arms around her, prepared for a storm of weeping and release, but none came. Possessed by a strange serenity, as of long practice, her passion withdrew behind a closed door. Not looking at him she straightened her gown, squared her pale shoulders and lifted her feet from the water, tucking them around her cushion.

"Tell me," he said mildly. "I'll listen."

He could watch her with a sideways glance, a friendly eye, giving her time to decide. When she began, without preamble or prologue, her voice was low and thoughtful, unhurried but almost as if she had been waiting for someone to ask.

"I miscarried the first time. The next lived only a few days. You know, British women—Trinovantian women—we're expected to be courageous, as fierce as the men."

"And so they are," Raven said, thinking he understood.

"Not everyone can be a warrior," she snapped, showing something of her younger self, he thought. The one not in perpetual mourning, shrouding her grief under the perfection of her household.

"And then what happened?"

"Titus came, and this time we were fortunate. Then the next year, it was Marcus and he thrived as well. Two stout sons to make the house of Gallio into a dynasty. Hilarion was beside himself with pride."

The ghost of a pleasant memory twitched up the corners of her mouth. "He was travelling all the time then, but in his letters, and when he was home, his every thought was on the boys, and practically his every word. He was so full of plans."

The ghostly smile fled. Raven thought he knew why.

"He spoke too often, and with too much pride?" he guessed. "There are powers that take notice of such things."

"We call them *y Bendyth*," she murmured, "the Blessing, though they are not often kind."

He was not permitted to take offense, knowing what it meant. Like Fair Folk, Good Neighbours, The Ladies And Gentlemen, a flattering term allows the whole of Faerie to be named, light and dark, unseelie and benign, without calling them forth.

"They are not all wicked, surely."

"Oh, of course not. I know the *ellyllin*, the little mischief-makers that pull my hair or trip a lazy servant, or tangle the horses' manes even after you watched them being groomed. But they can be helpful, too, when it suits them. They are like unruly children, like my disobedient child. They let me see them, sometimes, you know."

Of course.

"Tell me what happened."

Cool and detached, as if it had happened to some other mother, some other child, she faced him.

"No one believes me, but I know what I saw. They had been playing, Marcus and his elder brother, chasing dragonflies on a summer night. Titus came when he was called. But not Marcus…"

She coughed slightly, swallowing old tears. "We searched and we called…. To the north, we had gone as far as the spring, when we heard a scream like a hunting cat, or a horse in panic. I looked up and saw a winged shadow rising into the sky, very fast. Then a small thing…"

Memory caught in her throat, snatched her voice away.

"Such a small thing, it fell to the earth so quickly, like a star falling. It took another hour to find him. He was tangled in the rushes just over there, the little body still whole and perfect, with the print of a muddy hoof on his tunic, and a monstrous toad squatting on his chest. I thought at first that he was still alive, but the *ceffyl daur*, the water horse, had already snatched his soul away."

A swift frisson of recognition trilled across Raven's thought. The creature Ben had encountered on the Thames might have been such a thing.

"No one else saw this happen?"

The question ripped a bitter laugh from her throat.

"The whole household and half the valley was searching for him. Anyone who looked up saw it, but not my civilized husband. Or if he did, he denied it. He was devastated, and he was fearful, but not of the *Bendyth*. He saw no hoof print, not even the horrible toad. Nothing but a dead child—his second son and half his dreams, drowned. If you ask him, he will tell you—everyone will tell you—Marcus drowned."

Wisely, Raven held his tongue, adding new anger to the growing store.

Again remote, Veloriga told the rest.

"We mourned. We buried his ashes. It's a fact of a woman's life that from time to time we must give a child back to the gods before…" She shook her head ruefully. "Soon enough I was pregnant with Marina. I went to the temple of Isis to consult with their physicians and the midwives. She looks after mothers, you know, Isis. Then a priest there, a local man not an Egyptian, told me Marcus is one of the *Bendyth* now."

The words came swiftly now, tumbling over each other like the rapids of Faerie.

"He said because Marcus was taken from the Cyfla —that is this river's old name—he is with the Atami who bide here, he said. He might be right here, almost in my arms. I thought, if I could become one of them, I could find him there. I could beg the goddess to let him go, bargain with her. There was a way, he said, and he had a charm, but—"

"Wait, I know this one." The jewel-blue eyes glittered. "But it would be very expensive, and you must never doubt him, or it would not work?"

On a breath, she nodded.

"Lady, the magic of the *Bendyth* is what it is. It can't be bought or sold."

"But—"

"Shall I tell you the rest?"

More than any priest of Isis or Osiris, it is within the Raven's gift to know these things. He delivered them in the terms she knew.

"If all came about as you say, he is indeed alive in the Summer Country, though Marcus is no longer his name. He will have nine years of forgetfulness, and nine years of wandering, and nine years of remembrance before he can come to you, if he will. And then he will be so changed you will not know him. That is the truth of it, as well as it can be told."

She nodded, dry-eyed and fierce.

"I will be an old woman, or dead, before then. No. He will know me, if only I can come to him."

She held up the scroll, almost crushing it in her hand. "Aneirin, the priest, he taunted me with this for months. Every week he demanded more money for his time, his assistant, a translator, a copyist, a necromancer! Silver at first, then gold, then other things I would not give. That's when I denounced him to the high priestess before Isis herself, and she listened. When I got home, I had to tell my husband. He was furious, of course, about the money and the scandal. Then I gave him the scroll. He said it was rubbish and ought to be burned, but he could see it had some value, I guess, and hid it away. Marina was born, then Madog. And that is the end of it."

"But he copied the scroll, tarted it up, aged it, and then sold the copy," Raven said thoughtfully. "Clever indeed."

Eyes slipped sidelong, senses on alert. A small sound that might have been a badger's cough broke the air, louder than the croaking frogs and night birds hunting along the Fleet. A squirrel, probably, scrambling over the wall undeterred by faerie tricks. And maybe it was Ben, less stealthy than he hoped.

"Have I been a terrible fool?" Veloriga asked, all the energy drained out of her.

"Ah, well. You have given too much credit—and too much money—to a scoundrel, but who hasn't? Lady, are you well?"

Eyes glazed, she had begun to sway. He caught her shoulders to steady her.

"I'm well. I think… All right, settled now. How strange," she said, staring at him while her heart steadied. "So many things I have never told anyone. I have been afraid for so long, but not any more. Who are you?"

He smiled enigmatically, and held the papyrus up to the light.

"I am your friend. Now, the first charm is damaged, but it is not meant for you, in any case, human child."

"I am no child."

"Of course not," he said, soothing, "but to the spirits, to the *Bendyth* of the earth and the sea, you are very young. Now attend. This second part is meant to allow a mortal, such as your worthy self, to spend an hour with them, free of human sorrows."

"But it doesn't work."

"Doesn't it? You have said the words, but there is more to it. Here, you see?"

He tilted the scroll again. "You see these marks here and here?"

Patiently he explained it all—the words, the music, the rules which were not, thankfully, too many or too difficult for a play-loving creature to remember.

"And will it make me as they are?" Veloriga asked finally, tilting her head toward the misty river where a pair of buxom river maids, shimmering in fine scales green and bronze, alternately turned somersaults and toyed with the jewels in their hair.

Raven shrugged lightly, though he was pleased to see them. "So it says here."

The girls in the river shook their heads energetically, which also bounced their fulsome breasts and made them giggle.

Who is like us, little bird?

"One hour only, you must not forget."

Impatient to begin, she cut him off.

"Yes, yes, I will remember."

The longing in her voice was as palpable as her grip on his arm. In the dark, something moved in response. Raven's hand went up for silence.

"Hush a moment!"

With an oath and a quick gesture, he did what he should have done at the beginning, and warded the landing against eavesdroppers. He'd raised a wall to hold back the river mists while they talked. Now on a whim, he let the fog seep back over the edges of his barrier to twist the vision of any idle watcher, or any diligent one, for that matter.

Content with his handiwork, he held out his hand for her to take.

"Come into the water."

She touched his fingers and stood, then stepped down gasping as the cold water hit her thighs and stomach, soaking through the fine light wool of her tunic.

"Oh! It's so cold."

"Not for long."

When it reached her waist, the skirts billowing about her, she turned to press the scroll into his hand.

"Keep it safe, will you? Hilarion will go mad if he finds it missing."

"You should not lie to your husband, lady," Raven said severely.

With a haughty sniff, she flipped her braid over her

shoulder, half-Atami already.

"He should not have taken it from me. Now I am going to find my son. Now teach me the song, please, Corax."

So he sang, delivering the pure notes as a kind of chant to make it easy for her, and using the Latin text to be sure the magic would respond to her will. Then he nodded to Veloriga. She sang it back to him, tentative at first.

"Something is happening," she whispered.

Go on!

Go on!

Go on!

Her hobgoblins, her *ellyllin*, had crept to the edge of the lawn, the boldest standing at the Raven's feet to cheer.

Trembling, she sang the words. Then she turned to face the stream and the waiting sirens and lifted her arms to the moon now scudding through the gathering clouds, and sang it through a third time:

"*Anat, Ashtart, Ata'r*, bid my tail to rise, open my eyes, let my soul drink the waters. Ata'rathi calls me to the waters."

Her face turned up to him filled with surprise and shining like the moon.

"How do you feel?" he laughed.

"I can feel…I feel…"

The change had begun even before she reached the end where the last notes hung sparkling with enchantment. Waist deep in Cyfla's water, the air shifted and flickered, twisting the light.

"Oh Isis! This is wonderful!"

Raven knew what it felt like, and longed for the release of his own transformation, but he had seldom watched it happen, and never to a human so willingly changed.

Carefree for the first time in years, the laughter spilled from her with each new sensation: as the night air caressed her naked breasts, youthful and firm again. From her hair to her hip bones a glimmering light spun down into her legs. A spiralling rainbow painted the lines of her cheekbones, throat and shoulders, the backs of her hands with a shimmer of silver scales over green and gold and rose.

"How do you feel?" Raven called merrily, though he knew the answer.

"It tickles!" She yelped, startled and fell back, splashing into the river. "Thank you!"

Like ribbons of blue-green light, the flukes of a shimmering, translucent tail flipped up behind her as she sounded, the tatters of her clothing streaming behind. The river girls on the opposite bank cried out with delight and laughing, flipped up their tails and dived to greet her.

"Only an hour, remember!" He sent his voice after her. "And give Cyfla my compliments and…"

The mermaid had already turned her back on her home to follow the sirens deep into the stream, deeper than the river itself, into the waters of Faerie. He laughed and conjured an hourglass of falling sand that glittered like diamonds as the seconds sped past.

Night and silence closed in. Would she come back, he wondered, now that she had what she wanted? Would she even remember? It occurred to him that the word he had translated for her as free of human sorrows might be better rendered as 'unmindful'.

ii

To the immortals an hour is never long, Raven thought, pacing the landing with impatience unsuitable to a lord of the Great Fae. Except when it is. The seconds that had poured so speedily when first he'd turned the glass now moved with impossible slowness.

Was this how fathers felt, waiting for a child to come home from a date? What would happen if she were deep under water when the time ran out? Would the magic spit her out on the nearest shore and hope for the best? Or would she be frolicking one moment and drowning the next? What if she fell in love with a sailor? People with wishes never think about consequences.

He sat on the step and reached into the swiftly moving water, letting it ripple through and between and around the long fingers barely noticing the icy chill. His mind settled, his heart clear, he merged his song with that of Cyfla's river and spoke the words of summoning, begging an audience with the river goddess, and waited. Nothing answered, though a gauzy, moth-winged nymph glared at him from her bower under a stand of hollyhocks.

Sorting through what they knew, he recalled Ben's story of the chariot race. The man had called the girl by some other name, Oriana, but that meant nothing. Romantic twaddle from a man who thought "princess" wasn't good enough for a… All right, perhaps not good enough for a goddess, but twaddle still. Whoever he was, Raven realized, the man must be an immortal, or near to it. And from the description, it could well be someone he knew. So saying, the raven-boy scowled and called to mind his personal shortlist of Faerie's Most Annoying.

In the mansion, the towers, the M.C. Escher galleries of his thought, he examined the shaping pattern again, letting stories and names, music and light float and shift while he tweaked his perspective.

"Somewhere in all this shit there's got to be a pony," he muttered. Then he kicked over the metaphorical table and let the pieces fly.

Baffled beyond bearing, he rolled down onto his stomach and, resting his chin on one arm, swirled the other hand in the water, and formed the call. Again, utter silence filled what should have been an open channel. She'd gone out and left no forwarding address, forgotten to set her voicemail. The image amused him. He'd been spending too much time in the mortal world, obviously. But the lack of response was troubling.

Where was she? And where was anyone? Even the *ellyllin* had wandered off.

Right here, Boss!

At the high-pitched sound, like a vinyl record played back at high speed, he looked down to find that a lanky manikin, almost two feet high, in a green suit and with Pinocchio's nose, had sat down next to him, dangling long legs from the edge. Twiggy-fingered hands rested on its knees. No more substantial than the top branches of a hawthorn tree, it kicked its heels against the face of the step, quite as if it were the most ordinary place in the world to find a Dartmoor pixie, as the creature seemed to be.

"Is there a message?" the fae lord asked politely.

Aubrey says, A'right, me handsome. Need any help?

"Ah, no, I think we're fine. Making progress."

Well snap it up then, he says. We're burnin' daylight! Make it work!

The raven-boy sighed mightily.

"Please present my compliments to my lord and say…"

Here she comes! Hooray! The creature hopped to its feet with a back flip. *I must away ere break of day. A toora-lye-ay! Mae fy hofrenfad yn llawn llyswennod!*[2]

"Sorry?"

It cartwheeled away in a babble of mock-Welsh until it stopped under the arbour, executed a tight ice-dancer's spin, and *pop*, it disappeared.

At last, a stirring in the waters, a ripple, a whoosh and splash, and she appeared in a shower of dark water and long red hair. Escorted by the sirens she'd left with, accompanied by a long-limbed nereid, a sea maid who might have been Veloriga's twin, but for having two legs, and what looked like jewelled gills at the side of her neck. Perhaps the many-times-great-grandfather hadn't been lying about his mermaid liaison after all.

"Corax!" Veloriga cried in a voice now young and light as her own daughter's. "I think I am early, but I had to tell you, Atius Corax, you have set me free! I am free! Look look look!" She lifted the golden hand of one of the girls then the deep brown of the other. "This is Cleridis and this is Parthenia."

A fountain with a nymph in it erupted almost in her face. Crowned with a pile of curls as black as the raven's, she threw ice white arms around Veloriga's neck and kissed her hungrily while the water sluiced over them. Without letting go, the

---

2 My hovercraft is full of eels! Pixie humour much resembles Monty Python's.

nereid flung a coyly smouldering look over her shoulder at Raven.

"You spoke true, Valoraemaiah. He is a pretty one. I love you already, pretty one!" she called, and flung one hand toward him. "Come, come! Come play with us!"

"Come play!" the others cried.

A night-black eyebrow arched while Raven considered the possibilities. He was an excellent swimmer.

"This is my very distant cousin Kyraeth," Veloriga said, detaching the nereid and passing her off to Parthenia, or possibly Cleridis.

"You have a new name again, I see."

"Oh yes, it is my Atami name, or part of it. Their real names are much longer, of course, and very beautiful, but they must be sung under the water." She swam to him with a single flick of the gossamer tail. "Oh, I love you, Corax, and I am in your debt."

She ducked under the rippling surface and arrowed towards him, letting the river wash back the thick mass of her hair. The braid had been loosed and replaited in dozen of tiny braids stuck with river flowers pink and gold. Without a single strand of grey the red-gold ends floated curling over her shoulders and between the bobbing breasts, and made a nimbus around her on the water.

One of the naiads burst into a trilling song, and the other joined her. Veloriga listened only for a moment, then added her voice in a complicated harmony. Then she broke off again to say,

"I didn't want to come back, but they said I must."

"Thoughtful girls." He threw them a smile and a wave.

An adorable shrug.

"I don't know why."

"So that you do not drown, lady. Wait, I have an idea."

They took his salute as an invitation to blow kisses and flirt and flaunt and, really, he had the will but not the time.

From a pocket of Faerie, Raven pulled four pretty combs and as many again of round jewelled mirrors. All the watery ladies squealed with delight in Icthylean harmony and reached their webbed hands to him greedily. Three sets he threw as far as he could downstream, and let them race after them, tumbling and leaping. The last he held out to Veloriga, now as eager as her sometime sisters, then he pulled it back.

"If you are good you shall have it. Come sit here and tell Uncle Corax what happened."

Raven reminded himself that talking with nymphs always takes patience, and she would be one for a little while yet.

"You look happy," he said. "Did you find your son?"

The golden tail curled around her in the water, the flukes a gossamer veil. She flipped it and brought it down just to hear the music in the water as it fell.

"Who?" She shrugged like a ripple of the tide, content to toy with her hair. "Oh, he isn't there. Journeying, or heroing, or something. Whatever the third thing was. Or the second thing."

"I see. And Cyfla?"

"She's gone away. Everyone knows that. That priest was an idiot."

"Well, yes, he was. Veloriga… No, dear, don't do that."

She wasn't listening. She had decided she'd rather plant little kisses on his toes. One slightly webbed hand, warm blood under chilled skin, started to travel from his ankle to calf, coaxing aside the silken wool of the tunic on the way to his thigh, ordinarily a most efficient way to his heart.

A fae glow flared around him that lit up the yard like daylight, then dialed quickly back as control overcame delight. Somewhere over the garden wall a rough Frisian voice shouted in alarm and called for back-up. Heavy boots scraped the ground. Back-up told him how drunk he was, and the voices and armour clattered away.

Raven took both her hands in his and lifted them firmly away.

"Valeria Lucila," he said, capturing her eyes in his. "It has been," he kissed one hand, "an adventure." He kissed the other, and though she pouted very prettily, that was all.

Before she could take a breath to reply, he was outside her reach, poised under a mischievous grin half way to the house, his radiance reduced to a shimmer at the edge of her awareness.

"Live well" he called.

"Wait! Come back!" she cried, stretching her pale arms to him, beseeching. He started toward the house, his walk an easy saunter.

"Make love to me, Corax."

"I really can't," he said over his shoulder.

"But I know how it's done, now! Only let me show you."

That made him turn, all right, with a widening grin.

"Sweetheart, if only there were time."

When she tried to lift herself out of the water, he put a finger to his lips, then pointed it at her.

"Now you stay right there. No, right there, and silent until the glass runs out."

The Raven laughed and reinforced the order with a constraint he seldom used to hold her quiet and still without harm. In two minutes, no more than three, when Valeria Lucila was herself again, Cinderella would be home from the ball with her griefs resolved. Or perhaps not. Either way, his part in her story was done.

"*Vale!*" he said with a cheery wave, and he was gone.

iii

A tool shed within the river garden wall had given the watcher cover from the rain all afternoon, though the floor stood half an inch in water over the unmortared tiles. Cramped and wretched, he huddled on a wooden bench barely cushioned with some sort of coarse sacking. Hatred and madness stood in the red-rimmed eyes. After all he'd been through, all his suffering at the hands of men in every age, every fearsome day wasted in the pigsty called the Mermaid Stair recovering from his hurts, seeking back and back through time— after all that…this? His thoughts grew dizzy and collapsed. After all that, the demons had still robbed him.

He needed only the last spell, the hidden spell. In all his study, only Isidore of Seville had even alluded to it, preserving the single phrase, "the doleful charm unsend," which Isidore claimed to have found in some writing of Pliny the Younger, referencing an even older work now lost. The final spell, as Isidore wrote in the prevaricating words of speculation, had been hidden because it would undo the whole brothel kingdom of the Atami. And that, thought Silence Carew, was all he wanted.

So he waited while the rain drove all into the house that had greeted him with such cold hospitality. He was soaked through and freezing, but he had learned a kind of patience.

Still, he jumped when his angel spoke, the great booming bell of its brazen voice, as always calm and sure.

ALL WILL BE WELL. THE ABOMINATION WILL BE DESTROYED.

He'd not understood at once, but late one night while he lay racked with marsh fever in some Saxon pig-sty of a monastery, apprehension had come. An angel stood over him, vast and black behind the veil of its celestial perfection. It never slept and would never leave his side. It spoke seldom, showed itself rarely, but the other badgering, cajoling voices had fled before its mighty wings. The name had appeared in his mind in searing letters: FILEAL, whom God had sent to oversee his holy mission to rid the world of Atami. Fileal who carried a human soul on its tongue to bestow once it was earned, when the task was done.

So Silence had waited in the dark and the wet of Roman Britain, watching through a knothole in the wooden door and the one narrow window in a cracked, lime-washed wall, until the house was silent. When the woman came out, his lips drew up in a horrible mockery of a smile. This Valeria, the unnatural wife to a dishonest merchant, she would know. He would wait.

She had chattered earlier with him about the mermaids, showing off the disgusting murals and mosaics in the house, reeking of the Atami pestilence, inconstancy, depravity. She had revealed her shameful secrets, though she knew it not. She might wear the guise of a true woman, but that too was a filthy lie. The whore knew perfectly where the Ata'rathi scroll was kept, and she would give it to him before she died, broken and screaming, under his hands.

Fileal said nothing, but Silence felt its approval warm as a cooing dove. There was movement on the landing.

"Who's this?" he hissed. A young man joined her out of nowhere, obviously her lover.

The angel said: LISTEN.

All they did was talk. Lovers' nonsense, surely, though the man never touched her. What was there to learn, except how a wanton seduces an corrupt man?

WATCH.

Silence put his face to the window, blinking hot eyes. The distance and the damp made the sound dull, hard to make out. For a long time they only sat and talked, partly in a swift, light Latin, partly in something he thought was Welsh. He thought they must be plotting to kill her husband.

Smirking, the goggle-eyed whore handed her lover a gift, a letter maybe, or the deeds to the house, or the devil's contract signed in blood.

I will write letters in her blood, he thought, and strained to listen.

Then an insect bit the watcher's ear to make him jump; the bench he sat on scraped the tiles. He gasped out Christ's name, then clapped a filthy hand over his mouth, pressing himself to the wall.

The air stank suddenly of magic. When he looked out, the lover's hard eyes, filled with flame, slipped sidelong until they came to rest on the shed where Carew held his breath and prayed.

He heard a click, a buzz. The man, the demon, had not moved, nor made a gesture nor spoken any spell. And yet the world went quiet as if his ears had been stopped with wax; so quiet he could not hear his own heart beat, though he could feel its hammering. A rippling wall of air swept toward him, flung sharpened spears of light that made him duck and snap the streaming eyes shut. When he opened them, his world was black and nothing more, and all his senses failed him. Panic-frozen in the small space, he dared not move when every tool and pot and nail, every shard of broken light would betray him to pain and death.

SLEEP, said the angel.

He may have fainted, but either way, Silence slept.

✳︎✳︎

Even before the handsome Corax vanished into the house, Valoraemaiah, Veloriga, who was feeling rather more like Valeria as the sands sped through the glass, had forgotten why they'd been talking. She'd wanted something from him, wasn't that it? Of course, he wanted to kiss her. Cold flesh warmed at the thought.

She heard her name. One of her names. Atami voices so well beloved were calling, shouting at her.

Look out! Valoraemaiah, swim away! Swim away!

The laughter bubbled up but she kept it to herself. She couldn't swim away. She had to stay right here being pretty and happy for just a little longer. What a fuss they were making. She would turn to look in a minute. Right now she would sit under the stars looking down at the lights in the water rippling, trickling, tickling across her breasts, making tall brown islands of her nipples, half submerged.

The last grain of sand ran out of the bottle, all spells complete. The magic rose up rejoicing, returning her to her husband, her children, her life. Remembering all, retaining all their grace, Valeria kicked her legs free of the enchantment and turned to blow a last kiss and wave, all pink and white again.

"Farewell, sweet friends!"

Her friends screamed, eyes wide with horror, and dived tails up into the deep streams. Valeria Lucila's world began to end.

From behind, a hard arm went tight around her throat to crush it. A hard voice cursed her on stinking breath. She squirmed and tried to kick as he dragged her naked from the water. Her hands tore at the sinewy arm to pull it away, to let her breathe. But the man was strong and well-practised, the arm knotted and slick with old scars. She was dangling in the air, disoriented and fainting, and his iron arm never let go.

A line of flame erupted in her side. She tried to scream for the guard, for anyone, but there was no air. No air. No light.

Oh Isis, what is happening?

The world spun, the light whirled down to precious points

no more than sparking fireflies.

Barely conscious, Valeria felt her stomach lurch in those airborne seconds while she fell, knew when the graveled earth reached out to slam her head to the ground, bruising, cracking, tearing across her cheek. She clawed into the moss, trying to rise. The fire in her side exploded when he kicked her. Her body rolled and skidded almost to the water's edge, to the blessed water's edge. Again she tried to move, to crawl over the brink. But his fingers gripped into her braids and pulled her head up.

Her head raked back, slender throat exposed, she could scarcely breathe. Then, he threw her back and the air slammed out of her. His fist cracked across her jaw. He let her fall. Blood, thick and tasting of metal, sprang into her mouth.

She had still not seen his face, but she knew him. Knew the amulet that hung around his neck. Knew the scars on his arm.

"P- Placidus? W-Why?"

He growled and dragged her further into the shadow of his hiding place, and flung her on her back. Kicking her ankles apart, he dropped to his knees between them and leaned forward, pressing the tip of a cold black knife between her thighs.

"Where is the last spell?" he hissed. His breath stank of vomit.

"W–what?" she gasped. Her swelling tongue snagged on broken teeth.

"The true scroll with the last spell, you Atami slut!"

The torn lips moved, but nothing came from them but bubbling blood.

"The man, your demon lover. I know he is called Fitzroy, for he named himself to me long ago. The token that you gave him, was that it?"

Not everyone can be a warrior. Between blows and imprecations and unending pain, she told him what little she knew, and even where the demon had gone, though she had no idea.

He hadn't finished with her, not by half, but a glance up toward the house reminded him how exposed they were.

Servants, gardeners, anyone might appear at any minute. Besides, more rain was coming. Fat raindrops splattered on his bloody hands. He had other, more isolated shelter where he could complete his task unmolested. Then he would find Sir Rafael bloody Fitzroy, and the scroll and the spell, and he would destroy them all.

Growling with frustration and violence delayed, Silence closed a hand over the woman's bloody mouth and nose, muttering imprecations. Too weak to fight him now, she fainted soon enough.

31
At the Nymphaeum

i

Restless, Ben dozed on the reading couch listening to the house settle, grow silent while the lamps guttered and long shadows flared. Guests found their beds, some of them already occupied by the playmate selected for them. Whispers, shuffling feet, some other noises, more shuffling. No one came to look in on the patient, and even his partner had a task to occupy him. Intermittently, snips of conversation reached him from somewhere outside. After awhile, he felt the subtle cloak of enchantment descend, muffling the sound in cotton wool as if an open door had been abruptly closed. Probably best, even without knowing what Raven was up to.

Against the quiet, he could feel the tightness in his chest grow stronger. The harp string hum thrummed in his blood, clear at last without the interfering magic of the amulet. It called him towards his goal without promising exactly what he'd find. Ben thought he could be sure of it—if London didn't slap out the tuning peg as it had in the past.

Barring that, he knew he'd waited long enough. In the failing lamplight he gathered up hood, cloak, and satchel, and put his hand to the garden door. He paused, listening; what had changed? The song had become a blended note, like two matched voices wound together. Ben grinned and shook his head. The very complexity only made him more certain.

However it worked, wherever it came from, the note, the need, could not be plainer. It was time he went after it.

*
**

From the garden gate someone had carved a path down to the Fleet, or the Pistrinum, or the Cyfla, and laid flagstones along the marshy bank for the ease of the mistress's dainty feet—and future pilgrims' feet, once Hilarion had his way. Smooth as a good Roman road, it straightened out the curves of the wandering stream, turning nature into art and making the journey quicker and decidedly less muddy than Ben had expected. Still wet, of course, and mortally dark though a moon must be riding up there somewhere. A modest shrine or a marble bench appeared out of the mist every so often to let a traveller rest or take in what must be a view on a clear day.

Up, said the unwavering pull, so up he went unchecked through a darkness nearly absolute, through the meadow scents of mud and marsh grass. A bit of a breeze swept past his ear, and a nightjar's mating trill, and the shuffling of the night-time residents of the heath. The path as it lifted gradually met the ridge that embraced the Villa Hilarion, moving ever north and east.

With the narrowing Fleet no more than a dark reedy line at his left hand that meandered away and looped back, the land rose gently, skirting a low hill thick with youthful oaks and even younger apple trees. The orchard, he supposed, that someone had been trying to lead him to. Once or twice as he moved along, the clouds parted for a stray shaft of moonlight that let him check his bearings, avoid a collision, let a fox scuttle across the path. Then it closed in again.

A fat drop of rain landed on his cheek, as cold as old tears.

He'd never been very good at judging distance without a map, and the tattered mist wasn't helping, but he thought a mile must have passed in this way, keeping his head down, marking the light crunch of his boots on the wet path to keep from wandering off, his own heart thudding steadily in time. A mile or even two. Then the slope curved up, the angle sharpened. The finished path gave way to packed earth gone muddy, packed gravel replaced by short planks where the builders needed more traction. Ben stumbled and nearly pitched to his knees. The hand that shot out to steady himself found a waist-high pile of rubble and discarded stone disks.

He was breathing hard as he straightened, beating the crap off his hands, and listening hard for the clatter of Frisian armour or the bark of a challenge. All he could hear was the slide and hiss of tumbling pebbles through the debris, and from far away the bubbling voice of a fountain.

Then the racing clouds opened; a lively breeze tossed the ground mists. Ben looked up, and felt his breath catch in his throat. Across a small minefield of discarded building materials, the milk-pale moon fixed a ring of fluted columns in a noose of light, the nearest only a few muddy paces away.

"Is that it?"

Picking his steps he clambered up the slope to the pavement of a Classical colonnade, only partly complete, which circled a shallow pool filled to overflowing with water. At its center, the lady of the lake rose with the waters of Avalon with the spring gushing from her cupped hands. Not magic, just Roman engineering, he thought, and a marble statue.

Behind her, barely visible, a grey shape floated, a filigree of polished stone and caryatids floating spectre-like out of the hill behind it. Low steps traced the curve around the reflecting pool, reaching to join hands with the unfinished colonnade, a full-moon circle for the source of the Fleet. Then the fog thickened and closed in, leaving only a faint glow where the moon had to be. He could see his hand in front of his face, but that was about all.

Ben snorted a little. Avalon, right. Or Brigadoon. *"Pull up a hay bale, kiddo."*

Who used to say that?

He was trapped there, in a way. Between the mist and the wet uneven ground, the mundane unknown was quite enough to hold him in place awhile. Stalled, he leaned against a rain-streaked column breathing in the musky smells of the heath.

Now what did that smell remind him of? He took a deeper breath, holding it, letting his mind slip.

An old tune came into his throat, a song he'd known all his life, and after a moment's quiet humming, Ben felt another voice join in—familiar, a match for his own, but older and more mellow. Perhaps it was just his own voice reverberating in the all but unseen *peristylium*, the temple court. Perhaps it was a memory of trees.

It was cold spring now, his breath a white haze; it had been warm back then, and late summer. The patter of raindrops shaken from a tree branch on his left was the echo of old applause. A shrew squeaked; or was it the creak of wooden boards under foot on a September night, when the footlights were Coleman lanterns, and the seats a hillside of musky hay bales among the white birch.

The rest of the memory washed over him faint but unmistakable: the crisp metallic ring of a Caswell harp, the applause, and the genial voice inviting him, a faire brat of sixteen, to the stage.

"Hey, everybody, it's Rosie Harper's boy, Ben. Pull up a hay bale, kiddo. No, not out there, up here. Come on, and bring that guitar."

So long ago. Chris was gone now, and those days as well. It took a minute for Ben's throat to open enough to clear it, reminded of the soggy here and chilly now.

"One of my old teachers used to say," Ben repeated softly, and the matched voice seemed to be with him, *"there's a song for every purpose, and a purpose for every song. Let's warm this place up!"*

He felt the strings under his hands, heard one foot tapping out the time.

> *As I walked out in Chester city*
> *At the late hour of the night*
> *Who should I see but a fair young maiden*
> *Washing her clothes in the clear moonlight.*
> *Madam I'm a darlin', a die row dither-o*
> *Madam I'm a darlin', a die row day.*

He sang quietly, watching the gloom shift with the weather.

> *Oh first she washed and then she squeezed 'em*
> *Then she hung them out to dry*

And then she folded up her arms
Saying, "Oh what a fair young girl am I."
O Madam I'm a darlin', a die row dither-o
Madam I'm a darlin', a die row day.

And as he watched, a freshening wind unstitched the mist from the ground, drew it off in lacy rags, until across the lake or pool or pond the nymphaeum appeared, garlanded in goddesses, haunted by shadows but more real than it had been. It was closer than he'd thought, and smaller, a jewel in the wilderness. The wet and freezing wilderness and the muddy building site, the landscape barely finished and nature not yet invited back. He left off singing, his heart warmed and ready.

Now where the hell was Raven?

A rattle of wings, a disturbance of air, a pricking of cold sharp claws through the thick wool on his shoulder. There he was.

"Oh good, I've always wanted a pet."

The claws lifted and feathers flipped his hair. A mocking laugh, and Raven was standing beside him.

"So how do we get in?"

Ben didn't bother answering. Lazily he flicked a nod towards the building.

"Door."

"Yeah?"

"This walk swings round to the front porch, but it's…" He caught a slight quiver in the fae lord's glow as if he were suppressing an urgent desire to laugh.

"So you got it, the scroll?"

The corners of Raven's mouth twitched in the gilded dark.

"Of course. Most of it."

"So we're still not done."

"Of course not. That's why we're here, isn't it?

"I have no idea. I just get the call, I don't get to ask questions."

Neither of them moved, each waiting, considering. Anticipation and the gathering storm hovered together like the orchestra watching for a cue.

The stroke came down with a terrific crack. Lightning tore

open the sky, followed almost at once by a peel of thunder like the whole timpani section rolling together, folding and unfolding and rumbling at last away. Another sheet of lightning, more drums crashed and died.

Ben blinked, and rolled his eyes upwards at the sound.

"We're going to get wet again, aren't we, Watson?"

"I'm afraid so, Holmes."

"We should move."

The wind pushing the storm front across the Thames valley became the yelping rush of the Wild Hunt, whipping the rain into stinging needles that drove them around the *peristylium* at a sliding run, skirting the riffling waves of the pool toward shelter.

ii

Oddly reluctant to proceed, unwilling to step back into the sheeting rain, they stood behind the doors that had opened without complaint. Not bronze, as it turned out, but thin sheets of copper, greening from the damp, beaten over carved oak— heavy enough but less timeless. Unlocked, they swung outward at the fae lord's lightest word. But the black inside was absolute, and Ben's primitive back brain rebelled.

"You go first," he said.

The raven-boy punched his shoulder and stepped inside with ease. Grumbling a little, Ben followed the faint elven glow into the dark, the same step but no further; and the harp string tension wavered in his chest, and went out. Destination achieved. Great.

"God damn, it's cold."

Even against the hammering rain, Ben's voice rang back from a lofty ceiling, dank and invisible in the airless black. The sharp reek of dirty laundry and old gym shoes crept sourly into his nose and mouth.

"Is that mildew?"

"It feels like a hole," Raven observed with distaste. He scanned the hall seeing more than his friend but less than he liked. "I can hear running water. I thought this was supposed to be a temple in the classical mode. This is…"

A ball of light leaped up from his open palm to the ceiling where it hung, spinning slowly. Flames sprang up in low cressets. Shadows flung themselves across the mossy face of an earthen wall reaching two storeys overhead, closer than it should have been. Half-blinded, Ben winced and turned to see Raven shimmering beside him, lowering a graceful hand along with the light level.

"Well, that was dramatic."

The boy shrugged lightly.

"A Druid cave with Roman appointments, there's dramatic for you. Hilarion will call it a grotto, I suppose. The Governor won't like it, but I expect Valeria is pleased."

The light revealed a wide chamber, not very deep, with a low altar in the middle. On each of the rocky side walls, smoothed panels featured a few unexceptional cult paintings: a fair-haired goddess in her chariot attended by nymphs and satyrs, receiving offerings among her maidens, or doing honor to the greater gods.

"It's smaller than it should be, isn't it?" Ben said, keeping his voice low as he crossed the chamber. Even the timing of the echoes felt wrong. Building the new recording studio last summer had sensitized him to these things.

He jumped when Raven sang out a jaunty tune.

"My Johnny was a shoemaker and dearly he loved me!" Cocked his head. Gave a listen. Shook his head. "Acoustics are crap too."

"Floor's nice," Ben said, striding across still more frolicking dolphin mosaics. "And this would be the actual spring."

Behind the altar the far wall had been left rustic, if not exactly as nature made it, hacked into the hillside. The mossy surface glinted with silver steams trickling to a bed of grey and purple stones. In the midst of the jeweled catchment, clean icy water jetted two feet or so out of the ground to be collected in a wide stone basin. It splashed into a gravel base from which it sank, presumably, into some mechanism below that fed the fountain in the reflecting pool.

"Slate," Raven pronounced. "Some amethyst scattered around for luxury. The rest is flint. The Tears of the Goddess, they'll call it, you'll see."

"Oh, please!" Ben was disgusted. He knocked the rock face and smirked. "This whole wall is a fake. It's not rock, it's plaster and paint. It's a stage set!"

"What have we here?" Raven tapped a smooth space in the wall, and felt it bounce back. "Ah. We have a door."

"A secret passage? Or a backstage?"

Raven threw pale blue lights up the passageway as they pushed through. Every few feet an alcove or a closet opened out; changing rooms, storage for ritual items.

"A good cult needs a good story," the fae lord went on, "properly mythic, with solemn music, especially if their goddess is gone."

"She could be stolen by a god in a golden chariot," Ben suggested.

"Been there, done that," Raven said dismissively. "Look for an annual ritual, though, conjuring her return, and then again to make her go away when the river floods. They'll want a proper chorus. I'd put the chief priestess in a mask and... Oh look! A mask!"

He popped out of a closet wearing a wig of dancing yellow curls. Over his face he pressed a mask made of hammered copper, hilarity carved into its flowing features. Aristophanes' ancient words boomed from the round hole in the mouth, deep and powerful, filling the little room.

"*Brekekekéx!*" he intoned. "*Koáx Koáx!*"

"Go Stanford!" said Ben.

"What?"

Raven flipped off the mask and tossed it aside, sending the wig flying after it, then strode back out to the main room, the sanctuary.

"There's nothing here. Come on."

Ben caught each piece out of the air, like the juggler's boy. Then he shrugged and let them fall anyway as he hurried to catch up.

"Tickets will be pricey!" Raven assured him, still madly envisioning the scene in front of the spring.

"But the costumes," said Ben, "will be fabulous."

"Titania would love this place. But she will insist on being chief priestess."

By the time the echoes from their laughter had died, they had explored all there was to see, and Ben was doubting his gift again. Had it snapped off because he was where he needed to be, or what? What were they doing here?

When the sarcasm had run down a bit, he said, "It's May Day; that's Beltane. Can't we invoke her, or something?"

The boy shook his head.

"I've been trying all evening. Either she isn't in, or she doesn't care to answer, and she won't be summoned."

"Look, a staircase," said Ben, taking a torch off the wall. "We can go up!"

They went up.

The upper floor with its galleries over the spring held a few bedrooms, most already furnished; at least one had already seen some profane use. Raven's scandalized remark fell on dead air since Ben had taken his torch the other way. He found chests of linen towels, enameled boxes of incense, silver offering bowls in need of a good polish, even a bunch of desiccated grapes some frolicking builder had forgotten. He also found a nest of mice, newly established, and left it alone. Not his problem.

They patted corners for more secret passages, stuck their hands into pigeonholes and cupboards. At the raven-boy's touch, each locked box opened on its secrets, each cupboard revealed its contents, and each time they were disappointed. Nothing they needed was here.

"Hey!" Ben's voice rang above the muffled rain on the roof tiles. The latest storm might be letting up. "Hey," he said again, appearing in the doorway. "I found the office. But I need better light, come on."

It took a while to go through everything, since the whole project seemed to be stored in this windowless room. When for a moment Ben thought he might have hit the jackpot, a box full of scrolls turned out to be Etruscan pornography.

"We should go through each one," Raven said, nodding soberly over the first painted sheet, and turning it sideways for better analysis. "You know, to be sure our scroll isn't rolled up with something else."

Ben grinned and punched him in the shoulder.

"How old are you?"

"You don't want to know. What's this—ah!" he hissed. The casket he'd picked up banged to the floor, cracking the lock. "Gods below!"

"What is it?" Ben stooped to pick up a document box and a bunch of papers. He winced on his friend's account when he realized it was bound with iron bands. "You okay?"

Raven nodded as curtly as he could with two burnt fingers in his mouth. He took them out, shaking the sting as the feeling came back. He'd already tasted enough iron for a faerie lifetime.

"I hate being taken by surprise. What's in it?"

"Work statements, waybills, invoices," Ben said, flipping through the sheets. "Some preliminary sketches, the builder's agreement, a bill from the sculptor for the repairs to the goddess in the pond when the fountain system was installed. Cost over-runs, kickbacks, delays. I have a friend at the Museum of London who would kill for these."

An amused sneer flitted across Raven's lips as he lifted a packet out of a drawer.

"No wonder he keeps these records here, our benevolent husband. Letters to some temple in Rome asking advice on managing a pilgrim center. With a few terse replies from their head priest. He really is going to need a choir and all that backstage area. It's not meant to be private at all." He let the papers tumble carelessly from his fingers. "Ben, there is no magic here, and precious little religion. Nothing we need. Except this, maybe."

He held up a long ivory box carved with medallions of griffons and centaurs pursued by hunters, latched with an ivory pin on a silken thread. When he shook it slightly, it rattled.

"Pretty," said Ben wearily. "How does that help?"

"Sadly, not at all." Raven lifted the domed lid and shook out the contents: a handful of ivory dice and gaming pieces, a few silver coins. "Unless you feel like a round of backgammon."

The American wasn't listening. The stale air was getting to him, and his clothes itched. Shivering and sweating at the same time, Ben stepped into the hallway, hoping for fresher air or even another place to search.

"I keep feeling like we should go up another level, but there isn't one, is there? Damn it, I know there's… I can almost hear it, but…" He started to sway, and threw an anxious glance over his shoulder.

"Let's get out of here. You look terrible."

"I feel terrible," Ben said, and wiped sour sweat from his forehead with the back of a sleeve.

They went down.

The thunderstorm had eased a little, judging by the noise level in the sanctuary, though a spattering wind still swirled through the bronze-covered doors. Raven closed them with a wave, refreshed the lighting, then found a pair of curule travelling chairs in the prop room, and a table so Ben wouldn't fall out of his. Sadly there was no wine.

In a minute or two, Ben's head had stopped swimming and he felt less haunted, his breath less ragged. The high-ceilinged chamber was more frigid than ever, but he could think again.

"You're keeping the ivory box?" he said at last.

"I thought you'd never ask." Pleased with himself almost beyond bearing, Raven pulled the little scroll from his tunic.

Ben wanted to snatch it out of his hands, but did his best to remain unimpressed, even while his whole mind strained after the story it sang. He smirked.

"Did you play chess for it with Hilarion? Or, no. You said you charmed the wife!"

The boy made do with his most modest grin.

"To be fair, it didn't take much. Clever girl, she nicked it from the heartless bastard so she could be a mermaid."

"And it worked?"

"I even watched until her hour was up to be sure she was all right."

"What a hero." Ben had enough energy left for sarcasm. "So what have we been scratching through the dust and mildew for? What am I still hearing?"

"No idea." With each shake of the close-cropped head, the boy's usual black curls fell closer to his shoulders. "I don't hear the things you do," he said, and there seemed to be a note of envy in the simple statement as he handed the thing across.

As his friend had before him, Ben knew what it was almost before he touched it. The song was there in the ancient mode, the tale of its travels and its hurts, a chiming bell and a whiff of burnt cinnamon. But as he listened, really listened, he realized the tale had done a kind of hiccup, like an old-fashioned record needle skipping on the label, repeating the last bit again and again.

When he unrolled the unfinished scroll, so much smaller than he'd expected, the skipping stopped. No, it changed. Now when the song hit a flaw, it came round to the beginning again like an earworm that won't resolve. And somewhere underneath, another voice pattered along, almost in synch but limping—that was the only word for it—until it peeled away with a kind of sigh.

"Here and not here," Ben murmured, and looked around, a little dizzy.

"What do you mean?"

"I mean you're right. It's not complete. There really is a missing piece, and it's right here except…except, it's not here. I mean, not now. I mean—" He looked up, radiant with discovery, all dizziness burned away. "Don't you get it?"

The boy scowled, unhappy.

"Apparently not. Where is it, then?"

Excited, and a little manic, Ben tried to put the pieces in order as they came to him.

"Right here, but not now. I don't know, but I do know we have to take this one with us."

"We can't take it out of the time stream, Ben. You know that. It's got to be there in 1595 for us to find, and so on. And then we'd lose it anyway when Carew puts it on the fire."

"No, no, we won't. Don't you get it? Because this isn't that scroll."

"I'm confused."

The excitement rolled off of Ben like a wave as the details shaped into words.

"There was only ever one unique original, and that was on the wall of pearl in Ata'rathi's first temple. (God, the hall where I met the Mothers must have been modelled on it!) When it was finally written down, a dozen were made, and one of them came to Robert Cotton. But this isn't that one. This one came from her own hand, if you believe such things."

"We don't have much choice, do we?"

"Look again, see? The papyrus is practically new, the ink is bright black."

"So either it is a brand new fake or…"

"…or," Ben finished the sentence for him, "it's preserved by magic. Exactly. You don't hear the things I do, and I can tell you that Cotton's had no magic in it."

Even the King's Raven seemed impressed, but he frowned as he rolled the scroll up tight and dropped it into the ivory case. The lid clicked into place; he set the pin in the lock.

"So we can take it away."

"We're meant to! We're the next step. It has no where else to go."

"But I thought the *Gwragedd Annwn* sent us here to find the thing that would make Carew come to us."

"Did they?" Ben wondered.

"He's here, isn't he?

"But not following us."

Raven stopped, not liking the images that came to him: Valeria quiet and still by the riverbank, waiting for the sand to run out.

"But he is on his way, I think."

"Better here than at the villa."

Ben was shaking his head, still trying to sort it out.

"We haven't been paying attention. I asked about the scroll. Amphitrite told me to find Cyfla. I followed my gift, but what if…"

"Shh!" Raven put a hand up for silence.

Over the patter of rain, rough noises penetrated the temple precinct. It wasn't just the scurrying of badgers or the drizzle of drains. Someone was out in the *peristylium*, shouting and cursing in English. A coarse voice stopped and started as if in conversation; some other disorganized sounds; the troubled whickering of a pony and the scuffling clop of unshod hooves on pavement.

At a sharp gesture from Raven, all the lights went out as he stepped to the bronze-covered door, except for a red glow on the altar. When Ben joined him, that light snapped out, too.

Silently the door opened to show a sliver of light, no more, the dawn hovered behind the rain. Then a sickening smack echoed over the court, a vile oath and horrible chuckling, scuffling, shuffling, a light splash. Ben went cold.

Raven closed the door with a thought, leaving them in the enfolding dark. By his own light, all his senses tuned, the fae lord stepped back and waited.

iii

Silence had found the heathen place, stumbling and sliding along the path as often off the paving stones as on them, and hanging on to the half-frantic pony until at last he came to the marble pillars and the pool. Giggling to himself he stomped through the beautiful pool to wash the filth, the clay and blood and worse things from his head and hands. Then opened his trews to piss over the feet of the goddess, only regretting he had no worse offering to leave. Well, besides the whore, the false wife, Valeria.

Relieved and refreshed, he went back to the pony where it trembled near the curb edge of the pool, and cut the ropes that bound the pale body to the beast. She—it—slithered to the ground, a broken doll, blood still oozing from every wound. The head, patched and bleeding where the prideful hair had been hacked away, bounced on the curb with a crack, and he thought she moaned.

Impossible. How could she be alive? Then the body tumbled over so that the horror of the shattered face, the black-crusted eyes stared up at him like a witness to hell. He had seen it already, and sneered. But from somewhere, the ruined thing mustered the breath to whistle in horror. The awful sound bubbled in her throat, then stopped. She drew no inward breath.

Ah, God, he thought, how her satanic master must love her! Well, she will see him soon enough.

He made sure of it with a fist, then shoved the thing face-down into the pool, watching with cold satisfaction as the blood ribboned into the rain-pocked water. When he reached for the pony's leading rope, it shied, and started away. He swore and raised a fist, but a thin curtain of rain sheeted over the fountain, and the pony had had enough. It broke and ran.

"THERE WILL BE ANOTHER," said the angel, chanting as Silence cursed the wretched thing. "BURN THE HEATHEN WITCH IN HER TEMPLE. BURN IT IN GOD'S NAME. DESTROY THE FALSE IDOLS AND RECEIVE YOUR SOUL."

With a scornful cough he looked back at the body, then up through the curling mist at the curving grace of the temple, seeing nothing of value on either side. Perhaps there was firewood inside, or papers, anything that would burn once he had claimed the scroll. Belike there was even food. He was cold, all the heat had drained out of him, and he could do with a nice fire.

Silence started up the steps to the bronze doors glazed with mist, then stopped. The doors were closed. What if they were locked?

They weren't locked. Carew put his fingers to the gilded handles and started to pull.

With a roar of thunder and Faerie rage they burst open, flying from the hinges. One heavy panel caught his jaw, the other threw him back and launched him high into the air. It carried him screaming across the pool, beyond the marble colonnade. Raven fired again from the portico, shouting curses in dead languages then flew after him.

Horrified, he stopped by the water.

"Oh, God, Ben!" he shouted. "See to the girl!"

Something must be protecting the bastard, how could he

still be running? There was movement along the swollen stream as it poured off the hill, something in the shadows under the bay trees. Another blast flew that would have destroyed him utterly, if only it had hit him. A stand of hazel exploded instead. Another blast, and another, a willow, an oak flared like candles as thunder rolled and exploded overhead.

"Dis and all his dogs! Come out, you bastard!"

"Raven!" Ben yelled against the clamour.

The pure white center of a godlike inferno, the boy's arm came back to throw another. At what he hoped was a safe distance, Ben put two fingers in his mouth and whistled, then snapped,

"Raven!"

The fae lord whirled on him, his face a mask of unearthly fury.

"No!"

Panting with frustration, he brought the beautiful hands down, clenched into hard fists, the light around him diminished.

"Damn it, Ben! How can he be gone? I must have hit him! How can I not have hit him?" The rain poured like tears down his cheeks.

"Raven?" Ben said, just loud enough to reach his friend over the rattle of the rain. The boy stared at him, breathing hard, with eyes still as wild and dark as the tempest.

"What?" Raven snarled.

Ben nodded and stared back steadily.

"The woman. She's not dead. Or she wasn't a minute ago. Come on."

The boy gulped, and scooped dripping black hair out of his eyes and said again,

"What?"

Quickly, they strode back to where Ben had hauled Valeria from the water. She was unconscious, but still, somehow, shallowly breathing. It was too much to look at. He had spread his rough freedman's cloak over the worst of the damage.

Kneeling, Raven raised her gently on one arm, humming and stroking the air above the ravaged skin while his tears fell.

Ben could practically hear the power in the simple gesture, but even he could see that nothing changed.

At last the fae lord rocked back on his heels and wiped his cheeks.

"She sleeps now, true sleep without evil dreams. He will not haunt her as she passes. That's the best I have within my gift, except…one thing, maybe. If Amphitrite aid me."

The fae glimmer strengthened as he stood and looked down at the wreckage of the good wife, the sorrowing mother, and started to sing. Then choked on it, swallowed, and started again.

This time his voice was true, his power resurging. The song in the Icthylean mode was brief and wordless, plangent with sorrow. With a wave, he flipped aside the blood-stained mantle. Slowly, he lifted both hands and the tragic body followed, floating on air over the ungentle curb, until he laid it in the water at the statue's marble feet. The fountain water fell across her ruined face as he directed, cleaning the filth away.

Silent for a long minute, at last Raven pointed one long finger and sang three words on three descending tones—a minor chord of A, Ben told himself while observing, altogether irrelevantly, that the rain no longer fell on the three of them. As if it mattered. Whatever his friend was trying to do, he couldn't watch.

A slithering plop and a splash drew the harper's attention again, and there was the answer. Where Valeria had lain broken, now swam a little trout with a pale pink and white belly, a shadow of red and gold above. It moved sluggishly at first, then flipped its tail and darted away across the pool, across the exquisite mermaid mosaic, and out into the Fleet itself.

"She had so little life left in her," Raven was saying, almost to himself. "Not quite the same as saving her, I realize."

"But not bad."

Weary and wet beyond all belief, Ben watched her go, then slouched back to the temple portico to pretend that getting out of the rain would make a difference. After a while, Raven joined him.

"Well, here's another place we can't come back to," Ben said, watching the tree fires sputtering out as the latest downpour washed across the clearing in chattering waves.

"Hmm," Raven agreed, and hunkered down next to him on the doorstep. "I still don't understand how he got away from me. I don't miss, you know?"

"You were over-wrought. Also—" Ben held up a finger before the boy could object. "Also, there's a morven stone down there. I saw it in a lightning flash when I came up."

"So he was already gone."

"Probably. Broke his arm, though, I think. Or worse."

"Yeah. But now he's basking in the sun on the Mermaid Stair, healing up. Stay till he's healed, the vicious bastard, then pop out wherever he wants."

"At least, he'll be following us."

Echoing drips from the eaves filled the lengthening silence. The rain, the insidious, appalling British rain was slowing, the iron clouds breaking up, the Milky Way in its glory spilling into view. Off to the west, the crown of the setting moon bathed the Chilterns in a farewell glow as the eastern sky began to pale.

Ben breathed more easily, relieved to see his clothes were dry and were, in fact, plain jeans and jacket again, though his butt was cold from sitting on the granite steps, and his legs twitched with aching.

"Long day."

Knees drawn up, Ben laid his head on folded arms and thought about sleep. A seriously long day.

A thought struck him.

"What about C. Hilarion Gallio?"

"Fuck 'im," Raven muttered, then rubbed a hand over his eyes. "No, sorry. He was fond of her. We always have to leave loose ends, don't we? At least he'll never have to see her as we did."

Ben knew the image would never leave him.

"We can't stop Carew till we find the Fleet. Amphitrite told me three times and I keep…"

"She also said to go to the Roman city. And that's turned out so well. Any ideas?"

"One. Maybe even two," said Ben, and paused. "What if we call on his mother?"

Raven started to ask what that would accomplish, and thought better of it. Gradually, stars replaced the rain, and the fires died. They couldn't just sit here.

"Okay," he said.

They got to their feet, and Ben went to fetch his sushi bag from the sanctuary. A clank when he picked it up made him look inside. A strap must have come loose. Nothing should be rattling around.

Reaching in to check each of the bag's many closures, he felt his wedding ring chime against something metallic and smooth, and brought up the silver flask, round as an apple, etched with his name and the words *King's Man* in flowing script. He'd given the last of the wee man's water to the old lady when she asked for it. As one must, he thought with a generous smile.

He pressed the flask down into the basin around Cyfla's spring, watched the bubbles escape until it was full. When he tasted it, sweet and pure, cold as the snows of Faerie, he felt his mind settle, his thoughts clear. He took in a deep breath and let it out.

"Trust the water," he said as he capped the flask and secured it. The words so lightly spoken echoed his steps as he re-crossed the cavernous hall. "A quick chat with Mom to verify something, maybe check in with his Grace, and then... here, but not here. Are you coming?"

"Oh, yes!"

32

Issa

The King of Faerie's gentlemen had once stumbled onto the Mermaid Stair by accident, finding a fantasy island in the arms of a dozen streams and terraced cataracts under the great roaring falls that dropped out of Faerie three times the height of Yosemite Falls. It had been a watery world hedged with fern and light-limbed trees sketching the sky, smelling warmly green and spicy, singing with water that rushed, pounded, sighed into placid pools, tinkling over stone. Not any more.

"Son of a bitch!" Raven spat as if honey had turned to bile in his mouth.

The next time, Aubrey had dropped them off in rustic simplicity, all redwood and sugar pine like the mountains above Santa Cruz. Lovely and restful, exactly what Ben needed except that what should have been unspoiled had become brittle and sere. It was worse now.

"Forget to pay the gardener?" said Ben, but the joke fell flat even before he finished saying it, and his glasses went dark in the harsh sunlight. "This is way worse that I expected."

This third visit brought them ashore on a sugar-sand beach surrounding a secluded lagoon framed in tall palms. It might once have been the model for Hawaii or Costa Rica. Of the many dark tracks that marked where streams once tumbled through the ferns from mountains to the sea, only one had any life to it. Any others were reduced to an algae-clogged trickle without rainbows. On those damp tracks, the flowers were sun burnt, their heads broken, petals bruised and withered. The palms swayed with their leaves draped in brittle skirts around dead cores.

Ben raised his face to catch a breeze, but all he got was a lung full of hot metal, the air still and dead.

"Oh, God, this totally sucks."

When he glanced over at his friend, Raven looked strained and deeply unhappy.

"We're too late," he said hoarsely. "Carew's not here. Neither is anyone else. Let's go."

Ben was already on one knee tracing the *morven* marker at his feet. This time, instead of trusting to chance, he set his mind on a goal. Seconds later they stood on a sandy path above the Dart in springtime crowded with a dozen shades of green. Broad-limbed trees loomed overhead, reaching the shade across the river under a clear blue sky. Here the air was cool, the water at the bottom of the slope lively.

Laughing suddenly, Raven flung out his arms.

"Dartmoor! Ben Harper, I love you!" He threw his arms around his friend, then took Ben's face in his hands and planted a great smooch on his forehead. He stepped back and blew a huge sigh of relief. "Home! Or near enough as makes no matter."

"Mmm, maybe. Maybe not," said Ben, scanning through the trees. "What's the matter with the sky?"

Raven's eyes followed his, brow furrowed. Great slashes crossed the bowl of the sky stained with murky red, like cotton wool dabbing at bloody wounds.

"I'll just go and see, shall I?"

Before Raven had quite finished speaking he was in the air, powering nearly straight up. Ben watched him, a dwindling speck, wondering how far a raven, even a magical raven, could fly towards the stratosphere. He found a comfortable boulder and sat down to wait and think.

It wasn't long. A harsh scream with an edge of panic broke the quiet, followed by a crash, and a few seconds later another. Ben stepped back from the riverbank as a black bundle crashed through the boughs of a vast beech tree. Just under the last broad bough, the Raven's head came up, the wings cracked open to full expanse. The beak shook out a fierce, angry yell, and he pulled up almost at Ben's feet. The bird soared up again, backed and stalled, and finally tumbled through the branches of a young fir tree.

"What the hell!" Ben ran to where Raven, a boy again, lay swearing and muttering on the ground.

"It's broken," he gasped, and took Ben's hand to find his feet.

"What's broken?"

"Hang on," said Raven, stumbling down to the river's edge to fling himself into the water, with Ben following close. He lay there for a moment, gasping.

"Those aren't clouds. They're rents in the fabric of this place. Whatever magic holds it all together, something is pulling it apart, like all the others."

"What's on the other side?"

"No idea," the boy rolled back, still winded, with water streaming through his hair and clothes. "As cold as this is?" He grabbed Ben's hand and thrust it into the icy river. "It was worse."

Ben yelped and pulled back.

"Christ, yes, I get it."

"That's a tropical ocean by comparison. I… God, I'm still shivering. And I don't get cold! We need to see the king."

"Issa first."

This time Raven had to ask, "Why?"

"Come on, shift."

The track rose and fell as the channel beside them cut twenty, thirty feet into the Dartmoor hills; the path along the edge remained clear enough, if a man were mindful, or preternaturally sure-footed. They fell into step, watching for any signs of play, or sweetness, or joy. Any sound of music. But all they heard was a melancholy wind whispering through the trees.

"Hang on," said Ben, with a hand on his friend's arm. Their walk had become an angry march above a bank growing ever higher above the rushing river. Only the chattering of water over stone reminded them it was there.

"Haven't we been here before?"

"Holne Bridge," Raven said, pointing through the leaves. "Or Holne Bridge as it is here. Only we were down there, and it was springtime."

"So where is Issa?"

Raven scowled, setting off again.

"What good will it do? The Mothers have already told you what she did."

"They told me what they know," said Ben, holding his ground, "but they didn't know everything. Can you stop fuming long enough to listen for her?"

"I think I can do both. All right. This way."

They found her in a clearing under a tree that had no business on her river; its fat pink and purple flowers dripping from dense, dark foliage, richly colored and thriving only by virtue of her presence. Draped in heavy folds of pale green and faded violet, she sat with her knees drawn up to her chin. Long slender hands covered her face in despair and shame.

"Will she even talk to us?" Ben wondered. The weeping seemed endless. "Can she talk to us?"

"I'll find out," said Raven, and took a hasty step toward her, jaw clenched. But his friend laid a restraining hand to his shoulder and he stopped.

"No, let me," Ben said.

The boy nodded tightly, reining in his anger.

"Right."

"My lady?" Going to one denim-clad knee beside her, Ben dared to pull her hands gently away from her face and held them. Incurious, the timeless, ageless grey eyes turned up to him, red-rimmed and brimming.

"My lady, please, will you speak to us?"

Issa blinked, and tears spilled down the heart-shaped face of a twenty-year-old woman whose delicate beauty never changed. With ill-timed humor, Ben knew what Mellis would say: *Only a goddess could give herself over to weeping for uncounted days without showing a puffy red nose.* That brought to his lips and eyes the merry smile which legions of female fans had found irresistible, but the nymph had no response to it.

Issa glanced past his shoulder to the sullen, black-clad elven lord glowering a few paces away. She coughed slightly and looked at Ben again.

"Who are you?"

"My name is Ben Harper, lady, and I serve the lord Oberon. This gentleman is the King's Raven."

Remembering his manners, the Raven straightened and bowed slightly. She returned his courtesy with a bewildered nod. She blinked.

"What does the king of Faerie want with me?"

"Oberon the King and Father Thames himself" (she gasped a little) "have set us a task, and only you can help us." She waited, the tears for the most part in check, so he went on. "We seek your son, the man called Simon Carew."

Her breath caught in her throat.

"Are you his friends?"

"We are not!" Raven snapped, then shot up into the air with a raucous cry and a whomp of black wings before Ben could tell him to shut the hell up.

"What do you want with Simon?"

"Madam, I think you know. He has done great harm. Terrible murders."

In swift strokes he described the latest victim, not sparing her feelings while scorching his own. Before he was done, she had closed her eyes.

"This very sanctuary is dying because of his crimes," Ben concluded. "So I must ask you in Oberon's name to tell me where he is, if you know. And what will stop him."

The nymph was rocking back and forth now where she sat on the ground, keening like a marsh bird. With a *whoof*, Ben sat back on the grass and prepared to be patient. She was the man's mother. This wasn't going to be easy.

"Simon was here," she said.

"When was this?"

"You know time here is more flexible than in the mortal world. It may have been days ago, perhaps a few hours, I cannot tell."

"Or both," Ben muttered.

"He came here in great pain, beaten and bruised. He was so kind to me while I mended his broken bones. What you say cannot be true."

"It is, I'm afraid."

"No, no, he… My Simon is so alone, so sad, is it any wonder he is angry! But it is all my fault, not his!"

There could be no sympathy, only hard truth.

"He tortures and kills nymphs and sirens, all to gain a soul he has already blackened beyond recall. The fault is his own."

"No!"

"Yes. And he is destroying the Atami Stair. How can that be your fault?"

"You do not understand. It is the charm that I spoke over him as a child."

He knew that. So much the Mothers had told him already. But he was right. There was more. And bit by bit, with the focused patience he gave to his music, Ben plucked the details from among the rambling recriminations and sniffling tears—the details only she knew.

The Lore Mothers understood that Ata'rathi's third charm was too devastating to circulate, and had sent it to the ends of the earth for Issa to keep safe and secret. But there had come a time when a man, a beautiful man, had set up to work by her ford—a smith newly come into his mastery. All fire and flame, he was, black hair and blue eyes, with a great black beard curling above the powerful chest, and shoulders like the men of olden times.

She had spoken to him shyly. He had been most respectful. After a while and many meetings, they had become comfortable together. She told him who she was, and he told her his dreams. She had taken lovers many times since first awakening in the dawn of the world. This time, she fell in love.

Now among the Atami, love is a light-hearted thing, freely given and easily set aside. Issa cared for Giles Carew too deeply to want to give him less than her whole heart, but she had no heart to give. So she told him of the charm that would let her love truly for a year and a day. For his sake, she accepted the cost; disbelieving, so did he. Issa went to live with Giles as his wife, and bear his child.

When the time came, Issa had not wanted to leave her little family, and yet there was no choice. Her heart that loved with mortal intensity was breaking with a pain unendurable and unending. How could humans bear to live with such grief?

But what if they could avoid it? Surely, she had reasoned, the spell that gave a breakable heart to the Atami would have the contrary affect on her mortal son. He would be invincible, proof against hurt and heartbreak. And so she laid the charm on him in the cradle.

The Lore Mothers would have advised her of the peril, but she had not dared to ask. They would have told her that a hard heart saves a man from heartbreak, and from compassion too, but not from anger, fear, or resentment; or the fire; or the knife. Or from a world that tells him he has no soul.

Too late, she had given the charm into another's care, and thought herself well rid of it. Now Issa mourned not for her lost love, but for the child she had broken on the wheel of her foolishness, and for the world he was destroying.

So yes, Ben thought, it was her fault. It still is.

He stood up without a word and paced along the bridge to lean over the grey stone, staring for long minutes at nothing at all.

"What did she tell you?" said Raven into the silence just about two feet behind Ben's shoulder. Ben started at the sound, and turned as the mobile rang from the depths of the sushi bag.

Soberly holding his friend's gaze, he got out the phone and tapped it open.

"Yes, sir?" He nodded, listening. "We're on our way."

"Are we?" Raven asked, as Ben rang off.

The harper's sober expression folded into a grim smile.

"I know how to stop him."

Part Four

London

"A place both for the beauty of the building, infinite riches, variety of all things, that excelleth all the cities in the world."
--John Strype

33
Saturday, reporting in

"He will stop, I know he will," the lady of the Dart had pleaded when they left her. "When he has what he wants, he will stop! Promise me you will not hurt him!"

They could have made such a promise, to make her feel better. It would have been all kinds of a lie. Raven would not have given such a promise even if he could. And Ben had no desire to ease her pain at the expense of others. Instead, he parted the gates between the worlds with a lugubrious Puritan hymn, and took them home.

Seated but not relaxed on the upper deck of the *Gates of Dawn* in its guise as an elegantly appointed houseboat, the boys drank good beer and made their report to Father Tam and Aubrey. The river god was not happy, even when they produced, with forgivable pride, the scroll in its ivory box. The second charm had boxed his ears when Valeria Lucila made her transformation, two thousand years ago and yesterday afternoon. His dismay grew in the telling, until they got to the part where Raven went to investigate the torn curtains of the sky above the Mermaid Stair.

He had been letting them talk, taking turns as he knew they would, while platters of steak and chips slowly disappeared from in front of them.

"What did you find there?"

The deep melodious voice rumbled like thunder in a kettledrum.

Raven shook his head.

"Nothing, sir. It was as if—" He paused, weirdly uncertain. "It was like nothing I've ever encountered before."

"You're young," said Tam, tilting the beer bottle back to finish it off.

"No, sir," said the raven-boy, then caught himself. "That is, yes, of course I am. But I doubt if even you have seen such a thing. Sky on either side but nothing... nothing in between. Not outer space, no stars, just a cold that reached into my bones." He reached for words, unaccustomed to the lack. "I could approach it, see its edges. But when I tried to fly in, it threw me back. I nearly fell out of the sky."

"No, you actually did fall out of the sky," Ben murmured, though his friend threw him such a look!

"Are you all right?" said Aubrey quietly. He had said very little so far, content to let Tamesis conduct the debrief.

"Aye, my lord. Though I can tell you I haven't felt so dizzy since I was dragged backwards through a mirror into an iron cage."

Tam raised an eyebrow in the king's direction, who waved it away. Another story for another time.

"What then, Mr Harper?" Aubrey asked.

The harper was staring at his plate and at the remains of a meal he didn't remember eating.

"You're really going to hate this part, sir. Father Tam, have you heard of any other Atami deaths in the last, say, twenty-four hours? Subjective time, that is. It might have been anywhere in the time stream."

The river god frowned with remembered pain.

"One. Here in London. Your own London."

Raven snapped to attention, alarmed.

"Who? Not Teifi, the Walbrook?"

"No, she is well enough, though grieving in her hall. We lost one of the little Islington girls, along the Regent's Canal. She was found just as... Just as she was fading away. Terrible, but not so much as the one you have described." As ancient as he was, he shuddered.

"Then it's here," said Ben. "Amphitrite sent me to the Roman city. But she didn't say the Romans would still be here, did she? Carew is here, and from what Issa told him, he knows that he is looking for Cyfla." Throat weary and dry, he pleaded: "Sir, I wonder if I could trouble you for a large whiskey?"

Swearing, Raven flung himself to the drinks cabinet to find Ben his drink—and one for himself. The anger he had carefully set aside was not so far away after all. Aubrey noticed.

"What did you do to her, boy? To Issa?"

"Nothing!" the kid shouted back.

He had changed his clothes again, returning in black jerkin, frilled black shirt, and black leather jeans. When his king blinked in response, Raven took a deep breath and let it out, chastened. His mouth creased in a tight grin. "Mr Harper wouldn't let me."

Ben shrugged and sipped at his drink, letting 30-year-old Jameson's burn away the strain.

"I didn't want to deal with the paperwork," he said.

Living through it all had been bad enough. Recounting it in the kind of detail the king required was too much like doing it all again, but of course, he did it anyway.

After a long, thoughtful minute, Ben turned to Tam.

"My lord, I had a vision, or a dream, or something the first time we were here. Do you remember? I didn't understand it, or maybe I forgot, but Ata'rathi charged me especially to find the Fleet and wake her. Cyfla is in London, right now, somewhere. Think, sir, what drew her from her river in the first place? Where else would she go?"

Aubrey had risen, pacing the perimeter of the great room while his henchmen talked. Now he looked at Ben.

"You said you know how to stop him."

The harper nodded, not quite as sure as he had sounded, then took his drink and went to lean on the balcony rail. Issa had given him what he needed, but he was still guessing.

"The Lore Mothers have disowned him. Cyfla has the missing piece, and I have the scroll it comes from, which will lead us to her. This bastard will follow, and we'll have him."

He took a deep breath and let it out, sipped again at golden whiskey smooth as chocolate, and let his mind go. What could he hear? The ripple and slap of the river on the dock below. The rhythm of the *Gates of Dawn* rocking slightly at its mooring. The hooting of sea girls watching *Strictly Come Dancing* on the outdoor screen below. And then there was the music in his head. The tune Ata'rathi had given him. But why?

No more questions. His mind opened and dived into the waters, and the words flowed in. Words the mermaid goddess had given him already. He turned back to his friends, and without preamble sang softly.

> *In the meads upon the heath*
> *my fleet-foot daughter lies*
> *and dreams alone, unknown.*
> *She sleeps, O let her wake!*
> *Wake her. Bring her home.*

The last note hovered on the night air along with the tang of wood smoke from someone's fireplace and the musky scents of autumn coming early to the river. It was Aubrey's turn to raise a quizzical eyebrow while the river god caught his breath.

"Yes," Tam said under a thoughtful frown.

"Sir?" Ben said, shaking back the sense of mystery and magic.

"As you know, the River Fleet runs almost entirely underground. The spring these days is an unmarked patch of boggy wetland beside a pond on Hampstead Heath. The stream runs under open air for perhaps a quarter mile, then slips into the sewer system. That sounds vile, I know."

"Fleet Ditch stank to make a man throw up his gorge," Raven said. "I didn't care for it much either, I can tell you."

"At least the end product is processed and sweetened, and harmeth none."

The harper smiled at his phrasing.

"But she isn't there—not actually in a pond on Hampstead Heath, is she?" he asked. "Nor under it, nor reigning over the sewers? She's here, but not here."

"The Roman city, as London still is, hides her in more ways than one, yes. In one place at least Fleet runs close enough to the surface to be heard by a man who stops to listen."

"That would be me, sir," said Ben.

"So it would," said Aubrey. "Listen for the water, listen for her song. Then…"

"I know, sir. Follow my gift."

"Trust the water." The king of Faerie, just some guy in faded jeans and a hand-made silk shirt, smiled paternally, then the watching eyes narrowed. "When did you sleep last, Ben? You look like hell."

Father Tam raised his mellow voice over one shoulder.

"Llyea! Make up a guest cabin, if you please."

"Yes, Father," came the answer from somewhere.

"Your Grace, with respect," Ben objected through a yawn. "There's no time to waste!"

Aubrey didn't feel obliged to explain himself. A few good hours of sleep would give his henchman an advantage that the murderer, the monster, did not have: a fit body and a ready wit. A good workman, thought Aubrey, takes care of his tools. His own people could watch the waterways tonight.

Ben's wakefulness persisted long enough to let him stumble into bed under his own power, and turn out the light. Without further encouragement from Faerie, he surrendered to dreamless sleep.

34
Sunday: Clerkenwell

When the sweet-breathing spring unfolds the buds,
Love flies the dusty town for shady woods;
Then Tottenham fields with roving beauty swarm,
And Hampstead halls the City virgins warm.

—John Gay (1685-1732)

Early on a crisp Sunday morning, street traffic in the city was minimal, thank goodness. First stop, the old Victorian district of Clerkenwell, where they stood under a slate-grey sky in front of the Coach and Horses (est. 1855) contemplating a pumpkin and four mice on the swinging sign over the door.

"Oh!" Ben exclaimed. "*Cinderella's* coach! I thought... Why am I surprised?"

Raven shook his head.

"Cinderella. Very whimsical," he said, sounding a bit like Aubrey. "You know Dick Turpin used to stop here? Well, not here exactly, but the first coaching inn that stood here. There was a Bear Garden right next door. And everything from this corner as far as you could see was wild heath. It hasn't always been quite this charming. Now where's this famous listening spot?"

The old inn, now a genteel gastropub, had set its dining room doors just where Back Hill turned the corner into Ray Street. A few neat redwood tables sat out on the pavement for fair weather dining, and opposite them a twelve-inch square grate was set into the middle of the road. Deep below, the water echoed in its brick-lined conduit.

Standing directly over it, the stark urban avenue around them still and cool, touched with last night's rain, Ben smiled. Wild heath or city street, Fleet danced along, and the sound of rushing water came to him as clear as when he had stood on its banks almost two thousand years ago. It took no special gift; any passer-by who listened could hear it, if the traffic noise abated.

"What is it?" Raven asked, watching his friend's face with interest.

"Just appreciating the vastness of time," said Ben. He waved a little vaguely up and down the street. "Could you, uhm…keep us from becoming a statistic?"

The boy nodded, and with a click of his fingers, the sounds and distractions of the urban world were muffled. Then a lone jogger rounding the corner in front of the pub almost bounced off of them when he decided to step off the curb and cross the street. Frowning, Raven used both slender hands to mime widening the space in front of him, and the shimmer of a barely perceptible perimeter expanded. Nothing vulgarly physical, no force field, but a dissuasion from being in this part of the street. And silence.

City traffic, delivery trucks unloading, the clank of crates at the Russian tea-room across the way, even the hum of the morning breeze, faded till all they could hear was their own breathing, and the song of the Fleet: Cyfla singing in her sleep.

"That's it," Ben said, quite softly, and squatted down to listen, really listen. It was stronger than he expected, the song carried along under the music of the water itself, and as the city fell away around him, the song swept him along. He waited. Then he had it. Felt it. The tug of his gift giving him the direction and for a change, an actual location.

Oh yes, he thought, this is how it's supposed to work. Today, London was on his side.

"Okay," he said, and stood up, dusting his hands, brushing down his jeans. "Let's go."

35
Hampstead Heath: Oakwood House

"That's it."

The house loomed above them on the ridge, enormous, ancient, and derelict. How it had survived the Blitz, no one could say, then or since. Looking at it from the bottom of its overgrown hill, Ben thought of *Psycho,* with screeching violins.

"The House of the Seven Gables?" Raven asked.

"Oakwood House," said Ben, thankful this time not to the diary but his production crew. "We wanted to use it for *Now or Never,* but Elaine couldn't track down an owner."

Raven's boots crunched through what had long ago been a neatly groomed gravel drive, exploring the lower reaches.

"You do know where this is, yes? Where we are?"

Ben looked around thoughtfully, until he was suddenly overcome by a broad, aching grin. "You're kidding."

The boy nodded. "We were right here, dig down three or four meters. The foundations of Hilarion Gallio's villa are under there somewhere, undiscovered."

"Which means the nymphaeum is down there, too, I suppose." Ben stared northwards, but thinking about the layers and depths of time made his head hurt.

"Cheap materials, labor disputes, and no…"

"And no mistress."

The terrain had changed a good deal in two thousand years, even in the last four hundred; filled in, leveled, terraced, undercut, bombed. No matter how much you tried to see them, the ancient silhouettes were gone. But the hills and the ridge were still there, reshaped but still embracing the valley of the Fleet as it rambled toward the Thames. Some of it was the wild land of the bathing ponds and bike paths; and up here, just within the Council warrant that protected Hampstead Heath, the spring itself.

And then there was Oakwood House, looming above the lost villa. The house had a history, the diary had said, but it didn't matter. She was there in a room over their heads, unaware of her peril.

"I can see a shimmer," Ben said, squinting up at the fanciful gables and the faux Norman tower. "Is that... Is it warded somehow?"

Raven had been kicking trash around a squatter's camp at the foot of the slope. Generations of children had built forts in all this, and the homeless had found shelter. He glanced up, eyes narrowed, and shrugged a little too casually.

"Yeah. Come on."

The grade of the old drive was steep, but made somewhat easier by a couple of turns along a wide path cluttered with wind-blown trash among the wild mustard and Queen Anne's lace, weeds and fallen branches. Eventually they stood at the foot of a ruined *porte cochère* where horse-drawn carriages and long chauffer-driven cars had used to deposit great ladies and gentlemen, generals and statesmen, and now and then a king.

"No one owns it. No one even knows it's here. How do you hide something this big, even in a city this size, for... I dunno. Decades, maybe."

They picked a way around the weedy perimeter, undeterred by fences or walls. Stout boards had been nailed across a door above a broad marble staircase, and *Keep Out* notices plastered over. Raven surveyed it for a minute, gave what passed in him for a grunt, then strolled on.

A trail of red bricks, the mortar mostly perished, led them round more blank, staring windows masked with whitewash until they came to a tradesmen's entrance and a peeling wooden gate, mud-spattered and broken but like the rest, curiously free of graffiti. But there were also signs of shuffling boots in the loose dirt that drifted at every doorway, handprints on every window ledge along with the marks of passing…what? Cats, probably. Cats are seldom impressed by enchantments.

Eventually they completed the circuit and a bit more, stopping at the double pair of classic Palladian columns that framed the street doors. Well, three of them did. At some point one had succumbed to wind and weather, possibly termites, and collapsed. Disintegrating, it lay buried in the tangled jumble that had been the front lawn, locked in bindweed, dotted with yellow flowers. The gilded doors behind them, though, however dull with inevitable London grime, might almost have been new.

"Maybe not so long after all. What if…"

"Yes?"

Raven sighed dreamily, as if he'd forgotten to breathe. "What if from time to time, she rouses. Or someone rouses her. Maybe she looks about, hoping the world has changed. It always has, of course, but never to her advantage. She wanders off, looks at the shops. Or who knows, maybe she goes out clubbing! Then she finds a new place. Sets her wards, and sleeps again."

"So why can no one can find her?"

The fae strode swiftly toward the cliff edge.

"I'll tell you why." He called over his shoulder. "Look how far she is from the water up here!"

Abruptly, he was back at Ben's side, chewing on his anger.

"Shut up," Ben said softly and, ignoring his friend's sulk, stepped back for a better view of the tower. "Can you hear it now?"

Shuttered, the little gabled windows on the topmost level—the level Cyfla must occupy, Rapunzel in her tower—turned closed eyes on the world, but he could hear her song, oh very faint under the sounds of the city, the rattle of dry leaves, the hum of a new rainstorm coming in on the breeze. Her song, and something else, descant or continuo, that he didn't understand.

A sharp nod from Raven. "I can."

"And?"

The raven-boy had nothing more to say, for now.

Ben had led the way all morning, taking faerie shortcuts instead of the Tube, using his gift and Cyfla's song, however faint, to guide him. He had done all he could; no faerie vail remained that would let him inside.

Now he caught his partner's eye and nodded significantly toward the door. No need to break in when you have a faerie prince on your team, right?

"Over to you." He waited. "In your own time."

Strands of long black curls lifted in the damp breeze as Raven tilted his head, birdlike, considering the problem.

"Right. Step back a bit."

"Carew's not in there?"

"No, no. In fact… No."

Tension crackled in the air as Raven laid a hand flat against the door, crusted with grime and peeling gold leaf. Then he sang a single clear note and extended his will. Waves of power splashed across the surface, lighting it up in the grey morning.

Nothing else happened. The fae muttered under his breath, and chose another note, then a sequence, then a complicated phrase.

"Oak and bloody ash!" The flat palm became a fist and pounded uselessly on the door.

"You lads looking for something?" a raspy voice enquired.

Both gentlemen froze, then turned to face an older man— older than Ben by a few hard decades—hands comfortably hidden in the pockets of a clean but ill-fitting tweed jacket. In his seventies perhaps, thin and sprightly with the cheekbones and clear grey eyes of the Celt above a trim white beard, he reminded Ben a little of a professor he'd had in grad school, without the elbow patches. This man, though, had a stubborn, nervous look about him, as one who has lost more battles than he's won but still can't help manning the barricades.

Nothing the man had said was challenging, nothing about him offered a threat, but Raven, Ben saw, had drawn himself up very straight, his mouth a thin line. The sapphire eyes glittered and for a moment, the suggestion of a slender golden band glimmered on his brow—a mark of rank Ben had never seen before.

The old guy bore a hint of the eldritch glow that marked the fae, as well as the red-threaded nose of a long-time drinker. That nose had been broken, too, sometime long past. So now what?

Right. A question had been asked. Better jump in before Raven could say anything haughtily unforgivable, which looked imminent. Ben thrust out a friendly hand.

"Good morning, sir. I'm Ben Harper," he said, leaning a bit on his American accent. "Maybe you've seen me on television."

"Don't have one," said the man, whose hands remained resolutely in his pockets. "Never saw the point." His accent had a touch of the Welsh lilt, but barely a touch, as if he had been away from home many years.

"Okay, well, I host a programme where we help people get organized. My assistant gave me this address so we could... Well, it looks like I wrote it down wrong, doesn't it? And you are?"

"He is called Glas," Raven said thickly, almost swallowing the *g*. "It means, the color of the sea under the wave. Son to Gwydion, you know."

"I'm sorry?"

Both a bard out of legend and a master of magic, Gwydion had taught Sparrow one summer, briefly. Ben was still in awe.

"Mmm. No more than I am. Treasons, stratagems, and spoils."

"Gods, what a memory!" said the man.

"Glas and I are old—"

"Not friends, are we, my lord?" said the old man through an easy smile.

The light around him shimmered, his appearance shifted. The glamour of deep lines and great age fell away until he was just another young man, as tall and very nearly as pretty as Raven, but otherwise quite opposite: very fair, with pale eyes and hair like beaten gold lifting in the breeze. And his expression was sunshine over the blue sea, bright and open.

"Brothers in arms?" he suggested, "Partners in crime? Schoolfellows?"

"I was going to say adversaries."

The other boy laid his hand over his heart.

"My lord wounds me!"

And the fae lord relaxed slightly, finding a tight smile of his own.

"Not yet. What are you doing here?"

"Living here! Perhaps you saw my camp at the foot of the hill? Mine by right. Squatter's rights, y'know." For a moment, the old man flickered in his place, raspy voice and all. "Greater London Council finally confirmed it. Twenty years, and I'm still here. Caretaker, me."

Ben pushed his glasses up his nose, and closed the distance between them to peer through the glamourie.

"Aren't you the…" He looked at Raven, then back again. "You're the guy from the chariot race. And that couple in the park. And all those times you've practically ridden me down. But I saw you on the *Gates of Dawn*. You're one of… He's one of Tam's people!"

Glas had the grace to look uncomfortable.

"Not exactly."

"I know what he is." Raven took up where he'd left off. "And what is it you're taking care of, exactly?"

"This bit of land. The hillside." The smallest hesitation. "The house."

"And the river below? That's not your proper calling."

"I say she is."

Ben watched his friend, whose grim attention was entirely on Glas, his face impossible to read.

"You cannot know how much danger she's in."

"You mean the Puritan? That freak?" Glas laughed, but there was no humour in it. "She was rude to him once, and he's been stalking her ever since, poor sod. Now he's found her, god knoweth how, but he has no power except invective and threats. Of course, he's frantic. So what?"

"So he went out to Regent's Canal and tortured and killed another nymph, instead."

That stopped the laughter.

"I am sorry for it. But that's not my concern."

His English was lilting and might have been lovely, but Ben detected a long weariness. Ben was weary too, and wished they'd get on with it.

"He is half Atami, did you know?" Raven asked coolly. A hand went to the talisman at his throat. "And he has one of these."

That caught Glas off guard, which also threw him on the defensive.

"So what? We set the wards here, my lady and I. He cannot get in. No more can you."

"But you know I will eventually."

There was a long pause while their eyes never left each other, then Glas nodded.

"Very likely. I drove the gibbering bastard off with flashing lights and scary noises, even conjured up the Wild Hunt. Not the sort of thing to work on you, is it?"

"You're such an idiot. Why are you here?"

"You don't get it, do you? Maybe you've heard of the Ata'rathi Scroll, the gifts of the mermaid goddess?"

"We've heard of them."

"Of course. You have always known everything," Gwydion's son sneered. "Like that little incident with the earthquake."

"And the volcano. I lost track of you after that."

"I hate class reunions," Ben muttered. He plopped the Swadeshi down on the porch and sat beside it to watch with his chin in his hands.

"Aye, and the volcano," Glas went on bitterly. "And everything else that was ever my fault, oh most noble. But all that has changed."

"Cyfla loves you?"

"That," snarled the magician's boy, "will be something of which you know nothing!"

Power of some sort sparked around his hands, gathering his anger.

"Gods of the air!" Raven rocked back and laughed for what

felt like the first time in days, but it wasn't pleasant to hear. "You fell in love with a nymph, and she has the last part of the scroll! That sodding charm again. Cyfla cared for you, you rhyming juggler, just as Issa did for her coal-black smith! So of course…"

"She's a goddess, and she loves me, you pompous magpie!"

The spell flew from Glas's fingertips. It broke over the raven-boy in a shower of rainbows, feeding the faerie glow that pulsed around him.

"Oh, thank you," the Raven breathed happily.

At his thought, a silver-hilted rapier out of Oberon's own workshops appeared in his hand. Its mate lay at his feet, gleaming and razor-edged. Never taking his eyes from the adversary, he flipped it spinning through the air between them. Glas caught it expertly and came at once on guard.

"I don't want to fight," he insisted, glancing nervously up at the tower.

"Oh, but I do," said Raven, balanced easily on the balls of his feet, feeling the grip mould to his hand as it had long ago. "Come on then."

Ignoring them, Ben let his mind drift while the words of Glas's anger, Raven's mockery, and the chime of steel faded from his awareness. She's a goddess, he thought. Not just a nymph, but a river goddess. The Fleet herself. And the river ran to a song, the repeating song.

Bright-eyed and slightly manic, he grabbed the sushi bag and ripped open the latches. The ivory box came into his hand and opened almost on its own. The song reached out for him as for a friend, without his even touching the papyrus. Ata'rathi's charms. Fleet water, and the lost river, the river and the lost girl.

Find the Fleet, Amphitrite had said. The Fleet, not the Thames. The girl not the river. The girl who was there, and not there. Trust the water. Bring her home. O let her wake, reverse the charm.

The scroll itself didn't matter. Nothing in it could destroy the Stair, only Silence. But to reverse the charm…

"Reverse the charm!" Ben leapt to his feet as the pieces

finally tripped into place, and the whole mechanism of their quest began to stagger towards an end.

"Gentlemen!" Without looking, almost without caring, he stepped out, inserting himself much too close to the circling singing steel of their swords. "Gentlemen, hold!"

Antique and razor-edged, a very real, non-metaphorical rapier whistled past his nose, and Raven cried out, "Ben, for oak and ash!"

"Tell your boyfriend to get out of it," Glas snarled across Ben's shoulder:

"Yeah," said Ben, blinking. "Okay, you've got old issues here, I can see that."

They both glared at him, scarlet with long anger and breathing hard with the sincere desire to hurt something.

"He's owed a lesson!"

"I don't care! And neither does Ata'rathi. You can race for pink slips some other time. Killing him—or whatever—is killing time. Stopping Simon Carew, that's the mission, remember?"

Glas, pink-cheeked and insufficiently instructed, threw down the sword.

"This is bollocks."

But Ben was shaken by a revelation he couldn't explain any better than he had at the nymphaeum.

"It's not about the scroll. It's not about the girl. Or well it is, but it's certainly not about this guy."

"Oi!"

"It's the song. Here and not here, remember? Because parts of the scroll are in the same place at different… I mean were in different… Oh, never mind," he snorted when Raven started to roll his eyes. "It will all make sense when it does."

"This is the company you keep now? This idiot child?"

"As for you, Glas ap Gwydion, you think you're afraid now? If you have been hiding her all this time, then you've got a lot of explaining to do."

"What, to you, sweetheart?"

The harper's laughter faded to a knowing smirk.

"No, kitten. To her mother! Now open the goddamn door!"

36
Sleeping in her bower

The vast reception and ballroom of Oakwood House, boarded up against time and the weather, sat lost in shadows until Raven threw some of his little lights into the air to dispel the murk. The magic already in the house fought back, reducing the effect to a kind of *chiaroscuro*. No matter, each of them gasped, as much in pity as in wonder, as the light flickered on marble, gilt, and milky glass.

It had been gorgeous once, they could see that, though the vast medallioned ceiling and its wedding cake chandeliers dripped with cobwebs as thick as Spanish moss. The last decorator had apparently favored a Land of the Pharaohs theme, and staring ushabti figures in ebony and gold lined the bannisters of the curving double staircase. Dust and mouse droppings piled in drifts along every floorboard, lingered at the feet of a grey metal desk and caressed the tall grey filing cabinets. The RAF had been here last, and evidently cleared out in a hurry.

A crunch under someone's foot betrayed the skeleton of a long-desiccated vole. The sound echoed; crusty, bitter dust kicked up. Ben coughed and closed his mouth against who knew what sort of crap, feeling like Indiana Jones on a bad day.

Still, as the three men stared in the middle of the broad, polished floor, dulled with the penalty of years, the remnants of that beauty could still strike awe in one of them at least.

"This room is as big as my house," Ben breathed with a

laugh. A snort from the bard's son showed what he thought of that.

"Quiet," said Raven with an air of command. "Listen."

The song was there. Thready, but undeniably there. The laughter in Glas's throat caught suddenly, and broke. He swallowed unsteadily and said, "This way."

"No, wait. Listen, I said."

Something was looming in the shadows at the door they had foolishly left unsealed. Before they could move, Silence Carew had slammed it open and stood framed in the doorway.

"At last!" he growled, and his voice was a handful of gravel. "You, and then the witch, and the rest of your whole benighted race!"

Clutching the iron knife as if it held his whole world, he threw himself snarling at Glas, as if the other men weren't even there. As if it didn't matter.

It mattered.

"Go!" Raven shouted, and shoved Glas up the stair. Before the fae could turn again,

Ben Harper, unarmed and out of practice, dropped into a fighting stance and stepped toward the puritan, then put a shoulder into his gut, grabbed a leg and stood up. Carew flipped and slammed into the floor. Ben moved to stomp the knife hand with a booted foot, but Silence pulled it away a fraction too soon, and slashed upwards. Ben tumbled to avoid the blade and slipped on the vole. He went down sliding, slammed up against the cold foot of the desk. He thought he heard a crack, but the pain was too distracting to be sure.

Silence scrambled to his feet, the greasy strings of hair pasted with cobwebs, frantic to get to his goal.

In any ordinary fight, they would have faced off, started again, but Carew didn't care about anything but getting past. When Ben hit the ground Silence retrieved the knife, sought a new path. He started to run, the leather boots slipped on the marble floor. The American grabbed his foot and twisted, to bring him crashing down. This time Ben got a grip on the wrist of the knife hand, slamming it back to the floor again and again until the fingers loosened. Then he snatched the knife and held it to the man's throat. Ben Harper had never killed a human, but he longed to drive it home.

Carew screamed and grappled again, knocking the knife away, but Ben's advantage held. Furious, he drove a fist into the cadaverous face that knocked it back to the marble floor. Then did it again, for good measure. The man went limp, unconscious at last. Gasping for breath in the airless room, Ben rolled aside then dragged himself to his feet, shaking the sting out of his right hand.

"No *glissandos* for a week."

"Don't forget the weapon," Raven said. He was standing neatly out of the way looking dapper and most of all uncobwebbed. "Over there."

"I'll come back for it." Ben glared at him between raspy breaths. "You couldn't have helped?"

"No time for fine tuning. I'd have had to blast you both."

Slapping at his clothes and peeling grit and filth in furry rolls off his face and out of his hair, Ben winced. His side ached. A rib had probably cracked.

"I could have lived with that,"

"Not today," said Raven, and turned to head up stairs. "At least, you wouldn't have liked it. You okay?"

Ben took a step, wincing. "Mostly."

"Carry on, then."

The grand staircase that Raven mounted so lightly rose to a from the broad landing, suitable for an impressive entrance. Ben imagined the stately thump of the Marshall's staff calling attention over a room filled with glittering guests. The precise enunciation of ancient titles and noble surnames ringing down the centuries. Plumed headdresses, impeccable tailoring, false smiles and covered whispers. Their images assaulted him and their muttering voices, even a shrill burst of ethereal laughter.

It was also remarkably steep, and his legs a bit wobbly. A trickling itch under his shirt made him think he might be bleeding somewhere, but he wasn't quite sure. So he used the hand rail to haul himself up.

When he reached the top where Raven waited, the harper stopped nonchalantly for a breath, looking back. The ground floor was a breathtakingly long way away.

"He's not dead, you know," Ben said.

"That's not my office."

"I see. We'd better move, then."

They went up.

A narrower stair from the private rooms muttered with the staccato of a ghostly telegraph, the rumble of voices reading dispatches, dictating orders, latest word from the front. The clatter of Morse code, the squee and crackle of the wireless being tuned in, an echo of Winston Churchill's sonorous tones.

Up again by another, still narrower stair to a slender corridor and a cramped passage to the servants' quarters: chambermaids and footmen endeavoring to be invisible and perfect all at once. Falling into bed at all hours, rising before the sun, and lucky to have the employment.

A winding stair brought them to a single open door on a dark turret at the very top of the house, shared the rafters with pigeons and squirrels. Through shuttered French windows ringing it like a lantern, a watery light was working hard to urge the tiny room to brilliance. Dust motes drifted.

An iron bedframe made Raven step back, then force himself forward, denying the atavistic chill. He'd awakened in an iron bed once not so long ago, and the memory would live with him, a persistent, humiliating fear. But no amount of courage could make him immune to its poison. To the goddess, perhaps it merely worked to keep her hidden, but the faery lord swore and retreated.

Ben stood in the doorway until his eyes grew accustomed to the gloom, then whistled low. No fairy princess was so well appointed, or so sad. Cyfla, lady of the Fleet, lay like Snow White on her bier gowned in silk, first white, then shimmering under the fitful light with every shade of blue, cushioned on downy pillows, a faery embroidered counterpane folded at her feet. The walls that had in their time been papered in the cheapest stuff glowed with opal light. Flowers filled every corner, sweetening the air.

"Not Rapunzel," Ben said, his voice a whisper among the echoes. "Sleeping Beauty. It's beautiful."

"Everything she could need, in case she should wake," said Glas, "and I not by her."

His own face wet with tears, they found him on the bed, supporting her golden head and shoulders on his knees. She might have been dead, she was so pale and still, except for the slow rise and fall of her breast. He, or someone, had bound her hair into a long braid shimmering over her shoulder almost to the dainty ankles.

The free-range anxiety was making Ben restless, so his appreciation was short lived. He'd found the girl. What of the final charm?

The place was hardly as big as a good-sized dressing room—which meant his gift had become as specific as it was going to be. He started opening boxes and turning over pillows, listening for the rest of the song.

Raven, unimpressed, leaned in the doorway, posing his question to Glas over folded arms.

"Did you do this to her? This enchanted sleep?"

"No! Not the way you think," Glas said, more quietly, brushing a loose strand of gold away from her face. "It was her idea. She loves me, you see. Enough to risk the charm. And then…" He choked on the memory.

Raven waited, saying nothing, senses on alert.

"Her own music, and mine. You couldn't understand. We make a harmony so perfect that we…"

The voice trailed off, the pause lengthening while they watched him, watching her. Raven cleared his throat and shifted his pose to encourage efficiency in the telling.

"All right. For a while we were every day together, squandering our days as thoughtless as children, but then… She thought, if we sang it together, in a particular harmony, we could alter the spell— cheat the magic, you know? If we had only a year and a day, we wouldn't take all the days at once, but spread them out along the centuries. We could be in love for all time."

"She gave up the river, her charge from time out of mind.

She gave up her nature. For you?"

"Yes!" Glas snapped. "As I did for her. Raven, I have bent my whole nature to loving her, to protecting her. I…"

The tears were real, whatever their source, the fae lord thought. Aloud he said, "And what else?"

Glas ap Gwydion, who might have been a hero, pulled himself together.

"Once every hundred years—more often in these busy times—she wakes for a few days, a week or so. We go dancing, we make love, we travel."

"Ride down ordinary mortals in the street," Ben muttered.

"Then, at need, we find a new haven for her, and she sleeps again. I keep her safe. Gods below, man," he cried suddenly. "You cannot understand. You have never loved!"

Raven shrugged his contempt.

"You're still an idiot."

"I do know you, I…" Glas said, expecting an altogether different response. His grief fueled by frustration, he added sullenly. "You don't know anything."

"This is not about me. It doesn't matter whether I understand, nor my lord the king, nor Father Tamesis. She is not yours to keep."

"She is!"

"She has betrayed her charge," Raven went on placidly. "It is not her fault that Silence Carew became a monster. Cyfla did not write that story. She is not even part of it, but she holds the key to it. And, as Issa intended, only Cyfla can turn that key. That's what Ben was trying to say before. Yes?"

"More or less."

Wracked with misery, holding her as close as he dared, Glas stroked her hair murmuring.

"What am I supposed to do? What can I do?"

"Let her go," Ben said quietly from the shadows. "Wake her. Let her go home."

"I can't."

"Of course you can. She wakes to your voice when you call her."

"No!"

"You must," said Raven, with absolute certainty.

Ben, watching this preternatural exchange, felt another *click*.

"I'm not sure he can, not like this. But you know what?"

Raven cocked his head quizzically, and the harper nodded towards the sushi bag where it slumped by the door.

"Kick that over here, if you please."

The boy had taken charge of the satchel since the fight began downstairs, and put it down only when they entered Cyfla's silken bower. Now he did as he was asked.

When Ben reached in, to his delight, he drew out the little silver-strung harp that was Oberon's, which he had carried through so many hard places, and which had its own enchantments. The final charm and its antidote were still hidden, but the instrument was in his hands, and Ata'rathi's tune in his head.

Gasping a little—that bruised rib or whatever it was reminded him it was there—he lowered himself into a hard chair beside the bed, and began. Sweet music filled the little room, the ancient tune meant for Ata'rathi's daughter.

> *In the meads upon the heath*
> *the fleet-foot daughter lies*
> *and dreams alone, unknown.*
> *She sleeps, O let her wake!*
> *Wake her. Bring her home.*

And nothing changed. Though the room brightened slightly, after a minute or two, Raven laid a hand on his shoulder.

"This pattern has many parts, hasn't it? Trust the water."

The harper's mouth twisted, the two lines of a frown creased his brow. Ben met the jewel-blue gaze for a second, then slapped his forehead.

"Of course!"

One more time he dived into the impeccably organized satchel and this time brought out a gleaming silver bottle, round as an apple, etched with his name and honors. He held it out to Glas, who flinched as if it were cold iron.

"What is it?"

"Water from her own spring," said Raven. "From before the pollution, before the sewers. From the very day, I suspect, when you took her away from there."

"What do you want me to do with it?"

Ben shrugged.

"You're the magician, Glas ap Gwydion."

"But it will break the spell."

"Glas," Raven said gently. "Brother. You know you must."

Yielding at last, Gwydion's son nodded and reached for the flask as the harp began again.

The harper chose a sprightly tune this time, quite at odds with the clouded, dreamlike atmosphere all this enchantment, all this antiquity and sorrow, had engendered. The key changed. His foot started to tap out the time. Raven, finding a smile about him somewhere, sped up the slatted shutters one by one in time with the tune, and threw open the windows inviting in sunshine and the light breeze off the heath. The room breathed in; they all did.

Oblivious to all else, the magician's boy filled his hand with the icy water.

"*Cariad*," he whispered, his voice a caress.

Slowly he tipped the water over his lady's head, watching it sheet across her eyes and back along the neat channels of her hair. Almost at once he felt a tiny catch in her breath.

"Oriana."

Another handful, her name again, and a tremulous shiver passed across her limbs. On a third baptism:

"Cyfla."

She gasped, the translucent eyelids flickered.

A terrible sound broke Glas's voice in panic and despair, but he put the flask to her lips anyway and, whispering lovers' nonsense, encouraged her to drink, to accept, and to wake while Ben Harper played.

37
There and not there

It was done. The sweet face flushed with roses. The dark eyes grew wide, graceful hands fluttered up in dismay at her wet hair. Cyfla murmured sleepily, "What? Is it time already?"

"It's all right, *cariad*," her lover said, smoothing the water away from her face with a handkerchief. When she shook her head, blinking in confusion, and struggled to sit up, he helped her.

"I know that song!" she said happily. "Oh, my dear! Have we tarried so long?"

His hands tightened, pressing the memory of lithe muscles under silken skin into his heart, willing her not to go. But the spell was broken. Glas let his hands drop as she leapt away from him. Light-hearted she twirled a pirouette, spinning out the embroidered bands of her nightdress like a flower on its stem. Then she caught her breath, and stopped. She reached for his hands and drew him into her arms, covering his face with kisses.

Unmindful as the sorcerer's apprentice, he let the silver bottle fall. It tumbled to the wooden floor, its contents streaming away across the carpets towards the door.

"Amadis, dear heart," she whispered. "I must go home!"

Raven, seeing his cue, came forward and took her hands, and kissed them.

"My lady," he said, smiling. "I believe I can be of service."

"Oh, kind sir! Do I know you?"

She giggled, a silver sound like the bubbling waters of the Fleet's many wells.

He gave her his name and style, and Ben's; the harper stood, and bowed, and snatched the harp and his bag out of the rising water that streamed out now from her feet.

The rosebud mouth rounded with delight.

"O, excellent! I have seen you before, human child!" she said, brightening further, if that were possible. She put her hands around his face and kissed him on the mouth, then spun away.

They watched her dance out of the tiny room without a single glance back to her silken pillows and satin caps, her fine embroideries, and her lover standing shattered with his face to the wall. Whim carried her, and little moth wings that lifted her so she scarcely touched the floor, down one stair and the next.

Ben and Raven, both speechless, could only follow beatified and awestruck. She was taller than they had thought, or perhaps she grew as she became more and more herself, Cyfla, goddess of the Fleet, sister of the Thames.

There was one thing remaining, Ben thought, with her kiss still tingling on his lips. He'd remember it in a minute. Raven, laughing, wild and utterly fae, slapped Ben on the shoulder.

"Tarry not, old son!"

All around them, the house was changing, morphing through a sparkling haze, swelling, greening. The water, as if pouring from the spring itself, followed down the stairs behind her, dropping through the floorboards, filling the mouseholes, swelling the files in their abandoned drawers, flooding the walls with the waters of the Fleet.

Enchantment hung from Cyfla's every step, and with each step her spring and its waters rose about her. And in minutes, seconds, the great house in the middle of London had dissolved, or disappeared, or simply been left behind; and she walked instead over the springing grasses, among the yellow irises of Hampstead Heath at the place where it intersects with Faerie. Where the fine homes of the Highgate should have frowned over the hill, apple trees grew starred with white blossoms, and piles of bluebells nodded at their feet.

Following with a heart less giddy than hers, Ben's breathing slowed and he remembered.

"My lady, if you please!" he called, hearing his own voice as a dull clang against the crystalline walls of the world. "You have one of Ata'rathi's charms in your care, a slip of writing."

She stepped and twirled with delight on what was still almost a green marble floor just as it became wet green grass, then she hiccupped and caught herself.

"I do!" she said, "Oh, yes, I remember that, I do!" Then a dainty frown troubled the dainty features. "Issa gave it to me, I don't remember why. Why do I have it? Glas?"

But Glas was nowhere to be seen.

"Never mind. It's around here somewhere. Oh, I know! I left it… I left it…"

The air shifted in a way Ben recognized. She turned a liquid sort of arabesque and every stitch of the silken nightgown disappeared from her thought and thus from her person, and a scrap of pale old papyrus fluttered to the ground.

"Oh, here it is!"

She bent to pick it up, then gave a sly teasing look under her arm before she straightened. Solemnly Ben held out his hand.

"Do you mean this? Do you want it? Have to catch me!"

But Raven, imagining himself less subject to her attractive powers, laid gentle but catching hands on her shoulders. Grey eyes sparkling, she raised full lips to his, and stood on tiptoe to kiss his mouth well and thoroughly. Then she stood back and, shy as a schoolgirl, held out the papyrus on the tips of her fingers.

"Ben?" said Raven, almost blushing. "Over to you."

The harper stepped up to claim it before anything else could happen. Their eyes met, and the boy's rolled. But he let her kiss him again, highly aware of the lithe little body she pressed into his.

Ben ignored him and walked in under the apple trees, studying the page. His lips, unencumbered by river goddess, drew into a thin smile.

"*Addendum: A charm contrary to the last,*" it began.

Applying the focus that had made him an organizing guru and the skills that had made him the king of Faerie's own man—and standing well away from the growing influence of the goddess—he processed the charm in the Latin translation with the English commentary scribbled next to it. Compared it to the two charms he already knew. Began to cast it up in a kind of verse wrapped around a tune.

"Got it," he said quietly, and looked around for Raven.

By his sacrifice, Glas had broken Cyfla's enchantment; that task was accomplished. One more remained, and now a party seemed to be starting around Cyfla's spring. Either that, or he'd walked into an old Disney cartoon.

As lithe as a Theban acrobat, as giddy as a teenager at her first rock concert, the river called her nymphs to join her. One by one by twos and threes, boys and girls, nymphs and satyrs and water fae of all sorts, woke from the Fleet's long dream, shaking the rushes and the long shafts of iris. All the laughing children returned from hiding, rushing to Cyfla with noisy delight. Music began to rise.

Below the bubbling surface of the growing pond, glimmering with faerie light, the rippling image of Amphitrite appeared, the Lore Mothers in shadow beneath her. Oberon, too, had sensed the change and arrived in kingly panoply, crowned and smiling, to welcome Cyfla home.

Father Tam strode forward to embrace his lost sister, and Teifi of the Walbrook and all London's rivers came to her as well. Only Issa of the Dart, veiled in violet mourning, walked apart from the rest.

Then Tamesis looked up, his senses shaken by something no one else could see.

"Hold!" he said, in a voice that crashed through them all like a wave. Even the satyrs ceased their dance. "Stand away from the *morven!*"

The air around the granite marker shimmered and turned black as a mirror. Sick with terror, furious with shame and his destroying god's unfulfilled mission, Silence Carew roared through the portal and fell with a splash like an explosion into the water. He surfaced, gasping and swearing.

Nymphs and sea maids screamed and dived under the lilies, while Raven was whispering in Ben's ear.

"See what he has around his neck?"

The puritan struggled to gain some footing, water and muddy roots streaming over his face and shoulders. Swinging free over the ruin of a linen shirt, hung three suns and three lions, symbols of the world he rejected, with the *morven* pendant glowing like a star in the middle.

Raven snarled. "I thought you got rid of that damned knife."

"Yell at me later. Here, take this," Ben handed him the counter-charm. "And give me your amulet."

The baleful glare of Simon's eyes found Sir Francis Bowne, pulling the knots of a jewel close around his throat, a jewel that was mate to his own. Next to him the demon Fitzroy was tucking the missing papyrus into his doublet. Yes, he would kill them, too, as soon as…

And there she was, so close he could nearly touch her nakedness, the tilted grey eyes, the heart-shaped face that had haunted his nightmares through the long years. Beautiful and hateful, never forgotten, the witch of the apple tree, bright in her brothel.

"Oriana, at last." He almost wept as he raised a hand to point the black knife at her. "Oriana!" He coughed and gagged on the name. Spat it out and barked again, "Thou drab! Harlot! Sorceress! Witch!"

From overhead, a shower of apple blossoms caught the breeze and swirled around her, dazzling the eye as they had before, clothing her in a fluttering white chiton stitched with pale pink, touched with green. Cyfla, delighted, whirled before she heard the shout, and hushed the chattering nymphs around her.

"What did he say?"

"I say thou keep'st a bestial court among these jades! Where is thy lord, thy buffoon, thy apish playmate? What—"

A lake in a storm, the air around the goddess frothed as she drew herself up, summoning her silks, her lace, her fine array as he had first seen her. Collared and glittering with diamonds, she strode toward Carew, no playful child. Two bright spots of anger flared in the pale cheeks.

"What tuneless creature is this that spoils the peace of our spring? That name is not for him to use!"

"Lady." Ben stepped forward with a courtier's grace and an answer. "This is Issa's son, that might have been your cousin, your loving brother. He chose instead to torture and murder with that black iron knife. The *Gwragedd Annwn*, your mothers, have condemned him."

Half-starved, half-mad, Simon called on what threadbare dignity he had left to him. He pointed at Ben.

"You are none of this company. Give me the witch and her master, and you shall be spared."

Ben indulged in a small smirk as he turned his back and walked away, while behind him Tam nodded sharply. The water itself grabbed Simon Carew and splashed him down again. Cursing, he struggled to get up. No one laughed except the satyrs, who think everything mortal is hysterical.

When he tried to slog through to dry land, Tam shrugged and pulled the muddy bottom from under the man's feet. This time the terrible knife flew from his grip straight to Oberon's hand, who cared nothing for the touch of cold iron.

At his side, Raven flinched as it flew past him.

"Target practice, sir?"

A wry smile crossed the king's face.

"If you like," he said, and threw the knife into the air.

The ball of power that overtook the thing high overhead left only Raven with a tingling hand and a self-satisfied expression, but nothing else.

"Father!" Silence gurgled as it vanished. "Fileal, aid me! Fileal, for god's sake honor your oaths!"

But there was no aid. Watchers saw the red-rimmed eyes flood with angry tears, the hopeless mouth shape three words that might be *You have failed.*

Ben Harper stood a while in thought resting his hand on the Atami amulet, feeling the resonance with Carew's. He felt slightly light-headed, suspended almost in a moment between moments. To one side he was aware of Raven winding the last piece up of the scroll with the rest to store in the ivory box. The rest was silence.

As if he were quite alone under the apple trees, Ben sat down on a mossy rock with Aubrey's silver-strung harp nestled between his knees. He struck one note, and he began to hum. A slow scale at first, testing the Icthylean mode. Then the tune emerged, and found its way to his supple fingers and the song he had made for the charm.

In front of him figures of fae and Atami and one frantic man stood poised as if caught in a single frame of film. Vaguely he was aware of Issa's pleading voice, Oberon's deep replies, but they were nothing to do with him. It was time and past time to end this.

Utterly certain, he lifted his voice in the ancient mode.

Atargatis Ata'rathi Ashara!
The doleful charm unsend
All sorrows end
Sad heart abide no more
Light heart restore
Tears fly away
Old love forsake
New pleasures take
Become yourself again
Rabbatu atiratu yammi

Carew stopped ranting, frozen as the king's harper sang, His face twisted with horror as his enchantment broke, his locked soul creaked open, and understanding streamed in.

In terror and pain each monstrous act enfolded him; the monster he was crashed helter-skelter along the blood-stained corridors of his mind, searching for a single instant of kindness or pity. He screamed,

"God! God, what have I done?"

The Atami crowding now around him had no answers, only their fury surging towards him. Long-fingered hands plucked at his clothes and pulled at his limbs, though he slapped them away. Their tiny voices buzzed in his ears, and the winged faeries like stinging insects flew at his eyes.

Frantic, Carew whirled to find the king of Faerie speaking gently to Issa, her soul also unbound, her weeping ended.

"My lord!" Simon sobbed. "Is there no pity neither in Heaven nor Fairyland? Will no one speak for me? I am but the man she made me—she and the witch. Oh God, she abandoned me! Left me to be mocked among my own people! This is all of her doing."

"Sir?" Ben inquired on a rising note.

Oberon kissed Issa's cheek and handed her, a bright-eyed girl in a lavender Grecian dress, to Father Tam. Then his expression hardened and he nodded curtly to Ben. The heath fell silent for the one purely human voice among them.

"I know your story, Simon Carew," Ben said, pitching his actor's voice to carry. "I could read it in the things you've touched. I read it in your bones and in the scars on your body when we fought. Three suns and three lions have showed me your mind, and may I never in my life see such a thing again. Other men have begun with less and yet become men of good heart, no matter what mouldy magic they stumbled into. Your choices have been your own, and you will pay for them."

He paused and ran his eye around the fauns and satyrs, naiads and nereids, goddesses and sea maids ringing the lake, and he lifted his open hands to encompass them.

"Remember where you are. Pity is not the principal attribute of Faerie."

On the bank, Oberon watched coldly, blinked once, and turned away.

"Wait," the man called through his tears, but no one marked him.

Grim and trembling, Glas appeared at last at Cyfla's graceful shoulder, determined to do his lady one last service while she still remembered his name, and his love. He whispered to her, and saw at last what Raven had seen in Teifi, the goddess behind the girl, and blushed as if he had forgotten it until now.

"Simon Carew!" Glas ap Gwydion shouted.

His chest heaving, the man almost fell again, crazed with

despair, worried at by creatures as angry as little dogs.

"My lord!" the cracked voice cried. "Have mercy, for the love of God! I am like you! I am one of you!"

"Not quite" said Glas ap Gwydion coldly. "I've never blamed my mother for anything."

Then he handed his lady a long bow of ivory and horn. He took from Ben an arrow tipped with flint, with a small bronze amulet bound behind the point. He spoke a few words in her ear.

With queenly poise, Cyfla nocked the arrow then leant around the string to kiss his cheek. She turned to Simon Carew.

"Mercy? I have it here, you son of a bitch."

In a single fluid motion she bent and loosed. The dart whistled as it sped swiftly to Simon's chest, shattering the amber Atami disk, and buried itself in his heart.

The cry that burst from him could in no wise match the cries he'd caused for sorrow and despair. No hearts were softened to hear it. Piranha-like, the furious Atami swarmed over him and bore him down until he disappeared under the boiling surface of the water. After a moment, the water was still.

With a satisfied squawk and a rattle of night-black feathers, Raven leapt into the air and soared out over the sunlit heath.

38
A Sunday in November: Cornwall

"The Best English Folk & Roots Band in Ten Years"

"Best Up and Coming Folk Artist of the Year"

"The Other Ben Harper Rocks the Harp"

"You do know it's November, yes?" Raven said as he jumped out of the sleek black van and slammed the door. They'd had this conversation already, but it was worth repeating. Sometimes the motivations of mortals just escaped him, even Ben Harper whom he knew well.

Ben was grinning, feeling much the same about the raven-boy.

"And no one goes to the beach in November, I know."

He slung Moytura in her case over Raven's shoulder and set off down the steep asphalt path that led from the road to the strand.

"And yet, here we are. They say this coast of Cornwall is warmed by the Gulf Stream. See? Palm trees." And so there were.

"And why am I here?"

"You're the roadie." When Raven sputtered, Ben added, "Besides, you're part of this."

"Part of what? Why are you so mysterious?"

Ben stopped the headlong rush with a look, and met the enquiring sapphire eyes.

"Because it might not work. But it's the only thing I can

think of that makes any sense."

"This is sense?"

But that was all he would say.

Raven thrust his hands into the pockets of his jeans and marched sullenly along, matching pace with his friend. Apparently Ben was right. The sea was a brilliant blue out to the horizon, gilded with the declining light of a golden sunset. The onshore breeze was rising, stinging his ears.

The beach wasn't crowded, but it had been on this surprisingly sunny autumn day. To be sure, most of the people, judging by the bright red British tans on some of them, had already enjoyed their day and were packing to go. Only one group appeared to be setting up and getting a bonfire going in a fire ring instead of breaking it up.

"There's Mellis and Sparrow." Ben threw up a hand to wave. "All right, Dinah and Tom brought the kids. Cool, they all came! Come on, Watson. Family night!"

The Folk and Roots music festival had been a triumph. Over the last few months, *Faerie Reel's* first CD had made a slightly remarkable but not entirely unplanned cross-over to the New Age lists with a couple of haunting original songs, including one that none of them exactly remembered writing.

So while they were too new to be featured headliners this year, their reception had been enthusiastic, and they had played exceptionally well. Before heading home, he'd made an executive decision (together with Dinah, of course) and declared it was time for an unplugged beach party. Just families. No playlist. Just food and beer and music for its own sake—for their own sake.

Being autumn, the sun went down quick and early, which meant the bonfire could light up the night that much sooner. Stars winked into place, few by few; not the busy, untroubled starfield of olden times, but still pretty impressive. There would be a meteor shower later, they said. Perfect.

Raven slipped away for a few minutes while everyone was eating, and after a while, when the music had gotten going, he was back with his fiddle, and with Aubrey, and as time went on a few others dropped by whose features were sharper, their ears slightly more pointed than the Saxon profiles of the band.

Those who weren't playing were singing, and those who didn't sing could dance. The dancing mostly involving hopping, a bit of spinning, and occasional falling down, but even the smallest got up again giggling. After a while, someone called on a woman with long dark eyes who said her name was Sinadubh—one of Dinah's friends, or maybe one of Raven's—to show them what dancing really looked like. Which she did then, laughing.

After a while, she borrowed a bodhrán from Brian Hobbes and set a new rhythm to the night. They bounced through jigs, they ran through reels, they made stuff up, and where one musician sat down to breathe, another took their place. Not that the fae ever needed or often wanted a break, but it was only polite.

The beer never ran out, and the bonfire never seemed to die down or need much in the way of fuel, thanks to Aubrey's good will. No more sand got into the potato crisps than was tolerable. And then when the moon rose, three days off the full, she tilted her pock-marked approval at their revels.

Ben took that as his cue. They had laid out a few loading flats to create a hard surface to keep the instruments out of the sand, and Ben had perched on a milking stool with Moytura balanced in front of him. He sat back now, rocking the harp forward onto its feet. Thinking to hand it off, he glanced up at the nearest of Aubrey's gentlemen, a lad who hadn't named himself. A slender hand reached up to push aside a long wisp of pale hair, stained, he thought, a kind of sea-foam green.

"Glas?"

The magician's son had been watching him play, a kind of hunger in his eyes. Ben nodded.

"You don't mind?"

Ben shrugged as he got to his feet, but thought it best to ask,

"Does Raven know you're here?"

"He said I should come along. Something about bygones

being bygones." A mocking smile finally broke across the kid's lips—another impossibly ancient kid. "But I'm on best behavior."

Well done, Raven.

"Cool." Ben leaned over and touched Dinah's elbow, and when she looked up, he said, "This is, ah…"

"Charlie."

"Charlie Glass. Friend of Raff's. He's okay."

And without waiting for a response, Ben stepped down onto the sand, caught up his bag, and found his lovely wife listening to Sparrow tell the other children a story, something with dragons in it. He crooked a finger and she came. Together they strode down to the fire pit. Shortly, Raven and Aubrey fell in beside them.

"What are we doing?" Mellis asked.

"Not leaving you out. You'll see."

The fire was crackling, a big golden red blaze of flames like autumn leaves reaching into the night, fragrant with resins from the sweet woods brought by Aubrey's crew. The air was crisp with autumn and the landward breeze brought with it the scents of salt sea and far-away lands. The four of them stood in silence for a while, watching the flames, and the curling breakers crashing beyond.

Then Ben slipped the lacings of the satchel and withdrew a long ivory box carved with medallions of griffons and centaurs pursued by hunters, latched with an ivory pin. He slipped the pin, and the scrolled parchment, all the parts restored, fell into his hands. He had tried to return it to Tamesis, but the river god protested. It was too perilous and he wanted no part of its care. Oberon likewise pointed out that it was not really within his remit, even as king of Faerie, though he had repaired it. No, it must be returned to Ata'rathi, though no one could say exactly how Ben was supposed to do that. It had sat on a shelf for weeks in his office, waiting for some kind of clue.

Now, on a night full of falling stars, he thought he knew what to do.

"We're all agreed," he began, "that this thing is too danger-ous to stay in the world, right? Well, if Ata'rathi has removed herself from the world, and her priests and her temples are long gone beneath the waves, there aren't a lot of options. So I thought, with your permission, sir, burning would be the best thing. Safest, anyway."

While Ben was talking, a star fell, a short flare of light streaking across the sky. Before he had finished, there was another. Then two more. Behind him, someone shouted,

"Blimey, look at that!"

The music came to a ragged halt as everyone looked up at the lightshow coming out of the constellation Leo. The meteor shower had begun. After a startled moment, Moytura's liquid voice sounded, mellow and sweet under the skillful hands of Glas ap Gwydion, and the universe had a soundtrack.

Ben Harper smiled, not minding the interruption. Then, as he watched, one star fell aslant the rest, crossing the sky with powerful grace until it seemed to touch the horizon and fall into the sea almost in front of them. The path of reflected moonlight along the ocean's surface shimmered with power. Something within it was moving with purpose towards the shore.

Aubrey touched Ben's hand, taking the scroll and rolling it back into the handsome case.

"I think you are being given a better answer than the fire, human child."

Magic seldom surprised Ben any more. Seldom, but not never.

"Sir, shouldn't you do this?"

Aubrey gave him an odd look, and shook his head.

"It was your quest, and your accomplishment. Go. Trust the water."

Ben took the scroll again and walked down the pebbled shore until the sea foam broke against his knees. And there she was, rising in front of him on her twin tails, Ata'rathi wreathed in stars. Her hair, the color of the deep ocean, coiled in ringlets tight to her head and the rest of her, flesh and scales, shimmered gold and green, and her black eyes were bright. About her throat, a necklace of blushing shells reflected the firelight. Ben thought she might be smiling.

He bowed as he knew how, and held out the scroll.

"You have done very well, human child," she said. "The king of Faerie is well served."

"I have done what I could, madam," said Ben. The sand under his bare feet kept shifting with the incoming tide, though he held his footing. "His Grace and Father Tamesis agree, though, that these charms are too perilous for the world in these times. So I return them to your care, if you will have them."

The siren goddess nodded, then, and accepted the ivory case from him.

"They were meant to bring joy," she said, "but the world has changed. Thank you, Ben Harper, and to the King's Raven as well."

She glanced over his shoulder towards Raven, who bowed gravely.

What else was there to say? Well, one question, perhaps.

"Madam, what of the Mermaid Stair?"

She tilted her head, as if assessing his need to know, then said, "It will recover. It is recovering now, though the damage was great. You will not see it again. No human will, no matter how much Atami blood runs in his veins. It is closed."

Though her tone hadn't changed, Ben could feel anger hovering there. He had his answer, that was enough. Then she smiled, if that was her smile.

"But for you it might have been utterly destroyed. I am grateful that it was not. There is a debt between us, Ben Harper, which you may claim at your will. And so," she said, "farewell."

She was gone, the stars of her coming now no more than the foam sparkling on the wave. Ben turned and sloshed back to the tideline, feeling drained. He took Mellis's hand.

"Did you see her? Ata'rathi?"

There were tears standing in his wife's golden eyes, brimming to fall.

"No," she whispered while the stars shot tracers across the sky. "I heard a kind of whisper, or something, and some strange music, but...no."

Behind her, Aubrey was shaking his head. Some things cannot be shared.

"Let's go home," said Ben.

Epilogue

1592 Richmond Palace

The Queen of England was dining in private this evening, a late light supper in her Privy Chamber over looking the river. Her only guest was Sir Walter Ralegh, richly dressed, his deep brown beard curled and scented with Hungary water, which he knew to be her favorite. As royal rooms go, this one was intimate, more a withdrawing room than an audience chamber, a table for two by a pair of lead-paned windows. A single gentleman of her Household would serve to wait on them, no more. Upon the opposite wall, the virginals sat on an oaken table waiting for her accomplished touch, though she would never play for others.

She'd had her cousin the Lord Chamberlain's players in the afternoon, among them that Shakespeare fellow whose work she so fancied, and a ridiculous farce called *The Comedy of Errors*. She was still laughing about the man and his dog as she arranged her broad embroidered skirts around the bench and sat down to the first course, a dish of parsnips and marigolds cooked with oranges.

"Faith, he was so like Sir Christopher Hatton with his sorry face, I near thought him before me on the platform."

Ralegh laughed with her.

"Perhaps because they are both clowns?"

"Nay, Water!" she scoffed lightly, giving him his nickname. "Lackwit, I mean that he was like the dog!"

When the musicians arrived, she glanced at them with interest. Someone new. Excellent.

"Who have we here, Master Rafael?"

The gentleman of her Household who was waiting on them stepped forward, smiling out of sapphire eyes.

"If it please your Majesty, Lord Aubrey sends his compliments with the music, and Sir Thomas Weston recommends them to your pleasure."

She nodded with grace and addressed the man directly.

"Sir Thomas has some credit with us, in sooth. Lord Aubrey even more. Say what is thy name, fellow."

"I am Sir Francis Browne, madam."

Ben Harper gave his best high court reverence and rose, standing easy, holding his cap in his hand as was the custom. The heart pounding out a galliard in his chest was probably customary, too.

"Sir Francis Browne?"

She quizzed him a bit on his family, his background, whence his knighthood came and at whose hand, to which he had ready answers. Why had she not seen him in her Court till now?

Meantime, Ralegh ground his teeth under a light, courtier's smile. To be a royal favorite is to be always a little on edge in the presence of other talented, intelligent men. Did he detect some change in her? No, she was only being Gloriana, as always, charming another acolyte. She might be rising sixty, but she still drew people to her. And at least this green-liveried fellow was no young buck, no real competition.

The woman, now, wasn't she interesting? Tall, perhaps too tall, but fair and modest in her plain blue gown, waiting to be noticed. The tawny eyes when she raised them engaged Ralegh's a bit too boldly, perhaps, before looking hastily away. The fellow said her name.

"My sister Margaret, your Majesty," said Francis Browne, and gave Mellis his hand to draw her forward. It also gave her an anchor as she sank into a deep curtsey. Her nervousness was almost but not quite visible, and her fingers were cold. But nerves are natural when meeting a queen. She had not had his long years of preparation for this adventure, but she'd be fine, he knew.

Mellis hadn't liked having to pretend to be Ben's sister, and had said so over more than one planning meeting in the kitchen at home. But the Queen was notoriously hard on the wives of men she liked. They had taken the safer course. It seemed to

Maggie Secara

be working, for the Queen gave her a question to answer as well, which she fielded with hardly a stammer.

"It may please you to hear her play on the virginals," Ben said when asked. "I, the cittern and the harp, though not both together, of course."

She chuckled a bit, approving.

"And belike we'll sing for Your Majesty, as you will."

And so, while Raven attended her with utter and silent perfection, Ben and Mellis brought their several talents together to sing and play on a summer night at the Queen's palace of Richmond. The initial nerve storm had passed. After that, all their choices must have been golden, for she did seem pleased, singing along sometimes and tapping her little foot. For himself, Ben was in heaven.

At last the Queen grew weary, and dismissed them most cordially, Master Rafael bearing a pretty purse with two gold sovereigns in it with Her Majesty's good will. As they were packing up, they heard a murmur, a question, her sudden laughter. Ralegh bowed and retired scowling, but Raven, acting on the Queen's whim, unlatched the windows to let sweet air into a chamber grown stuffy, and Ben's heart lifted even further.

On the riverbank below, mermaids were singing.

THE END

The Ata'rathi Scroll

Taken from the English translation (1763) of the Latin transcription of the original Urgic-Akkadian as rendered into Homeric Greek by the Author. (Oxford, 1916)

'Tis said in all reports that Ata'rathi's temple was once partly in the sea, where she was attended by both mortal and immortal men and maidens. The scroll was writ at Ata'rathi's own command for the benefit of all those who honored her. Kept in the Holy of Holies, it was used very seldom. Finally it came to rest in the great library at Alexandria, whence all know what became of that place.

THE FIRST CHARM

For the Atami to get a human form for to walk in human lands, she must first be altogether on dry land and sing these words in the Icthylean mode. The transformation will end when the charm is sung in the Dorian mode, or at Ata'rathi's call.

> *RABBATU ATIRATU YAMMI*
> *From Ascalon to far Urhaal,*
> *my feet to walk, my voice to talk,*
> *mine eyes to blink, a mortal soul*
> *to drink the air until my mothers call.*

Commentary: The Icthylean mode was known to the ancients as a mode peculiar to the Atami or water fae, similar to the Aeolian mode but more watery.

Atami appeareth by all accounts to be a word among the water folk for their own kind, notwithstanding its exact translation has been lost to the Wise. Likewise the cities or perhaps temples of Ascalon and far Urhaal remain unknown.

Of the words *rabbatu atiratu yammi*, the most ancient books say that this is a most ancient name or title of grace signifying thus: Lady Goddess of the Sea.

THE MIDDEST CHARM

For a mortal man or maid to dance as the Atami do for the length of one hour by sun or moon, sing these words three times in the Doric mode.

> *Anat, Ashtart, Ata'r*
> *Bid my tail arise, open eyes wide,*
> *my soul to drink the waters.*
> *Ata'rathi calls me to the waters.*

The transformation thereafter may be made once in a mortal day with only these words spoken: *Yammi Atiratu Rabbatu.*

Commentary: The most ancient texts being mere speculation must suffice that dancing among the Atami may be best apprehended as swimming, bathing, or elsewise frolicking upon the waters. Another more vulgar hath reported the words *my tail to rise* to be of more potent portent, especially among the males of all species, referring to the act of procreation.

THE LAST CHARM

That a child of the Atami may love truly and with a full heart as do mortals, bind on a talisman of three suns and three lions having employed the first charm if required, and sing these words in the Icthylean mode only. To use it otherwise is to invite great danger and even death.

> *Rabbatu Atiratu Yammi*
> *Be blood for burning,*
> *soul for yearning,*
> *home forsaking,*
> *Touched by lightning,*
> *leave off sighing,*
> *heart delighting.*
> *Atargatis Ata'rathi Ashara!*

The charm abideth for a single year and a day by the maiden moon, then must Atami's child return to the Mothers' halls, and no more live among mortal men.

Commentary: This giveth to a siren or nymph a heart that can be broken, for though they often may be seen to fall in love with mortal men yet they oftimes be unmindful and drag them to the depths where perforce they drown them. The charm hath effect for a year and a day only that is to say thirteen moons of the lunar calendar as counted by the men of old and of some even today in Moorish lands. It cannot be renewed, so protective is she this Ata'rathi of her children. The suns and lions of the talisman are supposed by scholars to be beads of gold and of sulfured amber framed in what shape the bearer liketh best.

Addendum: A charm contrary to the last

Here followeth an expedience for countering the third charm before its term expire, in that mortal men, being vain and faithless by nature, soon cool in their affections or light upon another love, or in the course of time be killed in wars or by sickness, in all ways cruelly abandoning the Atami who has sacrificed a light heart for his sake.

To reverse the charm, go home to the sea or what homely waters thou wilt. Sing these words in any mode thou pleasest so it is soon ended, and all shall be restored.

ATARGATIS ATA'RATHI ASHARA!
The doleful charm unsend
All sorrows end
Sad heart abide no more
Light heart restore
Tears fly away
Old love forsake
New pleasures take
Make me myself again
RABBATU ATIRATU YAMMI

About the Author

Maggie Secara started out wanting to be an archaeologist. Then a reporter, then an international spy, a poet, an opera singer, a novelist, a historian. She ended up being a bit of each, earning a Masters in English and becoming involved with historical costume and improvisational theatre. When all those passions came together at once, she decided to be a novelist again, and so she did. Her short fiction has appeared in a variety of publications, including *New Realm*, *Unsung Stories*, and *Daily Science Fiction*.

Maggie lives in Los Angeles, California, with one adoring husband, two goofy cats, and half a million English words to toy with.

You can find Maggie in all these interesting places:

Facebook   facebook.com/groups/maggiesworlds
Twitter   @MaggiRos
Tumblr   maggie-secara.tumblr.com
Pinterest   pinterest.com/maggiros
Amazon   Author.to/MaggieSecara

And of course
www.maggiesecara.com

www.ingramcontent.com/pod-product-compliance
Lightning Source LLC
Chambersburg PA
CBHW070617260626
47161CB00007B/2475